NORTH TO ALASKA
The Memoirs of H.H. Lomax

Book 6

PRESTON LEWIS

WOLFPACK
PUBLISHING
— EST 2013 —

WOLFPACK
PUBLISHING
— EST 2013 —

Published in the United States by Wolfpack Publishing, Las Vegas

Wolfpack Publishing
6032 Wheat Penny Avenue
Las Vegas, NV 89122

wolfpackpublishing.com

Paperback ISBN: 978-1-64734-051-3
eBook ISBN: 978-1-64734-050-6

NORTH TO ALASKA

For Spencer and Madlyn,
Great Friends

INTRODUCTION

When I first started work on *The Memoirs of H.H. Lomax* a quarter century ago, I never expected that the project would result in six volumes and keep me editing and laughing for so many years. But alas, Henry Harrison Lomax provided a unique and humorous perspective on the people and events that have grown in legend—if not in fact—since the closing of the American frontier. Lomax's ability to find humor in some of the Old West's most legendary and sordid events was surpassed only by his talent for being there to begin with. He was like thousands of other Old West vagabonds that roamed the frontier in search of fortune and adventure. Lomax found more of the latter than the former. While he did at times come into money, he seldom kept it for long, either being swindled out of his earnings by the unscrupulous or squandering it on the dissipations common among the drifters of his era.

In his later years, Lomax put pencil to Big Chief Tablets and recorded his recollections of his times on the frontier. Ultimately those pencil-lead meanderings came to reside in a prominent university archives on the American Southwest. So as not to cover the same background explained in earlier volumes, I will refer the reader to those books, beginning with *The Demise of Billy the Kid*, for more detail on the Lomax papers and their provenance. I must admit again that I cannot vouch for their complete authenticity, a fact that has scared away many academic historians of the Old West from giving them a fuller examination. With my education in journalism, a profession known these days as much for "fake news" as for legitimate facts, I had fewer qualms about editing and publishing Lomax's recollections as he told a good story, even if he shaded the truth, shaved the facts or shamed the innocent. His proclaimed circle of acquaintances in past volumes has included Billy the Kid, John Chisum, Pat Garrett, Frank and Jesse James, Doc Holliday, the Earps, Big Nose Kate, Wild Bill Hickok, Bat Masterson, George Armstrong Custer, Crazy Horse, Calamity Jane, Jesse Chisholm, Joseph G. McCoy, Johnny Ringo, Buffalo Bill, and dozens of lesser known and less colorful frontier characters, including many females of questionable values.

If there has been a criticism of Lomax's memoirs, it has been that I included the bawdy sections of his reminiscences. Fact is, Lomax frequently wound up in the beds of willing women and even worked in a brothel in Waco, Texas, for a spell. I have left those encounters in his recollections as I felt the passages were necessary to understand the man and his times. It was not that Lomax didn't seek a traditional relationship with a good woman, but rather that those attempts were always foiled by other factors. He abandoned his childhood sweetheart in Northwest Arkansas for his own safety and hers, in the aftermath of the Civil War and then fell in love with another decent young lady before leading the first herd of longhorns to Abilene, Kansas. When he returned to Texas flush with his cattle drive earnings to marry her, she was gone. Had either of those relationships been consummated, Lomax would never have compiled so many adventures and so entertaining a narrative of life on the frontier.

This book, too, introduces Lomax to another woman of easy virtue in Mattie Silks, the queen of Denver's night life and perhaps the most famous madam in the Old West. Lomax claims to have been at the wounding of Mattie's lover Cort Thomson, an encounter that in subsequent years has been amplified into a supposed topless duel between Silks and Kate Fulton, another madam competing for Denver's red-light trade and for Thomson's affection. Lomax remembers the shooting more as a fully clothed drunken brawl than a blouse-less duel. Following his fruitless search for the easy riches that would solve his periodic financial difficulties, this volume takes Lomax from Denver to Leadville and ultimately to Alaska and Skaguay, or Skagway as it is now spelled and as I corrected in his memoirs for consistency.

Most of Lomax's adventures center on him trying to make a name for himself or a fortune that would set him up for his final years. He had his financial ups and downs throughout his life, but was at times better off than the numbers suggest today. Using an inflation calculator, for instance, I determined a dollar in 1877 when this saga begins was the equivalent of $24.62 in 2020 money. By this tale's end two decades later, an 1897 dollar equaled $31.16 today.

As a stampeder drawn to the Yukon for Klondike gold, Lomax uses an alias for the first time in his life and meets a bevy of characters up north, including one aspiring writer I take to be Jack London. This is how Lomax began his recollections on that meeting. "On the beach in Dyea guarding his and his partners' gear, I met a fellow named for a European capital. It was Jack Paris or Jack Madrid or something like that and he proclaimed he was a writer, but it looked to me he was more of a reader, resting on the tarp-covered gear and devouring a copy of *The Origin of the Species*." If my speculation is right, and Jack London was indeed in Dyea at about this time, Lomax influenced London's first great novella, *The Call of the Wild*. But while Silks and likely London are peripheral characters, Lomax's principal antagonist in this tale is legendary frontier conman Soapy Smith, whose career in crime and corruption ended unceremoniously on a Skagway wharf.

Like *First Herd to Abilene*, the previous volume in *The Memoirs of H.H. Lomax*, this story was stitched together from scattered reminiscences I compiled into a single narrative. I hope it holds together well for the reader as I tried to minimize any enhancements other than a few edits to improve the transitions. I had trouble coming up with a title for this account as the best one had already been taken—*North to Alaska*—for a John Wayne movie. As that was one of my favorite movies by the western actor, I opted to use that title for this book. That decision seemed somehow appropriate as I have for years taken Lomax's words for my own as well.

Though I am no authority on the Klondike Gold Rush as my strength is more in Texas and Southwestern history, I find Lomax's account lines up generally with the facts published in the more substantial accounts of the peak years of 1897 and 1898. By 1898 half the continent was dead broke after the Panic of 1896 and the other half was trying to get to Dawson City by any means possible to better their economic situation. Like many stampeders, Lomax never made it to Dawson City, deciding the White Pass and Chilkoot Pass routes were too demanding for a man approaching fifty. Instead, Lomax parlayed his resources into a saloon and theater that would mine the prospectors before they ever left Skagway to prospect the Klondike. Bartending and saloon keeping were nothing new to Lomax, who had tended bar in Beaver Smith's cantina in Fort Sumner, New Mexico Territory; mixed drinks in a Waco, Texas, brothel for the clientele; and owned a saloon in Tombstone, Arizona, Territory, before a lawyer swindled him out of the business. His account of the characters and chicanery in Skagway generally parallel the facts, and his version of Soapy Smith's death lines up closely with more recent research on the shooting rather than the explanations posed by Skagway residents at the time. I'll leave it to readers to make their own assessment of Lomax's story and any discrepancies in the recollections of a man who was born in 1850 in Arkansas and died in 1933 in Texas.

As to the further origin and provenance of the Lomax papers from which I have compiled the previous five volumes in *The Memoirs of H.H. Lomax*, I will refer the reader to the introductions in *The Demise of Billy the Kid*, *The Redemption of Jesse James* and *Mix-up at the O.K. Corral*. Those three books provide substantial details on the derivation of his journals. Subsequent volumes *Bluster's*

Last Stand and *First Herd to Abilene* supply additional details on his life. While some may question his credibility as an observer of the occurrences Lomax claims to have witnessed, no one should doubt his ability as a storyteller of the first rank. I like to say he was a chronicler of the historical and the hysterical West.

I have enjoyed my work with *The Memoirs of H.H. Lomax* over the last quarter of a century. What has made it especially enjoyable is the fine people I have worked with in publishing these papers. I must acknowledge the contributions of Greg Tobin, Don D'Auria, Paul Block, Tom Beer, Sally Smith, Elizabeth Tinsley, Pam Lappies, Tom Burke, and Billy Huckaby. I am also indebted to the fine folks at Wolfpack Publishing for continuing the saga of H.H. Lomax. So, a special thanks goes to Mike Bray, president and publisher; Rachel Del Grosso, associate publisher; Lauren Bridges, associate editor; and Paul Bishop, acquisitions editor. They are a great pack to run with.

As always, I must acknowledge my wife, Harriet Kocher Lewis, whose contributions to my success have been immeasurable. Harriet and I not only share our lives together but also a wonderful family with daughter Melissa plus her husband John Kemp and with son Scott plus his wife Celeste. Their marriages have produced "The Grands," Jackson, Carys, and Cora Kemp and Miriam and Hannah Lewis. The Grands remain an ongoing joy in our hearts.

Finally, I must thank the many readers who have found H.H. Lomax as amusing as I have and who continue to follow the trail he blazed through the legends of the Old West.

Preston Lewis
San Angelo, Texas
May 2020

Chapter One

Shooting a man in the back was frowned upon in the old days, though sometimes you lacked a more honorable option to survive a vendetta. Over the years, I was blamed for one back-shooting I didn't commit and never got credit for dispatching the one crook I *did* shoot from behind. Now I'm not complaining, and I'm not saying I'm proud of all the choices I made with a gun, but I never marched around boasting about my killings or defacing my pistol with notches on the grips or scratches on the barrel to represent the men I'd put in a grave. Some fellows bragged so much about all their enemies they had dispatched that if they'd carved or scratched notches in their weapons for every fellow they claimed to have killed, all they'd been left with was a pile of splinters or metal shavings instead of a revolver.

No, sir, I never bragged about those things because you seldom knew when a lawman might be eavesdropping on such arrogance, intending to avenge the death of some hombre that likely needed an express ticket to hell to begin with. Nor did I claim to be a shootist as I didn't want a reputation that would dishonor my momma and her teachings, as she was a Godly woman who believed in the Good Book. Even if I was her prodigal son, she'd have been humiliated by me breaking the Fifth Commandment and shooting another human being in the back. The odd thing about the two times I was involved in back-shooting incidents, though, is that they were both related, despite coming some two decades and twenty-five hundred miles apart.

And making matters worse, both instances happened because of an insect bite. Yep, I'd gotten severely bitten by the gold bug twice on the frontier, winding up first in Colorado and later in Alaska, which was colder than a suffragist's heart. I should know because during my Leadville, Colorado, stint I encountered Susan B. Anthony, who opened my eyes to how mean a woman could be. I much preferred the sugar and vice of Mattie Silks and her soiled doves in Denver to Anthony's dire and brimstone over the plight of women in the newest state and the other thirty-seven. Those were raucous days when Colorado had first joined the Union, and the suffragists attacked the God-given rights of the male citizens of the new state.

As misguided as Susan B. Anthony might have been, she was halfway honest, unlike the most despicable fellow that ever trod upon the plains or mountains of Colorado—Jefferson Randolph Smith the Second. Known as Jeff when I first met him, but later as "Soapy," he was crookeder than a barrel full of rattlesnakes and twice as mean. What he lacked in integrity, he more than made up for in cleverness as he could've swindled Satan out of his horns, tail and pitchfork without the devil ever knowing what had transpired. He possessed enough charm that shills and hooligans attached to him like metal shavings to a magnet so you always had to be careful in any town that Soapy worked because his ruffians were on the lookout for anyone they might defraud or scam. Such tricks played out best in mining towns where everyone was looking for a quick buck and sudden riches.

My time in Deadwood, Dakota Territory, had shown that hard money came to prospectors with a bit of luck and grit while easy loot accrued in the pockets of men who earned their living by serving the cravings of the miners. I'd visited the Dakotas in 1875 with two telegraphers I'd met in Texas. Those fellows, Douglas Wolfe and Brian Dreban, obsessed on finding gold until our partnership broke up because they thought I was crazy and seeing ghosts. They were robbed and returned to their telegraph keys while I accompanied George Armstrong Custer on his ill-fated excursion to the Little Bighorn. Unlike the boy general, I survived the military expedition with my scalp intact and an Army mule beneath my bottom. I named my ride in honor of General Bluster, calling him Ciaha, an Indian name I made up to stand for "Custer is a horse's ass." Ciaha helped me out of several tight spots with the Sioux and Cheyenne before I headed to Deadwood to stop James Butler "Wild Bill" Hickok from spreading vile rumors about me. Our differences started after our first acquaintance in Springfield, Missouri, right after the War Between the States, and then ballooned following a brief encounter a couple years later after I led the first herd of Texas cattle to the new trail town of Abilene, Kansas.

The bad blood between us kept me alert in Deadwood until the day Hickok was in a card game paying more attention to me than to Jack McCall, who slipped up behind Wild Bill and plugged him in the head. Satisfied that Hickok would never spread another lie about me, but concerned that one of his friends might think I had plotted with McCall, I rode away from Deadwood early one morning, planning to move to healthier climes. But as I pointed Ciaha south, I pondered how fate had made some men rich that surely didn't deserve it. Now I never was nor ever claimed to be a college professor, but in Deadwood I saw guys a lot dumber than me walking around like they owned the world. Even if they didn't have title to the earth, they had enough money to purchase a substantial portion of it. I figured I deserved to share such riches. After all, I was smarter than most of them. If I matched their luck, I knew I'd be wealthier than them.

As I meandered south by southwest, I kept hearing about mining possibilities in Colorado, which had become a state the day after Wild Bill Hickok had played his last hand of poker. As Deadwood was practically lawless, I figured the new state would have enough law to guarantee I might keep my wealth, once I uncovered it, without needing to look over my shoulder with every step I took. My experience in Colorado taught me that when money was at stake, I could trust no one, not even myself.

About a year after I left Deadwood, I found myself in Denver, having worked my way south, doing odd jobs to keep food in my belly, to pay for shelter during the cold winter and to provide for a few drink and recreational dollars in my pocket, if only for a short spell. By the time I reached Denver in August of 1877, I had just less than three dollars on me and a hunger for grub for me and Ciaha. Memory tells me Denver then had 30,000 residents, maybe half of them sober. The rest, like me, were drunk either on liquor or on dreams of getting rich by squeezing gold out of the Rocky Mountains, which towered to the west like giant tombstones over the city. A gravestone was a fitting description of the Rockies as they were the burial spot for so many visions of wealth and security, including my own.

On the outskirts of Denver, I started asking people for jobs or tasks I might undertake for a meal or a few cents, but got no takers. Seems the city folks cared little for honest work so I looked at other possibilities. I wound up riding into town beside one chap wearing a dark suit, black boots that shined and a larcenous smile that didn't. He nodded. I nodded. Ciaha even nodded, though not the man's pompous black stallion. I took the fellow as either a prosperous preacher or a broke gambler.

"You interested in making a dollar?" He tweaked the end of his thin, black mustache.

"An honest dollar or a crooked dollar?" I responded.

"They're one and the same."

I tilted my head and paused. Now I couldn't decide whether my newfound friend was a preaching gambler or a gambling preacher. "The Good Book might disagree," I answered, trying to smoke him out if he was a man of the odds or baptize him in my piety if he was a man of God.

"Ah, the Good Book," he mused. "What would I do without it?"

"You're a reverend then?"

"No, young man, I am an undertaker. While most men in these parts dream of getting rich taking ore out of the ground, I am wealthy from putting folks into the ground, all with appropriate verses from the Good Book, you understand. A burial without a Bible scripture is like a wedding without a bride, pointless."

"So you're a believer in the Good Book."

"Only in the goodness of the book to soothe the sorrows of the bereaved, to bring comfort in times of loss and to provide hope that the dearly departed will one day greet his loved ones in the great beyond. Beyond that, young man, I would call it hogwash."

I raised my head and studied the sky, relieved it was clear and cloudless for fear a thunderbolt might strike me down for riding with a man so blasphemous.

"You seem astounded, young man, but I can't believe what I can't see."

"And, I can't see what I can't believe," I answered, knowing it didn't make much sense, but stumped as what else to say.

"Ah, a philosopher," my mortician friend observed. "A deep thinker, you must be, but I only think six feet deep."

"Then what do you believe in, good sir?"

The fellow slapped hand over his heart. "I place my faith in Sam Doherty!"

"I never realized God had a name, much less that it was Sam."

The undertaker laughed. "No, young man, Sam Doherty is the fleetest man afoot in all of Colorado, a sprinter unbeaten in the annals of Denver foot racing. No offense to your mule, young man, but I am confident Sam Doherty would beat him in a hundred-yard race."

Ciaha rattled his head from side to side and brayed. I didn't know if he was insulted or just hungry, but his timing startled my companion.

"Your mule has a sensitive constitution."

I nodded. "It comes from being around so many jackasses."

"Then he may not want to accompany me," my saddle pal replied.

For a moment, I thought he was admitting he was a jackass, but he continued.

"I'm headed to the fairgrounds where there'll be two-legged jackasses aplenty. You never answered my question if you were interested in making a dollar, young man."

"I reckon. What must I do?"

"Wager every cent you've got on Sam Doherty. He's running against some fool Texan who thinks he can outrace Sam in a hundred- and twenty-five-yard run."

Not caring a whit for Texans, I decided to bet my meager three dollars against the Lone Star sprinter.

"I'm telling you it's a sure thing, like spitting and hitting the ground," said my new friend.

His comment forced me to reflect on the sure things I'd been involved in since leaving home in Cane Hill, Arkansas, a dozen years earlier. None of those certainties came through for me, and I walked away from them much poorer than I had gone in. Even so, I decided to accompany the undertaker to the fairgrounds and then determine whether I'd cast my fate with the sure thing or the long shot. "Lead the way," I offered.

"My pleasure," he said. "Now let me introduce myself. I'm Thermopylae Spade, named for the great Greek battle."

"Never heard of a battle named Spade," I answered.

"No, young man, the battle of Thermopylae, the Alamo of the Persian Wars," he explained.

"I know nothing about the history of Paris other than it's the capital of France."

Spade shrugged. "Not Paris, but Persia. What did you say your name was, young man?"

"H.H. Lomax. I was named for a president, William Henry Harrison."

"He was a short-lived commander-in-chief, living only a month in office. I hope your luck is better than poor President Harrison's."

Shrugging, I replied, "I don't suppose we'll find out until we get to the fairgrounds."

"Luck's not required when you bet on Sam Doherty, the Denver Dart."

I rode across town with Thermopylae Spade, listening to his outlook on life and death, him profiting most from death, telling me that undertakers were like shootists, best remembered for who they had put in a grave. He rattled off a few of the well-known locals he had planted six feet under, but seeing I was unimpressed, he scratched

12

the back of his neck.

"I'd give anything to bury a president," he said, "even one like William Henry Harrison who only served thirty-one days in office."

As long as he didn't lust to inter someone *named* for a president, I didn't care.

"What about Sam Doherty? Assuming you could catch him after he died and stuff him in a coffin, would he be a big enough name for undertaker immortality?"

Spade pondered my question like it was sincerely offered, but never gave me a definite answer. The more I rode with the macabre mortician, the more I came to dislike him and his outlook on life or was it his outlook on death? We spent a half hour crossing town together, and I finally spotted a wooden grandstand that I took to be the fairgrounds in the distance.

As we approached the weathered bleachers with a shingled covering, I saw hundreds of other people converging on the park. They came afoot, atop horses and in buggies, all intent on seeing Sam Doherty outrun and outsmart the upstart Texan. I didn't know if Sam could beat his opponent in a footrace, but I knew he would win in a battle of smarts. To my way of thinking, Texans were dumber than stump water. If a bird had the brain of a typical Texan, he would fly backwards.

Everybody aimed for the racetrack with its white-washed fence circling the perimeter. I debated whether to stay with Spade, who greeted everyone he saw as a potential client. I finally decided I best accompany the undertaker. Despite his warped outlook on life and death, he remained my only acquaintance in Denver. He pointed his horse for an open spot by the fence where we dismounted and tied our animals to the rail before working our way with the crowd toward the bleachers. Every time Spade acknowledged a fellow citizen, I wondered if he was measuring him for a pine box or thinking of the scripture to read at the guy's funeral.

We squeezed through the throng to the grandstand, staying close to the fence rail which separated the spectators from the racetrack. Spade steered me to a break in the crowd, and we studied the two sprinters warming up for the match race.

My mentor lifted his gnarly finger and pointed to the taller racer, a muscled athlete who looked like he had been chiseled from stone by God himself. Shirtless, the competitor wore leather suspenders to hold up his loose-fitting black pants that came midway down his calf, meeting the white stockings that fit snugly inside his fleece running shoes. "That's Sam Doherty, a fine specimen of masculinity, known far and wide for his broad stride, his blazing feet and his strong lungs. It's a sure thing to bet on him." Spade paused a moment, then laughed as he gestured at his opponent.

I chuckled, too. This unusual example of Texas manhood wore an outfit I might expect to find in a circus or a brothel, but not out in public, even among the worst citizens of Denver. The lean Texan sported a tight pink bodysuit that bared his shoulders and the upper reaches of his chest and back. Over the leotard, as Spade called the body suit, he wore a pair of the shortest pants I'd ever seen, extending from his waist to the middle of his thighs. His royal blue shorts were emblazoned with a smattering of gold stars, and his running shoes in matching blue looked like those a ballerina might wear. He stood a palm shorter than the Denver Dart, with rakish eyes beneath a sandy mop of hair and over a neatly trimmed handlebar mustache. Though well proportioned, the foot racer's physique would never be mistaken for Doherty's perfect form.

"His name is Corteze Thomson, but he goes by Cort. Says he's never lost a footrace. So it'll be a showdown between two undefeateds, Denver against Texas, the mountains against the desert, good against evil."

I studied the racing pair, Doherty attended by three men, two carrying towels and the third a bucket of water with a dipper clipped to the rim. By contrast, Thomson relied on a single attendant, a short female with a pleasant plumpness accentuated by her rounded face beneath a curtain of brown hair that tumbled down to her shoulders. She carried a purple silk umbrella that matched her lace-trimmed dress of the same color and fabric.

Beside me, Spade pulled out his pocket watch from his vest and opened the cover. "Twenty minutes until the race starts, plenty of time to make any bets you want," the undertaker said. "It's a sure thing."

I pointed at the woman attendant. "Who's she?"

The undertaker cleared his throat and shook his head. "Thomson is a kept man. That is his keeper, Mattie Silks. She's a new madam in town, been here a year or less from what I've heard. Operates a fancy house near Holladay Street. Cort lives with her and spends her money."

"Not a bad job to have," I noted.

"You're running out of time if you aim to walk away with some easy winnings," Spade informed me, then announced to the spectators. "Doherty's my man, the Denver Dart. Any takers for the Texas Tarantula? Five dollars to fifty bucks, I'll take all bets."

I turned back to the racecourse and watched Doherty jog twenty yards along the soft track. Then Thomson moved to the starting line and dashed forward, his feet churning like the driving wheels on a locomotive, kicking up dirt as he ran until he took a misstep and tumbled to the earth, screaming and grabbing his ankle.

Mattie jogged to him, tossing her umbrella beside him, kneeling over him and dirtying the hem of her silk dress. Thomson thrashed about on the ground, grimacing and shaking his head, as his opponent with his three assistants raced over to check on their rival. The crowd fell silent. Another man carrying a megaphone sprinted to Thomson as Mattie helped him to a sitting position, his face contorted with pain or, I thought, good acting. Now if the race were run, it was more of a sure thing for Doherty. That's when I realized I had to bet on Thomson, even if he was a Texan.

As Mattie arose from the dirt, Doherty and his colleagues gathered around his opponent and helped him to his feet. Thomson forced a smile at the crowd, then limped toward the starting line, shaking his head vigorously as the man with the megaphone questioned him. Finally, Thomson shrugged and sighed, then swatted at the megaphone as the fellow lifted it to his lips.

"Ladies and gentlemen, due to the unfortunate fall we will postpone our race a week."

The crowd booed, some even throwing rocks at the contestants. "What about the bets?" Spade yelled.

"Cort Thomson must forfeit all stakes," the announcer proclaimed.

Half the spectators cheered, but the remainder jeered and hissed.

The announcer shrugged, uncertain what to do. Mattie looked from Thomson to the crowd to the announcer, then back to Thomson. She whispered to him, then moved to the announcer, taking the megaphone from him and raising it to her painted lips.

"Ladies and gentlemen," she called in a voice too soft and dainty for her hard profession, "Mr. Thomson has promised to run the race in spite of his injury and risk of permanent damage to his ankle. He promises to cover all wagers lost on him if he's permitted three-to-one odds."

The Texas Tarantula waved to the crowd and nodded his agreement, then limped toward the starting line, dragging his right foot as he advanced.

"Is that fair?" Mattie called above the murmuring spectators.

Most folks liked their chances if they were Doherty supporters or the odds if they were Thomson backers. That's when I decided to bet on a sure thing.

"I'll take those odds," I cried out, "and Cort Thomson for up to a hundred dollars." Four bettors around me took up my offer. Then I saw Spade and made my way over to him. "I'm taking the kept man for fifty dollars if you'll take Doherty at three-to-one odds."

The undertaker laughed. "Are you loco, Lomax? It's even more of a sure thing now."

"I believe in the healing power of God Almighty and three-to-one odds," I answered.

Spade grabbed my hand and shook it. "Easiest fifty dollars I ever made. When the race is over, you'll be the latest jackass to arrive in Denver."

Making my way back to the rail, I took more bets than I could keep up with and many more than I could

16

pay if the Texan lost. If Doherty won, I realized I might not escape the fairgrounds alive since my three dollars wouldn't stretch enough to cover my wagers. On the positive side, I at least knew an undertaker.

As I worked along the rail, I encountered Mattie Silks making her way down the fence in the opposite direction and taking bets I couldn't afford. When I passed her, she looked me in the eyes and winked. "See me when the race is over. I'll reward your faith in my Cort."

I touched the brim of my hat. "Obliged, ma'am," I replied as I kept accepting wagers, until the bugle call announced the impending race. Rather than move to the finish, I stayed by the starting stripe so I could make a quick getaway if my racer lost. Then I remembered Ciaha was tied at the opposite end of the track past the finish line and realized I, too, might be finished.

Doherty strode up to the starting line as confident as a crooked accountant with a good eraser, thrusting out his chest and taking in the deep breath of victory even before the race began. Meekly, Thomson lined up beside him.

The announcer marched up to the line, lifted the megaphone and outlined the rules. There would be up to three starts. Any racer that got off ahead of the gun would be disqualified after a second false start, and his opponent declared the winner. The starter would cry mark and set, then fire the starting pistol to initiate the race. Both men nodded their understanding and agreement. With the megaphone at his mouth, the announcer pulled a pistol from his coat pocket and held it above his head.

"On your mark!"

Both men leaned forward.

"Get set!"

Anticipating the start, Thomson flinched then, darted ahead, tumbling to the ground.

Doherty's supporters laughed and began counting their certain winnings as the Texan got up and swatted the dirt from his pink tights as he limped back to the starting line.

"One more false start and you're disqualified," the starter informed him and the crowd.

Thomson nodded as he took his place and leaned forward, his eyes focused on the finish line a hundred and twenty-five yards distant.

"On your mark!"

Both runners gritted their teeth, determined to best the other.

"Get set!"

The crowd held its breath.

BANG! went the pistol.

Doherty shot away from the line like a cannon ball, but in one of the greatest miracles ever to occur outside the Bible, Thomson exploded like a meteor, his feet churning and kicking up dust as he raced. He stayed even with Doherty for twenty strides, then sped past him, putting five yards between himself and his slower adversary by the halfway mark. At the finish line, Thomson was a full twelve yards beyond Doherty. As he broke the ribbon that confirmed his victory, he turned around and ran backwards for another thirty paces, raising his arms in exultation and sticking his tongue out in spite.

I started working my way back along the fence rail, collecting three times what I had risked. Having made so many bets, I couldn't remember all the faces and didn't collect near what I was owed, but that was fine because I now had enough money for a decent stay in Denver. I saw the undertaker ahead in the crowd and called to him, "Wait up."

Spade turned and shook his head at me.

"A sure thing, was it?" I asked.

He spat at the ground, his spittle splatting on his shiny boot tip.

"Where's my hundred and fifty dollars?"

"I was just going to get it from my saddlebags. Give me a minute and I'll be back."

Though I intended to follow him, I felt a hand grab my arm and tug me around.

It was Mattie Silks. She had a smile on her painted lips and a come-hither look in her eyes. Besides that, she was holding up her skirt by the hem as men dropped their losses into the purple silk pouch. "We haven't met," she said. "I'm Mattie Silks."

"H.H. Lomax is my name."

"I intend to thank you for your faith in my Cort."

Shrugging, I said. "I did nothing other than believe in miracles over sure things."

"To the contrary," she replied. "Your support of Cort inspired more to bet on the sure thing."

"Only it wasn't so sure a sure thing, was it?"

"Exactly," she replied. "I'm inviting you to our picnic tomorrow to celebrate my Cort's victory. It'll start at four o'clock at Olympic Park."

"I'm new to Denver and don't know my way around."

As we talked, losers kept dropping their money in Mattie's skirt pouch. She so many bills in the silk fabric she held the hem with both hands to keep the winnings from spilling out. "It's off Fifteenth Street just before you get to the river. You can't miss it. The park is outside the limits of Denver, so the local constabulary won't hassle us."

"I'll be there," I replied, "but now I've got to collect more of my earnings."

She smiled. "Me too."

We went our separate ways, me looking for Spade and her claiming a fortune.

By the time I reached Ciaha, I figured I had three hundred or more dollars. I looked around for the undertaker, but his black stallion had disappeared and him with it. I never saw him again, but I would see plenty of Mattie Silks before I escaped Denver.

Chapter Two

Uncertain what to expect from Mattie Silks and her picnic celebration, I arrived a quarter after four the next afternoon at Olympic Park on the east bank of the South Platte where it converged with Cherry Creek at the Fifteenth Street Bridge. The park covered fifty acres, half a meadow that sloped to the river and the remainder a grove of box elders, cottonwoods and occasional evergreens. Horses, buckboards and fancy buggies were tethered along the street. I dismounted and tied Ciaha to a hitching post, taking in the surroundings. Across the street from the commons stood a smattering of saloons, pool halls and gambling dens, where men could purchase all known vices. Studying the field, I estimated over 300 folks attending, many congregating around three outdoor bars where vendors had put planks over empty barrels and served free beer. As I looked about, I realized the attendees were not the cream of Denver society, but rather the dregs of the city's underworld, a mixture of pickpockets, scam artists, cutthroats, gamblers, crooked lawmen, schemers and the ladies attracted to those professions. On the positive side, I didn't spot a single evangelist condemning sin or another undertaker intent on profiting from the wages of such transgressions. Eventually, I spotted Mattie in a yellow silk dress holding a matching silk umbrella over her head to protect her fair skin from the afternoon sun. She flitted around a blue-and-white quilt in the center of the park, gripping a bottle of champagne by the neck, occasionally tipping it to fill the proffered mugs or wine glasses of her fellow celebrants or raising it to her lips for a healthy swig. I looked for Cort Thomson, figuring he would be celebrating with the woman who supported him, but instead observed him fawning over another young lady of Mattie's profession, though this demimonde sported hair the gold of fine corn silk and a narrow body that accentuated her heaving bosom. While she may have had better looks than Mattie, she lacked better sense by messing with another woman's man in such an open fashion.

Except for the undertaker, Miss Silks remained my only acquaintance in Denver, so I ambled her way. I watched her drain the last swig of champagne from her bottle and toss it aside like a customer when his time was up. As she yanked a second bottle from an ice-filled bucket, she spotted me. Grinning, she threw open her arms and ran toward me, as excited as if she'd found a long-lost brother.

"Lomax," she cried, "I'm so glad you've joined us. I couldn't have hired a shill to do as good a job as you did yesterday in convincing those fools to take your bets even at three-to-one odds." She approached me like a stampeding buffalo and wrapped her arms around me so tight I thought she'd pop my lungs.

Squirming free from her grasp, I caught my breath and smiled. "I won almost three hundred dollars."

She started unwrapping the foil from the neck of the wine bottle and grinned. "I took in over two thousand, thanks to you and my Cort. Have you seen him?"

Playing dumb, I shrugged, not wanting to start a feud between her and the gal with corn silk hair. "Glad it worked out for you. I sure needed the money."

"Who doesn't, Lomax?"

She had a point and a smile on her face until her gaze moved beyond me and focused on her man conversing with the golden-haired harlot. Her cheeks reddening and her nostrils flaring, Mattie bared her teeth and brushed past me, taking a healthy swig from the fresh bottle of champagne, then throwing it away as a half-drunken reveler dropped to his knees to salvage what he could from the discard. "Follow me, Lomax," she ordered.

I complied, figuring it best to stay on her good side and perhaps see a cat fight as a bonus.

Approaching her lover, Mattie stepped between Cort and the other woman and scowled. "I've someone for you to meet, Cort," she announced, turning her back on his companion.

Thomson cocked his head and winked at the blonde, who planted her balled fists on her firm hips and glared at Miss Silks.

"This is H.H. Lomax," Mattie said. "He backed you yesterday when few others would, bettering the odds in our favor."

Before Thomson could speak, his blonde acquaintance stepped beside him, sliding her arm inside Cort's. Mattie scowled, releasing the yellow silk umbrella, which tumbled to the ground.

"Aren't you going to introduce me to your friend, Mattie?" the interloper cooed. "I bet I can steal him from you just like I can take Cort away."

Mattie's empty umbrella hand slipped inside a fold of her silk dress and returned with a small pearl-handled revolver clasped in her fingers. Mattie waved the pistol at her competitor's nose. "This is the trollop Katie Fulton."

"Strumpet," Fulton shot back.

"Easy, ladies." Thomson reached for Mattie's hand and pushed her weapon down until it pointed at the ground. "No harm here, Mattie. We were discussing prospecting opportunities in Leadville. The gold may be played out, but rumor has it they're finding silver, as much as a hundred ounces per ton and that's from low-grade ore."

Katie grinned at me. "The prospectors mine the ore. We girls mine the miners."

Mattie scowled. "Why don't you take your business to Leadville, Katie? You'd fit right in being a low-grade whore!"

Katie's eyes spat venom that would've killed a rattlesnake.

Thomson jumped between the two competitors. "Ladies, let's stay civil. We are celebrating my triumph afoot against the legendary Sam Doherty. Put away your pistol, Mattie."

"Stay away from my man," Mattie growled as she

returned the weapon to the pocket in the folds of her yellow silk outfit.

"He's your man only if you can keep him, Mattie," Fulton shot back.

"I'm everybody's man," Thomson replied with a smile that could've softened granite, though not the hearts of the two prostitutes. He leaned over and picked up Mattie's umbrella, closing the canopy and offering it to his benefactor.

Mattie accepted the sunshade, curtsied to Katie and turned away from her rival, placing her other hand on the shaft. I thought she intended to open the canopy again, but she lifted the shaft, cocked her arms and with a mighty heave spun around and whacked Fulton in the nose. Katie stumbled backwards, her nostrils spewing blood and her lips profanity as she tumbled.

I backed away as Mattie lifted her umbrella over her head and strode to Katie, intent on massaging her bleeding face even more. Cort lunged for her, wrapping his arms around his meal ticket and preventing her from striking Fulton again. Just as he got her under control, a gentleman friend of Katie's stepped in and swung his fist for Thomson, missing him and grazing Mattie's cheek. She screeched like a wounded mountain lion, flailing her umbrella like a yellow fringed sword as Katie staggered to her feet. By then several others swarmed in, pulling the women apart and holding them.

Once the combatants were separated and a line of men screened them from each another, the situation calmed for the moment. While most of the men hoped for a good cat fight, Mattie was providing the free beer and drinks so no one wanted to risk the refreshments for an encounter that might end the celebration.

Thomson finally convinced Mattie she had nothing to worry about from Katie as a romantic rival, as he only had eyes for her. I came to learn that his eyes may have belonged to Mattie, but the rest of him was available to any cute young lady that caught his fancy. After Mattie bought his assurances, she shook herself free from his embrace, straightened her dress and opened her umbrella, one panel of the yellow silk stained with blood from

Fulton's nose. Mattie smiled at the scarlet mark of honor and marched around the park, twirling her umbrella to draw attention to the red stain. She returned to her quilt as many fellows comforted her with their observations that she far exceeded Katie Fulton in beauty and class, though I suspected they were buttering her up to keep the free beer flowing.

I meandered through the crowd, checking out the assembly of men and women, but avoiding intoxicants as I realized I needed to keep my senses around this bunch. I suspected many remembered I had won large wagers the day before, and the revelers looked like they were more interested in relieving me of my winnings than in celebrating my good luck.

As for the females, they were of a class that circumstance had led me to in the past with mostly satisfactory results, though you never knew for sure. One comely young lady with an ample waist and a narrow bosom winked at me and offered me a calling card that read: CONSTANCE NOBLE, ACTRESS, FILLE DE JOIE. I examined it, then looked into her green eyes and smiled. "Where do you perform, Miss Constance?" I asked, thinking she might be worth a visit to work the kinks out of my system.

"Miss Katherine Fulton's," she answered, batting her long eyelashes at me.

"Katie Fulton?"

She nodded. "One and the same."

I returned her card, not caring to risk offending my host. "I'm guest of Miss Silks. I best decline your generous offer, Miss Constance."

She shook her head. "I took you for a man with more starch in your britches than that."

"It's not the starch in my britches as much as an umbrella in my nose that worries me."

My new friend grinned. "Such a pity. I could've shown you a wonderful time. Don't you think I'm worth the risk?"

"No offense, Miss Constance, but I can find another girl easier than I can find another nose," I answered, fighting an urge to scratch the sudden itch on my nose.

Noble lifted her beak in the air. "Too bad because I doubt Mattie will survive the ride home. Miss Katherine's plenty mad about her broken nose and plans to put a couple bullets in her. I'll be surprised if Mattie's not lying on her back for good by the end of the evening." She smiled and sauntered away, her fine hips swaying with each step.

While her gait sure tempted me to retrieve her calling card, her threat perplexed me. I didn't care to get between two feuding madams, but Mattie had done well by me, inviting me to her celebration. So, I waited until she had calmed and ambled over to her blue-and-white quilt where she reclined on her elbow beside Thomson, who rested on his back staring at the clouds and sipping more champagne. Miss Silks had planted her unfurled umbrella at the edge of the quilt for everyone to see her rival's blood stains.

Others in the crowd maintained their distance from the couple, and I understood why as Mattie remained incensed.

"You stay away from Katie. She's meaner than a momma bear with a sore tit."

"Don't you mean a sore nose?" Cort laughed, then swigged on the champagne.

"It's not funny, Cort, you chasing after her like a schoolboy."

Thomson put his thumb on the bottle's neck, shook it before removing the stopper and showering the sky with champagne, which fell as a gentle mist upon them. Mattie punched his shoulder and sat up, reaching for her umbrellas to shelter herself from the sprinkle. She spotted me and grinned. "Lomax," she called, "please join us."

I walked over and toed at the edge of their quilt with my boot.

"What's bothering you? You look like your dog was run over by a train."

"One gal said Katie's threatening to shoot you."

Cort sat up on the quilt and shook his head. "Katie'd never do that."

Mattie tossed her umbrella aside and turned to Cort. "You think any girl that smiles at you is virtuous, even if

25

she's a whore. Katie's flattering you to find out what she can about my business and success."

"She's not that smart," Cort responded.

"Didn't say she's smart," Mattie countered, "just conniving as hell. Don't let her gold hair, big bosom and narrow waist fool you. She's using you like you use me."

Cort grinned. "But Mattie, I make you considerable money with my racing."

"Not as much as you cost me!"

If Mattie fretted more over Cort's attentions to Katie than my warning her rival planned to shoot her, I figured I should find Ciaha and ride away, leaving the lovers to settle their differences outside of Katie Fulton's gun range. I tipped my hat at Mattie and stepped back, certain the madam was ignoring me. Before I turned, though, she chastised me.

"Don't wander off, Lomax. You need me," she called.

Uncertain what she meant, I shrugged, fearing she was suggesting something unbecoming. I'd been around enough to know loose women could get a man in trouble faster than a gang of the dirtiest outlaws anywhere. "What do I need you for?"

"A job," she replied. "I'm hiring you as a bodyguard to protect me from Katie Fulton."

I pointed at her beau. "Doesn't Cort protect you?"

Thomson cocked his head and swiveled it from side to side. "I can't keep my eyes off Mattie."

If I were Miss Silks, I'd be less worried about where his eyes looked and more about where his hands went, I thought.

"He's just sweet talking me," Mattie replied, "but I know Cort can't keep his eyes off skirts, no matter who's wearing them. He won't do for a bodyguard. I'll pay you four dollars a day and even buy you new duds and guns so you appear respectable. To be honest, your appearance is shabby. You need to exude class if you work around me and my girls."

I hesitated, glancing down and studying my attire, which looked dirty and ragged, but I had worn worse. I wasn't sure whether I would be guarding her or keeping Cort from flirting with other women of Mattie's class. My hesitation paid off.

"Okay, five dollars a day, Lomax, assuming you can handle a gun. Now don't think I can't manage a revolver myself. I can, learning from the best, Wild Bill Hickok himself—God rest his soul—in Abilene, back in seventy-one."

A smile cracked my lips. "I taught Wild Bill how to shoot in Springfield, Missouri."

"Don't be funning me," Mattie chided, "because you're losing your believability."

I countered, "Did Hickok teach you how to draw and fire over a mattress?"

Cort jumped up from the pallet and doubled his fists. "Don't insult my Mattie!"

"I'm not," I answered, then looked at Mattie. "Did he stand you beside a bed to practice drawing and firing?"

Mattie nodded. "He did."

Now I cocked my chin and grinned. "I taught him that. When I first met him, he was practicing fast draws outside of Springfield, dropping his revolver every other time or so. Half the time his pistol discharged, killing a gopher or squirrel when it hit the ground. He wasted a lot of ammunition and varmints before I showed him how to practice over a mattress, making it safer for himself and the little rodents."

"I'll be damned," Mattie said. "That's how he instructed me. If you taught Wild Bill, you must be quite the expert."

"I manage," I answered, trying to downplay my meager gun skills so I wouldn't get a reputation that sent every shootist aiming for me.

Turning to Thomson, I lifted my right hand to the butt of my revolver and threw him a narrow-eyed stare. "What were you saying about me insulting your Mattie?"

Cort gulped and stammered. "I was protecting Mattie's fine reputation, but I didn't know you were a shootist of note."

"Keep it to yourself, Cort. I don't brag about it for everyone's safety."

He nodded. "Yes, sir, Mr. Lomax."

Glancing at Mattie, I said, "I'll take your job provided you and Cort don't spread my reputation around because it'll make things harder. And, I want a week's pay in advance—"

"Agreed," Mattie answered.

"—and you provide lodging and meals."

"That can be arranged," she said. "And, you'll find there are other benefits in staying at my house." She arose from her quilt and stuck her hand inside her sweetheart neckline and pulled out a roll of bills the size of a goose egg. She peeled off thirty-five dollars and handed me the cash. I took the bills, still warm from her bosom, before she returned the rest to her dress. "As of this moment, Lomax, you're hired."

"Now get to work," Cort commanded.

I spun to face Mattie and extended my hand with the payment between my fingers. "I'm not taking orders from Cort. Here's your money back, and I'll be on my way."

Madam Silks shook her head and refused my offer. "You take orders from me only."

"Tell your boyfriend that," I demanded.

Mattie pointed her finger at Cort. "Lomax works for me, not for you. He only takes my commands. Do you understand?"

Cort nodded, but I could tell he resented the situation. If the rumors were true, Thomson was nothing more than Mattie's hired hand like me, though likely better paid and with mattress benefits from his boss.

"You satisfied, Lomax?"

"Yep."

"Now get to work," Mattie commanded.

Turning around, I decided my first duty was to find Katie Fulton and determine what she was up to. I wandered among the revelers, enjoying the coolness now that the sun had dropped behind the Rockies. Far from dissipating, the crowd had grown as more men and women strolled through the park, drinking, laughing and celebrating, their merriment coming more from the free beer than from Thomson's victory over Sam Doherty. Ambling through the celebrants, I spotted beneath a box elder, Katie Fulton being attended by the man who assisted her after Mattie plastered her nose with the umbrella. Fulton's snout remained red and swollen as she attempted to wash away the humiliation of her attack with mugs of beer provided by her gentleman suitor.

So as not to be too obvious about spying on Katherine Fulton, I meandered through the crowd, running into Constance Noble again. I smiled.

Constance answered with a flirtatious grin. "You changed your mind, have you? I can sure take the starch out of your britches?"

"Maybe," I said. "Who's the fellow that's attending Miss Fulton?"

"Sam Thatcher. He dotes on her."

"Like Cort Thomson on Miss Silks?"

Constance shook her head so hard that she flung an earring off. I watched the jewelry hit a burly man on the neck ten feet away, then fall to the grass at his boots. As I strode over to pick up the adornment, he finished the dregs from his mug of beer, dropped it to the grass and doubled up his fists, spreading his legs apart in a pugilistic stance.

"What did you hit me with, fellow?"

"Nothing," I advised him. "My friend's earring flew off when she shook her head." I pointed to the ground where the golden orb had landed, but he never took his eyes off of me.

Constance scurried over. "It's true, sir, it was my fault."

My opponent looked from me to Constance to the grass to me again. I could tell all the beer he had consumed had left him itching for a fight. He took a step toward me.

"No harm intended," I offered, though I could see revenge rather than forgiveness in his bloodshot eyes.

As he neared me, another fellow ran up and grabbed his arm. "Hold your horses," the new arrival said, pointing at my revolver, then yanking his hand down. "He's a shootist that taught Wild Bill Hickok the fast draw. He's deadly with a pistol."

I was as shocked as my burly opponent, whose eyes muddied with confusion as he pondered whether to pound me with his fists or apologize for offending such a noted pistoleer. I wriggled the fingers on my right arm and let them brush against the grip of my revolver.

The fellow stared at my hand and swallowed hard as he unclenched his fists. "That true?"

"You care to find out?" I challenged.

Shaking his own head, my challenger answered with a nervous smile and my own words. "No harm intended." He bent and retrieved the earring, stepping toward Constance and offering her the jewelry. "Here, ma'am," he said as he meekly dropped the trinket in her hand.

"Thank you," Constance whispered.

"That's better," I said. "Now have another free beer on me."

He turned and walked away with his pal while Constance looked at me with newfound respect. She strode over and took my hand.

"Dangerous men thrill me," Constance said.

She squeezed my arm and drew me closer. "Tell me how you became a gunman. How many have you killed?"

"It's not something I talk about or am proud of," I answered, angered that Mattie or Cort had spread my story. I suspected Cort had told it so someone might challenge and dispose of me because I refused to take his orders as I had related it to no one else in Denver or before.

Constance squeezed my arm even tighter. "Silent and dangerous," she mused. "I like that even more in my men."

What she liked most in fellows, I suspected, was a wad of bills, and I had to make sure she didn't pick my pocket while she was drowning me in flattery. Yanking myself from her grip, I told her, "It's for your own safety. Men are gunning for me, and I'd hate for you to get hurt."

"Dangerous, silent and sensitive," she said. "I'm liking you more by the moment, but I never caught your name."

"Lomax," I said, "but keep it to yourself. I don't want my enemies to learn I'm in Denver. It'd only create trouble. A lot of innocent people could get killed, yourself included."

"You're so thoughtful, Lomax."

I tucked my gun hand in my pants pocket and confirmed my race winnings plus Mattie's pay remained secure. Just like my money, Constance was still there, but unlike my cash I had to get rid of her, especially after I lost sight of Katie Fulton and Sam Thatcher. I stopped suddenly. "Damnation," I said.

"What is it?" she asked.

"Over by the trees I spotted Shotgun Jake Townsend," I lied, creating a phantom enemy. "He's sworn to kill me, and you don't want to be around if he fires his shotgun. Stay calm and walk away. Don't attract attention to yourself or me as you leave. If you hear a shotgun blast from the trees, don't come looking for me because I won't be a pretty sight."

Constance grabbed at her throat. "Be careful." She scurried off.

Clenching my lips, I nodded, being the dangerous, silent and sensitive type of gunman that I was. I headed for the trees near where I had last seen Katie Fulton and Sam Thatcher. I searched for them without success as dusk settled in, then started back for Mattie and Cort who were gathering up their quilt and champagne bucket as well-wishers dropped by to thank them for the free drinks and good times. The crowd dispersed toward the buggies and mounts tied along Fifteenth and the intersecting street where I had left Ciaha.

As I neared my new boss, Cort glanced over and strode my way while Mattie accepted the gratitude of her dwindling guests. "Where the hell have you been?"

"Looking for trouble," I said.

"There's a rumor going around that Shotgun Jake Townsend's hunting for you," Cort informed me.

Damn if rumors and lies didn't travel faster in Denver than any place I'd ever visited. "Is that a fact?"

"Can't say I've ever heard of Townsend," Cort continued, "but if I'd known you had that kind of man on your tail you I'd never let Mattie hire you."

"Shotgun Jake and I go back a long way. He's a back shooter if ever there was one, and he leaves a mess when he's done settling scores."

"Then don't ride too close to us when we leave for our place."

"Don't you mean Mattie's place?"

Thomson ignored my observation as Mattie hugged a pair of her lady guests and shook the hands of their escorts. Looking around at the park as the stragglers headed for their rides, I searched for Katie Fulton and

Sam Thatcher, but they had disappeared into the evening. About the only ones left were the saloon keepers taking down their temporary bars and stacking their empty kegs for retrieval in the morning light.

Miss Silks came over. "Are you gentlemen ready to go?" she asked.

"Lomax isn't a gentleman, or he'd carry the quilt or the champagne bucket."

"Gotta keep my gun hand free," I replied.

"Quit riding him, Cort." She pointed to a buggy on Fifteenth near the saloons. "That's our rig."

"I'll meet you there when I fetch my mule."

"A mule?" Cort exclaimed. "You're riding a mule? I bet it won't take long for Shotgun Jake Townsend to catch up with you. Damn, Mattie, you hired a hell of a bodyguard."

"He costs me less than you, Cort."

As I walked toward Ciaha, I wondered if I could convince him to kick Thomson to death. Mounting my mule, I discussed the possibility, but Ciaha ignored my request to assault a fellow he'd never met. As I rode to Fifteenth Street, I saw Mattie take the reins of their buggy and turn it around. I caught up with them and pulled in beside the buggy as we started for her place.

"Why don't you ride behind us?" Cort suggested. "Nothing's lower class than a man on a mule."

"Unless it's a kept man," I responded.

Mattie laughed. "If your bullets are as accurate as your words, you're just the guard I need." She paused and smiled. "We're both drunk, but stay behind us and we'll be fine."

"Yes, ma'am," I said, letting Ciaha slip ten yards back of their rig. Everything went well for a block until we neared the Denver & Rio Grande Railroad tracks. Behind me, I heard a galloping horse and the rattle and jangle of a wagon running loose. Ciaha jumped to the edge of the street as another buggy with its top up passed. As soon as it did, I saw an arm with a pistol extend from the side. Once the speeding rig evened up with Mattie and Cort, the gun exploded once, then again, as the assaulting wagon raced away.

Mattie screamed as her buggy careened to the side of Fifteenth where it came to a halt. She bounded from the buggy into the road, pulling her pistol from the folds of her dress and firing blindly at the escaping assassins, disregarding everyone else in the street.

Reaching the conveyance, I jumped from Ciaha and saw Cort slumped over in his seat, the white collar of his shirt red and sticky with blood. He had been hit in the neck and would bleed to death if I didn't do something as Mattie focused on reloading her gun and firing it along with curse words at the attackers.

I pulled Cort from the buggy and stretched him out on the ground, wrapping my hands around his neck. If I gripped too hard against his wound, I would strangle him. If I didn't press hard enough, Cort would bleed to death. The way I figured it, either way I came out a winner.

Chapter Three

After Mattie emptied her pearl-handled revolver the second time, she looked at me with flaming eyes that misinterpreted the situation. She lifted her pistol, pointed it at my nose and pulled the trigger.

Gritting my teeth, I awaited the blast.

CLICK!

The gun was empty. I thanked God for my reprieve and prayed she wouldn't fetch her umbrella from the buggy.

"Quit choking him," she yelled.

I raised my sticky, bloody hands and wriggled my fingers at her. "I'm trying to stop the bleeding." I put my hands back over his neck wound.

"Oh, my gawd," Mattie screamed, spinning around. "Somebody get a doctor." She squatted down beside me. "Cort, Cort, don't die on me!"

I feared he was about to breathe his last as he remained as still as a corpse. Then Thomson blinked his eyes and regained some senses. Confused that I was strangling him, he grabbed my wrists with his hands and tried to fling my fingers away. I felt the blood flow quicken. If he fought me, he would bleed himself to death. Despite my efforts, he resisted. I let go with my right hand, yanked my pistol from its scabbard and conked him on the head.

"Why'd you do that?" Mattie screamed.

"I'm trying to save him," I cried, dropping the weapon by his ear as he went limp. Then I gripped his neck again, as a gaggle of curious, chattering spectators gathered around me, some lighting matches to better see in the encroaching darkness. Moments later someone brought a lantern and placed it on the ground beside us.

Mattie gasped when the ball of jaundiced light revealed the crimson stains on his collar and my hands. "Don't die on me, Cort," she implored, then paused. "I'll kill that Katie Fulton for this," she announced, lifting her revolver and ejecting the hulls from the cylinder. She stepped around me to the buggy, looking for something.

Figuring it was more ammunition, I called to her. "Put away your gun, Mattie, I think Cort's coming to." I lied, but I didn't want her pulling the trigger at my nose again, this time with a loaded revolver.

She thrust the pistol in her dress, then squatted down by her lover, whose blank eyes stared somewhere beyond Denver. "Hold on, Cort; hold on for me," she pleaded.

From the back of the murmuring throng came the call of a louder voice. "Make way for the doctor. Make way for the doctor." The chattering crowd parted enough for the physician to squeeze through. He was a portly fellow, smoking a cheap cigar and carrying a worn leather case, wide like him, with the implements of his profession plus a corked whiskey bottle rising above everything else. He pushed Mattie out of the way and barged to my side, where he fell to his knees.

"Cut himself shaving, did he?" the doctor asked.

"No! He was shot," I answered.

"I know, son. It was a joke."

Neither I nor Cort was laughing.

He yanked his cigar from his mouth and ground it into the street, then pulled the liquor from his bag, yanked the cork out with his teeth, spat the stopper back in the case and took a healthy swig from the medicine. "Now move your hands, son," he commanded.

The moment I removed my hands, the doctor poured whiskey on Cort's neck. The sting brought movement to his eyes, then a groan from his lips. Nudging me aside, the physician bent over him, studying the wound on the right side of his neck. "Hold the lantern up for me," he ordered. I grabbed it by the handle and lifted it, bathing

Cort's pale face in a sickly yellow glow. The doctor sat the liquor bottle down and reached into his medical case, pulling out a wad of bandages he untangled, then tore off a strip about a foot long. He folded the dressing in thirds and then pressed it against a two-inch gash on Cort's neck.

"It's not as bad as it looks," the physician announced, "and it seems to be clotting, so he should be okay after a few days' rest."

Mattie clasped her hands and smiled. "Thank gawd!"

"Nope," the doctor corrected, "you need to thank the good Samaritan here that staunched the flow. Your man would've bled to death before I got here if he hadn't stemmed the bleeding." He looked up at me. "You've a physician's gentle touch, son. You had any medical training?"

"None!"

"Where'd you learn the perfect feel to stop bleeding?"

"I've nicked myself shaving on occasion."

The doctor laughed. "I've heard that joke before. You don't have to explain it to me."

Mattie interrupted our discussion. "Can't we get Cort somewhere to a bed?"

Twisting his head up at Miss Silks while maintaining pressure on the bandage, the doctor nodded. "Go ahead, if you intend to kill him."

"Of course not," she harrumphed.

"He's best where he is until I'm sure the bleeding's finished and we can apply a permanent dressing," he answered. "Have you reported this to the police?"

Mattie tittered. "Just because he cut himself shaving, why should we report that to the law?"

The doctor nodded. "Plan on settling it yourself, do you?"

Tossing her head in the air so that her rich brown hair tumbled over her shoulders, Mattie laughed. "I can afford to pay others to handle my business when needs dictate."

Though I knew she was right, after watching her empty two loads of bullets at Katie Fulton, I figured she'd want the pleasure of handling this matter in her own way.

"Well," the doctor answered, "word's going around that Shotgun Jake Townsend's been seen in Denver today. I'm told he never misses."

Unable to contain a laugh, I chuckled and shook the lantern.

"Keep the light still," the physician ordered. "There's nothing funny about Shotgun Jake Townsend."

Mattie eyed me and nodded. "I like a man that laughs at death, especially when he's hired to guard me and Cort."

"I don't remember Cort being part of the deal," I said, deciding I'd rather face Shotgun Jake in a duel than protect Thomson.

"Ten dollars a day then," Mattie offered. "Anyone that'd laugh at the mention of Shotgun Jake Townsend must be worth that kind of money."

"A week in advance," I countered.

She nodded. "Once we get Cort taken care of."

The doctor lifted the bandage and studied the gash on Cort's neck. "It's clotted up enough to travel once I secure a fresh dressing."

"Then I'll take him home," Mattie announced, "and put him to bed."

"I bet you will," some wiseacre called from the crowd, drawing laughs from the men and a few giggles from the women among them.

"I'd advise against that," the doctor cautioned.

"Putting him to bed?" Matte responded.

"No, sitting him in a buggy. He needs to stay on his back as a precaution so the wound doesn't reopen and start bleeding again."

While Mattie pondered the restriction, the physician tore another strip of bandage and folded it in thirds, placing it over the bullet gash. He looked up at me. "Son, squat down here and hold the dressing while I unroll enough to wrap it around his neck two or three times."

As I placed the lantern on the ground and dropped to assist the doctor, he noticed my blood stains. "When we're done, take my whiskey bottle and wash off your hands."

"That's a poor use of good liquor."

The doctor shook his head. "It's cheap whiskey, good for little more than steadying my nerves and washing wounds." Taking the long run of bandage he had pulled from his leather case, he wrapped it over the wound and then around Cort's neck four times before tucking the loose end inside the dressing itself and freeing my hand.

The physician looked at me as I rinsed my hands with his low-grade whiskey. "Sure you wouldn't like to take up the medicinal arts and assist me?"

"Does it pay ten dollars a day?"

Pursing his lips, he shook his head as he glanced at Mattie. "Saving lives doesn't pay as well as ruining them." He sighed. "You've got the touch, son, to be a doctor. Best of luck to you, though. You sure saved this man's life." He paused. "And I don't even know your name. Mine is Page, Dr. Carl Page."

"Lomax," I said. "H.H. Lomax."

"Well, twist my tail, son. Aren't you the one that taught Wild Bill Hickok the fast draw?"

"That's what's been told about me."

"Maybe if you'd given him poker lessons," Page mused, "he'd still be alive."

I shrugged, afraid to admit that if Wild Bill had been paying less attention to me than Jack McCall in Deadwood's Saloon No. 10, Hickok might have survived his last poker game.

As the physician stood up, he stroked his chin. "Just a last word of advice, Lomax."

"Shoot, Dr. Page."

"I hear Shotgun Jake Townsend arrived in Denver today to settle a score with a fellow named Lomax. If that's you, be on the lookout. I'd hate to patch you up because a scattergun blast is untidy."

Nodding, I patted at my pistol but drew only leather. Then I remembered I'd left my revolver on the ground beside Cort after I had cold-cocked him. "This might come in handy," I noted as I bent down and picked up the weapon, sliding it back in its scabbard.

Page turned to Silks. "Who's paying for services rendered? You, madam?"

"Thank you, doctor," Mattie answered as she shoved her hand in her sweetheart neckline and pulled out the wad of bills she'd paid me with earlier.

"Your thanks should go to Lomax," Page replied. "He saved your beau."

Mattie uncoiled the roll of currency and counted out twenty-five dollars, then handed him her payment without him ever having announced the cost. "Dissipation pays well," she said.

"Indeed it does," Page answered, "that being five times more than I would've charged. For the next three days, keep your fellow on his back, no excitement or sudden moves, including carnal activities."

I thought those were strange instructions, there being no carnival in Denver to my knowledge, but he was the doctor, and I was new to town. "While you got the money out, Mattie, you might pay me another thirty-five dollars in advance for guarding Cort. I'll make sure he doesn't go to any carnival."

Page slapped his knee and bellowed. "That's another good joke, Lomax. You ever thought about making you living on stage?"

While I'd considered holding up a stage a time or two when I was broke, I'd never judged acting on stage as honorable a profession as robbing one on the road.

Mattie counted off my salary increase and handed me my raise, though I was having second thoughts. While Miss Silks was all right, I'd seen cases of smallpox I liked better than Cort Thomson. Hell, if you were gonna steal from a woman, at least have the decency to do it behind her back when she wasn't looking rather than robbing her face-to-face with your charm. Less gossip that way.

After she settled up with me, she turned to the crowd and waved the bundle of bills over her head. "I need a wagon and someone to deliver Cort Thomson to my place on Holladay Street. You can't miss it as it's the finest parlor house in town. I'll pay ten dollars."

Nobody stepped forward to accept her offer. After all, it was Saturday night and there was plenty of whiskey waiting to be swallowed across the street or elsewhere in Denver.

"Fifteen dollars," she announced, drawing no takers until she sweetened the pot. "Twenty dollars and an evening with one of my fashionable young ladies." Her final offer drew more responses than she could accept, finally accepting the proposal of four men, who promised to load Cort in their freight wagon, deliver him to Mattie's place, unload him and transport him to bed. In exchange, each would earn five dollars and a roll in the hay to boot. Mattie accepted their offer, even paying them in advance as she knew the mattress romp would give them plenty of incentive to complete the deal.

When the negotiations concluded, Mattie instructed me to stay with Cort and make sure he made it safely to her place as she didn't trust Katie Fulton not to attempt to assassinate him and her again. I told her I'd do it until I looked around and missed Ciaha. "My mule's gone," I said, panic in my voice.

"I'll buy you a fine steed tomorrow," Mattie offered.

"But I need him tonight, if I'm to guard Cort."

"Anybody seen my mule?" I cried, turning to the crowd.

Mattie picked up the lantern and handed it to me. "See if you can find him."

"Hey, that's my lantern," said a thin man wearing a barkeep's apron.

Without missing a beat, she peeled off ten dollars from her roll of cash and gave it to him. "I'm buying it from you. There's enough there for you to purchase two or three new ones."

I grabbed the lantern and started calling for Ciaha. Then I worked my way back through the park, figuring he was more likely to head there than to walk deeper into Denver. Shouting his name dozens of times, I finally detected a familiar bray down toward the river and ambled that direction, swinging my lantern in hopes he would recognize me in the light and come trotting my way. Instead he waited for me to approach him down the sloping bank of the South Platte. When I found him, I grabbed the reins and walked him away from the sloping bank before extinguishing the lamp and mounting Ciaha for the return to Fifteenth Street.

Over the last eighteen months, I had grown to love that mule, my one constant companion in all the days since I left Fort Abraham Lincoln against my will as part of Custer's final Indian hunt. He had been my confidant and friend the entire time, from the Little Bighorn and

Custer to Deadwood and Wild Bill and to Denver and Mattie Silks. Some might think it pathetic that a man can't do better for a pal than an old army animal, but Ciaha was dependable, unlike most friends, and didn't argue politics like others.

Ciaha and I made it back to Mattie's buggy, where she was impatiently snapping the buggy whip in the air. "Where've you been?"

"My mule wandered all the way to the river. I couldn't help it."

"Well, Cort's feeling poorly, and he's impatient to get into bed, carnal relations or not."

"He'd be getting in a coffin if it wasn't for me," I reminded her.

She flicked the whip on the flank of her gelding and the buggy lurched forward, followed by the freight wagon that carried Thomson and his four attendants. The quartet hollered and whistled, as excited as if they were going to the carnival after depositing Cort in bed.

Denver's streets were lit from the lamps of saloons, pool halls and other dives that did a booming business on a Saturday night. We turned on Holladay Street and drove a few blocks before Mattie pointed the freight wagon to her brothel. "Go around to the back," she commanded. Her block stood quieter than many we passed, as if she expected a certain dignity among her male clientele and a definite sophistication among her ladies. I'd worked a spell in a Waco brothel, and I'd had occasion to visit ones now and then when the urge struck me, so I was aware of the services offered. Mattie's place didn't measure up to the refinement I had encountered in Waco, but it wasn't a hog ranch either. Only a year earlier I had learned that my oldest sister, who ran away from home in Cane Hill, Arkansas, before I got to know her, had become the most successful madam in Deadwood. So, I had developed a soft spot for these working gals as long as they stayed off the laudanum, opium, morphine and liquor. Those that abstained from those intoxicants were some of the finest people alive, while those that didn't were among the meanest and dirtiest you'd run into anywhere. To

Mattie's credit, she kept a decent house that treated the girls as fair as could be expected.

It wasn't Mattie's handling of her gals that bothered me as much as it was her maintaining Cort Thomson as a kept man. I just didn't have any respect for him, leeching off of her like the bloodsucker he was. He was not only fast afoot but also quick with the wit and charm. In the coming days, I heard her scold him for wasting money or chasing other skirts. Cort, though, would say something funny that would tickle her and make her forget her original complaint. Thomson was so slick that he could pick her pockets even when she was naked.

As the four freight men slid Cort out of the wagon onto Mattie's blue-and-white quilt, she jumped down from her buggy, grabbing her furled umbrella and pointing to the rear entrance. Cort moaned, and Mattie stepped to his side, asking if he was okay and offering to do anything he needed. He groaned louder. The quartet carried Thomson up the steps and into the house, as Mattie mother-henned him all the way inside. I dismounted, tied Ciaha to a fence post and walked in the back door into the kitchen overheated from a wood stove in the corner and the harsh words Mattie shot at her help when they stared at Cort as he passed.

"Let us through, dammit," Mattie cried, wielding her umbrella as a general would use his sword leading men into battle. "My Cort's hurt; needs rest. Take him to my bedroom, fellows."

The four carrying him looked at one another with questioning eyes. None of them knew where her room was and appeared too scared to ask, likely for fear Mattie might smack them in the nose with her umbrella or renege on her promise on private time with her girls. I trailed behind the caravan. The men hesitated.

"Get moving," Mattie cried, waving her umbrella in the air. "My Cort has suffered long enough. Put him on my bed."

"They don't know where your bedroom is," I informed her.

Mattie spun toward me. "Who are you?"

"Your bodyguard. The fellow that saved your Cort from bleeding to death."

"Oh, yeah," she mumbled. "Now I remember."

The shock of Thomson's wounding and the haze from all the champagne she had consumed had scrambled her memory. I was glad I had been paid in advance and hoped her deteriorating recollection of the day's events might allow me to slip away and pretend none of this had ever happened because the more I was around Mattie and him, the less comfortable I became.

Turning her bewildered face from me, she directed her four temporary hands through the parlor where eight clients took their gaze off the young ladies they were propositioning and watched Cort and his escort pass by. As I followed them, a randy client asked me what was wrong with Cort's neck.

"He cut himself shaving," I offered.

"Don't fun me," he responded.

I sighed. "Can't pull a fast one past a man as sharp as you, now can I?"

The fellow swelled up his chest, proud that his brilliance had been recognized by a dumber being. "Now tell me what happened."

"Mattie tried to slit his throat for asking too many questions," I responded, watching the guy swallow hard then turn back to the soft flesh he was propositioning.

We marched through the parlor and around the staircase, then along a dim hall to a far door that Mattie opened, scurrying to the opposite side of the room where she tossed her umbrella by her vanity and lit a lamp as the men moved toward the bed. Mattie flung back the covers, exposing the cleanest and whitest sheets I'd ever seen. She grabbed a pair of pillows, equally white, and fluffed them, placing them at the head of the mattress so her devotee could recover from his wound. The quartet eased Cort onto the bed, gently pulling the quilt from beneath him as Mattie sat on the edge of the mattress and tried to remove his stained coat and shirt. He groaned each time she lifted his arm. I suspected he was feigning pain to draw more sympathy from his woman and stick his fingers deeper into her pocketbook.

"I can't bear to hurt him more," she said, looking at the four who had tended him. "What are you waiting on? Get out of here so my Cort can recover."

"Ma'am," one of them stuttered, "you promised us a girl apiece if we delivered him to your place. We want our due."

Stunned that these men valued their lust more than her man, Mattie pushed herself up from the mattress and strode to her vanity, opening up a drawer and grabbing four bronze coins. She returned to the quartet and gave a token to each. "These tokens are good for a poke with one of the girls. Take them and be gone."

"Yes, ma'am," they answered in unison and charged past me out the door like it'd been a spell since they'd had a woman.

I thought I'd slip out behind them and abandon Mattie and her sleazy companion, but she stopped me.

"Lomax," she said, "be a dear and fetch Lupe. Tell her to bring me my sewing basket."

If she remembered my name, her mind wasn't as muddled as I had hoped. I might not escape her clutches so easily. I nodded and departed, retracing my steps down the hall into the parlor. "Lupe? Lupe?" I called. One of girls pointed me to the kitchen. I marched there and saw a broad Mexican woman placing a pot of coffee on the hot stove. "Lupe?" I asked.

She turned around and smiled. "*Sí.*"

"Miss Mattie requested that you take her sewing basket to her room. She must be planning to sew something for Mr. Cort."

"Tsk, tsk, tsk," she replied. "That man is no good, but I'll deliver her basket."

"*Gracias,*" I said, answering with my limited Spanish. I started back to Mattie's bedroom and found her planting soft kisses on Cort's cheek and forehead. "Lupe's coming."

Barely had the words left my lips than she marched in, carrying a basket of sewing materials. She placed her freight on the bed, and Mattie picked up a pair of shiny sewing shears and cut the sleeves and sides of his suit so she could slide the attire off in pieces without having to move him. Then she started cutting at his bloody shirt.

"Anything else, Miss Silks?" Lupe asked.

"Yes, Lupe. Please show Lomax where to stable his mule. He's a gunman I've hired to guard me and Mr. Thomson from Katie Fulton and Sam Thatcher. They're the ones that did this to my Cort."

"*Si*, Miss Silks," Lupe replied.

"When you're done with that, Lupe," Mattie continued, "please see that a mattress is placed in the hallway outside our door. I want Lomax to sleep there tonight for extra safety. No telling what Katie might try to do. She's crazy enough to kill Cort and me in our own bed."

"Yes, Miss Silks."

"And another thing, Lupe. Have the girls be on the lookout for Shotgun Jake Townsend. He's been spotted in town."

"Who's he?" Lupe replied. "I've never heard of him."

Mattie just shook her head. "He's as mean a killer as has ever been to Denver. Just let the girls know to be careful, especially if someone comes in with a sawed-off shotgun."

"*Si*, Miss Silks." Lupe backed out of the room and motioned for me to accompany her.

We retraced her path to the kitchen, and she took me out the rear door, pointing to the small stable at the back of the lot. I led Ciaha there and tended him, removing my gear and leaving him with a trough of hay and a full bucket of water. I carried my belongings and carbine inside and found a mattress with clean sheets and pillows on the floor outside Mattie's door where I dropped my load and collapsed on the bed, keeping my weapons handy in case my imaginary friend showed up.

It took a while to go to sleep, primarily because of the moaning from Cort Thomson. I couldn't tell if he was hurting or was dreaming of some carnival ride.

Chapter Four

By morning when I awoke, I felt like a watchdog sleeping on the front porch. With brothels being a night business, I was the only resident up at a regular hour, except for Lupe in the kitchen tending the stove and boiling a pot of coffee. "*Buenas dias,*" I said, startling her.

Lupe spun around and smiled. "I didn't hear you come in," she said. "Nobody rises early in this house, save me."

"Most folks don't sleep on the floor," I replied.

She laughed. "Some do, either passing out or preferring it to a mattress."

"You're pulling my leg."

Opening a cabinet and taking a fancy teacup from a hook, Lupe carried it to the stove where she grabbed a potholder, picked up the pot and poured me a cup of coffee. "No, *Señor* Lomax, it is true. One of the richest cattleman in Colorado brings his bedroll when he visits and throws it on the floor, preferring to sleep and do business with the girls there." She placed the cup on the table and gestured for me to sit.

Taking my seat, I picked up the mug and blew on the steaming liquid, then took a small scalding sip of the weak brew. I smiled at Lupe. "Good coffee. Most folks brew it too strong."

Lupe grinned. "The girls prefer it weak. Miss Silks likes it that way so I can get more cups out of a pound of coffee and save her money." She frowned and shook her head.

"You against saving money?" I asked.

"No, I am frugal myself, but what she saves on coffee she wastes on Mr. Cort, giving him fine gifts and nice things. He doesn't care, just uses her for his pleasure and abuses her for his amusement. He's a good-for-nothing man."

"A leech!"

"¡Sí!"

I grinned. "You and I see eye-to-eye, Lupe. Does Mattie know how you feel?"

"What I have told you I have shared with Miss Silks," she replied. "Many times. He is a sheep in wolf's clothing, that's what Mr. Cort is!"

I didn't understand if she meant to twist her comparison or not, but she pegged Thomson better than me and in fewer words. I dipped my coffee cup at her in a toast of agreement.

"Now, *Señor* Lomax, let me ask you a question." She pulled up a chair opposite me. "Is this Shotgun Jake Townsend as mean as they say and is he after you?"

Surprised by her inquiry, I glanced around the kitchen and dining room, then toward the parlor, confirming no one else within hearing range. I leaned across the table. "Can you keep a secret, Lupe?"

"*Sí.*" She nodded.

"I made him up. He doesn't exist."

She looked at me with stern lips, which gradually softened into a broad, toothy grin. "*Señor* Lomax, I am so proud of you, telling such a tale that hooks Miss Silks. She's shrewd and you're the first one that's been able to pull the wool over her eyes."

"Maybe it's the wolf hide over her eyes, Lupe, but don't you go share this with anyone else as Shotgun Jake may come in handy before I'm done here."

"Oh, *Señor* Lomax, let me use his name now and then, *por favor.*"

"What for, pray tell?"

"To scare Mr. Cort."

My lips parted in a wide grin, and I nodded, realizing that having both Lupe and Shotgun Jake in my gang could work to my advantage in getting out of the high-paying mess I'd gotten myself into. "You can, Lupe, but only when I'm around."

The cook jumped from her chair, came around the table and hugged me. "*Gracias, Señor* Lomax, *gracias.*"

"You, Lupe, just became my favorite among Mattie's girls."

She marched over to the stove, strutting like a mother hen leading her chicks to eat. She fixed me a meal of boiled eggs, sausage and biscuits, as she explained that she cooked two meals a day for the house, breakfast served at eleven-thirty and dinner at five. As she prepared the morning meal for the girls, we giggled about our shared secret over Shotgun Jake. Around eleven, Mattie strode into the kitchen to spoil our conservation.

"Lupe," she ordered, "take a break from breakfast and gather up everything for my sewing basket and get it out of my room, along with Cort's bloodied clothes. Also, remove that mattress from the floor by my door."

"*Si*, Miss Silks," she replied.

"Let me help," I said, rising from my chair and finishing my third cup of coffee.

"No, Lomax, you wait here," Mattie commanded. "I want you to visit the city marshal and see if he's arrested our Katie Fulton and Sam Thatcher."

"If you and Cort hadn't been too embarrassed for me to ride my mule at your side, I could've screened you both from the bullets."

"What's done is done," she replied. "After you find out where they are, tell me as I may want you to kill them."

She said it so matter-of-factly, I thought I had misunderstood her. "What?"

"When you locate them, I'll decide if you should murder them both."

Lifting my hand and waving it in her face, I shook my head. "I hired on to guard you, not to slaughter your enemies."

"At ten dollars a day you'll do what I tell you," Mattie informed me.

Standing behind her, Lupe grimaced and shrugged.

"Then I'm resigning."

"You walk out on me, Lomax, and I'll inform Shotgun Jake Townsend where you are."

Coughing and stifling a laugh, Lupe shook her head as her boss glared at her. Lupe shrugged. "Shotgun Jake is a very bad man!"

Mattie turned to me. "Get moving or I'll find Townsend."

I nodded. "Let me grab my things." I accompanied Lupe to Mattie's room, helping her pick up the single mattress and carrying it around the stairs, through the parlor and into the kitchen where she opened a door and backed inside.

"This is my place." Her modest room featured a metal bedstead with mattress on one side and a naked bedstead on the opposite wall. We dropped the mattress on the metal frame and returned to Silks' bedroom.

"Time's a wasting," Mattie declared, tapping her foot on the floor as I passed.

"I'm getting my carbine and belongings," I explained.

"Be quick," she demanded.

As I reached Mattie's open door, I bent over and grabbed my things, pausing a moment as Thomson growled at Lupe.

"Bring me a cup of coffee, now," he ordered like he was king of the house rather than its biggest leech.

"*Si, Señor* Cort," Lupe replied, "but let me grab these rags first as Miss Silks requested."

"No," he snarled. "I'm thirsty right this minute. Move, you meskin!"

Lupe turned for the door, but I jumped inside and stopped her.

"I'll get your coffee, Mr. Cort," I said. "I'll be quick."

"You damn well better 'cause I'm parched, Lomax."

I raced to the kitchen, dropping my carbine and saddlebags on the table.

"What's started a fire in you?" Mattie demanded.

"Your Cort needs a cup of coffee. He's mighty thirsty." I grabbed a mug from the cupboard and filled it with the scalding liquid. I headed back to Cort.

"Don't spill it on the parlor carpet," Mattie ordered as I passed.

I didn't because I wanted Cort Thomson to get every drop, especially after I entered the room. He had kicked his covers away and was lying there indecent in front of Lupe as she picked up the bloody remnants of his clothes. Mattie had cut every inch of his clothing off because he was as nude and as proud as a peacock of his modest charms. I was embarrassed for Lupe.

"It's about time, Lomax," he noted. "You're slow for a fellow making ten dollars a day."

No sooner had he spoken than I tripped and tumbled toward him, the hot coffee spilling as I lunged at the bed, splashing his groin with the scalding potion.

"Dammmnnnnn," Thomson squealed as the steaming liquid splashed on his pride.

"I'm so sorry," I cried, slapping the mug against his waist as I tried to put out the fire.

Mr. Cort cut loose a shrill yell. "Don't hit me with the mug," he cried as I attempted to swat away the burn, though my efforts only increased his agony.

Glancing at Lupe as she carried the bundle of stained clothing toward the door, I winked and she snickered, just as Mattie barged into the room.

"What's going on?" the madam demanded.

Cort thrashed around on the bed, grabbing the covers and pulling them over his midsection, an overdue display of modesty. "Lomax threw scalding coffee on me."

"I tripped," I explained. "Poor fellow had nothing covering him."

"Then he hit me with the mug," Thomson called, rubbing himself through the sheet.

Shrugging, I acknowledged the accusation. "Just trying to ease his pain."

"Get him out of here," Cort demanded, "before he kills me."

"He's got a lot on his mind," I noted. "Certainly more than he had on his waist."

"Go on, Lomax, and find the marshal like I told you," Mattie ordered.

When I stepped outside the room, she closed the door to minister to Cort's wound. As I rounded the stairs for the kitchen, several of Mattie's gals leaned over the banister.

"What happened?" one asked.

"Cort spilled his coffee."

"He's taking it like a baby," she said.

I stopped and shook my head. "It's not that he spilt it, but where he spilt it."

Three of the girls chuckled. "So he was preening without the sheets," another one said.

"Yep," I replied.

"He's proud of himself," said a third young woman.

I walked into the kitchen and spotted Lupe with a smile as broad as a rainbow. "*Gracias, Señor* Lomax, for taking Mr. Cort down a notch or two. He displays himself to all the girls when Miss Silks is absent."

"Why do you stay here?"

"Her work pays better than anything else I can find." She walked over and hugged me. "*Gracias, gracias.*"

"It was worth it, to see the expression on his face," I admitted. "Now I best find the city marshal's office and determine what Katie and Sam are up to." I picked up my carbine and saddlebags.

Lupe accompanied me to the back door, giving me directions to the marshal's office. As my destination was only a few blocks away, I decided to walk, so I carried my saddlebags out to the stable and left them on the stall by Ciaha, who seemed satisfied with his trough of hay, though I refilled his water bucket. Emerging from the shed, I walked to Holladay Street and looked at Mattie's place. Like her girls, the structure appeared less striking in the sunshine than it did under dim light. I then marched away looking for the marshal's office.

Denver was a bustling city barely two decades old and one of the West's oddest mining towns, much like Skagway would be in another twenty years. While Denver served as a hub for the state's mining industry, I knew of no mines in the immediate vicinity. The Pike's Peak Gold Rush in 1858 had spawned Denver in the eyes of sharp promoters speculating in towns rather than minerals. Pike's Peak led to Central City and all the subsequent boomtowns that produced enough riches to buy Colorado Territory's way to statehood the year before I arrived in Denver. The mining towns carried names like Trinidad, Caribou, Ouray, Telluride, Creede, Durango, Montezuma, Oro City, Eureka, Silverton, Georgetown,

St. Elmo, Alma, Gold Hill, Ophir, Pandora, Congress, Tincup, Capitol City, Breckenridge, Tomboy, Querida, Ward, Jamestown, Cripple Creek, Jasper, Kokomo, Lake City, Crested Butte, Russell Gulch and Fairplay, the most deceptive name of any boomtown anywhere as there was no fair play in the hunt for precious metals. But no matter what it was called, each mining town carried the promise of quick riches instead of the reality of backbreaking labor, exorbitant prices, drafty lodging, incessant frauds, a scarcity of decent women and an abundance of rodents.

The mining enclave of the moment as I searched for the marshal's office was Leadville, southwest of Denver. Everyone from soiled doves to ministers was talking about it. Gold had been discovered in the area after the Pike's Peak stampede, but it had petered out in the ensuing years. Now rich deposits of silver were rumored at the headwaters of the Arkansas River in the heart of the Rockies. When I learned that the high plateau spawned the Arkansas, I felt a touch of homesickness, missing my folks and the people I'd grown up around, no matter how mean they had been during and after the war. I decided I'd visit Leadville, just to spit in the river, understanding the current would carry a little of me back to the Ozarks, even if the rest of me stayed in the Rockies. My pa had gone to California during the Rush of 1849 and had returned to home poorer than when he left, but at least he made it back home. His party's other members were never seen again. Like my pa, I dreamed of riches immeasurable. Dreams, though, come much easier than paydirt.

Besides the residents, Denver also had a vagabond community of men and women passing through on the way to the mining towns. Another segment of the Denver populace, a group well represented at Mattie's picnic the day before, was the crooks that tried to scam the unwary in their quest for riches. I once heard a mine described as a hole in the ground with a liar at the top. You didn't have to get to mining country to find liars because a sizeable number of them moved in and out of Denver, congregating around the railroad station and trying to pick the pockets of new arrivals either with a sleight of hand or with a sleight of a pen on paper on "legal" documents. The schemes that trapped the naïve were profitable enough that the thieves could pay off the law and still make a good living at the expense of the newly arrived suckers. Most of the dupes were too embarrassed to admit to the authorities they had been conned. As a result, many crimes remained unreported, but occasionally a mark lacked shame and tried to convince the authorities to rectify the matter, creating a stir among the newspapers and upsetting the law over the bad press rather than the crime itself. So, dealing with the lawmen in Denver was an iffy proposition as you never knew if you had an honest broker or a blatant profiteer from the very misdeeds the peace officer had taken an oath to resolve.

When I reached the marshal's office, I walked in and inquired if anyone had been arrested for the shooting near Olympic Park the previous evening. The clerk shrugged, explaining he wasn't on duty then. He called for a deputy marshal, who came out and asked me my name.

"H.H. Lomax," I said, studying the lawman who looked vaguely familiar.

"Don't mean squat to me," he replied.

"I'm working for Miss Mattie Silks," I explained. "She was attacked last night and her partner shot in the neck by Katie—"

The deputy raised his hand for me to hush. "So that's how he cut himself shaving," he noted.

I realized that this was the fellow that had accosted me in Mattie's parlor and asked all the questions about Thomson's wound. From his bloodshot eyes, I gathered he was still suffering from a hangover, either from lust or actual drink. "Yep, that's how, courtesy of Katie Fulton and Sam Thatcher."

"Never realized they were barbers," the deputy said to himself, still as confused as a gelding at breeding time.

"Have you done anything about the shooting? I must inform the victims."

"Katie and Sam turned themselves in this morning," he advised me.

"How long will they stay in jail?"

"They already paid off the marshal, I mean posted their bail. The marshal released them within an hour of their arrest."

"While they are running around Denver, Miss Silks remains in danger."

"They left town on the ten-thirty train, headed for Kansas City. Mattie and Cort have nothing to worry about now."

Then an odd notion struck me. "Far from it," I countered.

"Say what?"

"Last night Katie paid Shotgun Jake Townsend five hundred dollars a head to assassinate both Mattie and Cort. That's why they left town so no one could blame them for the murders when Townsend finished his business."

The deputy whistled. "Shotgun Jake Townsend. I've been hearing terrible things about him the last few days. Word is, he's a bad one."

"As mean as they come. He'd back shoot his own mother if the return was right. Gossip says he's killed people for a nickel, so the price doesn't have to be very high."

My friend's eyes widened. "It's hard to make a living shooting folks for a nickel a pop."

Nodding, I agreed. "He makes up for it on volume. If Denver's population drops, I'd bet my honest word that Shotgun Jake is behind the decline."

"Let me get my boss." The deputy rushed past the eavesdropper with gaping eyes and mouth, and burst through a door marked **CITY MARSHAL.**

Swallowing hard, the clerk at the counter asked in a nervous voice. "Is Townsend as mean as they say?"

"Can't vouch for the truth of the story, but I heard that Shotgun Jake fell into a den of rattlesnakes back in Texas, and every rattler that bit him died before sundown. As for Jake, he climbed out of the pit, dusted himself off and went about his business. Some folks said all that venom in his blood improved his disposition, making him a mite friendlier than he'd ever been."

The clerk paled and looked at his desk, shuffling papers and catching his breath.

It took longer than I thought necessary for the deputy to return with the marshal, but I figured the lawman must have still been counting Katie's bail money. When the office door opened, the marshal emerged, a tall, strapping figure with black hair, black eyes, black handlebar mustache and teeth blackened from his chewing tobacco. The deputy trailed in his boss's wake like a puppy on his first hunt with his poppa. The marshal eyed me up and down as if he was inspecting a horse he considered purchasing.

"So you're H.H. Lomax," he said.

I nodded.

"No offense, Lomax, but I was figuring to find a tougher looking hombre." He continued to size me up.

While I was expecting a man with whiter teeth, I held my tongue for fear the city marshal might splatter me with the chaw he was working like a cow chewing cud.

"Rumors say you taught Wild Bill how to shoot and that when things turned sour, you dumped chamber pot drippings on his hair. Any truth to those stories?"

Playing coy, I grinned. "Could be."

"I don't indulge games, Lomax." To emphasize the point, his trigger finger poked the silver-and-gold badge over his heart. The word MARSHAL was engraved in the gold star beneath an arc embossed with **DENVER CITY**.

"Nor do I, marshal."

"Now what about Shotgun Jake Townsend?"

"I'm in Mattie Silks' employ, hired to protect her. Word is when Katie Fulton and Sam Thatcher failed to kill Mattie and Cort last night, Katie employed Shotgun Jake to finish the job. Then Katie and Sam left town to avoid suspicions when her rivals are murdered."

"Why is it I ain't heard much about him until the last week or so, Lomax?"

"Not sure he's ever been to Colorado before. He's better known in Texas, Indian Territory, Kansas, Wyoming and Dakota Territory."

"Are you certain he's in Denver now?"

"He's been tailing me for a year from Deadwood through Wyoming and into Colorado."

"How come?"

"He picked up some of the rumors about what I did to Wild Bill's hair and blames me for his death in Deadwood. Bill's demise was all Jack McCall's doing, but Shotgun Jake got it in his head that I distracted him from McCall."

"So you've seen him in Denver."

I nodded, knowing I was fibbing and hoping God didn't hold it against me. "Let's just say that if he was 'Buffalo Gun' Jake Townsend I'd be dead, but I don't let him get close enough to kill me with a sawed-off shotgun."

"Seems a rifle would extend his range and do the trick a lot faster."

"He likes the splatter of scattergun in the back from what I've been told."

"He's been said to kill a man for a nickel," the deputy informed his boss. "Bad man."

"What else would you expect from him?" I asked. "He's the offspring of that inbred breed of mongrels known as Texans. They're dumber than a Comanche working an arithmetic problem."

"Can you describe him?"

"The Comanche?"

"No," the marshal replied, rolling his eyes, "Townsend."

"He's is a short fellow, four maybe five inches at most over five feet tall. He wears wire-rimmed spectacles without the lenses."

"Huh?" The sheriff and deputy looked at each other.

"He's got eyes as sharp as a hawk, so he doesn't need glasses. He wears the wire-rimmed frames as a disguise. He looks like an out-of-work schoolteacher instead of a hired killer."

"What about his weapon?"

"He wears a frock coat so he can hide his 12-gauge Parker shotgun with a sawed-off barrel and stock. He's screwed a metal ring into the stock and secured a leather strap to the ring. Townsend hangs the strap over his shoulder and under his frock coat so the weapon hangs at his side, ready for use whenever he gets a murderous inclination. An evil man."

The marshal took a deep breath. "Sounds like a mean one."

I nodded. "Without a doubt."

"I'm sure you'll keep watch on Mattie and Cort."

Grimacing, I raised my shoulders and exhaled slowly. "That's why I came to see you, marshal. Mattie doesn't think she's in danger unless by Katie Fulton's direct hand. I've tried to explain to her the truth of the matter, but she thinks she's safe."

"What about Cort? Can he convince her?"

"Cort's too lazy to try."

"That sounds right on Cort," he answered.

"Would you drop by her place this afternoon and give her a warning? I don't care if you warn Cort or not, but please tell Mattie this is serious business."

The lawman nodded. "I'll be by about four o'clock before Lupe serves dinner and business picks up."

"Thank you, marshal. That'll mean a lot to me and to Mattie. Just don't tell her I sent you." I turned around and started to leave.

"Lomax," the officer called, "you tell us if you see Townsend anywhere, and I'll put my men on the lookout for him.

"Yes, sir," I answered as I marched out the door.

I walked around Denver until I found a gun shop and stepped inside, purchasing six 12-gauge shotgun shells and sliding them in my pants pocket. They would come in handy before I left town.

Chapter Five

Mattie Silks crossed her arms over her ample bosom and shook her head vigorously. "I don't believe that, Lomax." She stood in the doorway to her bedroom, angered that I had knocked and awakened Cort from his nap.

"You hired me to protect you and Cort. That's what I'm trying to do, Mattie."

"Katie's too dumb to hire a killer. She'd only find pleasure in shooting me herself. It sounds like a rumor she made up to scare me. I ain't falling for it."

"You're wasting ten dollars a day in my pay if you won't listen to me."

Mattie's nostrils flared. "My Cort needs his rest to recover. We can talk about it at dinner." She closed her door just as a pounding echoed down the hall from the entry. Mattie called to me. "Lomax, see who's out front and tell them we don't open for two hours."

I started for the entry, grinning at the marshal's punctuality. At the entrance I cried, "We open at six. Go away and let the ladies rest."

"Open up," came the officer's voice. "It's the law."

Unlatching the door, I cracked it and winked. "No problems here, marshal."

"I must speak to Miss Silks." He turned and spat tobacco juice off the porch.

"She's in a bad mood," I said as I allowed him in. "Mattie's in her room."

The marshal headed straight to her bedroom and

rapped on her door.

"Go away, Lomax," she screamed. "Cort needs his rest if he's ever gonna recover."

"It's the city marshal, Mattie. We need to talk."

The door cracked with her peeking out, then widened when she recognized the officer. "We've had no trouble nor caused any here, marshal."

"It's about threats made against your safety," he told her as he stepped inside.

Her face flushed with fear as the lawman entered. She stared at me as she shut her room.

"Do you want me to bring cups of coffee?" I called.

"Hell no," screamed Cort.

"Suit yourself," I said, turning and walking to the kitchen where Lupe worked over the stove on supper.

While no one else was in the room, I described Shotgun Jake Townsend to her and suggested while serving dinner she might mention such a fellow snooping around the place that afternoon, especially spending time by the side window in Mattie's bedroom. She nodded.

I sat at the kitchen table, and Lupe brought me coffee. Taking a sip, I complimented her again on the brew and told her how I'd offered to deliver a cup to Cort.

"So that's what he yelled 'hell no' about?"

"Yes, ma'am."

"Maybe he'll stay covered around me from now on. He's not as charming as he thinks."

"Working men get blisters on their hands," I said. "A kept man gets blisters elsewhere."

Lupe laughed. "That is a good one, Señor Lomax. If the blister is that sore, he'll be idle for a spell."

We visited for twenty minutes before I heard Mattie escorting the marshal to the front and thanking him for the warning. She let him out and joined us, her face clouded with worry.

"Is everything okay?" I asked.

She looked at me in a daze. "You were right, Lomax. The marshal said word's going around that Katie hired Shotgun Jake Townsend to kill us."

Lupe gasped. "Shotgun Jake Townsend? He's known

among my people as a ruthless killer, shooting Mexicans for the fun of it."

Mattie's face lost its color, except for the rouge on her cheeks.

Crossing herself, Lupe turned to the stove to stir a pot of stew.

"I told you this was serious."

She nodded. "I can see Katie hating me, but why would she want to hurt my Cort?"

"That might be the best way to hurt you, Mattie. Did you ever think of that?"

"How would I cope if I lost Cort?"

Probably save more money for yourself, I thought but didn't say. "You want me to sleep outside your door again?"

"No, you can bed in Lupe's room, but I want you to keep a watch for strange men."

"Like your nightly visitors? That's an odd request from someone running a brothel," I observed.

Lupe turned from the stove and wiped her sleeve over her brow. "I did see one man snooping around today, but he was a short fellow, not much of a threat."

Mattie shot her gaze at me, then back at Lupe. "A small fellow?"

"Yes," she replied, holding her hand midway between her waist and shoulders. "He barely came to here. Didn't look like he could hurt a fly, though I don't think he was all there."

"All there?" Mattie asked

Lupe placed her hands on her abundant hips and stared at her boss. "In the head, I mean. He was wearing spectacles, but there was no glass in the frames. I don't know why a man would wear glasses without the glass."

Mattie turned even whiter, the rouge seeming to pale to pink. "Shotgun Jake Townsend?" she whispered.

I asked Lupe a question to ease Mattie's fears. "This bespectacled fellow, he wasn't wearing a frock coat, was he?"

"*Si, Señor* Lomax. It was much too long for so short a man."

Clasping my lips together to keep from snickering at Lupe's performance, I turned to Mattie. "Likely a coincidence, but to be safe, I'm quitting and leaving Denver tonight."

She leaped to me and grabbed my wrists. "No, you can't leave me and my Cort."

"I'll repay six days of your advance before I depart."

"No, no," she pleaded, dropping my hands. "Keep the money, stay here and protect us."

"He's more interested in me than you and Cort."

"That's not what the marshal said."

"You didn't believe me to begin with. I can't work for someone that thinks I'm telling stories. Besides, Shotgun Jake's been tailing me for going on a year, trying to ambush me."

Lupe walked over. "No, *Señor* Lomax. He never mentioned your name, just Miss Silks' and Mr. Thomson's names, just theirs, not yours."

"What?" Mattie cried, stepping to her. "What did you tell him?"

"He asked if this was where Mattie Silks and Cort Thomson stayed," Lupe said, then paused. "I told him we have many visitors but I seldom know their names and wasn't familiar with those two names." She shook her head. "This little fellow couldn't hurt a fly."

Mattie turned back to me. "Please stay, Lomax, and protect us. I'll double your pay."

I reached in my pocket and pulled out my roll of bills, which was nothing compared to hers, and counted off what I owed her for six days of unfinished labor. "Ten, twenty, thirty—"

"No, Lomax, please stay. I'll pay Twenty dollars a day."

"—forty, fifty, sixty dollars," I counted, pulling the bills from my wad and offering them to the madam.

Shoving my hand away, Mattie clutched her throat, looking from the back door to the side window by the stove. "He could be outside right now."

"Yes, he could," I said, wagging the cash in front of her nose. "Take the money. I agreed to protect you from Fulton and Thatcher, not Townsend."

Lupe crossed herself again by the counter, then picked up a stack of fine porcelain bowls that she carried into the adjacent dining room where the girls would take their supper.

Mattie pleaded with me. "Keep the money. You owe

me a week's work."

I dropped the bills on the floor, and Mattie fell to her knees, begging me to stay as she grabbed them and thrust the cash at me.

"At least finish your week and give me time to make other arrangements. You owe us."

Lupe trod back to the counter for spoons, murmuring, "Shotgun Jake *es muy mala.*"

Figuring I had strung Mattie along far enough, I gave in. "I'll stay for the next six days, but I can't promise anything beyond that." I took the money and offered her my hand to help her up from the floor. When she stood up, I told her to deliver a message to Cort. "I intend to teach him a few more manners if I see him indecent with Lupe again. You tell his sorry ass that."

"*Gracias,*" the cook said as she marched back to the dining room with the eating utensils.

Mattie nodded, "Okay, Lomax, okay. I will as long as you protect us."

"For six more days. I promise nothing after that."

She sighed. "That'll give me time to work something out, maybe bribe Townsend to leave us alone."

Shrugging, I said, "That's up to you." Bless her heart, though, she had given me an idea, one that could fill my pockets with money to secure a claim in Leadville and make me rich.

My boss retreated to the dining room as the girls filtered in for dinner. Lupe filled a large serving bowl with stew and sat it on the table that seated ten. She returned for a ladle and a platter of cornbread muffins. As her girls took their seats, Mattie explained the threat facing her and her Cort while she dipped out bowls of stew and passed them around. When all the ladies had a bowl, Mattie nodded, and they picked up their spoons and ate.

Once they started dinner, Lupe filled two tins with stew and sat them at our table. We ate and grinned, listening to the conversation in the next room. As the girls dined, Mattie described Shotgun Jake Townsend as short and wearing spectacles without lenses. Saying he was a mean man with a lust for blood, Mattie described him better than I could have. One girl asked what she was to do if she saw this despicable character.

"Find Lomax," Mattie answered. "I've hired him to kill Townsend."

"Lomax don't look like much of a killer," the girl answered.

"Neither does Shotgun Jake Townsend, but he's as mean as they come."

Lupe and I smiled as we consumed our stew and corn-bread. "I bet Shotgun Jake Townsend never eats this well," I told her. We enjoyed our supper and our secret together.

After everyone finished, the girls arose one by one and headed upstairs to straighten their hair, paint their lips, rouge their cheeks and shadow their eyes before returning to greet the customers that would trickle in once Mattie unlocked the front.

Mattie asked Lupe to take a tray of supper to her room so Cort could eat.

"Do you want me to carry the scalding stew to Cort?" I asked.

"No, no," she answered. "You might excite him too much after the coffee spill. He's still red and blistered down there."

I turned to Lupe. "You tell me if he's not draped with a sheet this evening, and I'll teach him more manners until they take."

"He'll be covered from now on," Mattie assured me.

Lupe fixed a tray and delivered it to him, reporting back to me that Cort was a true gentleman for the first time in her memory and didn't treat her like a Mexican slave. "*Gracias*," she said. "He fears you."

"That's doubtful," I answered. "All he's scared of is losing Mattie's money."

"Who fears losing my money?" Mattie said, barging into the kitchen, a gold sash around her waist. I noticed the ivory handle of her revolver poking out from the top of the wrap.

"Cort's afraid you'll cut him off," I said, pointing to her pistol. "That peashooter won't stop Shotgun Jake Townsend."

Mattie smiled. "No, but you will. Now start guarding the place."

"Pay me the additional ten dollars a day you owe me for my services," I responded, knowing this was the easiest job I'd ever have, protecting her and her Cort from an assassin that didn't exist, except in the fears of Denver.

"I will, once I open for business." Mattie retreated from the kitchen.

Lupe cleared the tinware from our table, then the porcelain dishes from the dining room as she heated water on the stove to wash the tableware. After unlocking the entry and greeting early arrivals, Mattie returned to the kitchen, giving me another sixty dollars. Thanking her, I added the bills to my cache and stepped outside to check the house.

I ambled to the stable to inspect Ciaha, who was as content as a bandit with an open strongbox. After I forked hay into his feed trough and dumped water in his bucket to quench his thirst, I filled the two buckets for Mattie's buggy horse. Remembering the shotgun shells in my pants pocket, I removed five and tucked them in my saddlebags. I would use the remaining one in my pocket later that night.

Marching up the back steps and into the kitchen, I accepted Lupe's cup of coffee.

"Is everything okay out there?" she asked.

"No sign of Shotgun Jake Townsend," I informed her, "but I'm worried about tonight." I sipped my drink.

Lupe giggled as she washed the dishes. "I can't wait."

Once darkness sat in, I began regular rounds, circling the place in search of the imaginary assassin. I never found him, even though I checked the stable and the perimeter of the brothel. On my third trip to the horse shed, I emptied the two water buckets for Mattie's horse and carried them to the side window that opened into Mattie's room, where Cort recuperated. I placed the two pails upside down beside the shaft of yellow light that leaked from the window. The buckets would come in handy around midnight when I had a gut feeling Shotgun Jake would attack.

When I returned to the kitchen after each inspection, Mattie slipped back to meet me, asking if everything was okay. I reassured her that all was well, but reminded her that Townsend was as sneaky a killer as ever walked on Colorado soil, and we couldn't be too careful.

Around midnight when the place was full of celebrants enjoying wine and women and Mattie was checking Cort, I confirmed a full load in my pistol and started my next inspection. Circling the place twice, I picked up a stone on the second revolution, went around the back past the kitchen door, then up the side by Mattie's window. With the rock in my left hand, I used my right to lift my revolver from its holster. I approached the shaft of lamp light that seeped through the curtained glass.

Nearing the two buckets I'd positioned earlier, I checked the street to make sure no one was walking by. When everything was clear, I cried out, "What are you doing there? Get away!"

I raised the rock in my left hand and smashed it against the windowpane, the shattering glass tumbling inside Mattie's room and a shard cutting my thumb and forefinger.

"Drop that shotgun," I screamed, kicking at the overturned buckets and furthering the commotion. I lifted my revolver over my head. I fired in the air once, twice.

The inside lamp fell dark, and I heard Mattie scream from her bedroom.

I shot my pistol a third time overhead, shoved it in my holster and extracted the shotgun shell. I tossed it on the ground by the overturned buckets, then raced back to the kitchen entry. Someone had locked it. I banged on the door. "It's Lomax, let me in," I cried.

Lupe unlatched and flung open the entry. I raced by her into the parlor, startling the customers, two of whom jumped up and darted out the front door as I raced around the stairs toward Mattie's darkened room. I heard her panicked voice, peppering Cort with questions.

"Are you okay? Were you hit? Did you see who did it?"

Cort stammered, "Yes ... no ... no."

"Your nerves are shot," Mattie soothed him. "It's all right."

I burst inside the room, making out the form of Mattie sitting on the edge of the bed by Cort. "If a cup of coffee'll soothe your nerves, I'll fetch you one Cort," I offered.

"Hell, no, Lomax." Cort screamed at me. "You

should've saved me!"

"I did," I replied. Stepping up to the lamp on the bed-side table. I took a match and lit it, watching it glow and cast a sickly jaundiced light across the room.

Mattie glanced at me, yanking her hand to her mouth. "You're hurt, Lomax."

I looked at the lamp globe and saw red smears on the glass, then studied my left hand, still bleeding from the cut from the window shard.

"What happened, Lomax?" Mattie arose from Cort's side and stepped to me, taking a handkerchief from her blouse and wrapping it around my thumb and forefinger.

Catching my breath, I started explaining. "I was mak-ing my rounds when I came to your side of the house and spotted a short man stepping up on two buckets by your window. I screamed at him, wanting to know what he was doing. He was loading his shotgun, but before he could shut the breech, I shoved the gun barrel toward the window, breaking the glass and knocking him off bal-ance. As he tumbled to the ground, I fired twice, though I couldn't see him that well. I must've missed because he leaped to his feet and darted to the street. I shot again but lost sight of him after he turned down Holladay."

"Was it Townsend?" Mattie wanted to know.

I shrugged. "I didn't see his face, but he was Jake's height, and it looked like he was carrying a shotgun, so I suppose it was him."

"Damnation," Mattie said. "What are we gonna do?"

"We ain't sleeping in here anymore," Cort told Mattie. "Have a girl vacate her room so I can rest upstairs with-out being shot through the window."

Mattie nodded. "I'll do that, Cort, but shouldn't you thank, Lomax? This is the second time he's saved your life?"

"That don't make up for the coffee burns," Cort com-plained. "Those blisters still sting."

"I don't need his thanks," I said, "because I take pride in knowing I did what you hired me to do, Mattie."

"Cort, you should be more gracious like Lomax," Mattie chided her beau.

"You should find me another room to recuperate in,"

Cort countered.

Mattie hugged me. "I'll thank you, even if my Cort won't."

Seeing an opportunity here, I extracted myself from her arms. "When you find Cort another bed, why don't you stay with him there, and I'll sleep in your place with my gun ready to shoot Shotgun Jake if he returns."

She hesitated to accept my offer.

"If you'd rather risk it in your own bed, that's fine with me, but it proves one thing."

"What's that, Lomax?"

"You've got more grit than Cort."

Thomson scowled as Mattie accepted my offer with a smile.

"Something else, Mattie. I want clean sheets on the bed first."

Nodding, Mattie said, "I'll have Lupe change them."

"While she's doing that, I'll look outside your window with a lantern."

Mattie indicated she must check on business, walking out of her bedroom into the parlor, assuring her girls and their remaining suitors that everything was okay.

I looked at Thomson. "I'll still fetch you a cup of coffee, Cort, if you like?"

Cort arose from the bed, pulling the sheet off and wrapping it around his naked body. "You stay away from me, Lomax."

"Why don't you step over by the window, Cort, in case Townsend returns, prove to him and me that you're not afraid of dying?"

Instead, Cort scurried to the door, awaiting Mattie's return. Rather than her, Lupe entered carrying clean sheets. "Miss Mattie said for you to meet her in the kitchen."

Cort stepped out of the room. "Not you, but *Señor* Lomax."

I strode past Thomson. "Now don't you go dropping your sheet in front of Lupe. If you do, I'll save Shotgun Jake Townsend the trouble of shooting you." I marched to the kitchen where Mattie had a lit lantern on the table. She lifted it and started for the back door. "You sure you want to go outside, Mattie? I doubt Townsend would hang around after failing in his first try, but you never know."

"I'll risk it," she said.

Before we exited, I pulled my revolver and released the cylinder, shucking the hulls from my earlier encounter with Townsend and replacing the empties with three new cartridges. "You can't be too careful," I said, "when it comes to Shotgun Jake Townsend." I opened the door and stepped outside, cautiously looking around, then motioning for Mattie to follow me. As she emerged from the kitchen, a ball of yellow light enveloped us as we moved to the side of the house. I pointed to the overturned pails.

"Why the buckets?" she asked.

"He's too short to see in the window. He had to stand on them to aim." I bent over to grab the bucket handles and paused. "Look what I found?" I said, squatting and picking up the shotgun shell I had discarded after the incident.

"What is it?"

"One of Townsend's calling cards, a 12-gauge shotgun shell." I handed it to her. "He was trying to load it when I spotted him. Had he succeeded, this shell might have killed Cort."

"Oh, my gawd," she said. "What are we going to do?"

"We're gonna get a good night's sleep and figure out our next move tomorrow."

"Should we report the attempt to the marshal's office?"

I delayed answering to let her think I was contemplating the options. "Let's give it a day or two. You might show the shell to Cort, and I'll carry these buckets back to the stable as I suspect that's where he got them." I picked up the pails and took the lantern from Mattie when we reached the back door. When she stepped inside, I returned to the horse shed.

When I finished, I figured I deserved a good night's rest in the best bed in Mattie's place. I had considerable thinking to do as Mattie's suggestion of bribing Shotgun Jake Townsend gave me an idea of how to make more money and get away from Cort Thomson.

Chapter Six

Lupe and I may have been the only ones to rest well that night, but I don't remember a better sleep on a softer mattress than on Mattie's, even if Cort Thomson had tainted it. When I awoke midmorning, I kept thinking of Mattie's idea of bribing Shotgun Jake Townsend to buy hers and Cort's safety. If money was to be made on Shotgun Jake Townsend's evil reputation, I thought I ought to be the one to earn it. I spent the morning lying in bed with the fluffiest pillows I'd ever dreamed on until I heard voices outside Mattie's broken window, then watched two men nailing planks into the frame, eventually blocking out the morning sunlight. When they finished working on the side, they moved to the back and planked up that bedroom window too. I realized this was my last rest on such a fine bed.

Getting up, I dressed and emerged into the hallway, marching past the stairs as a pair of the girls, a redhead and a brown-haired gal, came down for breakfast. They made a big to-do about my bravery in fighting off Shotgun Jake Townsend and saving Cort Thomson's life at the risk of my own.

"It wasn't Cort I was thinking of," I answered, "it was Mattie and you ladies. I'd hate for such a scoundrel to hurt one of you lovelies."

"Ooooohh," they cooed.

"That's so sweet of you," said the redhead.

"You're a man I could fall for," answered brown-top.

Though I'd had the favors of working girls in the past, I

declined to partake in the goods in Mattie's place as I loathed Cort Thomson so and didn't care to share his womanizing reputation. I escorted my new friends to the dining room where they joined their madam and sisters in sin.

"It's about time you got up," Mattie said. "I'm paying you to protect me."

"You aren't dead, are you?"

"Not yet," she answered.

"Then I'd say I've done my job."

"Cort and I are reclaiming my bed tonight, now that our room is boarded shut."

"I figured as much," I said. "The banging on the windows woke me this morning."

"My poor Cort had a terrible night's sleep upstairs. He must recover and become himself again. The gunshot wound to the neck and the scalding at the waist have left him a mite touchy."

"You'd be burying him today if I hadn't scared off Shotgun Jake Townsend last night."

"That's twice you've saved him, Lomax," she said, a touch of humility in her voice. "I'm indebted to you."

"Doing what you're paying me for," I replied as Lupe passed with a platter of pancakes.

I moved to the kitchen table where Lupe had not only covered my plate with three flapjacks, but had also slathered them in butter. After Mattie distributed the morning rations to her girls, Lupe came in and forked a single flapjack from the stack still warming on the stove and dropped it on her plate. After fetching both of us a cup of coffee, she sat and pushed me a can of syrup. I drowned my pancakes in the amber sugar and bit into the tastiest flapjacks I'd ever eaten. "Lupe, I tell you, if I were the marrying kind I'd take you as my wife this very day and let you fix me pancakes every meal. These are delicious."

Lupe smiled. "Oh, *Señor* Lomax, I could never marry you, not with Shotgun Jake Townsend out there waiting to make me a widow."

Damn, she bluffed well. I'd hate to face her in a poker game because she could bluff the britches off a priest and have him believing he was the sinner.

"Don't worry your pretty head, Lupe. After I'm done with breakfast, I'm saddling up my mule and hunting Shotgun Jake Townsend. I'm ready to settle this."

"Señor Lomax, you so brave."

"I'm doing it for all you ladies in this house," I said loud enough for all to catch.

"Ooooohh," came a collective coo from everyone in the next room, save for Mattie.

"Sure you're not planning on running out on me and my Cort?"

"I'll not abandon a man as helpless as Cort," I promised, drawing giggles from the girls.

Mattie silenced their merriment with a stare that could've cracked granite. "You be back before dark, Lomax."

"If I find Townsend, should I bring his corpse back so you can confirm the kill or just his empty glasses?"

"I trust you, Lomax, as I've never known you to lie."

Lupe choked on a sip of coffee, and I returned to my pancakes, savoring my breakfast. When I finished I fetched my hat and carbine, then headed out to the stable where I greeted Ciaha and slipped a bridle over his head and a saddle on his back. I attached my saddlebags to the rigging and slid my long gun in its scabbard. Leading him outside, I realized Ciaha was as excited as me to leave this place, if only for a few hours. Mounting up, I turned my mule to the street and started exploring Denver. Instead of looking for Shotgun Jake Townsend, I sought a stationer as I needed writing paper. Mostly, I wanted time away from Mattie and Cort.

Hearing a train whistle, I headed toward the South Platte and the Denver Pacific Railroad tracks. When I spotted the depot, I saw a train emptying new arrivals. I rode that direction, watching the passengers disburse, many finding friends or family, others encountering the con artists waiting to relieve them of their cash and their dreams. Twice I dismounted Ciaha and led him down the street near pedestrians, eavesdropping on their conversations. Some men were obviously scammers while more sophisticated crooks spread rumors about mining stocks, either trying to sweeten the cost of their own companies or gut the value of their competition's paper. The theme I kept hearing remained that Leadville was the next sure thing with promising silver strikes, though I still craved gold. If gold had been found around Leadville in the past, I suspected more was out there, and I intended to find it where other men had fallen short. I failed to decide if it was the gold bug that bit me or the desire to get away from Mattie Silks and Cort Thomson, even though I had only known them a few days and had profited handsomely from that brief acquaintance. I decided they would fund my prospecting expedition, thanks to Mattie's suggestion of bribing Townsend.

Re-mounting my mule, I started toward the center of town, finally spotting a stationer that advertised books, newspapers and writing implements. I tied Ciaha outside and stepped in the small store where a short clerk shaped like a potbellied stove in wire-rimmed glasses greeted me. If his frames had lacked lenses, I might have mistaken him for a bloated Shotgun Jake Townsend. I informed the proprietor I needed a sheet of stationery and something to write with. He advised me he didn't sell single sheets of paper, and I must purchase a half dozen minimum. I explained I couldn't afford more than one sheet, and I had no writing implement. Still he hesitated until I told him my mother was dying at home in Arkansas, and I must let her know I was well and thinking of her. If I didn't get it in the post by this evening, it might never reach her in time.

He gave in and offered me a free sheet with a torn corner. He pointed me to a pen and inkwell, but I wasn't skilled enough to write the letter with a pen without getting ink on my hands and that would ruin my plan. I requested a pencil, saying my mother couldn't read ink that well. He looked at me funny, then stepped behind the counter, pulling out a drawer and retrieving a nub of a pencil. Approaching me, he gestured for me to sit at his desk and write my missive. I took a seat, stuck the worn point of the pencil to the paper and wrote:

Silky,

It's Lomax I want dead. You and Court don't matter. Pay

*me 15 hunert dollars and I won't kill you both. Answer soon
or I'll blast you aways first, then kill Lomax later. SJT*

It took me a while to draft my letter, partly because
the snoopy clerk kept hanging around me, trying to see
what I was writing. He must've gotten a look or an idea
because after I arose, he shook his head.

"Poignant note you wrote to your momma," he said.

Fearing he'd take my letter as a threat and might turn
me in to the law, I scowled. "I don't take kindly to people
reading my mail, especially when it's to my momma."

The clerk offered me a sickly smile. "I wanted to correct your spelling so you would impress your mother
with your command of the written language. I meant
no harm."

"What's your name, fellow, so I'll know who to hunt
if word gets out about my visit?"

He gulped hard, stuck his index finger in his collar and
tugged at the tightness. "Jerry Lander," he said, yanking
his finger from his shirt and removing his wire-rimmed
glasses. He cleaned the lenses with a handkerchief he
pulled from his pocket. "What's your name?" he asked.

"Jake Townsend," I said, throwing him a menacing look.

Lander dropped his glasses on the floor, and when he
straightened up after retrieving his spectacles, I saw beads
of sweat popping up on his forehead. "You're Shot—"

"That's right." I offered him a sinister nod of confirmation.

His pale face turned even whiter. "I'd heard rumors
you were in Denver, but I never expected to meet you."

"Thank my momma since she's always glad to hear
from me, but Jerry, I better not learn of you telling another soul about meeting me or reading my letter. As
wide as you are in the britches, I couldn't miss you, not
with my scattergun. In fact, I might return and shoot you,
anyway. You're broad enough I could inspect the pattern
of all the buckshot in your back. That's something I've
always wanted to see, but most of my clients have been
skinnier than you. I might ambush you just to check out
the spray pattern."

Lander's fingers trembled as he finished cleaning his
glasses and hooking the frames over his ears. "What …

did," the clerk stammered, "you say … your name was? I already forgot."

"I'm mighty glad to learn that, Jerry. You might live to be an old man, assuming you don't eat yourself to death."

Lander offered me a mealy-mouthed grin and an inquisitive look.

"What's on your mind, Jerry?"

"How many clients have you had over the years?"

I shook my head. "You're the second fellow to ask me that question in the last ten days. The other one inquired in Cheyenne, and the poor fellow became my ninety-ninth client. You might be my hundredth victim, I mean client, Jerry."

He nodded vigorously, sending waves trembling through his flabby frame.

"Now, Jerry, you think you might have a ball of twine or string to sell me?"

"Yes, sir, Mr. Town—"

I cleared my throat. "I thought you'd forgotten my name, Jerry."

"Now I have, I promise, and you can have a roll of string for free." He retreated behind the counter and pulled out a spindle with string coiled around it. Lander tossed it to me. As I snagged it out of the air, he said, "Thank you for your business."

"You'll be getting more of my business," I informed him, "as I'll be back tomorrow to confirm you've forgotten we ever met." I took the letter and wrapped it around the spindle, then slipped both in my shirt pocket. I tipped my hat at Lander and exited his store, a smile working its way across my lips. Reaching Ciaha, I opened a flap on my saddlebags and pulled out one of the shotgun shells. Next I retrieved the letter from my pocket, removing it from the spool and wrapping it around the shotgun shell, tying the paper firmly with a length of string I cut from the spindle. Finishing, I slid the shell in my britches pocket and tucked the spindle in my saddlebags.

I untied and mounted Ciaha, deciding to spend the rest of the afternoon exploring Denver and finding me an eatery for supper before returning to Mattie's place. I ambled back to the train depot, figuring I'd watch whatever show the con men put on to fleece their latest quarry. After tying Ciaha outside the train station, I wandered among the crowd, picking up offers for sure-thing mining stocks, accommodating women, three-card monte, shell-and-pea games, strong whiskey and other amusements.

I found myself drawn to the oratory of one shyster who had set up his tripod and suitcase or tripe and keister as he called his rig, on a street corner opposite the depot. Of all things, he was auctioning off simple penny cakes of soap. "Cleanliness is next to godliness," he announced with a squeaky voice that could use a squirt of oil, "and nothing cleans better than my soap. If you want to get closer to God or your girl, you can't afford not to buy a cake."

At the time I didn't know it, but that was my first encounter with Jefferson Randolph Smith the Second. Of slight build, he stood maybe five feet, six inches at the most, with closely trimmed black hair, mustache and beard and piercing, hypnotizing black eyes. That squeaky voice and those mesmerizing orbs attracted a crowd, and I found myself drawn to him. It was, after all, a free show, provided I didn't get suckered into purchasing any soap. Then Smith made it interesting.

"Men and I'm speaking to you men only because God gave our women folk wisdom to know the value of a good soap in promoting cleanliness, you often need an incentive to do what's best for you and today nothing is better for you than buying a cake of the finest soap in all of Colorado. So, to give you a solid reason to purchase my goods, I'm placing a twenty-dollar bill in one wrapper so the lucky buyer will go home this afternoon with a cake of my soap and a clean conscious that he never made a wiser buy in his life."

With that, the crowd moved closer to his tiny table. Smith pulled out a crisp twenty-dollar bill from his pocket and held it up for everyone to see. He offered the bill to a spectator to inspect while he bent over his open satchel and extracted three dozen bars, laying them on his stand. Taking the money back from the spectator, likely a shill, Smith held it up for everyone to inspect, then picked up a cake of soap and removed the wrapper, sliding the bill inside and folding it back over the bar. He placed this cake among the other wrapped pieces and shuffled them like dominoes. When he finished, he stacked the bars in a pyramid and resumed his spiel.

"Is today your lucky day?" he called. "It can be if you bid on my soap. One of you will take home twenty dollars and even if you don't get the lucky bar, you still leave here a winner with the best cake of soap in Colorado."

At that point, he picked up a bar and held it above his head. "What's the offer on this wonderful cleansing elixir?"

The spectators remained silent until one stepped forward and cried, "Oh, hell. I'll bid fifty cents." Nobody else challenged his bid.

"Sold," Smith yelled to the lucky bidder, "for fifty cents."

As soon as he handed the coins to Smith, the purchaser grabbed the soap from his hand and ripped the wrapper away. "Yeehaw," he cried, holding up a bill. "I got a five-dollar bill."

Smith smiled. "Gentlemen, I forgot to tell you I slipped a few other bills inside the wrappers before I put the big bill in." He held up the second bar, "Who'll bid a dollar for a chance to make five or a twenty times that?"

The bidding started with cleansers being sold for a dollar or two, though nobody else bought a wrapper with money in it, even though some had paid up to five dollars for soap as the pile diminished to fewer than ten bars. Finally, Smith auctioned his way to the last trio of cakes. "Gentlemen," he cried, "there's a one-in-three chance of the lucky bidder getting a twenty-dollar bill. I'll sell off two more bars, and I'll let you decide what ones I put to bid." He spread them on the table, holding his right hand over the first, the second and the third, deciding by the cheers and applause which to auction next. The crowd selected the third and first bars to be sold in that order. The bidding on the initial bar stopped at eight dollars, but the purchaser left disappointed. "The odds are one in two, a fifty percent chance the buyer walks away with a twenty-dollar bill this time," Smith announced.

When the bidding stalled at thirteen dollars, Smith

shouted, "I'll bid fifteen dollars myself," and counted out the cash from his auction earnings and slid it under the item. With that, two men started competing against each other, one of them dropping out at eighteen and a half dollars. The triumphant bidder handed over his money and snatched his bar of soap like a drowning man grabbing a floating log. He ripped off the wrapper and came up with the most expensive cake of soap he'd ever bought. Angered, he threw the cake of soap across the street and wadded up the wrapper, dropping it at his boots.

"Oooohhhh, I'm so sorry," Smith told the sap. "Now I will not auction the last bar of soap because it's unfair to those that bid earlier, but I must show you that the bill is there." With that, he picked up the remaining cake, lifted it over his head and unwrapped it for everyone to see. Sure enough, as he exposed the soap the twenty-dollar bill appeared between the paper and soap. When the spectators saw the bill, they groaned. "Even if no one got the twenty," Smith called, "every buyer leaves a winner with the finest soap ever to bathe residents and newcomers to the Centennial State."

With that, the auctioneer put his earnings in his satchel, folded up his table and grabbed them both as he marched away. Though I didn't keep a tally of how much he had collected from the auction bids, I estimated he left with a forty-dollar profit, maybe more if the five-dollar bill went to a shill. Smith's skill in conning a crowd impressed me, but I resolved not to be caught by the lure of easy money.

As I walked back to Ciaha, a well-dressed man in a suit approached me with a carpet bag in his hand. "You, sir," he said, "are a discerning individual, not to be lured into buying penny soap for a hundred times it's worth."

This fellow was my height and build, but with a stubby neck and eyes that flitted back and forth. He studied me with those nervous eyes. Though he was an odd-looking man, he was sharp in observing I would never get taken for a sucker.

"And," he continued, "you look like a man who recognizes exceptional value."

He had me pegged for sure.

"Would you care to purchase champagne all the way from France?"

"Too expensive for my taste," I replied.

He reached into his satchel and pulled out a green bottle with silver foil wrapped around the neck and cork plus a fancy label that proclaimed the contents to be "*Vin de la Sève.*" With a name I assumed to be French, it had to be excellent champagne. Thinking I might ingratiate myself further with Mattie if I bought her a bottle, I listened.

"Only five dollars," he said, shaking it so it bubbled.

"My tastes aren't that rich. I'll go two dollars."

The fellow lifted his nose in the air and shook his head. "Never," he said, "not for such an exquisite liquid."

"Good day," I said, turning toward Ciaha until the seller grabbed my arm.

"You are a hard man to bargain with, but why should I deny a connoisseur of your discernment the pleasure of sampling such delightful champagne. I'll accept two dollars for this bottle, but please tell no one I sold such a fine wine at such an inferior price."

"The price just dropped," I replied. "I'm now offering a single dollar and nothing more."

The salesman grimaced and nodded. "You drive a hard bargain."

As I pulled out my wad of money and peeled off a bill, the salesman's nervous eyes widened and stilled. "I know where you can double your money," he whispered. "I've a friend that runs a rigged faro table."

I shook my head, handing him the dollar and returning the cash to my pocket. "Nope." I took the bottle from him.

"Why not? It's easy money?"

"I don't want to endanger anyone."

"How's that?"

"I'm being tailed by Shotgun Jake Townsend."

The fellow backed away. "Enough said. Good luck taking on Townsend."

Retreating to Ciaha, I stored the champagne in my saddlebags and started to Mattie's place. I found a restaurant that catered to a better class of folks than I was accustomed to being around and sat at a table with fine linens, bone china, crystal glasses and silver utensils where I dined on elk roast, glazed carrots, boiled onions and brown bread. Eavesdropping on the surrounding conversations, I learned the men were interested in politics and mining stock and the women were consumed with suffrage and the tour Susan B. Anthony was making in Colorado to support their cause. Now I could not understand why ladies wanted to suffer any more than the rest of us, but I had long ago realized I couldn't decipher females or their way of thinking. After filling my belly with the fare and my mind with the conversation, I returned to Mattie's.

I took Ciaha to the stable, tended him, then strode into the house with the bottle of champagne in my hand and the shotgun shell and message in my pocket. I marched in the back as the girls and Mattie were arising from the dinner table.

"Where've you been?" the madam demanded.

"Searching for Shotgun Jake Townsend. I didn't find him, but word's out I'm looking for him. That may scare him away for a spell."

I offered her the champagne bottle, hoping it would stop her from dogging me.

She shook her head. "Idiot."

"It's the finest champagne from France," I said.

"No, it's not. It comes from Denver," she answered.

I read the label. "It says '*Vin de la Sève*.'"

"That's French for fruit of the sap. It's nothing but water, brown sugar and yeast. It's sold at the depot, a come-on so shills can gauge your money roll to determine if you're worth swindling or robbing."

"My French isn't that good," I confessed.

"I'll take it, though, because we'll re-sell it for champagne when our customers get drunk." She yanked the bottle from my hand and marched into the parlor.

After Mattie and the girls cleared the dining room, Lupe came in and started removing the dishes. "Did you eat, *Señor* Lomax?"

I nodded. "Let's visit when we won't be overheard," I whispered, then went into the room where she slept and where I would sleep this night.

After a half hour, Lupe wandered in. I slipped the shotgun shell from my pocket into her hand and told her my plan. Sliding the contraband into an apron pocket, she smiled that she loved my scheme.

As the sun set, I began my rounds, leaving and entering the place through the front door so Mattie would know I had been outside. Once I walked down the hallway and knocked on her bedroom door, asking Cort if he wanted me to bring him a cup of coffee or a bowl of scalding soup. He yelled at me to go to hell, but I stepped out of the house instead.

Once it turned dark an hour, I passed through the kitchen and out the back door, nodding to Lupe. "Give me a minute." I walked to the front of the house and studied the foot traffic on the street. Then I heard the scream. It was Lupe. I raced to the back, pulling my pistol and firing twice in the air.

Lupe stood in the open doorway, shaking, as Mattie raced into the kitchen.

"What is it Lupe?" she cried.

"It was him!"

Mattie glanced at me.

"I got a couple shots at him, but it was too dark to know if I hit him as he ran away."

"Idiot," she said, endearing me further to her.

Lupe lifted her hand to Mattie. "He said to give you this."

Mattie opened her fingers, and Lupe dropped into her palm a shotgun shell with a note tied to it.

"It's Shotgun Jake Townsend's calling card," I informed her.

Mattie gasped.

Chapter Seven

Mattie looked at me, her eyes flitting from side to side as she gasped for breath. "What do I do?" She lifted for my inspection the shotgun shell and note.

"It's Townsend's calling card to scare his next victims. Read the note," I said.

Releasing a deep sigh, Mattie stepped into the dining room, faltering a step before she caught her balance. She fell into her usual chair, holding the shell up and studying it, as if she feared reading the message.

"Sometimes," I continued, figuring I should give her hope, "he offers his victims a chance to buy back their lives." I walked around to the side of the table where I could see her face as Lupe stood in the door behind her.

Mattie bit her lip as she pondered looking at the note. "I should get Cort."

"If I'm to defend you, I've gotta know what it says," I argued.

Shaking her head, Mattie placed the shell on the lace tablecloth and studied it a moment more before untying the string and sliding the paper free. She unrolled it and read it while I wondered if she would permit me to see it. When she looked up, the worry drained from her eyes and face.

"Is he extorting you?"

"Fifteen hundred dollars."

I whistled. "Mighty steep. Did he say anything else?" I asked, probing if she would reveal what the note said about me.

Mattie hesitated and shook her head. "Nothing beyond the bribe."

"Did he mention me?"

"Not a thing," Mattie reiterated.

"That's good," I countered, knowing she had lied. "He must not have recognized me when I scared him from your window. That may give me an edge to ambush him when he comes for his money."

Mattie slapped the table with her fist. "No, Lomax. I'm not risking mine and Cort's safety by double-crossing a known killer. I can make more money, but not another Cort."

Thank heavens, I thought, because the world didn't need another Cort Thomson, there being enough slackers as it was. "Want me to take the letter to the marshal to stop this?" I reached for the note, but she shoved it inside her blouse.

"I'll let Cort read it first, then you." She stood up and strode past Lupe, who moved out of her way. Instead of turning for the parlor, she marched to the opposite end of the kitchen, bent by the cook stove and opened the firebox door. She screened herself from me, but I knew she was reaching inside her blouse for the missive. "You need more wood, Lupe," Mattie announced as she flicked her hand toward the glowing coals.

"Yes, Miss Silks," Lupe said, stepping to the woodbox and handing her boss new kindling.

Mattie had destroyed the note so I would never know of the threat to me. She shoved the wood in the firebox and shut the firebox door, confident the paper had been consumed. Standing up, Mattie marched to the parlor. "I've must show Cort the message," she told us.

"Should I fetch him a cup of hot coffee to ease his nerves?"

She ignored my generous offer.

After Lupe heard her open her bedroom door, she walked to me. "She burned the note."

"I know."

"What happens tomorrow?" she asked.

"I'll tell you then," I replied. "It's time inspect the place."

Lupe grinned. "You be careful, *Señor* Lomax. *Señor* Shotgun is a mean man."

I stepped outside for my first round for what I knew would be an uneventful night. I was right. I slept on the extra bed in Lupe's room and rested until midmorning, then arose and ate the late breakfast with the girls, though Mattie stayed in her bedroom, ministering to Cort's needs.

When Mattie finally returned to the kitchen, I asked to see the note, but she waved my request away. "Cort has it."

"He could read it to me."

"Leave him be," she said.

I nodded, but informed her I must go purchase a carton of cartridges since I'd fired so many at Shotgun Jake.

"Don't you go looking for him. Things'll be fine when we pay him. I don't want you messing anything up before then."

"He'll get back to you when he's ready," I informed her as I walked into my room to put on my gun belt and fetch my hat. Marching back through the kitchen, I announced, "I'll return by dinner," as I left by the back door.

After saddling up Ciaha, I rode through the streets of Denver, enjoying the activity of people dreaming of the riches they might find in the impressive mountains to the west of town. I made my way to the stationery store and marched in as Jerry Lander was helping two fashionably dressed women pick out fancy papers for their correspondence. After Lander saw me, he never turned his back on me so I got to enjoy his profile, which looked like he was smuggling a hundred-pound bag of flour under his shirt and britches. I'd seen snowmen with better shapes than Lander. When the women completed their purchases and left, Lander came to me.

"You remember me?" I asked.

He hesitated, uncertain what the proper answer was. Finally, he took a deep breath and answered. "I've never seen you before in my life."

I grinned. "Very good, Jerry. I'm assuming you don't even see me now. Am I correct?"

"Whatever you say, Mr. Town—"

Cocking my head, I waved my forefinger at him. "Be careful with my name, Jerry."

He nodded.

"I won't be long, Jerry, provided you forget I was ever here."

"Done."

"Give me a free sheet of paper and a pencil so I can write another letter to my momma. And if I find you reading over my shoulder, I'll give you the treatment I'm known for."

Lander took a sheaf from the counter and gave me a pencil, pointing me to his desk. "Take your time, stranger."

As I took my seat in his chair, Lander marched across the small store and re-arranged boxes of paper, though never turning his back on me. After a few minutes of thought about what Shotgun Jake Townsend would say, I wrote my next threatening note, again with my left hand to disguise my writing.

Silky,

If proposal agreed to, send 15 hunert dollars by meskin cook to depot at noon tomorrow. No tricks or you and your lazy man friend will die anyway. Your pal,

Jake

Pleased with the note overall, I especially enjoyed insulting Cort in the process. I stood up and shook the paper like I had written it in ink, then nodded at Lander. "That's enough for today, but I'll be back tomorrow so don't spread any rumors I'm in town."

"No, sir, whoever you are, I would never do that."

"It's a shame, Jerry. You're such a broad target, I'd like to see my buckshot pattern in your back."

"I won't say a word about you, I promise."

"Thank you, Jerry. I'm glad you understand. See you tomorrow."

I had no intention of returning the next day, but Jerry didn't know that and would be careful not to identify me as Shotgun Jake. Before I mounted Ciaha, I untied a flap on my saddlebags, then wrapped and tied the latest note around another shell, which I stuck in my pocket. Climbing atop Ciaha, I killed time by riding over to the depot and watching the conmen try to rope in suckers. I saw Jefferson Randolph Smith the Second auctioning off penny cakes of soap and the fellow that sold me the counterfeit champagne.

When I tired of the spectacle around the station, I started back for Mattie's place, figuring out how Shotgun Jake Townsend would deliver his last message to Mattie. I decided Jake would throw it through the kitchen window. Problem was, how would Jake do it? The ruse would fail if someone saw me pitching it, nor could I risk paying somebody to do it. I thought for a while and realized I'd have to work from the kitchen.

Reaching the stable, I unsaddled Ciaha and tended him, then inspected the side of the house beneath Mattie's boarded-up window where I picked up shards of the glass I had broken trying to protect Cort and Mattie from the imaginary assassin. I also found and pocketed a rock the size of my thumb. When I entered, I saw Lupe busy finishing dinner. Certain no one was around, I whispered how the evening attack would play out.

"Oh, *Señor* Lomax, you are so cunning," she paused, "in a respectable way."

"That's how my momma raised me," I said, appreciating the sentiment, though I questioned how decent I could be working for Mattie Silks when she put up with such a rascal as Cort Thomson.

"Your momma would be proud," Lupe said, as Mattie marched in.

"Proud of what?"

Without missing a beat, she answered, "*Señor* Lomax's momma would be proud for how brave he is to stand up against such a mean man as *Señor* Shotgun."

"She'd be prouder if he ever killed the son of a bitch," Mattie shot back.

"I've come closer than your Cort has," I answered. "He's too scared to leave the house since Townsend tried to assassinate him. At least I've been out looking for the bastard."

"Okay," Mattie replied. "Perhaps I'm just terrified until we can pay him off and get things back to normal. Is everything on schedule for dinner?"

"*Si*, Miss Silks. I'm always on time."

The madam looked at me. "I feared Lomax was slowing you down. If he's bothering you, tell me."

"Oh, no, Miss Silks. He's the only one around here that treats me like a person rather than a servant. He's a good man."

I grinned. "My momma would be proud."

Mattie glared at me and strode into the dining room to await her crew. Lupe had boiled a pot of beans with ham hocks and had baked cornbread muffins. She had the table set and the serving dishes filled and in place when all the girls arrived. After Mattie seated and served them, Lupe joined me at the kitchen table, and we ate our dinner.

Once the ladies left the dining room to make their final tweaks for the night's male guests, I helped Lupe clear the table so she could wash the dishes. While she finished the cleaning, I marched outside and made my regular rounds to protect Mattie, Cort, and the others from the imaginary assailant that had served me so well since I had arrived in Denver. Around nine o'clock I implemented my plan, carefully removing the bits of glass from my pocket and placing pieces on the kitchen counter and other shards on the floor, while Lupe watched the parlor. When she was sure no one was watching, Lupe scurried over to the counter as I pulled the rock and shotgun shell from my pocket.

Drawing back my arm, I flung the rock through a lower pane in the kitchen window.

Glass shattered. Lupe screamed.

I tossed the shotgun shell against the wall opposite the window.

"*He visto al diablo,*" Lupe cried. "I have seen the devil."

From the parlor came the sounds of terrified men and women.

I yanked my pistol from my scabbard and rushed to the broken window. Sticking the barrel through the hole, I squeezed off a two shots.

Mattie bolted in. "What's the matter?"

"Oh, Miss Silks," Lupe exclaimed. "I saw the devil in the window, *Señor* Shotgun. He tried to kill me with a rock."

Mattie turned to me as three girls and a trio of clients poked their heads in the door. "I suppose you missed again."

"I was shooting blind," I said, defending my honor. "How many shots did Cort get off protecting you, Mattie?"

"My Cort's still recovering."

Lupe sat in a kitchen chair and fanned herself with her hand, then froze. Pointing to the floor, she screamed, "Look."

I followed her finger as I holstered my pistol. "It's another of Townsend's calling cards." I walked over and picked up the shotgun shell with the attached note and handed it to Mattie.

Mattie yanked the offering from my hand and unwrapped the note, dropping the shell on the floor. Carefully, she read the message to herself, mouthing the words as she did. Next she recited it to the rest of us: "Silky, if proposal agreed to, send 15 hunert dollars by meskin cook to depot at noon tomorrow. No tricks or you and your lazy man friend will die anyway. Your pal, Jake." She crumpled up the note and threw it at her feet. "What's he mean calling Cort lazy?"

"Must be he don't know him that well or it could've been worse," I offered.

"Shut up, Lomax," Mattie said, turning to Lupe.

"Don't make me go," Lupe pleaded. "He's the devil in person. I saw in his eyes evil like I have never seen until now."

"You've got to go, Lupe. I don't have any choice since he requested you."

"Please don't make me go alone, Miss Silks. You or Mr. Cort, please go with me. He terrifies me for what he might do."

"We can't accompany you, Lupe. He's threatened to kill us."

"Then send *Señor* Lomax or I quit tonight."

"He was threatening to kill me before you two," I answered. "Why should I go when he's said nothing about calling off his vendetta me?"

Mattie shrugged

"I'll quit tonight and take Lupe with me," I announced. I dug money from my pocket to return her pay.

"No, no," Mattie said. "You're staying Lomax. I'll pay you fifty more to handle this."

"In advance," I insisted.

She nodded, looking around the room. "Clean up this mess, Lupe, and stuff some rags in the hole in the window." Mattie turned to the spectators still standing at the door. "You girls get back to work, and you fellows forget everything you've seen and heard tonight or your wives might find out about your dalliances." They scurried away.

I brushed the glass off the counter onto the floor while Lupe swept up the fragments. I squatted with the dustpan to help her. When I had the debris, I stepped outside and dumped the broken pieces by the stable. Returning to the kitchen, I gave Lupe the dustpan, which she returned to the corner. After she checked with Mattie that she was no longer needed, Lupe retired to her room and blew out the lamp as both of us readied for bed in the dark.

"You're a good actress, Lupe. You ever thought about going on the stage?"

She sighed. "I've never been able to afford a stagecoach ride, Señor Lomax."

"No, I mean act in the theater. You were that good tonight. I believed every word you were saying."

"Gracias, Señor Lomax, but there is no lower class of people than actors. They pretend they are something that are not. Such is not for me. Being a cook is honest work, even if it serves a dishonest profession in a place such as this."

"If you had the money, what would you like to do, Lupe?"

She pondered for a moment as she settled into her bed. "Maybe I'll do something for the children. There are so many without homes. The girls here sometimes have babies, which they abandon. Every child needs a mother and if not a mother, someone who cares for them."

Without a doubt, Lupe had the biggest heart of any woman I'd ever met in a brothel. "You're a better person than me, Lupe."

"But not as devious," she answered before we dozed off for the night.

When I awoke the next morning, Lupe had already arisen and was preparing a simple breakfast of biscuits since she had a noon appointment with Shotgun Jake Townsend. I dressed and readied myself to guard Lupe against the deadliest killer who never existed.

Emerging into the kitchen, I saw Mattie counting out bills on the table, pulling fifteen hundred dollars from her wad of cash. She looked up at me. "Lomax, harness up my buggy to take Lupe to the depot."

"How about telling Cort to help?" I inquired.

Mattie scowled. "He's remains puny from his injury."

"I'll take him a cup of coffee, if it'll help," I offered.

"Never," Mattie replied. "His neck is fine, but he's still tender downstairs, thank you."

"I do what I can," I said, as I started for the kitchen door.

"Then hook up the buggy."

I walked to the stable and did my assigned chore, though I took time to move the four remaining shotgun shells from my saddlebags to my pants pocket. I led the black gelding and buggy around to Holladay Street, tying the reins and going to the back and entering through the kitchen. Mattie and the girls were eating biscuits and jam at the dining table, while Lupe sat at our table, motioning for me to take my seat. As soon as I sat, she got up and pulled out a pan of golden-brown biscuits. She placed the tin on the table and shoved a tub of butter my direction. I grabbed four biscuits and a knife, buttering the biscuits. As I spooned apricot preserves from a jar onto my biscuits, Lupe brought me a cup of coffee and joined me to finish her breakfast.

"You nervous?" I asked.

She nodded.

"I'll protect you from Shotgun Jake."

"It's not that," she answered. "I've never had so much money in my pocket."

"Maybe you should take up shooting people in the back," I said.

Lupe hesitated, then shook her head. "I'd rather be a stage actor."

We both laughed until Mattie came over. "Hurry and get going. I don't want this arrangement to go awry. If it does," she continued, "I'm blaming you, Lomax."

"I'll manage," I said, gobbling my biscuits and washing them down with Lupe's coffee.

"Don't be late," Mattie ordered as Lupe moved to the kitchen door, carrying a purse that was sewn from a flour bag.

I patted the six-gun at my side, then motioned for Lupe to follow me through the parlor and out the front entrance. She scurried behind me. At the entry, I unlatched the door and led her outside, leaving it for someone else to close as I helped Lupe into the buggy.

"That's the first time I ever went through the front door," she said. "Miss Silks always has me enter and leave by the back way."

Circling the wagon, I climbed onto the seat, loosened the reins and started the black gelding toward the depot, checking behind me to make sure no one was tailing us. If someone was following, I never spotted them. Even on the busy streets, we made it to the station in fifteen minutes, and I tied the buggy at the corner and helped Lupe from the rig. I slipped my arm in hers and we strode along the plank walk and into the depot where dozens of people sat on benches or mingled while they awaited their train. I guided her to an empty bench and told Lupe of my plan about keeping all of Mattie's money before realizing she deserved it more than me for all the indignities she had endured working in Mattie's brothel, while I'd only lived there a few days.

Opening the flap on her purse, I stuck my fingers in and counted out my share, slipping it in my pants pocket. "There's five hundred dollars for me, Lupe, but you should have the remainder, a thousand dollars."

Lupe's face looked as bewildered as if she had actually seen Shotgun Jake Townsend. I saw tears welling in her eyes. "Do you mean it?"

"Yes, Lupe. You can leave Mattie or buy whatever you wish."

She stared in disbelief, tears rolling down her cheeks. "You know what I want, *Señor* Lomax?"

I shrugged.

"A bank account," she informed me.

Now I looked bewildered. "Why?"

"All the wealthy people have a bank account."

"Must be why I'm not rich," I answered. "I don't have one nor any idea how to start one, assuming I could ever trust a banker."

"I'll find an honest banker and save more money until I can leave Miss Silks and do something on my own."

Smiling, I hugged Lupe. "You'll do well because you're as decent as my momma." After that we both sat on a bench while I explained the story we would tell Mattie when we returned. I aimed to have Mattie kick me out of her place before supper time. I figured I'd fattened my pocket as much as I could at her expense, though I felt better about my questionable earnings since it was money that wouldn't go to Cort.

Now my partner smiled. "Your momma raised a devious son."

"Nope, that credit belongs to me. I came about it on my own."

We retreated to the buggy where I helped Lupe to her seat. Then I pulled the shotgun shells from my pocket and offered her two. "You need to hide these and the money inside your blouse." As she did, I took out my pocketknife and pried the crimp open at the end of the other two shells, dumping the powder, shot, and wadding on the ground at my feet, grinding the residue into the dirt with my boot. Then I handed her the hulls. "Put them in your purse and tell Mattie that Townsend ordered you to give them to her."

She grinned. "Your momma would be so proud!"

I strode around the buggy and climbed in my seat for the return trip. After parking out front on Holladay, I helped Lupe down and escorted her up the steps to the front porch and banged on the door until I heard Mattie's voice.

"Go away," she cried. "We're closed."

"It's Lomax," I answered, "we want in."

The door inched open, then widened. "Why didn't you go around to the back?"

"I wanted Lupe to enter by the front after she saved Cort's bacon and yours."

"So you paid him off, Lupe?"

"Oh, yes ma'am. He was the meanest man I ever encountered. The fires of Satan burned in his eyes."

"But did he take the money?"

"*Si*, Miss Silks, he did, and he said to give you these." She slipped her fingers in her modest purse and pulled out the two hulls, handing them to Mattie.

The madam stared at them, uncertain what to make of the gift. "What's this?"

"It's his way of saying the deal's complete, and he won't be shooting you, just like he promised." I took the hulls from Mattie and slipped them in my pocket.

The madam sighed. "I can't wait to tell my Cort."

"But Miss Silks, there's bad news," Lupe interrupted.

Turning to her, I scowled. "I told you not to tell her."

"But I don't want to die," Lupe said.

"What is it, Lupe, what is it?"

"*Señor* Shotgun said he would not shoot you or Mr. Cort, but he would burn the house down if *Señor* Lomax stayed here."

"Dammit, Lupe, I told you *not* to let Mattie know."

"I don't want to die like burned biscuits," she countered.

"That's it, Lomax. Gather your things and get out of here once you tend the horse and buggy."

"I'm done now?" I countered. "Cort can unhook your rig. I saved his life twice, and this is the thanks I get?"

Mattie nodded. "I'll be forever grateful for that, but I can't risk him and the others getting fried over a vendetta between you and Shotgun Jake Townsend."

"I'm not returning your advance pay," I growled.

"Fine, just grab your things and leave."

I stormed out of the parlor, through the kitchen and into the back room. I slammed the door behind me, trying to stifle my laughter. Lupe had carried out her part perfectly. I gathered up my few clothes, my carbine, and my canteen, still smiling when I heard a rap on the door.

"*Señor* Lomax, may I come in?"

"I don't care," I cried.

The door eased open, and she slipped in, closing the entry. We both grinned at each other and shook our heads.

"I can't believe you told Mattie what I asked you not to," I shouted to be heard, then whispered, "You did so well."

"But I didn't want to burn to death," she yelled back before speaking softly, "*Gracias*," she said, pulling her take from her blouse.

"Hide the money and these," I instructed her as I gave her the hulls from my pocket.

"What for?"

"If Mattie or Cort gives you trouble, tell them you Shotgun Jake Townsend dropped by to say the deal was off. Give them a shell for proof."

Lupe grinned. "You are so smart. Your momma would be so proud." She came over and wrapped her arms around me. She whispered, "I'll hide the money. One day I'll slip away and open a bank account, maybe become rich."

"You deserve it, Lupe. It's been an honor knowing you." I kissed her on the cheek, then gathered up my belongings and walked into the kitchen past Mattie and out the back for the last time. Mattie slammed the door behind me.

I strode to the stable, saddled Ciaha, glad to be leaving Denver almost a thousand dollars richer than when I arrived. Leading my mule outside the shed, I left the door open and mounted, aiming Ciaha toward the Rockies, deciding I could grow my grubstake into a fortune grand enough not only to open a bank account but also to buy a bank of my own. I was heading for Leadville, delighted to be shedding myself of the leech Cort Thomson and equally glad to realize I would never see Mattie Silks again. On that count, I was wrong. I did encounter her again two decades later in Skagway. And, she would save my life!

Chapter Eight

Leadville sprouted up a hundred miles southwest of Denver, but I probably traveled three times that far to get there, following the crooked road that connected the state capital with the new mining town. I'd seen mountains before but nothing on the scale of the Rockies, which towered thousands of feet, some exceeding 14,000 feet in elevation. The way I figured it, if God took a flatiron and flattened Colorado out like a laundress working the wrinkles out of a shirt, the state would be bigger than Texas, which suited me because it would stop the incessant jabbering of Texans about their state's bulk. I suppose they had to brag about the size of something since their brains weren't big enough to fill a whiskey jigger, assuming they had any brains at all.

I took it slow into the mountains because the air thinned the higher I rode, making it harder to breathe. Some said the Leadville air was so thin that house cats died there. As I climbed the trails, I fell in and out with various travelers and learned Denver stood at an elevation of 5,000 feet while my destination was more than twice that high. I spent five days making the journey since Ciaha was having as hard a time breathing as me, and he was carrying a heavier load. We weren't the only ones intent on prospecting in Leadville as the road teemed with men, though many dropped out. Had I been traveling through Kansas or, God forbid, Texas the trip would've been a monotonous expedition with flat grasslands and a boring horizon. Here the rugged granite peaks and dramatic valleys with streams meandering along the bottoms made for striking vistas that caught my breath, even in the thin air. I spotted deer and beaver and an occasional elk, plus bighorn sheep which I'd never seen before. Pine, fir and later aspen as I ascended in elevation dotted the mountainsides. With the calendar having turned to autumn, the air carried a crispness in the late evenings through the early mornings before sunshine broke over the tall mountains and warmed the countryside.

On the third day out of Denver, I fell in with an old prospector who had been wandering the Colorado Rockies since the Pikes Peak stampede. He looked as if he had lost a fight with a wildcat with his disheveled hair, wild eyes, and a ragged beard beneath a shabby slouch hat. He wore a tattered army overcoat and scuffed boots and carried a Sharps rifle on his right shoulder while he held the reins to his burro in his left hand as he walked. As I rode by, he called out. "Son, you best get off and reduce the load on your mule." I ignored him until I heard a metallic snap that I took him to be him cocking the hammer on his weapon.

Twisting in my saddle, I saw he was aiming his Sharps at me. "Were you talking to me?"

"Indeed I was," he said. "You're gonna fag your animal, and you don't appear to be man enough to carry everything he's toting."

Deciding he had a point, that being the gun barrel aimed at my head I dismounted.

He lowered his rifle and snickered. "It wasn't loaded." He released the hammer and propped the long gun back on his right shoulder, picked up the lines to his donkey and started walking beside me. "It bothers me to see men abusing a splendid animal, especially a mule, which is more valuable in these parts than a woman."

I'd fallen in with a philosopher and figured to mine him for information about prospecting in the Rockies. "Leadville's my destination, planning to strike it rich."

"Bell, book, and candle shall not drive me back, when gold and silver becks me to come on," he replied, then paused when I didn't acknowledge his observation. "That's Shakespeare," he said, "from the third act of *King John*."

"Pleased to meet you, Mr. Shakespeare. I'm H.H. Lomax."

"That's not me. I'm Pops."

"Who's not me, err you?"

"I'm not Shakespeare, the Bard of Avon, don't you know?"

"Oh, him," I answered, as if I understood what he was saying.

"Glad you're a well-read man," he continued. "A mind for literature can help pass the icy nights we're headed for once winter arrives Around Leadville the snows arrive late October or early November and stay until May or later. Even when the spring melt comes, it's bad, the ground turning to a mushy soup."

Weather reports were fine, but I needed information. "What do you seek in prospecting?"

"Color," Pops answered. "Little flakes of gold that shine like the sun on a cloudless day."

"My pa went to Californy during forty-nine. Didn't find anything, but at least he returned home to Arkansas alive."

The old-timer studied me. "You don't look like much of a prospector."

"Most folks don't think I look like much of anything."

"Beauty provoketh thieves sooner than gold," Pops spouted, "Shakespeare again from *As You Like It*, Act One."

"Shakespeare must've been a good miner, if all he thought about was gold."

"The bard mined the English tongue," Pops told me. "As a poet and playwright, he was an alchemist with words, making golden nuggets of wisdom with the leaden language."

"Well, Pops, I didn't climb this far and high to write poetry. I came to find my fortune."

My new friend shook his head. "You're too late. Times are changing and mining with it."

"Explain without quoting Shakespeare."

"In the old days, you filed placer claims along the rivers and panned for gold. You could find good gravel with color and pan your way to a small fortune in gold dust, flakes, and nuggets. Mining's moving toward lode claims, giving you the right to dig for ore, but it's harder work and takes more men, machinery, and explosives than the old way. You're too late to the party."

"If I'm too late, why are you heading to Leadville, Pops?"

"I know what I'm doing, Lomax! You don't understand the difference between gold and pyrite, I suspect."

"Pyrite?"

"Fool's gold."

I shrugged. "Tell me."

"Gold is better because it's what makes fortunes. Pyrite is a false dream for the ignorant. Gold is heavier than pyrite, which is a dull, darker yellow, almost the sheen of brass, while gold is a rich yellow that'll reflect sunlight. Fool's gold is shaped like crystals with flat faces you see in rock salt. Gold comes in rounded, odd-shaped nuggets with no regular form or shape. If you're prospecting, keep a metal file on you. When you find a mineral you can't identify, rub it against the file. Pyrite leaves behind a smudge of blackish or dark greenish powder. Gold produces a bright yellow streak. Even you could recognize the difference."

"If you know so much about gold and what you're doing, Pops, why aren't you rich?"

The old-timer offered me a smug grin. "Who says I'm not?"

"You don't look it."

My traveling companion laughed. "If we went by looks, you have the face that should be behind bars, and I don't mean those in saloons."

"I've never been to prison, Pops."

"You just haven't been convicted yet."

Maybe he was right. I had scammed Mattie out of fifteen hundred dollars, but I looked at that as doing her a favor since it was money that wouldn't wind up in Cort's hands. "You ever jumped a claim, Pops?"

"I haven't been caught, if that's what you mean." He laughed. "Well, not convicted, at least. If you're serious about mining, you need you a lawyer to file your claim and make sure it's valid. Otherwise, you spend more time in a courtroom than a mine."

His wisdom, I had to admit, extended beyond Shakespeare. We camped the night alongside the road, and I arose the next morning with him, drank his coffee and ate his jerky before we continued the journey to Leadville, me leading Ciaha and Pops guiding his donkey. In the middle of the afternoon we came to a wide valley that spread out beneath the mountain peaks. My teacher pointed out that we had crossed the Mosquito Range with the 14,000-foot Mount Sherman to the south. He pointed west to another imposing line of mountains, telling me that was the Sawatch Range with Mount Massive and Mount Elbert vying for the tallest, both at over 14,400-foot elevation. Between the Mosquito and Sawatch Ranges stood a smattering of tall trees. Through the timber wound the headwaters of the Arkansas. I couldn't believe a river I'd seen in Fort Smith started this far up in the highlands. From what I saw, the greatest prospecting activity was between the pass where we entered the valley and the town of Leadville, halfway across this bowl of a valley.

I felt lightheaded from the thin air, but Pops, being so close to potential riches, stood as vigorous as a bull. He scoffed at the prospectors working the eastern half of the valley, saying he preferred to search for a bonanza away from the others. For all the activity on the road from Denver, I had expected a bigger community. The Leadville I entered had a dozen permanent buildings and a smattering of tents and shacks scattered around stakes that marked the planned streets for the city's growth.

Studying our destination, I observed, "Not much of a town."

"Not yet," Pops acknowledged, "but come spring and summer, it'll be booming. Word's getting out these are the new diggings, and folks from Oro City, Granite and the other unnamed burgs in this high valley will move here then. By this time next year, the place will be thriving."

"I don't see it," I responded.

"Well, Lomax, if you intend to try mining, you best get a claim in quick before the valley's overwhelmed 'em. Remember to hire you a lawyer to handle the legal papers so you can manage the mining work."

"You think we might go in as partners?"

"Nope. The more people in on a claim, the trickier it gets because you can't trust folks when it comes to money."

He drew no argument from me, not after taking Mattie for fifteen hundred dollars, though I felt good about the funds I had left with Lupe. That wasn't thievery as much as righting a wrong. With my share of the Shotgun Jake Townsend payoff plus my winnings from betting on Cort at the footrace and my pay for guarding Mattie and her kept man, I had almost a thousand in cash on me, though I realized I shouldn't flash it around, not in a town driven by greed.

"What about finding a room?"

"Good luck," Pops said. "There's never enough to go around in a mining town and often what you find's overpriced and not much better than sleeping on the ground, if you can afford it. You don't look like the type that's got money or the smarts to hold on to it if you did. That's why I gave you the free advice. I'm doubtful you'll survive the winter." He pointed to Ciaha. "I've got my doubts about your mule as he's frail. He may not make it through the cold and thin air unless you buy him plenty of fodder."

After all, we'd been through together, I didn't want to lose Ciaha, but I worried how much hay and grain would cost to keep him fed during the cold stretch. I'd figure out something as I always had. "Any other advice, Pops?" I asked as we passed tents and shanties that I doubted could withstand a sneeze, much less a howling winter wind.

"You need a heavy coat and some better boots before the snows come or you'll wind up frozen or diseased by spring."

"Anything else I should buy?"

"You appear armed well enough to protect what's yours, but for cooking you'll need a coffeepot, frying pan, bread pan, tin plates, and cups, utensils, a bake oven, a coffee mill, a knife and fork. For sleeping and wearing, you'll want a poncho, a regular suit of clothes, three or four double blankets, and a pair or two of good work overalls. Now for mining, you should buy a six-pound striking hammer, four steel chisels, an eight-pound breaking hammer, a long handle shovel, a pole pick, and three steel drills in lengths of eighteen, twenty-six and thirty-six inches. To make your work easier, you need a keg of powder and fuses, though I wouldn't care to be around when you handled explosives."

"I'm flattered by your confidence in me."

"I've seen what an ill-timed explosion can do to a man so I don't care to be near someone inexperienced with powder."

As we neared the principal street with the permanent buildings, Pops told me he had enjoyed my company the past two days, even if I was a high-country greenhorn. He wished me luck, especially if I handled explosives. I thanked him for his advice, even when unflattering.

"Coat, boots, and lawyer are the most important things," he reminded me. "Get them and you should do okay."

He was right on two of the three necessities.

"Remember you need to stake out you a claim fast before more men flood in and take the prime spots. For a lode claim, you must work it, digging a shaft in search of silver ore. You can't prove your claim unless you show you excavation is progressing."

We stopped at the street with the permanent structures and shook hands, wishing each other the best and heading our own ways, Pops trudging north toward the elusive bonanza he hoped to find and me down Leadville's dusty street. Half of the buildings lacked signs so it was hard to determine their purpose, but I identified the Tabor and Mater stores, a shabby log structure that claimed to be a hotel, a drug store, a combination livery stable and wagon shop, an assayer's office and Billy Nye's Saloon, the biggest building on the street. I led Ciaha down the dusty trail, debating whether to take him to the livery first or to stop in a store and buy me a tin of peaches or something else for supper, as Pops had only provided coffee and a single strip of jerky on the last leg of our trip.

Because I hadn't ridden Ciaha since breakfast, I figured he'd had an easier day than me so I opted for the store, deciding on Tabor's place as his sign identified the business as H.A.W. TABOR GENERAL MERCHANDISE & POST OFFICE, though it was disconcerting to see an open coffin leaning against the wall next to the door. I tied my mule to the hitching post outside and marched in, finding a couple I took to be in their late forties wearing aprons. The woman sat behind a metal cage and counter labeled POST OFFICE in the corner, sorting letters while the man stood on a stepladder stocking the shelves with tin goods. He glanced over his shoulder at me, shoved the tins in his hands on the shelf and retreated from his perch.

"Welcome to Leadville," he said, "I'm Horace Austin Warner Tabor or 'Haw' as most folks around these parts call me." He pointed to the female at the mail desk. "That's Augusta, my wife of two decades." She nodded at me.

I smiled and took in her long flat face and flat brown hair parted in the middle and plastered down save for the ringlets which fell over her brow. She was neither pretty nor ugly, just plain for a woman, though she might well be the best specimen of her gender in Leadville as I had yet to eye another gal. Tabor's visage looked like the work of a drunk sculptor, featuring a bushy mustache, bushy eyebrows, bushy sideburns and a receding mop of brown hair that didn't start until the middle of his head. He had the longest forehead I ever saw on a man.

"I'm H.H. Lomax," I announced.

"Planning on staying in Leadville a spell?"

"Until I make my fortune," I answered.

"Let me be the first to welcome you and ask for your vote for mayor in the election coming this January. And, if you strike it rich, I might suggest you contribute to my election coffers. If not, your vote'll be sufficient. Until election day, what can I do for you?"

"I need something to eat."

From the corner, Augusta lifted a handful of envelopes and scowled. "How about some mail for supper?"

"I was thinking more a tin of peaches," I answered.

Tabor stepped over and patted me on the shoulder. "Pay her no mind. She's frustrated with the stacks of correspondence we've got to sort. Half the country's coming to Leadville, and their kin's sending mail to them general delivery. The letters get here before their folks do." Tabor studied me a moment and scratched his whiskerless chin, as Augusta grumbled about the mountains of mail she had to handle. "Do you read by chance? Not everyone does and don't be ashamed if you can't."

"My momma wouldn't've let me leave home in Arkansas without being readable. I'm even familiar with Shakespeare. 'Beauty provoketh thieves sooner than gold.' That's from *However You Like It*." I pointed to Augusta. "I suspect you need a guard to keep the local fellows from stealing your wife, looker that she is."

Augusta smiled and tipped her head at me.

Tabor sputtered, "I didn't think Arkansas folks had ever heard of Shakespeare."

"He's one of our favorite miners," I said.

"Miners? He wasn't a miner."

"He mined the English language—did he not?—and produced nuggets of lasting gold."

"Yeah," Augusta interjected, "while Shakespeare's wife did the work he avoided."

"I can't read as well as you, Augusta," Tabor shot back.

"Then you shouldn't have taken the mail contract, Horace, and harnessed me like a plow horse with the chore."

Theirs was not a marriage made in heaven, I decided, figuring I should've gone to the Mater store across the street.

Tabor looked at his spouse with tight lips, then turned to me, his grimace dissolving into a sickly smile perfect for a politician. "If you can read, might you consider hiring on to sort the mail and give my wife a break, Lomax?"

Cocking my head and glancing at Augusta, I hesitated.

"We'll board you in the back room. You'll use mail sacks for a mattress and covers. Leadville is brutal in the winter. This store's drafty, but it'll beat sleeping in a tent until spring when everything muddies up with the thaw."

"Will you throw in one meal a day?"

Tabor nodded, "Though it won't be hot."

I pondered the offer, planning to accept it, but delaying the decision to see if I might extract more from Haw. "I need time to file a mining claim."

"Okay, okay," he conceded, "as long as you work ten hours a day six days a week organizing the mail, even if it's after hours when we are closed."

"And I want a dollar a day in pay."

Tabor hesitated until he glanced at Augusta, who stood

with her arms folded across her chest and her jaw clenched. If looks could've killed, we'd have been reciting Horace Austin Warner Tabor's eulogy at that very moment.

After realizing his future depended on hiring me, he nodded. "Agreed."

Augusta's stern demeanor melted into a begrudging smile as she dropped the letters in her hands onto the counter and stepped from behind the metal enclosure.

"I'll leave my things in the storeroom, take care of my mule. Tomorrow I intend to look around and file a claim, then I'll start sorting mail."

"I can live with that," Tabor acknowledged.

"So be it," Augusta interjected, "but I'm not handling any mail tomorrow. I'm done with that, and I'm done with not having any say in things, Horace." She untied her apron and threw it atop a stack of letters on the counter. "You're running for mayor and have asked a stranger for his vote when I can't even vote for you or your opponent if I so choose!"

"That's why you can't vote. You might make the wrong choice."

"And that's why I'm for women's suffrage so we're equal with men."

I scratched my head, uncertain why women would be so all-fired interested in suffering the same as the men. It made little sense to me.

"And that's why you'll go to Susan B. Anthony's lecture when she comes to town. You're gonna hear what she has to say whether you like it or not."

Figuring this marriage might soon come to blows and, based on the fire in Augusta's eyes, I decided she'd emerge the victor, so I excused myself, not wanting to be a witness if Augusta killed Haw right there. "I'll gather my belongings and put them in the back, then tend my other business," I said.

They both heard me, but didn't answer as they stared each other down. I backed outside and stepped onto the plank walk, wondering if one of them might have a use for the coffin propped outside. I gathered my saddlebags, carbine, and canteen, carrying them inside the store, which was frostier than when I first entered, the proprietors ignoring

each other and me as I made my way into the back room.
There must've been two dozen bulging canvas sacks of mail
stacked in the corner. A small window on the far wall lit the
storeroom. I dropped my gear on the wooden floor beside
the bags, startling a mouse that scurried away. I went back
to the street to get my saddle. After I added it to the pile, I
returned to Ciaha, untied him and led him across the street
to the livery stable, paying for three days fodder to be fed
him over the next two days to help him regain his strength.

Returning to the store, I made my nest in the storeroom corner, sorting out the six largest mail sacks and
arranging them on the floor, unfurling my bedroll atop
them. It wasn't as soft as Mattie Silks' mattress, but it
was better than the hard Colorado ground. As they were
closing up the place, Horace brought me a tin of peaches
and a can opener, telling me this would be my supper. He
showed me a lamp and pointed to a dozen empty crates.

"You might use those when you alphabetize the letters."

"Alphabetize?"

"Yeah," he answered, "put them in order. You do know
your A-B-Cs, don't you?"

"I know Shakespeare," I replied.

"Good night," he answered and left me alone for the
evening.

After fishing a spoon out of my saddlebags, I opened the
tin of peaches and savored the fruit and the sweet syrup,
then retired on my mail service mattress for a good night's
sleep. Once Tabor returned the next morning, I carried my
gear over to the livery stable and fetched Ciaha, rigging
him up and riding west out of town until I reached a broad
stream that flowed south. I dismounted and let my mule
drink the clear waters. I emptied my canteen on the bank
and stepped to the water's edge, dipping it into the frigid
waters of the Arkansas. When it was full, I lifted it to my
lips and savored the cool, pristine liquid. I had never seen
water so clean, unlike the muddy waters of the Arkansas
that reached Fort Smith and beyond. I re-filled my canteen
and started back toward town. East of Leadville I rode
among the scattered claims, looking for a site. The more
I looked, the less certain I was I wanted to file a claim as

there was too much physical work involved. Everywhere miners were digging shafts, hauling the debris out with A-frame windlasses and dumping the detritus. The men were dirty and their clothes ragged.

Come noon I smelled aromas from a lunch fire and found two prospectors that invited me to join them. I thought they were being friendly, but they were more interested in Ciaha than in me. If I had my own plate and spoon, they offered to share lunch. I dismounted and got the utensils from my saddlebags. They offered me a helping of pan-fried potatoes. They spoke in a thick German accent, identifying themselves as August Rische and George Hook, two former shoemakers who had met each other by accident during their prospecting endeavors and partnered up. From what I understood from their muddy accents, Rische knew mining the best and said their diggings offered promise. By their calloused hands I noted they were hard workers. As we finished our meal, they said they needed a mule to help them dig, but were broke. They inquired if I would consider becoming their partner so they could use Ciaha. I thought of Pops' warning about the fragile nature of mining partnerships and declined an outright partnership, since I failed to understand half of what they said. Instead, I made a counteroffer to lend them Ciaha, provided they kept him fed and worked a claim for me next to theirs. We agreed they had to work on my plot one day a week and begin a shaft that would go down ten feet or more for me to get full title to the claim. After lunch we staked out my claim adjoining theirs, and I pointed where the Lomax shaft would be dug. I told them to come to town tomorrow to retrieve Ciaha.

"If we get rich," I explained to my mule, "you'll never carry a load of any kind again."

After we concluded our agreement with handshakes all around, I returned to the Tabor store. Once I unloaded my gear in the storeroom, I led Ciaha across the street and stabled him, informing the liveryman that I would no longer be keeping my mule in his stable after next day. The following day, all I had to do was start sorting mail and find myself a trustworthy lawyer, if such an animal even existed in Leadville.

Chapter Nine

I sat on the stool behind the counter and the mail cage in the corner, uncertain what I was doing as I tried to sort and organize the correspondence. Noting my lack of progress, Augusta Tabor sauntered over, smiling with the knowledge she no longer had to do the task. "How's the alphabetizing coming?" she inquired.

Shrugging, I asked her, "What's your system of alphabetizing?"

"Same as everybody else's," she responded, not helping me a bit.

"Do you alphabetize a letter at a time or all at once?"

"Both," she answered.

I slapped my forehead that none of it made sense.

Augusta eyed me. "You know Shakespeare but not how to alphabetize?"

"We never needed the skill in Arkansas."

"I tell you," she said, "but then I want to ask you a question."

Nodding my acceptance, I listened as she explained that the alphabet can be arranged in order like numbers. The letter A corresponded to the number one and B equaled number two and so on through the alphabet. After that realization, I understood it was simply a matter of sorting the names on the envelopes and organizing them in sequence. She instructed me to alphabetize by last name, then first. It was a simple concept once outlined, and I picked it up fast.

When she completed my lesson, she said, "Now I have a question for you. Do you believe in women's suffrage?"

I had to shake my head. "No, ma'am, I believe women shouldn't have to suffer. It's not right."

"My thoughts exactly," she replied, "so you *do* support suffrage?"

This was the densest woman I'd ever encountered. I'd just said women shouldn't suffer, save maybe from childbirth and lengthy church sermons, yet she was saying they should. It was the darndest thing I'd faced in my entire life. I couldn't understand why she was thinking females should endure so much, but I didn't want to argue with her in case I needed more instruction on organizing and alphabetizing the bundles of correspondence that provided my mattress. Shrugging and offering a vague reply to what was a more complex question than I imagined, I announced, "I'm for what's right."

"Then you *do* think women should have the vote?"

"I don't know what voting's got to do with suffering," I replied.

"Voting is the cornerstone of women's suffrage," she said. "Without it we are doomed to suffer throughout the ages."

I stood there as confused as a Democrat at a revival and gave up. "I agree."

"Are you listening, Horace?" Augusta called to her husband as he prepared to open the store for the day's business. "Lomax believes in women's suffrage!"

"If I'd known that, Augusta, I never would've hired him."

To be honest, I was no longer sure what I believed about suffering or even women the way she distorted my words. I started alphabetizing as fast as I could, trying to avoid the verbal shrapnel in this marital dispute I didn't understand.

"You would've hired him," Augusta shouted back, "or you'd be looking for a new wife!"

"That might solve all our problems," Tabor said, pausing at the door to argue.

"Problems? You're running for mayor of Leadville, and you need all the support you can get. It'll help your campaign when people know that the governor and his wife will dine at our house for dinner before Susan Anthony's talk at the end of the month."

"Governor Routt would go anywhere for a free meal. Besides, he doesn't wear the pants in his family, Eliza does."

"Could be she's smarter than John Long Routt."

"I'm not letting you run my house, my store, or my politics, Augusta. All the men say Eliza, not the governor, is the reason suffrage will be considered in the legislature this fall because he isn't man enough to stop Eliza's foolishness."

"We women should put an end to your male foolishness," Augusta spat back. "Women want the vote from men, Horace, and men desire something else from us. Without us getting the vote we want, you men aren't getting what you want."

I'd been around enough brothels to understand that while husbands might not get it at home, they had other options.

"Lord, I know that to be the truth," Tabor shot back, still not unlocking the door, even though a customer rapped on the window. "Now be a dutiful wife for a change, Augusta, and greet our patrons with a smile."

As he opened up, his scowl evaporated into a politician's grin as he welcomed a dozen men to his store. Eleven of them headed straight for me. "Need my mail," said the first, telling me his name. If I had this many visitors all day, I would never get the sacks sorted for distribution. Fortunately, Augusta came to my rescue.

"If you'll sort the letters, I'll distribute them. I don't mind that."

At that point, I became a proponent of women's suffrage, whatever the hell it was. Of course, that was *before* I met Miss Susan B. Anthony.

We had a steady stream of customers throughout the day, some purchasing goods, but most checking on mail. Mid-afternoon, my mining claim neighbors August Rische and George Hook entered to check on their post. As Tabor's wife searched for their letters, I excused myself and headed across the street to the stable and returned with Ciaha on a halter as they exited the store, Hook reading a letter and Rische empty-handed.

We greeted each other, and I pointed to Ciaha. "Here's our mule. Are we still agreed that I loan you the mule and one day in seven you dig the shaft on my claim?"

"*Ja, mein herr,*" said Rische.

"Yah," Hook echoed.

"I'll drop by in a week to check on your progress."

"Yah," replied Rische.

"*Ja,*" answered Hook.

They untied Ciaha's halter and led him down the street toward our claims. I stepped back inside and sorted more mail in the storeroom, disturbing a few mice as they scurried about and hid among the bags. I tied with string all letters to the same individual and used empty wooden crates to organize the envelopes by each letter of the alphabet. With at least one new sack arriving every other weekday, I feared it might take forever to catch up.

That evening at closing time, I asked Tabor if he could recommend any lawyer to start the legal work on my claim.

"Cheap or honest?"

"Both," I replied.

"No such animal!"

"There's only two right now, but as word spreads we're the next boomtown, Leadville will be flooded with lawyers by spring, them and conmen."

"One and the same," I said.

"One's over in Oro City, a few miles away. The other's new, arriving last week. A fellow named Adam Scheisse, I believe it was. Supposed to know California and Nevada mining law, especially around the Comstock Lode."

Though this was Colorado, I figured I'd try Scheisse as I didn't have transportation now that I had loaned Ciaha to Hook and Rische. "Where might I find him?"

"He lives near the river in a tent, though I don't know which one. He rents a room in the back of Bill Nye's Saloon for an office. You might look for him there."

"I'll do that this evening."

Tabor nodded. "I'll loan you my key so you can secure the place when you leave."

"What about my supper?"

"Take what you want."

"One more question, Haw. Have you had enough of

women's suffering?"

Tabor lifted his hand to his chin. "Up to here, but don't tell Augusta."

I laughed and locked the door behind him, and stepped to the shelves, deciding I'd try a can of apricots for my evening meal. I carried the tin into the storeroom and opened it with Tabor's tool and spooned out fine pieces of orange fruit, then drank the syrup from the container. After sundown I put on my hat and gun belt and exited the store, locking it and walking down the street to Billy Nye's Saloon. I had to say Nye had faith in Leadville's growth because he built a place at least three times bigger than the next largest structure in town. I entered, drawing the stares of two dozen customers seated at scattered tables. He had too few tables and chairs for such a vast space, so the furniture stood like isolated islands in a vast sea. Inadequate lamps lit the place, so the span was dim in the corners. Nye's roughhewn bar nestled against the west wall near the single pot-bellied stove at the far end. The saloon would need more stoves in the coming winter to warm an area that big unless someone struck a bonanza and business picked up. Along the back, I saw three doors, one open with lamp light seeping out. Beside the door hung a sign for ADAM SCHEISSE/ATTORNEY AT LAW.

"Care for a drink?" cried the bartender as I headed for Scheisse's office.

I waved the offer aside. "I'm here on legal business."

"A jigger of whiskey will ease the pain."

Ignoring the barkeep, I reached the door and knocked on the sign for good luck, as this was my first time to require a lawyer on a civil matter.

"Enter only if you need the services of Colorado's best attorney," came a confident voice.

I stepped inside, uncertain what to expect. What I saw was a suited man leaning back in his chair with his feet up on a rectangular table that served as his desk. He strangled the neck of an open whisky bottle in his left hand.

"State your name," he commanded, drawing a swig of whiskey.

"H.H. Lomax."

"State your business."

"I need to file a claim on mining property."

"Placer or lode?"

"Lode claim."

"You've come to the right man." After taking a second swig from the whiskey bottle, he sat it on the floor by his chair, slid his feet off the desk and stood. He was tall and lean with a long neck that looked as if it had been stretched by a dozen unsuccessful hangings and with bug eyes that would've been the envy of a praying mantis. "I'm Adam Scheisse, esquire" he said, extending his hand.

As I shook his soft palm and fingers, I confirmed he'd never done a hard day's work in his life. Looking around the office, I saw a bookshelf with three legal books and a coal oil lamp.

"Drag yourself up a chair, Lomax," he said as he folded his frame back in his seat and picked up the whiskey bottle. Scheisse sat in the only seat in the room.

"I don't see one."

"Grab one from the saloon," he commanded.

Backing out of his office and heading for a chair at an empty table, I considered walking on out the door, but decided to hear Scheisse out. I carried the seat back inside and sat opposite him as he raised his feet up and rested them on the table corner.

"Now tell me how I can help you, Lomax."

"I need to file on a claim and make sure it's legal when I strike paying ore. I don't want to spend years in court squandering my wealth."

"You've come to the right lawyer, Lomax."

Looking around the sparse room, I shook my head. "I was expecting more."

"Sometimes you must travel light. You know how it is." He took a swig from his bottle.

"Where'd you last hang your shingle?" I asked.

"Virginia City, Nevada, but it's about played out. I'm seeking the next bonanza and fresh opportunities to help young men like you make a fortune and live a life of luxury."

His ideas of luxury and mine stood miles apart, but no busier than he was, I figured he could devote his full attention to my legal needs. All I was competing against was a whiskey bottle. "What's your services cost?"

"Fifty dollars, Lomax, and that includes the filing fee and my charges. Once you make preliminary filing, you must prove your claim by digging a shaft at least ten feet deep and beginning laterals in search of ore. Once you strike a paying lode, you dig wherever it takes you. I must inspect your plot first and confirm you've marked it appropriately."

I told him to find the claim abutting that of Rische and Hook.

"Near Fryer Hill?"

"Next to Rische and Hook."

Scheisse nodded. "Give me a few days, Lomax, and I'll find it. Right now, I'm backed up with clients, more business than I can handle by myself, but I'll keep plugging away until you have a legal claim that is rock solid. Are we agreed?"

I nodded.

"Where can I find you when I complete the paperwork?"

"At the Tabor store, handling mail."

"Then I'll be seeing you often as I have extensive legal correspondence."

I stood.

"Oh, one thing I forgot," Scheisse said. "I require half of my fee up front and the rest upon completion."

I made a mistake by reaching in my pocket and pulling out my roll of money.

"Damn," he cried, yanking his feet from the table and plopping forward in his chair. His bug eyes bulged even more when he saw my cash. "If I'd known you could afford more, I'd offered you more services."

I counted out twenty-five dollars and handed the bills to Scheisse. "I need a receipt."

The attorney looked around the room and shrugged. "I don't have any paper to write one, but my word's as good as my bond. You can trust me, Lomax, I assure you. Not only that, I'll expedite your business, put it at the top of my list."

"I thought you didn't keep paper."

He pointed to his forehead. "It's all up here. My list's in my head."

Uncertain if I was making the right decision, I shrugged and turned for the exit, figuring I'd give him a few days to see if he filed the paperwork. As I reached the door, he called me.

"Lomax," he said, "return the furniture, would you?"

Retreating, I picked up the saloon chair and placed it by the table where it belonged. As I marched for the door, the barkeep laughed.

"Fellow," he chuckled, "I warned you, you'd need a drink before you entered."

I walked back to Tabor's and lit a lamp in the mail room, watching the mice scurry for cover and then sorting mail until I tired. After that I smoothed out my baggy mattress and rested. Things fell into a routine for the next three weeks as I sorted mail and rented a horse once a week to check on Hood's and Rische's progress on my shaft. Ciaha seemed glad to see me, though sullen that I had consigned him to such work. At the store, I began to recognize the men and occasional women that came in and matched them up with their mail. I paid particular attention to my attorney's incoming mail. He had an entire stack from J.R. Smith of Denver. For a week, he didn't come by to collect his correspondence, always sending a boy to deliver his outgoing letters and pick up his correspondence. I refused to release the mail to the boy, insisting that the lawyer report in person for his missives since I was awaiting my legal papers.

Eight days after I met with him, Scheisse came in brandishing the documents that granted me ownership of my claim, provided I made the required improvements within the allotted time. Before he handed over the papers, he insisted that I pay. I told him I'd fetch the payment from the backroom so I excused myself to count the money away from his greedy bug eyes. When I turned around, I saw him standing in the doorway, licking his covetous lips from his brief glimpse at my roll of cash. He rubbed his elongated neck.

"This is a private area," I advised him.

"Nothing's private between a lawyer and his client, Lomax. I need to know everything to protect your interests."

Pointing him to the mail cage, I said, "I'll meet you over there and pay you."

He ambled around in front of the counter while I retreated behind it. At the mail cage, I gave him his money for the legal documents.

"Take good care of them," he said, "as they could make us rich."

"Us?"

"Believe me, Lomax, wealth brings a set of problems that only a lawyer can contend with. You'll need me."

"We'll see," I said, doubting I would use him. "Before you leave, get your mail."

"My courier told me you refused to release it to him."

"Can't take chances with the mail." I handed him a bundle that had eighteen letters from J.R. Smith of Denver.

"Good old Jeff," Scheisse said, "smartest man in Colorado."

"Thought you came here from Virginia City, Nevada," I challenged.

"By way of Denver," he said. "No trains into Leadville yet, unless I missed it. You take care, Lomax, and don't be reading my mail."

The idea never entered my mind until he admonished me, but at that point I knew one day I must open a letter to see what brand of chicanery he preferred.

After Scheisse left, Horace Tabor looked at me, shaking his head. "Do you trust him?"

"Can't say for certain."

"He's got a neck like a goose."

"Yeah," I acknowledged, "it's like he's escaped the noose a time or two. I'll start calling him 'Noose Neck'." We both laughed.

As the calendar neared the end of the month, the laughter died and tensions rose between Augusta and Horace, all of it related to the visit by the governor and his wife with Susan B. Anthony, who was scheduled to speak in Billy Nye's Saloon. Augusta focused on making a favorable impression, fretting that Horace would embarrass her in front of Anthony or Colorado's first family.

Augusta planned to host the guests at their modest house and fix the suffragist a fine supper before escorting her to Nye's for her talk. Horace rolled his eyes as his wife fretted over how to honor Anthony for her excellent work on behalf of women and whether she should provide a male escort for her guest. When Augusta decided that would be appropriate, she worried over selecting the right man for the job.

"Let me pick a prospector off the street. That'll do," Tabor said.

"Not on your life," Augusta replied, a threat in her words.

"Well, why not Lomax? He's dependable, hasn't robbed or killed us yet and is as good a young man as you'll find in a mining camp, Augusta."

Augusta stamped her foot on the floor and planted her balled fists on her hips. "Horace Austin Warner Tabor, I'm certain Miss Anthony is twice his age."

"Perhaps an escort of Lomax's charm could take the starch out of the old hen's bloomers," Tabor countered.

"He's from Arkansas," she said.

"Lomax knows Shakespeare," her husband replied.

Augusta eyed me from head to foot, her knotted hands falling from her hips. "He'd need better clothes and a haircut."

"I'm not spending money on new duds to escort an old woman to a speech I don't care to hear," I informed them, "not when I need a good winter coat and boots."

"Horace will cover your costs."

"Including a winter coat and boots?"

"Certainly," Augusta answered.

I turned to Tabor. "Thank you, Haw, that's mighty generous of you."

He shrugged. "I guess it's settled, am I right?"

"I've must give Lomax a lesson in manners. I don't want Miss Anthony leaving here thinking we are philistines in Colorado."

That was a band of Indians I was not familiar with, but I took Augusta's word for it.

"Starting tomorrow," Augusta informed me, "we'll spend half a day teaching you proper etiquette for such a distinguished visitor."

The following six days became a horrendous stain on my manhood as Augusta took me to their home in the afternoons and taught me how to pull out a chair for a woman and how to use a fork, spoon, and knife, though I had been using them for years. She told me not to belch and to say pardon me, if by chance I slipped and did burp. Next she instructed me how to converse with a woman of distinction such as Miss Anthony. She said simple minds talked about people, average minds talked about events and great minds talked about ideas and philosophy.

"I have a great idea," I informed Augusta.

She smiled. "Let me hear it."

"That we end this folderol so I can get back to work."

Augusta blanched, her smile slipping into despair so fast that I regretted the suggestion. She taught me that a proper gentleman looks for things to complement a woman on such as her hair, her attire, or her charm. Though she didn't come right out and say it, Augusta Tabor insinuated that it was okay to lie to a woman if its purpose was simple flattery. Until that moment I had always thought it was only proper to story a woman to get something you wanted, but Augusta instantly disabused me of that notion. By the afternoon that Susan B. Anthony arrived in Leadville, I was prepared for any potential catastrophe other than Miss Anthony herself.

At Augusta's insistence, Tabor closed the store at noon the day the governor was to bring his wife and distinguished guest to Leadville. He tacked a sign on the door announcing the mercantile was closed until the next morning and encouraging people to attend Anthony's lecture that night in Billy Nye's Saloon. As Tabor locked the store for the afternoon, seven miners stepped up on the plank walk demanding to get their mail before he left. They cursed and threatened him if he didn't, but Tabor glanced at Augusta, who stood scowling with her arms crossed over her bosom. I watched, holding my new outfit wrapped in brown paper, and realized Tabor was more frightened by his wife than he was seven muscled miners.

Looking at them, Tabor pointed to his wife. "Take it up with her."

Augusta glared at them, then took a step in their direction. They retreated as she lifted her finger and pointed at the nearest one's nose. "Be at Miss Susan B. Anthony's lecture tonight and applaud at everything she says."

"And what if we don't?" said the front miner, pointing his finger at her nose.

Slowly moving her head from side to side and clenching her fingers into fists, Augusta studied her adversaries and spoke in a low menacing voice. "Your mail might disappear or get marked deceased and returned to sender."

The prospectors looked at one another until one nodded. "We'll be there," said the leader, "and clapping, no matter the foolishness she discusses."

Augusta scowled her approval and strode toward them, the men parting for her to pass. I realized all this women's suffrage would lead to a lot of men suffering, but I held my tongue, following in Augusta's wake as we marched to their home, Tabor trailing us and reminding his customers, "Vote for Tabor come the January elections."

While most of the cabins around town were made of logs, the Tabors had a clapboard house that Tabor had skidded from Oro City to its Leadville location. It was small, but well kept, with a parlor, a kitchen, and a bedroom. As soon as we got home, Augusta charged into her kitchen and added more wood to the coals in her stove as she prepared the meal and boiled water so Tabor and I could bathe, Augusta insisting that we not only be mannerly but also clean. This was sure a lot of men's work for women to get the vote, but Horace and I went along with it, though it was awkward, me bathing in my altogether in the same room that Augusta was fixing supper. I never caught her peeping, however, as she was so intent on impressing Miss Anthony with her cooking and hospitality.

Once I was bathed, shaved, dried, combed and dressed in my union suit, she helped me into my new black pants, which were too big and kept slipping down my legs, and the whitest shirt I'd ever worn. As I held up my britches, she attached my paper collar to my shirt and buttoned it in front, forcing me to hold my chin and head up. I worried that maintaining that position might give me an elongated neck like my lawyer's. Realizing that my loose trousers might fall to my ankles and embarrass her, me and, most importantly, Miss Susan B. Anthony, Augusta fetched a pair of her husband's suspenders and pinned them to my pants.

When I was dressed, she made sure Horace was wearing his best suit and tie, then claimed the kitchen for herself so she could bathe, attend the cooking and be ready for the four o'clock arrival. Bless her heart, Augusta managed everything and was waiting in the parlor with her husband and me when we heard a buggy pull up outside the house. Augusta turned to us both. "Don't embarrass me," she warned, opening the door and stepping outdoors, Horace and me trailing.

"Welcome, Governor and Mrs. Routt and especially Miss Susan B. Anthony, our honored guest," she cried. When Augusta moved aside, I caught my first glimpse of our esteemed visitor. If ever a woman had been suckled on lemons and preserved in vinegar, she was it. I'd seen Sioux and Cheyenne warriors at the Little Bighorn with friendlier expressions than the one on her face. I prepared for a long, excruciating night.

Chapter Ten

After the governor helped Miss Susan B. Anthony down from the buggy, she stood there as Augusta introduced herself and her husband. The suffragist possessed dark, defiant eyes, a determined nose and chin, and a mouth downturned at the corners as if she always frowned. Before Augusta could introduce me, Anthony looked at me and said, "This must be your son. I hope you are raising him right with a belief in suffrage and temperance."

Augusta blushed. "No, this is H.H. Lomax, one of our employees. I thought it proper for you to have a male escort during your visit to Leadville. He knows Shakespeare."

Miss Susan B. Anthony eyed me from head to foot, and I realized she had as much use for me as a Sioux warrior had for fiddle lessons. She shook my hand limply, but the moment she released it the governor grabbed it and gave me a manly handshake. "It's always good to meet another Colorado voter, Lomax."

His wife poked his ribs with her elbow.

"Let me introduce my wife, Eliza Pickrell Routt," the governor said, "the fairest lady in all of Colorado."

Rather than acknowledge me or offer me her hand, she elbowed her husband again. "You forget, Johnny, that you'd have three more voters here, if you get the suffrage bill through the legislature."

"Indeed, I would," Routt said, "and no lovelier trio of voters in Colorado than the three beautiful ladies standing before me."

"That's why we're here," Eliza reminded her spouse.

I'd never met a governor before, though I wasn't sure he ran the state or just took orders from his wife.

"Why don't we step inside and visit before dinner?" Augusta suggested.

As Tabor opened the door, I gestured for Miss Susan B. Anthony to lead the way. She scowled at me like she had enough sense to figure that out on her own. The more I thought about women's suffrage with her as its leader, the more I realized it would be men that would suffer the most. She marched by with her nose in the air, her hair pulled tight against her head and tied in a bun in back. The suffragist wore a black dress as if she was in mourning, though it was topped with a high, white lace collar. I wondered if hers was as prickly as my paper collar and if that was the reason she was brassy as a new spittoon. If there was any honey in her, I doubted a thousand swarms of bees could find it.

As I passed Horace at the door, I whispered "Maybe a jigger of whiskey would loosen her up." I'd barely gotten the words out than Augusta strode over and yanked me back outside.

"Liquor is an abomination to Miss Anthony," she said. "Don't mention it again!"

Damn if women's suffrage wasn't going to make men endure the most when it was all said and done. After giving me a look that could've turned lava into a block of ice, Augusta exhaled deeply, wiped the frown from her lips and marched back inside with a smile. When I stepped by Horace at the door, he nodded and spoke softly, "You're right." He looked quickly to confirm that his wife had not overheard his comment.

Augusta pointed her honored guest to a padded rocking chair and the governor and first lady to a matching divan. The Tabors and I pulled out chairs from around the dining table that was set with everything but the food for supper. I sat and listened, wishing I had a keg of whiskey to help me get through this conversation.

"The world has been a blank to me these last ten days," Anthony announced. "I haven't read a single newspaper since

I've been in Colorado promoting suffrage. I hope men here are smarter than elsewhere, but we are making progress."

"Pray tell how," Augusta said, leaning forward in her chair toward her honored guest.

"We are optimistic that California Senator Aaron Sargent will introduce in January a constitutional amendment to provide women the right to vote once the states ratify it," she said.

"Isn't Sargent called the senator for the Southern Pacific?" Tabor asked.

"Remember, Horace," interjected the governor, "always to speak kindly of a fellow Republican."

Anthony nodded. "Senator Sargent has been called that by some, but we women must find our allies anywhere we can, if we are to ever get the vote."

After more exciting conversation than I could take, Augusta announced she had to finish preparing dinner so we could leave in time to reach the lecture hall for Miss Anthony's speech. I found it amusing she failed to describe the saloon for what it was. She stood up from her chair, hesitating a moment as she looked from Eliza to Miss Anthony to see if they offered to help. They didn't. "Lomax," she asked, "could you assist?"

"Certainly." Arising from my chair and turning to our guests, I said, "Excuse me, if you please," just as Augusta had taught me for whenever I left a room filled with distinguished guests. Escaping the dignitaries and the indignities of their conversation, I entered the kitchen.

With mitts on her hands, Augusta opened the cast-iron door on her stove and pulled out a baked ham and dropped the pan atop the stove. She retrieved a platter from a cabinet, grabbed a big fork and transferred the meat from the pan to the dish which she put on the small kitchen table. She pointed to a knife and asked me to slice the pork. "Not too thick and not too thin."

I grabbed the cutlery and chopped away, my slivers varying in width so that at least one would satisfy her. I eavesdropped on what I could hear of the conversation in the parlor and learned that Miss Susan B. Anthony had been against everything, starting with slavery, whiskey drinking, politicians who opposed her, newspapers that mocked her, labor unions that ignored women, ladies that sacrificed their opportunities for a husband, cops that arrested her and a dozen other injustices new to me. From what I gathered, she disliked everything except complaining about what she hated. As I listened and cut chunks from around the hambone, Augusta scooped boiled potatoes out of a pan and put them in a serving bowl, which she carried to the table. Then she returned and dumped a pot of canned green beans into a second serving dish, placing it on the table. Next she sliced two loaves of fresh-baked bread and added them along with a tub of butter and a dish of pickles to the feast. When I finished slicing the ham and discarding the bone, I toted the platter into the parlor. Augusta nodded her approval as she returned to the kitchen and put a new pan in the oven. She motioned me back, and I helped her carry out the water glasses.

Returning to the front room with the water pitcher that she sat on the table, she announced, "Please join us for dinner."

"Smells wonderful, Augusta," the governor said, his wife nodding her approval.

Miss Susan B. Anthony remained silent, just arose straight from her rocker and marched to the chair Augusta designated for her next to me.

As she approached, I grabbed her chair and pulled it back for her, just as Augusta had taught me. I drew an approving smile from her until Miss Susan B. Anthony snarled.

"Young man," she sniffed, "I am perfectly capable of pulling my chair out for myself."

I wasn't expecting this, not since I had practiced so hard to not only remember my assigned tasks but also to do them flawlessly. I thought about asking her if she was capable of pulling the chair out of her behind if I shoved it there, but decided against it, knowing Augusta would fire me, and I would spend my Leadville winter sleeping on the cold ground rather than on softer mail sacks.

Miss Susan B. Anthony shoved my hand away from the chair, pushed it back under the table, then pulled it out herself and sat.

"You're welcome," I mouthed, then took my seat as the others settled into theirs.

After we were seated, Tabor turned to his honored guest. "We say a blessing before our meals, Miss Anthony, would your object?"

"No, please, go ahead," she said. "I'm a Quaker."

At least she wasn't against God, I thought.

"We always hold hands when we pray to represent our unity," Tabor continued. "Would you object, Miss Anthony?"

I wondered if she was perfectly capable of holding hands.

"Proceed as usual and I shall honor the customs of the home in which I am a guest."

With that, I took the hand of Miss Susan B. Anthony by my side and Horace Tabor at the head of the table. He said a blessing that I cannot remember as I kept thinking how frail and cold Anthony's hand was. She saved her strength and heat for her causes.

When Tabor said his amen, everyone smiled and helped their plates. As Augusta had instructed, I did not fill my plate until after I had offered the dishes to Miss Anthony. She took a modest spoon of green beans, a single boiled potato, a single pickle, and a slice of bread, which she buttered.

When she passed the platter with ham to me, Augusta exuded concern. "Do you not care for ham, Miss Anthony?"

"It's not that," she replied. "When I travel I eschew any meats."

Finally, a topic I could speak on so I joined the conversation. "I generally chew my meat thirty times before I swallow. That's what my mother taught me."

Everybody looked at me, their eyes perplexed, until the governor laughed.

"That's a good one, young Lomax," Routt said. "You had me fooled for a second."

I grinned like I knew what he was talking about. Then everyone else chuckled, except for the suffragist, who grew stiffer in posture and demeanor as the evening progressed.

The value of the ensuing conversation assayed out to less than a penny for every ton of words. I didn't find it enthralling that Miss Anthony at her home in Rochester, New York, insisted on fruit, grain, and coffee for breakfast at seven-fifteen each morning; vegetables, four ounces of meat with the fat trimmed and water at noon for lunch; and fruit, crackers, and tea at supper precisely at six o'clock. Orange marmalade was her favorite table vice.

As soon as she said that, Augusta apologized that she had no marmalade, but confessed she was baking a peach cobbler in the oven.

While I ate and listened to the insufferable conversation, I realized why Horace Tabor stayed with Augusta. She was an excellent cook. Based on what I'd seen of Miss Susan B. Anthony, I wondered if she could even boil water, but she sure knew how to complain, returning often to how poorly she'd been treated by the press.

"One northeastern newspaper, the *St. Alban Advertiser* in Vermont reported an ill-founded rumor that I was abandoning my home in Rochester to live in Texas. While confirming what a hard community Texas was," Anthony harrumphed, "the editors noted that even Texas should not be subjected to such a punishment."

The women looked at one another in horror, while Tabor and I stifled laughs. A grin even worked its way across the governor's face until his wife elbowed him in the ribs.

We had a leisurely dinner as Anthony spoke of her trials and tribulations, then paused for Augusta and me to clear the table. We replaced the dirty dishes with clean bowls and Augusta brought out the pan with the peach cobbler. She'd used canned peaches and pie dough, and the savory taste only enhanced my opinion of Augusta's cooking skills.

By the time we finished, it was six o'clock, an hour before her speech was slated at Billy Nye's lecture hall. Augusta offered the ladies the use of her bedroom and slop jar while us men had to attend to business outside in the outhouse. It felt good to get away from them for a spell.

A half hour before the lecture, we stepped to the buggy. As the governor helped his wife aboard, I debated whether to aid Miss Susan B. Anthony, deciding she was perfectly capable of getting into the conveyance herself. I was wrong.

"Young man," she called, "aren't you going to assist me?"

I watched Horace Tabor roll his eyes. Augusta saw him too and nudged him in the side with another elbow.

After I helped Miss Susan B. Anthony and the dignitaries were seated, Tabor, his wife and I started walking by the buggy toward the saloon for a nice, invigorating ten-minute stroll in the crisp fall air. A line of prospectors, several holding their own stools or chairs, stretched outside the lecture hall as we arrived, starved for the sight of a woman even if they would get lectured by her for being the men they were. Reaching the building, I offered my hand to Anthony's as she got down from the buggy. "Thank you, young man," she said, as graciously as I've ever been thanked. Now I was more confused about her than any person I'd ever met. I didn't know if she was good or bad, saint or Satan.

Being younger than Tabor or the governor, I elbowed a path through the crowd so the star attraction could get inside. "Make way for Miss Susan B. Anthony, tonight's lecturer," I said.

Several men applauded, one even whistled as if she was a younger woman, drawing an immediate stare of disapproval from the suffragist. I figured the whistler was drunk, blind or both. When we got indoors, I saw faces we had encountered that afternoon, the men we had turned away from retrieving their mail. Two escorted us to the front row where they had saved seats for us while the others were directing spectators where to sit. Those seven fellows were starved for their mail. The rest of the crowd craved entertainment. They smoked cigars, cigarettes and pipes, and chewed tobacco, the ping in spittoons acknowledging their dirty habit.

As we took our places, the governor pulled out his pocket watch and kept up with the time. At seven o'clock he got up, dragged his chair over to the bar and stood on it, facing the sea of miners squeezed into the big saloon. I figured there might be four hundred people in the place. Billy Nye didn't need extra stoves with this many folks packed into his saloon as it the body heat and the smoke wafting to the ceiling made the thin air warmer and even harder to breathe. I noticed my lawyer leaning against the closed door of his office. Noose Neck sipped from the whiskey bottle in his left hand.

The governor stood on his chair and thanked everyone for coming out to hear Miss Susan B. Anthony and her message of suffrage. He implored the miners to support her movement as it would make Colorado better not just for women but also for men. Routt said our state was now leading the nation on the issue.

"Eight years ago, the Territory of Wyoming, our brother to the north, granted women the right to vote and the territory has thrived. We as Coloradans can do the same. In clearing the way for full suffrage, our state's new constitution allows women to vote in school elections to have a say in the proper education of their children. Now it is time we extend to the fine women of this young state the full right not only to vote but also to serve on juries.

"And if we grant full suffrage to the fair sex as Sir Walter Scott called maidens in *Ivanhoe*, then Colorado will attract women from all over the nation to live and to marry, to raise our children and cook our meals, to wash our clothes and keep our homes."

The audience applauded, but Miss Susan B. Anthony glared at the governor. As I took in the spinster's plain looks and stern demeanor, I doubted that Colorado needed more women like her or Mattie Silks, though the state could sure use more decent ones like Lupe.

Governor Routt explained that it was now up to the legislature to grant Colorado women full suffrage in all elections and that Miss Anthony was touring the state from Denver to Lake City and from Trinidad to Leadville to support that noble cause.

"Miss Susan B. Anthony voted in the presidential election of 1872," Routt announced.

"Then what are we here for?" cried a voice from the side of the room. I twisted to see Adam Scheisse shaking his fist at the governor. "Answer me that!"

"She was arrested for it, that's why. Her and fourteen other brave women in Rochester, New York, were charged with crimes for violating state and federal laws."

Two of the men Augusta had prevented from picking up their mail that afternoon walked over to Noose Neck and stood on either side of him, letting him know he should show greater courtesy to the governor and the honored guest. My lawyer suckled on the whiskey bottle, opened his office and slipped inside, closing the door behind him. I shook my head, thinking Miss Anthony would've been a better attorney for me.

Routt continued, "We do not want Colorado women treated that way, and that is why Miss Anthony has agreed to visit our state and tell her story. Gentlemen, I present to you Miss Susan B. Anthony."

Leadville's distinguished guest rose elegantly and stepped toward the governor. The seven mail men, as I called the ones whose letters we had delayed, jumped to their feet and applauded, turning around and imploring the others to rise and welcome Anthony. Routt offered her his hand so she could step up on his chair. Cheers combined with applause for a rousing welcome. Only when the mail men motioned for the crowd to be seated did the celebrants reclaim their chairs. As she talked, a miner from the back yelled, "I can't see. Stand on the bar."

"It would be unladylike to climb up there," she said, coughing, then holding her hand over her mouth.

Instantly, the seven mail men shot up and raced to her side, screening her from the crowd for a moment. Then the leader spun about and waved his arms in the air. "All the smoke's making it difficult for her to speak. After we put her on the bar, we'll pass around the spittoons. Throw your cigars and cigarettes inside and dump out any lit pipe tobacco," he commanded.

With that, he turned and bent with the other miners to lift the chair high enough for Miss Susan B. Anthony to step daintily onto the bar.

"Thank you, gentlemen," she said as she walked along the bar, fanning at the haze. The mail men then fetched four spittoons and passed them among the miners to extinguish their tobacco. A man stepped behind the bar and filled a mug, which he gave to her. I thought Augusta was going to jump out of her dress now that Miss Anthony had taken a slug of intoxicant, but the suffragist turned to the barkeep and said, "Thank you for the water, good sir."

When the mail men finished passing the spittoons and the smoke dissipated, Miss Susan B. Anthony strode along the bar, sipping water to moisten her throat before nodding to the front row. "Thank you, Governor Routt, for that fine introduction. I am honored to be among you but embarrassed to admit I was indeed arrested in Rochester five years ago in a high-handed outrage upon my rights of citizenship. In finding me guilty of voting, the court trampled under its oppressive boot every vital principle of our government. My natural rights, my civil rights, my political rights, my judicial rights were all ignored. I was not afforded a trial by my peers because the judge disallowed me that right. Even if I had been given a jury trial, it would not have been a jury of peers because not a single woman would've been allowed to serve. By the same means that slaves a dozen years ago secured their liberty by fighting unjust forms of law, now we, too, as women must grab the rights that the government will not give us. You have given the Negro the Fifteenth Amendment. Why not, as an act of justice, give the women an amendment? At least make women your equal instead of relegating us to the level of the Chinaman."

Anthony strode up and down the bar, her voice rising to make a point and then softening so that the audience strained to catch her words. I had never heard such a polished speaker, nor more powerful words emanating from such a petite frame. Then she spoke of the constitution and its promise to *all* citizens.

"In voting for the president of the United States five years ago, I committed no crime by simply exercising my rights as guaranteed to me and all United States citizens by the national Constitution with its preamble stating 'We, the people of the United States, in order to form a more perfect union, establish justice, insure domestic tranquility, provide for the common defense, promote the general welfare, and secure the blessings of liberty to ourselves and our posterity, do ordain and establish this Constitution for the United States of America.'

"It was we, the people, not we, the white male citizens; nor yet we, the male citizens; but we, the whole people, who formed the Union. And we created the constitution not simply to give the blessings of liberty, but to secure those blessings for all the people, not just the male half of the population. Those liberties are owed to the whole people—women as well as men. It is a downright mockery to talk to women of their enjoyment of the blessings of liberty while they are denied by this government the use of the only means of securing those liberties—the ballot."

The men sat enthralled, if not by the message, at least by the presentation and her mastery of the language.

"I present to you now the first section of the Fourteenth Amendment adopted nine years ago and added to our sacred Constitution. It states, 'All persons born or naturalized in the United States, and subject to the jurisdiction thereof, are citizens of the United States and of the State wherein they reside. No State shall make or enforce any law which shall abridge the privileges or immunities of citizens of the United States; nor shall any State deprive any person of life, liberty, or property, without due process of law; nor deny to any person within its jurisdiction the equal protection of the laws'."

She paused, her long silence increasing the impact of her words. Then she spoke softly. "The only questions left to be settled now is: Am I a person? Is any woman a person? And I hardly believe any of our opponents will have the hardihood to say we are not. Being persons, then, women are citizens; and no State has a right to make any new law, or to enforce any old law, that shall abridge their privileges or immunities."

The miners nodded in a room so quiet you could hear a mouse breathe.

"Then I submit to you I am a citizen, entitled to the same rights and privileges, including the right to vote and the right to serve on a jury, as you men in this room and in this new State of Colorado. To deny me and my women peers those rights and privileges means that the blessings of liberty are forever withheld from women and their female posterity. To them this government has no just powers derived from the consent of the governed. To them this government is not a democracy, nor a republic. It is instead a hateful oligarchy of sex that makes fathers, brothers, husbands and sons, the oligarchs over the mothers, sisters, wives and daughters in every household that ordains men as sovereigns and women as subjects. I am a woman. I am a person. I am a citizen. I am an American, and I should be treated as one with the rights and privileges I am due in my pursuit of life, liberty, and happiness."

The crowd paused as Anthony took another sip from the mug and lowered her head, signaling she was done. At that moment, the men jumped to their feet, clapping, cheering and whistling. They arose on their own without the mail men prompting their enthusiasm. If the vote for suffrage had been at that moment and the miners had been legislators, the audience so enthused with her powerful oration would've passed the measure and given women what they wanted if not what they deserved. When the mail men stepped to the counter to help Miss Susan B. Anthony to the floor, the crowd surged around her.

"The bar's now open," the saloon keeper cried and the men cheered even louder than they had for suffrage. After sips of whiskey and beer, all the men came to their senses except Governor Routt, who still had to watch his back around his wife. The mail men forced a path through the throng, escorting Anthony to the Routts and the Tabors. Augusta grabbed Miss Susan B. Anthony and hugged her, telling her how much her speech had touched and inspired her. Eliza Routt congratulated Anthony for another oratory well done. I fell in behind the two couples and Miss Susan B. Anthony, who turned to me. "Any thoughts, young man?"

"Powerful words, Miss Anthony. Have you ever thought of taking up mining law?" I asked, figuring she'd do a better job than Noose Neck.

"What an odd question, young man, when such deeper legal issues than mining law exist if this country is ever to become great."

"Mining law trumps everything around here, ma'am."

"You're not for suffrage are you, young man?"

Shrugging, I answered. "I never thought about it until the last few weeks when Augusta told me you were coming."

"Do you have a mother and sisters?"

"A mother and two sisters in Arkansas with another in Dakota Territory."

"Then you should be for suffrage, if only for them."

Perhaps she was right. My two Arkansas sisters had taken to book learning much better and faster than me. And my oldest sister in Deadwood did okay for herself in a profession she didn't care to write home about. All three were smarter than me and would know how to mark a ballot if they had the right to vote. I'd never participated in an election. The only person I'd ever known until then with aspirations for high political office was George Armstrong Custer, but he was so obnoxious I would've voted against him, even if his opponent was Miss Susan B. Anthony. "Maybe I should be for suffrage, ma'am, but it just don't seem right. It's not the way I was raised and, hell, I've never even voted. "

"That is your choice, young man," she said as we stepped outside into the night, "but allow your mother and your sisters the same choice in our system of government."

"My observation has been that politicians are crookeder than the road to Leadville."

Miss Anthony laughed for the first time in our brief acquaintance. "You are right, Mr. Lomax," she said. "They use us for their own benefit, but we must use them for ours. That's how democracy works, when you have the right to vote."

I nodded. "I'll give suffering more consideration."

Anthony chuckled a final time. "That's how most men look at it for certain, Mr. Lomax."

Approaching the buggy, I helped her into her place, then stood back as the governor seated himself with his wife and her in the conveyance.

"Augusta and I'll join you at the house shortly," Tabor said, as the buggy pulled away.

When I turned around to step back inside the saloon to wet my whistle, the seven mail men were standing there.

"We want our mail," the tallest one said.

"In the morning," Tabor replied.

"No," Augusta interjected. "They were so helpful to Miss Anthony, let Lomax open the store and give them their letters tonight."

Tabor looked at me, stuck his hand in his pocket and extracted the key. "Do as she says, and we'll see you in the morning."

"Yes, sir," I said as I watched the governor's buggy vanish in the night. I never saw Miss Susan B. Anthony again after that night, but I ran across her name in the papers for years to come. She did all right for herself and suffrage, but our brief acquaintance soiled my reputation for years.

Chapter Eleven

About six weeks after Miss Susan B. Anthony left the Tabor home following her Leadville talk, the Colorado Legislature voted on the suffrage bill and defeated it. Many women sulked over it and, so I heard, even cursed the elected bastards that had denied them the right to vote. Augusta Tabor took it hard, not speaking to Horace for a week and barely talking to me, unless she needed to get a message to her husband without delivering it herself. A lot of suffering transpired in the Tabor household because of the outcome. My ox wasn't gored, so I vowed to stay on Augusta's good side so she wouldn't toss me out in the cold.

Winter came to Leadville and the snows with it along with the first city election, which in January saw Horace Austin Warner "Haw" Tabor elected Leadville's first mayor. And even as more snow accumulated on the mountains and more votes were tallied for Tabor, the mail kept coming for sorting. Despite the ice, the town grew as new prospectors arrived with boosters and conmen, intent on either building a city or scamming its residents. Despite the frigid weather, construction continued into the spring with over thirty new buildings finished or nearing completion as the thaw set it. Somehow the freighters had navigated the narrow winding road from Denver to bring mail, supplies, and building materials, even in the horrific winter winds. Lode miners flocked to the area, staked out mining sites and dug their shafts to make good on their claims. Those unable to endure the backbreaking mine work in the bitter cold took on less strenuous work, building more structures in town. In addition to provisions and construction materials, mules were brought in by the hundreds to work the diggings, dozens of them animals were penned in the livery stable across street for sale. Never did I hear a bray night or day that I didn't think of Ciaha. By the time spring rolled around, Leadville was a different place than Ciaha and I had entered in the fall.

During the frigid months I used my new boots and winter coat that was part of the deal for escorting Miss Susan B. Anthony, wearing them when I ventured out to check on my claim. Both August Rische and George Hook kept their promise to work my property one day a week, at least until March when Ciaha played out and died. By then, though, they had depleted their money and carved up my mule and ate him to make it through the cold. I wished a better fate for Ciaha, but Rische and Hook were straight with me about him and their dire circumstances. I should've bought into their mine, but I had an adjoining claim and encouraged them to visit Tabor, who had been grubstaking miners down on their luck for an interest in their mines, should they ever hit a well-paying lode. The week Rische and Hook struck the arrangement with Tabor, he gave them a pick and shovel apiece, food enough for two weeks, a washtub to carry their supplies in and a jug of whiskey to keep them warm for the rest of the wintery weather. His initial expenditure came to just over $17. Subsequent provisions increased that total to $64. By mid-summer that investment started Tabor on the road to becoming the richest man in the state. As for me, a crooked but dead lawyer blocked my path to a Colorado fortune.

Along with everything else coming to Leadville, more mail arrived, a dozen or more sacks a week, so much so that Tabor hired another fellow, Pete Perez from southeastern Colorado, to help me sort and then distribute them. A Mexican like Lupe, Pete could read and alphabetize better than me. I asked him if he knew Lupe from Mattie Silks' house in Denver, but he said he was not familiar with her because he never frequented such places. I told him that Lupe was not a lady of easy virtue, but a hard-working employee that gave a fair day's labor for a decent wage. Pete seemed pleased to know of Lupe's righteousness. He excelled at reading the hen-scratching that folks called handwriting. And, he provided great backup when Augusta declined to pass out the mail or had a mad on for her husband, who kept squandering his profits on shares of claims that never came through or, if they did, would be denied by the dishonest miners that outnumbered the good ones. By March when Hook and Rische partnered up with Tabor, Leadville had three new saloons to compete with Billy Nye's, though none were as big. And Nye had earned enough money to buy more tables, chairs, gambling equipment and even a piano so that his place was the busiest and noisiest in town.

But I lacked the spare time to visit any of those saloons, working ten or more hours a day trying to keep up with the workload. For three weeks after the spring thaw all I dealt with was mail and mud, hundreds of men tramping into the store for their letters and leaving a trail of muck on the plank floor. At least we had floorboards as many early hovels and tents had only dirt for flooring so the men lived in sludge and squalor while they pursued the fortune that most never attained. After closing each day me and Pete scraped and swept the mud out of the store as Augusta insisted we clean the place daily so the hems of her skirts wouldn't be dirtied whenever she helped.

Noose Neck dropped by every other day to pick up his correspondence and send outgoing mail. I set his letters aside since he received a half dozen a day from various towns in Colorado. Each stack of correspondence I gave him always included a missive from J.R. Smith in Denver, and Adam Scheisse always posted a letter back to Smith whenever he delivered outgoing mail. Even though I disliked him, Noose Neck was familiar with my property and his visits offered me a chance to check on the status of my mining claim. He said it was progressing, pending completion of my shaft and the lateral extension necessary to prove I had struck ore. Progress, though, stopped after Ciaha's unfortunate demise as Rische and Hook devoted their time to working their own claim. Perhaps I should've quit clerking for Horace and Augusta Tabor and started digging myself, but I'd grown accustomed to a warm bed on comfortable mail sacks despite the mice and didn't want to wallow in the mud.

In late April Adam Scheisse came in to pick up his mail when the column extended out the door. Ignoring the queue, Noose Neck barged in, telling everyone he had goods to purchase, not mail. They let him through, but he stepped to the front of the line that Pete and I were feverishly trying to assist. "Give me my mail, Lomax," he said, drawing growls from men that worked hard for a living.

"Wait like the rest of us," complained one miner in mud-caked boots and stained overalls.

"This is legal business," Noose Neck replied, staring at his critic. "I'll see that the next person to complain is arrested. Where's my mail, Lomax?"

Pete rolled his eyes as I retrieved a bundle of nine letters from the pigeonhole and pointed to the end of the counter. He followed me as I marched that way. I handed him the stack while Pete scrambled to retrieve and distribute mail for the others waiting in line.

"What's the status on my claim?" I asked.

"No progress until you finish the digging. Start mining or hire miners to do it for you, men that know what they're doing," he said. After thumbing through his latest letters, he reached in his pocket and pulled out three missives, leaning over the counter to pass them to me, coming close enough that I detected liquor on his breath. "See that these go out with the next mail," he ordered. "There's important messages that must reach Denver as soon as possible."

"I'll put them in the outgoing mail bag."

Scheisse held up his hand. "Not yet. Drop them in the sack last so they'll be on top and the first removed when they get to Denver."

While I didn't know how the postal men in Denver handled mail, we in Leadville dumped the contents into a box and then sorted the envelopes. A letter on the top of the bag, wound up at the bottom of the pile, but who was I to question a lawyer, especially one that was handling my mining claim. "Okay," I said, "and to make certain they're on top, I'll keep them in my pocket until we close up the last bag." I slipped them in my shirt and turned toward the postal cage where my helper grew frustrated with the impatient miners.

"Good boy, Lomax," Noose Neck said in the condescending way of lawyers and others educated beyond their abilities or, in Scheisse's case, beyond his sobriety.

As I scurried to my helper, he shook his head. "I don't like that man."

Grimacing and nodding, I helped Pete distribute letters to a miner at a time. I should've found another lawyer after that, but I didn't have time as the mail kept coming along with the miners seeking their correspondence. The prospectors were a surly bunch, having to wait in line for mail from home when they could be digging up their fortunes in the muck or wasting their hours in the saloons. When work ended that night, Pete suggested we designate individual days of the week for certain letters of the alphabet. As he explained to Augusta, we would distribute five letters of the alphabet a day, starting on Mondays with A-B-C-D-E and ending on Fridays with the six letters U-V-W-X-Y-Z. Everybody was welcome to retrieve mail on Saturdays. We debated whether the method would work for everyone, especially those with business or legal communications. After Augusta outlined the system to Horace, her husband thought it improved our efficiency, and he suggested that those who wanted service outside their call day could pay a nickel a visit for the extra service. After Horace okayed the idea and the charge, he escorted Augusta home for the night, leaving me and Pete to finish the mail for the morning pickup and to alphabetize as much incoming as possible before bedtime. We lit a lamp and proceeded.

Just as I was tightening the cords on the mailbag, I remembered the three envelopes Noose Neck had insisted I put at the top of the outgoing sack. Extracting them from my pocket, I slid them individually into the sack, not recognizing the names on the first two, but hesitating when I saw the familiar address of J.R. Smith of Denver. As I was ready to insert that letter in the bag, I noticed the flap was open. I turned it over and saw that Adam Scheisse had dropped a dollop of candle wax on the back, but in his likely drunken state didn't notice that the drop had landed on the flap only, leaving the inside message accessible for snoops like me. When Pete wasn't looking, I slipped the folded sheet of paper from the envelope, opened it and read Scheisse's message to J.R. Smith of general delivery, Denver.

Friend Jeff,

The pickings are ripe in Leadville. Suckers abound, many with cash to invest in mining properties. Rumors of a major strike continue. Law is sporadic at best. Now seems a good time to visit. Plenty of opportunity for cappers, steerers, footpads, boosters, pickpockets, forgers, brawlers, gripmen and the usual trades. Please provide arrival date, if coming. Your friend,

Lawyer Adam

I knew what pickpockets and forgers were, but the other trades were foreign to me, though I suspected they were equally larcenous. "What's a footpad," I asked Pete.

"Something you put in your boot, I suppose."

"What about a capper?"

Pete shrugged. "Maybe a mining term for someone that handles blasting caps, I don't know. Where are you coming up with these terms?"

I held up my lawyer's correspondence and shook it. "Noose Neck's letter fell out of one of his envelopes."

Pete chuckled. "You're talking about your lawyer, right?"

"Yes, sir. He looks like the hangman stretched his neck a time or two." I offered Pete the letter, which he scanned.

"I'm not sure what these occupations are, but they don't sound like jobs an honest man would pursue. I don't trust your Noose Neck friend."

Taking the stationery from Pete, I folded it and slid it into the envelope, then closed the flap and found a candle I lit and tipped over the cover so that two drops of hot wax sealed the back. I extinguished the candle, then blew on the envelope to harden the seal. Next I placed the letter in the mail sack, tugging the cords tight for the bag to be picked up the next day. Pete and I worked another half hour on sorting mail, then retired for the night.

We spent the next week informing customers of our new distribution procedures. Though not excited about the rules, the men accepted them upon realizing they saved time waiting in line for their correspondence. When we initiated the system the following week, distribution improved so much that I had time to take a break from the store and stroll around town, which buzzed with activity as construction enlarged Leadville before my very eyes. The shouts of men and the sounds of hammers and saws plus trowels scraping against bricks assaulted my ears with the bulk of the new activity occurring where Main Street intersected with Harrison Avenue, which looked to surpass Main as the busiest thoroughfare in town.

As I walked along Harrison, I noticed a small crowd gathered at the corner on State Street. Moving that direction, I detected an enthusiastic but squeaky voice that I had heard somewhere. As I drew closer, I saw Noose Neck himself standing at the edge of the throng, as enthralled with the pitch as the others around him.

Drawing closer, I heard the start of a spiel I had first encountered near the train depot in Denver. "Cleanliness is next to godliness," the shyster called, "and nothing cleans better than my soap. If you want to get closer to God, or your girl, you can't afford not to buy a cake of my soap. My name is Jefferson Randolph Smith the Second, and I'm here to clean up Leadville like I cleaned up Denver."

Then I realized this was friend J.R. Smith of Denver, the conman who made his living by auctioning off penny cakes of soaps for whatever he got from the marks. I moved far enough away from the crowd to be inconspicuous, but near enough to hear the scam pitch.

Smith promoted his cleansing concoction and offered the incentive of folding a twenty-dollar bill within one wrapper of the two dozen cakes of soap on his little tripod table. He shuffled his goods and auctioned off the bars one at a time until he reached his last three bars. With one-in-three odds, the crowd kept bidding up the price until Noose Neck cried, "I'll offer nineteen dollars for that bar."

"Going once, going twice, sold for nineteen dollars," Smith announced to the spectators. "Will this be our lucky bidder today?"

Noose Neck stepped forward exchanged his cash for his purchase, which he unwrapped, lifting and waving in the air the twenty-dollar bill for everyone to see.

"Congratulations, my good man," Smith said, lifting the two remaining cakes of soap over his head. "Does anyone want to bid on these?" Drawing a smattering of laughs, he turned to Noose Neck. "Tell me your name, my good man.

My lawyer stepped toward Smith as he pocketed his winnings. "I'm Adam Scheisse, Leadville attorney at law."

"And what drew you to bid, my fine lawyer friend?"

"I intended to see if your game was on the square. These street-corner exchanges are usually scams."

"Are you satisfied that I am on the up-and-up?"

"Absolutely, Mr. Jones," Scheisse responded.

"It's Smith," the salesman corrected.

It was an excellent touch, Scheisse getting friend Smith's name wrong.

"My apologies," Noose Neck offered. "Let me make it up by buying you a drink one day soon. I office in Billy Nye's Saloon so stop by for one on me."

"Obliged," Smith said as he folded his table and picked up his suitcase while the disappointed bidders went their own way. Still a handful of men lingered around him and I wondered if they were cappers, steerers, footpads, boosters, pickpockets, forgers, brawlers and the usual tradesmen.

Returning to the store from my break, I spelled Pete for him to step outside and stretch his arms and legs. When he came back, I glanced past the six men at my mail cage and saw him open the door for another man. To my surprise, Jefferson Randolph Smith walked in ahead of Pete, carrying his tripe and keister. Smith studied the goods and marched to a soap-stocked shelf.

"Who's the proprietor?" Smith called.

Pete pointed to Horace Tabor, who ambled over to help his latest customer.

"I want to buy every cake of soap in your store," Smith said. "Might that be possible?"

Tabor scratched his chin. "It's a mite unusual."

"I sell soap on the street for a living, and it makes my job easier when I don't have competition," the conman explained.

"For a nickel a bar you can have them all," Tabor said.

Smith cocked his head and pointed at the sign. "It says a penny apiece. I was thinking you'd give me a discount, two bars for a penny, for buying your entire stock."

"No, sir, in my store, the more you buy the more I charge."

Smith scratched his beard, confounded. "Then I must do business with your competitors."

"Suit yourself," Tabor said, turning and walking away.

Looking like he had been slapped with a pound of raw liver, the crook spun about and marched out onto the street, slamming the door behind him.

Pete looked to Horace. "Explain to me what happened."

Tabor smiled. "He was a conman, plain and simple. He'd sell that soap for many times its worth to these hard-working miners. I can't abide that, not as mayor of Leadville. Now let's get back to work."

We resumed our tasks, handling the mail and assisting with whatever store chores Horace or Augusta asked of us. Over the next two weeks Noose Neck failed to retrieve his mail as often, arriving on Thursday like the other S's and picking up his letters, but seldom sending any.

As we entered May, I had been with the store for nine months, and Horace now had confidence in me, providing me with my key so I could come and go as I pleased while Pete was still building his trust with the Tabors. Occasionally, I left in the evenings to see how the town was growing or visit a saloon for a single drink. Though I always carried my money with me, which with my Tabor earnings totaled over a thousand dollars, I peeled off a couple small bills and placed them in my shirt pocket so I wouldn't expose my roll to men that might rob me.

One evening I entered Billy Nye's Saloon, figuring to have a quick drink at the bar, but before I reached the counter, I heard someone shout my name.

"Lomax, Lomax, over here," came the cry. I looked around and spotted Noose Neck standing there waving me to a table with three seated men. "Join us for a drink, won't you?"

Though I didn't care for my lawyer, I was open to a free whiskey, even with him. Marching over, I saw his friends and recognized Jefferson Randolph Smith the Second.

"Let me introduce you to my pals," Scheisse said, slapping me on the shoulder like we were bosom buddies. "Fellows, I want you to meet H.H. Lomax. He's the bravest man in Colorado, actually squiring Susan B. Anthony around during her visit to Leadville."

"Bravest or dumbest?" inquired the soap salesman I had watched on the street corner.

Noose Neck pointed to him. "This is Jeff Smith, and he sells more cakes of penny soap than any man in Colorado." Smith extended his hand and I shook it, feeling the soft palm of a conman who had never done hard work.

"Jefferson Randolph Smith the Second," he said. "Haven't I seen you somewhere before, maybe you've bought a cake of my soap."

"I can't afford your soap. Perhaps you saw me in Tabor's store. I work the mail there."

"Is that a fact?" Smith said in his squeaky voice, releasing my hand, scratching his close-trimmed beard, studying me with his dark eyes, then looking at his companions. "That might come in handy, fellows."

"Nobody posts mail better than Lomax," Adam Scheisse noted as he steered me toward another of his pals, a handsome gentleman with a face as guileless as an infant's despite the whiskey jigger in his hand. "Please meet John L. Bowers, Reverend Bowers."

The reverend put his unfinished drink on the table, took my right hand in his, then put his left atop mine and pumped warmly. "God bless you, Lomax. I'm so honored to make your acquaintance."

I studied his fancy suit and pressed shirt with a high collar over a silk tie with a diamond stickpin. He wore a derby hat and tweaked his waxed mustache. He was better dressed than any minister I'd ever met. "I didn't expect to find a preacher in a saloon," I noted.

"We men of the cloth must go where the sin is, Mr. Lomax." He pointed to Scheisse. "That's why Adam hangs his law shingle inside a saloon. As for the drink, I'm not a Baptist, their beliefs being too narrow for my interpretation of the Good Book."

Despite his explanation and fine words, I didn't see a Bible on the table nor a bulge in his fancy suit where he might pocket one.

"Reverend Bowers is as accomplished individual as you will find in Colorado, a member of numerous fraternal organizations," Scheisse informed me.

I should've been impressed, but I wasn't sure what a fraternal organization unless it was a religious group like the Methodists, Episcopalians or Republicans.

Noose Neck then pointed across the table to the third fellow. "That's George Wilder, a property man, who speculates on mining claims and real estate, making good money for all."

The speculator nodded, but didn't extend his hand. "Lomax," he said.

"Wilder," I replied. That was the extent of my conversation with him as he had a sullen look across his broad face and his narrow eyes. Before I escaped Leadville, I learned that Wilder manipulated property values by starting and spreading gossip about new or phantom finds. He also salted claims he acquired for pennies, later selling it for dollars. Rumors always flowed in mining towns because of conmen such as Wilder.

"Pull up a chair and join us," Scheisse said, and I moved to an adjacent table and stole a seat when the trio sitting there looked the other way. "Bartender," cried Noose Neck, "bring us another jigger for our friend."

"And an extra bottle of whiskey," Smith added. As soon as the barkeep brought over my jigger and fresh liquor, Smith grabbed them both, put my glass on the table, uncorked the bottle to fill my tumbler. "Drink up, Lomax, because it's on us."

"Thank you," I said, telling myself to limit my liquor to two glasses as I didn't trust these men, even if one of them claimed to be a preacher.

"Tell me," Smith said, "about your job handling mail."

"Not much to it. With incoming mail, we sort it and distribute it. With outgoing mail, we bag it." I took a sip of whiskey, which burned all the way down my gullet. I wasn't sure I could handle two jiggers of the cheap liquor, much less another sip.

"You ever read any of the mail?" Smith inquired.

"There's too much mail to read other than the addresses on the envelope," I answered, even though I had read one letter addressed to him.

Smith nodded. "I'm sure you do all that work and don't get paid enough."

"Never remember being paid adequate for any job I ever did."

"Lomax, we'd be glad to pay you to read and report to us on incoming and outgoing mail, say fifty cents a letter, unless we wanted you to hold it for us and then we'd give you a dollar."

"Can't do that, Jeff. That would be the wrong thing to do. My momma taught me that."

The Reverend Bowers patted me on the shoulder. "I knew you were an honest man, Lomax. Jeff likes to make sure his friends are trustworthy."

Smith nodded. "You passed the test, Lomax."

Noose Neck grinned. "Lomax can afford to be honest, fellows. He's got one of the most promising claims south of Fryer Hill." Scheisse listed all the miners around me, starting with Rische and Hook. "If his or any of those plots make good, he'll be able to buy every cake of soap you can find, Jeff."

They all celebrated that news about my mining property and my honesty, though I thought they were more sincere over the former than the latter, but it was free whiskey, even if the liquor could've gagged a maggot.

That was the first time I shared whiskey with them, and I did so many nights in the coming six weeks, all without incident until the very last time. Then I would be accused of murder and have to get out of Leadville quick.

Chapter Twelve

After my introduction to Soapy Smith, Reverend John Bowers and George Wilder, the spring of 1878 brought a flood of construction, rumors and mail, more correspondence than Pete, Augusta and I could manage. Men and a growing number of women now lined up outside our door each day to pick up their letters on our rotation system. At closing time we often had to lock out people still wanting their mail, angering them. Both Pete and I started wearing our side arms in case we had to deal with surly patrons either inside the store or when we ventured away. The stress of dealing with the unending arrival of more post drove me as many nights as possible to visit Billy Nye's Saloon and take advantage of the free drinks offered by the Smith and his cadre of friends. I made sure I never had more than two jiggers of whiskey because I distrusted Noose Neck and his acquaintances, but their offer of free whiskey meant I not only held on to my money but also increased it.

Each evening I approached Soapy's table, his circle of friends changed the conversation as if they didn't want me knowing their schemes. On most nights Soapy was in the saloon even if not at his gang's place because he was addicted to faro and spent much of his time and his ill-gotten gains trying to buck the tiger. While I kept my roll of money on me, I figured his growing gang included pickpockets, so I took to keeping my cash inside my sock and my boot.

At one of those saloon gatherings, Adam Scheisse advised me to finish my diggings to complete my claim so I wouldn't need another extension to gain full title. He offered to hire miners to handle the excavations for me. While sorting and distributing the mail was stressful, it wasn't dangerous, back-breaking work like digging in the earth. Noose Neck told me for $125 dollars, including his fee, he would hire and oversee laborers for me. I told him I'd think it over and let him know the next evening.

While I didn't trust him, rumors flowed that diggings south of Fryer Hill were turning up promising ore, a potential silver bonanza. Whether those stories had any fact in them or were George Wilder manipulating land and mine prices, I never knew. Considering that my total investment in the claim had been Ciaha and not a single drop of sweat, I accepted Goose Neck's proposal. After work that evening, I counted out $125 from my wad of bills and tucked that money in my shirt pocket before returning the balance to my sock inside my boot. Then an idea struck me to test the honesty of my newfound friends. I rummaged through one of the mail sacks until I came to a newspaper I figured the recipient would never miss and flattened it on the counter. Next I extracted two five-dollar bills from my money roll and used them as a template over the newsprint, which I cut in pieces the size of the bills with my pocketknife. When I had a stack of news clippings the thickness of the wad of money in my boot, I rolled them up with an actual fiver on top and bottom and tied the bundle together with a length of string. I stuck the roll in my pants pocket, telling him Pete I was going to Nye's to see my attorney.

"I don't trust him," he reminded me, "nor the crowd he runs with."

"They give me free drinks," I responded.

"Nothing's ever free, Lomax," he called as I left.

At the saloon Noose Neck, Soapy, Reverend Bowers and two other men I didn't recognize sat at their regular table. They welcomed me back as if I was the prodigal son, Soapy calling for the bartender to bring me a clean glass. Telling Noose Neck that I intended to take him up on his offer, I watched him and Soapy celebrate like I had made them both rich. I reached into my pants pocket, pulling out the roll of phony bills.

Soapy raised his hand. "Lomax, put away your cash. I'm sure Adam here has paperwork to complete before he takes your payment. Isn't that right, Adam?"

"You should've been a lawyer, Jeff. Keep your money, Lomax. I'll do the papers and bring them to Tabor's tomorrow for your signature."

Tucking my fake roll deep into my pants pocket, I extracted my hand and pointed to my temple. "I thought you kept all your legal matters in your head, didn't need paper."

"That was before my law business turned prosperous. Won't be long until I'll be moving out of the saloon into more prestigious quarters."

"What do we need papers for?" I asked.

"I need a contract allowing me to hire men for the job on your behalf and to pay them once they have met the requirements for finalizing your claim. We must have the paper documentation in case questions come up before the claims court."

Nodding, I picked up my jigger and downed it, this whiskey tasting better than previous doses I'd consumed in Nye's.

Soapy retrieved the whiskey bottle on the table and filled my glass again. "This calls for a second drink, anytime you agree to a deal."

Everybody congratulated me as I gulped my next drink.

"And another," Soapy suggested.

I held up my hand. "I've reached my limit and have mail to sort." As I arose from my chair, they stood up, slapped me on the shoulders, shook my hand or hugged me, proud that I had agreed to Noose Neck's proposal. I broke free from them and started for the door.

"I'll see you at Tabors tomorrow afternoon," Noose Neck called as I reached the exit.

Waving over my shoulder without looking back at him, I stepped outside into the thin Leadville air. I stretched my arms, reluctant to return to the mail, then stuck my fingers in my britches. The fake money had disappeared. One son of a bitch had picked my pocket! Slapping at my shirt, I confirmed they hadn't discovered the $125 to hire miners and pay their fees.

I returned to the store and sorted mail with Pete in the back room, which was growing more crowded with so many unsorted postal bags spawning more mice. I told Pete about accepting Noose Neck's offer and about the loss of my fake money roll.

"What did I tell you? Those guys can't be trusted, especially that lawyer," Pete said. "Whatever he brings in for you to sign, you need to read carefully."

After a restless night's sleep I arose the next morning and started work organizing the mail crates where we had filed the P-Q-R-S-T mail for Thursday. I was glad when Noose Neck showed up the middle of the afternoon, carrying a pine lap writing desk with ink stains on the top. Picking up his single letter from the past week, I met him at the end of the counter where he plopped the writing tray, opened the lid and offered me three sheets of paper. He wrote in an elegant hand, easy to read, so I reviewed the papers twice and confirmed the agreement sounded just as we had discussed. Though I was no lawyer, I discovered no tricky language that might override my title to the claim.

"Does it read okay?" Noose Neck asked me.

Catching a hint of liquor on his breath, I nodded, and he lifted the lid on the lap desk and removed a capped inkwell and a nib pen. After twisting the cap from the inkwell, he dipped the pen in the ink and offered it to me, showing me where to add my signature. When I finished, he pulled out another set of papers and had me sign them for my files. He blotted both signatures and gave me my copies. I fished the payment out of my pocket and gave him the $125 that was due. Scheisse gathered his material and told me he would hire and start workers the next day.

As he started for the door, he stopped and turned around, coming back to me and sticking his hand in his britches. He extracted a roll of money with a five-dollar bill on the outside. "This fell out of your pocket last night at the saloon. Soapy spotted it and wanted to make sure I returned it to you."

"Obliged," I said as I took the wad.

Noose Neck exited to finish the make-good on my claim.

That night I missed my usual trip to the saloon, staying with Pete to sort more mail. I told him about Scheisse returning the phony money. "Perhaps they're trustworthy after all."

Pete just laughed. "They're setting you up, Lomax, and once they realize you're keeping your real money roll in your boot, they'll figure a way to get it instead of the fake money."

"How'd you know I kept cash in my boot?"

"You walk funny, Lomax, with it in your boot."

Every time I visited Billy Nye's Saloon after that, I left my money in my saddlebags in the back room because I trusted Pete more than the men plying me with free drinks. Over the ensuing two weeks, I enjoyed the hospitality with Noose Neck, Soapy and their growing circle of friends. Each night, Scheisse confirmed that work was finished on the shaft and was advancing well on the lateral line with increasing signs of ore. Once we proved ore, Scheisse assured me, he would make the final claim on my behalf, and I stood to be wealthy beyond my dreams. He only requested that when I got rich, I keep using him as my attorney. With that he scurried away, and I dreamed of how I would spend all my newfound money.

Each night for the next week when I finished the mail or just grew tired of dealing with it, I headed over to Nye's Saloon for my two free drinks and to check with my attorney on the laborers' progress. He assured me his hires were nearing a vein that would make me fabulously wealthy, and even Reverend Bowers said he had ridden by the claim while he was trying to save souls and was impressed by the work.

A week later the German miners August Rische and George Hook came into the store, carrying a large envelope and wearing smiles wide enough to drag an ore wagon through. Even though they had eaten Ciaha to make it through the cold months, I offered to let them cut in line to handle their correspondence.

"*Nein,*" Rische said.

"Just looks like one envelope to me, not nine," I responded.

"No," Hook said, rolling his eyes. "He means no, we want to visit Mr. Tabor. In private."

I glanced around the store and didn't see him, then stepped in the back room where I found the mayor sitting on a wooden crate as Augusta lectured him on something. It looked like he was getting training to become the next governor.

"Pardon my interruption," I said, "but the Germans Rische and Hook are here to see you."

Horace looked up, a sigh of relief escaping from his lips. "Tell them I'll be right out, if Augusta doesn't strangle me first."

His wife scowled and motioned for me to leave.

"They said they wanted to meet in private," I informed him.

"Send them in," he replied.

Augusta folded her arms across her chest. "Fine, Horace, but I'm not leaving."

Tabor nodded, then turned to me. "Show them in."

I waved them behind the counter, and Rische and Hook marched past me, closing the door after they entered. I resumed distributing mail, assisting Pete with the task for another twenty minutes before the door opened and my claim neighbors exited, their smiles as big as ever. Excusing myself from my patrons, who cursed at my departure, I caught up with the two German miners. "How's the digging progressing on my claim?"

"*Nein,*" said Rische. "We do nothing since your mule died."

"No, not you two, but the new workers. How much have they done?"

"What workers?" Hook asked.

"The ones my lawyer hired to work my claim."

Rische shrugged, "*Niemand war da.*"

"I'll vouch for what August said because no one's been working your claim since we ate your mule," Hook answered.

I was madder than the devil at a church supper. Noose Neck had lied to me. I'd paid him $125 to finish the digging so we could complete the claim, and he had likely squandered the money on something else.

The two miners marched out the door, past the line of folks wanting their mail. I stood there, mouth agape, considering whether I should go find Noose Neck and just shoot him on the spot. I decided the law might look poorly upon such a rash decision, so I returned to the mail cage to help the next customer. He growled at me, but his timing was wrong because I yanked my pistol from the holster, cocked it and pointed it at his nose. "What was that?"

"Nothing," he said.

Pete offered a handful of letters to his patron, then turned to me, put his hand on my wrist and pushed the gun down. "Take a break, Lomax."

Gently, I released the hammer on my revolver and slid the pistol back in my holster. I turned and slipped into the storeroom where I found Horace and Augusta in tears and hugging each other. Figuring they were making up, I exited the room to go for a walk, but Tabor called.

"We've got something to tell you, Lomax, but shut the door," he said.

I figured they had decided to divorce and go their separate ways, but what they told me was even more shocking.

"Don't tell anybody, Lomax, but we're rich. August and George struck carbonate ore at twenty-seven feet. They showed me the assayer's report. The ore assays out at over two hundred ounces of silver per ton. A third of that is mine."

"Ours," Augusta corrected.

Tabor nodded. "Ours. Imagine that. I'm the mayor and I'm rich." He smiled, then looked at me. "I'm turning the store over to you and Augusta to run as I'm going out to the diggings tomorrow to protect my interest—"

"Our interests," Augusta reminded him.

"—our interests," Tabor concluded. "Word of this will spread fast and nothing'll stop crooks from trying to take what's ours."

I couldn't believe Horace Tabor would be rich because of a $64 dollar investment in two Germans who barely spoke English. Nor could I fathom I had the great fortune to file a lode claim next to theirs. I'd be wealthy too if my attorney had followed up on his promise. "I need to see my lawyer," I said.

"Can you do it after hours, Lomax, and help Augusta with the store and the mail?"

Though I preferred to find Noose Neck right then and strangle him, I figured delaying the meeting might give me time to cool off so I didn't kill Adam Scheisse or at least did it in the dark where fewer people could witness the murder. I nodded. "I'll wait until closing time."

"Thank you, Lomax. You'll need more help so you and Augusta can hire a clerk or two to assist with sales and with the mail as it's getting overwhelming." Tabor turned to his wife and hugged her again. "We're rich! Can you believe it, Augusta, can you believe it?"

I figured I'd be wealthy, too, once I found my lawyer and straightened him out. I returned out front to aid Pete and calm the surly crowd of mail-seekers. They were murmuring their dissatisfaction until I stepped back in the room because they hushed their complaints, word likely spreading that I had shoved a gun in the nose of the last person to bitch. Even though it was only ninety minutes until closing, the time passed slower than a prison sentence. I knew by the next morning that rumors of the strike would be the talk of Leadville. Though assayers were supposed to maintain confidentiality, few did, often because speculators and conmen bribed them for early information so they would make a financial killing. It wasn't right, but that's the way it was in a mining town where everyone sought an advantage in pursuit of a fortune.

When we closed the store, I apologized to Pete for abandoning him, then informed him that it looked like the Tabors owned a third of a mine that would offer fabulous returns in silver.

He grinned. "Don't you have a bordering claim to the Germans?"

"Once I get my lawyer to file the completed paperwork."

His face clouding, Pete grimaced. "I pray he's more trustworthy than my estimation of him. Otherwise, you'll still be sorting mail with me rather than building you a Denver mansion."

"I intend to put a burr under his saddle once I finish here."

"Tend your business," Pete said. "I'll handle as much as I can."

"Tonight'll be the last night for that. Tabor's told me to help Augusta run the store and to hire more help." I left Pete for the back room, deciding I'd leave my money stashed in my saddlebags, though I opted to stuff in my pants pocket the roll of fake cash I had cut from newspapers. After checking my revolver to make sure it was loaded, I grabbed my hat and escorted Augusta outside where she tacked a note that the store would hire sales and postal clerks the next day. I locked the store, stared briefly at the coffin leaning up against the wall as mules penned in the stable across the street brayed at me, and strode for the saloon, anxious to confront Noose Neck about my mining claim.

When I walked in Billy Nye's, I saw Adam and Soapy with three of their friends and an empty chair at their regular table. Several other men that ran with Smith's gang sat at an adjoining table. Noose Neck saw me and waved me over, pointing to the vacant seat.

"We saved the place for our guest of honor this evening," Scheisse said. As he spoke every man stood up and greeted me as if I was the belle of the ball. They shook my hand, patted my back and hugged me.

"What's this all about?" I asked as I slid in my seat, patting my pants pocket. The fake money roll was still there, but I knew I had to be careful.

"We're celebrating your newfound wealth," Soapy said. "Have a drink." He pushed a clean jigger and a full bottle of whiskey to me as everyone sat.

"What are you talking about?"

"Haven't you heard?" Scheisse asked. "Assays came back on the property next to yours at over two hundred ounces of silver per ton. As soon as I complete your claim, you stand to be one of the richest men in Colorado."

The Reverend Bowers smiled at me. "Remember, Lomax, that a tenth of your earnings goes to the work of the Lord."

"That's what I came to discuss, Adam, though I prefer to do it in private."

"Come on, Lomax, these are our friends, folks that've bought you drinks in the past."

I looked around as I downed my first jigger. The whiskey went down smooth as it was better than what they were accustomed to buying me.

"Don't pay us no mind, Lomax," Soapy said. "We're glad for you." He started talking to the Reverend, likely about religious matters as intense as they were in the discussion.

Looking at Noose Neck, whose protruding bug eyes showed he focused on me, I voiced my complaint. "No work I've paid for has been done on site. What's going on?"

"Have you ridden out to inspect the claim?"

"No," I replied.

"Well, I have," Scheisse said smugly, "and you're right. Then men I hired to do it stiffed me, but I'm gonna make it right for you. I'll be over in the morning to refund your money and sign all the corrective paperwork we'll need to satisfy your claim with the law."

I pointed to his door before realizing his shingle had been removed. "Why don't we step in your office now and finish the papers?"

"That's impossible. I've moved my business. I'm officed on Harrison at the corner of Main on the second floor of the Merchants and Mechanics Bank."

Pursing my lips, I considered the options. "Maybe I need to find another attorney."

"I'd be disappointed if you did, Lomax, but that's your choice. By my count Leadville now claims a hundred and twenty lawyers, give or take a handful. Good luck finding an honest one or even getting an appointment. The time it'll require for them to research your claim at the mining clerk's office will put you a week behind at least, perhaps as much as a month when other speculators are trying to hone in on your property."

Soapy interrupted his theological discussion with the preacher to offer his support to Noose Neck. "Adam's right, Lomax. Every minute you delay increases the risk of someone swindling you out of your claim, and that would be a tragedy if another lawyer of questionable repute stole your fortune." He filled my jigger. "Have another drink and think that over."

Downing the expensive whiskey, I shook my head as I put the glass back on the table. "I don't like it."

"Neither do I," Scheisse admitted. "I let you down, but it won't happen again. I'll refund your hundred and twenty-five dollars tomorrow when I bring the new documents over for you to sign. I'll even cover the cost of the laborers out of my own pocket."

"Adam's a man of his word," the Reverend Bowers added. "I'm a Godly judge of character, and you can depend on him to protect your interests and your fortune." The preacher picked up the liquor bottle and filled my jigger again.

Considering the suggestions and the help from my friends, I drank a third whiskey. "Okay," I said, "but I need to get back to work tonight." I placed my glass upside down on the table and arose, everyone standing with me.

They slapped my shoulders, shook my hand, hugged me and celebrated my impending wealth. I turned for the door, Noose Neck calling after me.

"I'll see you at Tabor's in the morning with the paperwork."

Exiting the saloon into the thin Leadville air, I returned to work, worried whether or not I had made the right decision. I didn't trust Scheisse, but I doubted I might find a trustworthy lawyer in Leadville. Finally, I decided I had no choice and I felt better about my situation until I slid my hand in my pants pocket for the store key. I found the key, but the wad of fake money was missing. At least I had my real cash safely hidden in my saddlebags, but from that moment on my stay in Leadville unraveled.

The next day we opened at the usual time, me, Augusta and Pete handling the regular sales and mail chores while five men came in asking about the clerk jobs. Flustered with more business than people to handle it, Augusta asked me to hire one for a salesclerk and another for a mail job so she could scurry around and help customers buying goods. I had to make sure the salesclerks could write and do arithmetic and to ensure the mail applicants could read and alphabetize, a concept I had to explain to two of them just as it was explained to me. Those two threw up their arms and left.

Right in the middle of my interviews, Adam Scheisse came in carrying his lap writing desk and leading Jefferson Randolph Smith the Second over to the corner where I was questioning a job seeker.

"I've got papers for you to sign."

Now I was flustered with so much going on. "Can it wait?"

"Every second's delay might cost you a fortune," Noose Neck said. "There's three documents for your signature. I'll transcribe copies once I get them signed and get yours back to you, but I must get these filed today."

"Three documents?"

"One abrogates the original contract you signed for me to hire laborers to work the claim. The second grants me the right to start a new arrangement with different miners. And the third asks for an extension of thirty days on your initial claim. I brought my friend Jeff to witness the signatures."

"I'd sign it, Lomax," Soapy said, "and let Adam file it before someone cross-files. Things might get messy."

"Okay," I answered leaving the job seeker and clearing a space on the counter for Noose Neck's his lap desk.

He opened it and pulled out the papers, then the capped inkwell and nib pen. "Take what the time you need to read the documents, Lomax. I want to ensure you don't see any problems."

Looking around at the crowded store and all the business, I just grabbed the pen and signed each place where he pointed. Smith signed as a witness after me.

Scheisse took each sheet of paper and blotted our signatures on each document, then held the papers in the air and blew on the ink so it was dry. After that he stacked the sheets in his lap desk and pulled out an envelope he opened and counted out what he owed me as Soapy watched. "Here's your money per our agreement," he said, louder than was necessary. "Count it to be certain it's all there, one hundred and twenty-five dollars for the sale."

I thumbed through the bills, confirming the amount, then rolled up the money, bent over and shoved the bills in my boot.

"I'll file the papers immediately, Lomax. Remember I'm here to help, but I'm busy as hell with all the mining activity now. If I don't return after two days with your copies, come see me at my office, second floor of the Merchants and Mechanics Bank. One of us is gonna get rich off this," Noose Neck said as he capped his inkwell, and placed everything back in his lap desk, then escorted Soapy out the door.

As soon as Scheisse and Smith left, I returned to my job seeker and completed that interview. By the end of the day I'd hired two more men to work in the store, though I didn't know what to pay them until I talked with Tabor. The following day Horace came in after the store closed and agreed to offer each clerk a dollar a day. He also told me that men had started working my claim with a flurry, and he hoped we wouldn't begin a competition that might ruin us both in trying to mine the same vein. As I understood mining law, a lode claim gave you the surface to find a vein, but once you found one, you could follow it anywhere it led. I worried that Noose Neck's delay might have diminished my chances to claim part of the strike, but was glad he had put men to work fast to give me a shot at getting my due.

Three days after I signed the papers, my attorney had yet to return with my copies of the documents. I told Augusta I had to visit Scheisse to follow up on some legal matters and left her with Pete and the two new helpers, who adapted to their jobs, especially the dollar-a-day pay.

On the corner of Harrison and Main, I spotted Scheisse's attorney-at-law shingle on the side of the building pointing up the exterior stairs to a second-floor entry. I traipsed up the steps, opened the door which jiggled a bell announcing my arrival. I walked in, surprised to see Adam Scheisse behind his mahogany desk and sitting in a cushioned chair. A fine office had replaced the sparse quarters in the saloon with a bookcase filled with leather-bound books, an elegant Persian carpet and a mahogany meeting table covered with papers and mining maps.

"Good day, Lomax," Scheisse said, leaning back in his chair and clasping his hands behind his neck. "How can I help you?"

"I came to get my copies of the papers I signed earlier this week on my claim."

"Your claim? What are you talking about, Lomax?"

"Making good on my lode claim, what I hired you to do three days ago."

"You didn't hire me to file your claim, you sold me your claim for a hundred and twenty-five dollars."

"What?"

"I told you to read the contract, Lomax, but you ignored my legal advice. I can't help you now."

Not knowing what to do, I stood there with my mouth agape. "My papers? I want my legal papers."

Noose Neck leaned forward in his chair and yanked his hands from behind his head. "Let me show you something, Lomax." He reached for a side drawer on his desk and pulled it open, lifting a sawed-off shotgun out and pointing it at my gut. "I suggest you leave right now or I'll splatter you against the back wall."

I backed away. "You stole my claim."

"You should've read the contract before you signed the documents. Lomax, you sold me your site for a hundred and twenty-five dollars. Jeff Smith was a witness. You didn't follow your lawyer's advice. You deserve what you get." He laughed. "Or, in this case, you deserve what you don't get."

Inching out the door, I vowed to get even with him, if he didn't shoot me first.

Chapter Thirteen

I descended the stairs outside the Merchants and Mechanics Bank, stunned that I had signed away my fortune. Cursing Adam Scheisse for being the crooked son of a bitch that he was and myself for not reading the documents before I endorsed them, I vowed revenge that night. Several of my postal clients greeted me as I walked back to Tabor's store, but I barely noticed them. As I stepped up on the plank walk by the line of men awaiting their turn to get mail, I stared at the open coffin that had weathered the winter by Tabor's front door and wondered if the lanky Noose Neck would fit in it. I'd gladly break his neck to squeeze him in. If Miss Susan B. Anthony had remained in Leadville, I'd have even hired her to focus her rage on Adam Scheisse.

After I squirmed past the mail seekers waiting in the door, I walked behind the counter and stood, bewildered by my sudden downturn in fortune. I still had more than a thousand dollars in my saddlebags, and I vowed I'd use every cent to get Noose Neck. As I remained oblivious to everything, Pete left his post and approached me, putting his hands on my shoulders and looking me square in the eyes.

"Are you okay, Lomax? You don't look so good." He steered me to the storeroom and closed the door behind us. "Are things all right?"

Biting my lip, I exhaled a deep breath. "My lawyer swindled me out of my lode claim. What I had is now his."

Pete whistled. "I never trusted him."

Rage coursed through my veins as my heart pounded. "I'm gonna kill that bastard."

"Don't do it, Lomax. You'll go to the gallows for murder. Let the law handle it."

Stewing over the fraud, I didn't care if I got hung as long as I sent Noose Neck to hell first. "The law?" I spat out. "The law's what swindled me to begin with."

"Sit and calm yourself, so I can return to work, but I'll tell Augusta you're not feeling good." Pete steered me to a crate and pushed me until I seated myself. "Don't do anything crazy, Lomax." He shook my shoulders to get my attention. "Promise me that, will you?"

I nodded. "Nothing in the daylight. There'd be too many witnesses."

"Don't tell me that, Lomax."

"But that's what I intend to do."

Pete shrugged and left, closing the door behind me and my misery. Moments later Augusta entered the room to check on me.

"Are you okay?" she asked.

"I'm upset," I explained, "my stomach that is."

"Well, take care of yourself. The new hires are catching on, though we're gonna need more help." She pointed to the mail sacks piled on the floor. "There's all those we've got to get sorted, but you rest the remainder of the day. Horace and I are grateful for all you've done since last fall."

"Thank you, Augusta."

She exited, closing the door behind her, leaving me to sort out what had happened. I stood up, walked over to the pile of mail sacks, turned around and fell back on the bundles that had been my bed for months. My only companion was the shaft of daylight that shown through the room's small window and the mice scurrying across the floor. For the rest of the morning and afternoon, I stayed in the room simmering in my anger. When the store closed, Augusta came to check on me before sending the two new clerks away and heading home herself.

After she left, Pete entered. "Augusta's worried over you, said for me not to sort any mail this evening until you get rested. Have you calmed down?"

I tossed Pete a scowl and without saying a word answered his question.

"You don't want to get hung or spend the rest of your life in prison, do you, Lomax?"

"I don't want Noose Neck to spend money that was rightfully mine," I screamed. "And tonight I intend to see that he never swindles another client."

Pete threw up his arms. "You should've listened when I told you Scheisse couldn't be trusted. Worse, though, you aren't listening to me now."

"Maybe not," I answered, "but what's it matter?" Vengeance is a bitter herb that can sour a man's judgment. I wasn't thinking straight, but I no longer cared. When it turned dark, I intended to stroll over to Billy Nye's Saloon and shoot Noose Neck, consequences be damned because Leadville and Colorado were better places with one less crooked shyster tramping over its rich ground. I must've checked the load in my pistol a thousand times as I prepared to murder my attorney. I dug my wad of cash from my saddlebags and stuck it in my boot, figuring I'd need the money to bribe the city marshal to turn me loose or—God forbid—hire me a lawyer to get me off the hook for the valuable public service I planned to perform. Waiting until an hour of darkness had settled over town, I inspected my revolver a final time and exited into the store where Pete sat at the counter sorting mail by lamplight.

"Don't go, Lomax," he pleaded.

"A man's gotta do what a man's gotta do," I told him as I strode for the front door. "I've got my key so I can let myself out."

"Don't get your fool self killed," Pete called as I pulled the door to and locked it.

After I shoved the key back in my pants pocket, I spit in Tabor's display coffin for good luck and headed for the saloon. Entering Nye's place, I found it crowded and noisy. I looked across the room to the usual table, expecting to find Noose Neck drinking and carousing with Soapy Smith and his gang. Adam Scheisse was nowhere around, but Smith gestured wildly to maybe twenty men seated or standing nearby. I marched that direction, my hand on the butt of my revolver. As I approached them, Smith pointed at me. His companions fell silent as they glanced my way.

"Where's Adam Scheisse," I cried. "I plan to kill him."

Around me the conversations stopped as I repeated my threat.

"I intend to kill that damned lawyer! Where is he?"

Soapy glared at me. "That's what we're asking ourselves. The son of a bitch hasn't shown tonight."

"He swindled me, and I'm gonna get even," I shouted.

"Damn, Lomax, keep your voice down," Soapy ordered, "or everyone in Leadville will know you're planning to murder Adam. Have a seat." He commanded one of his men to give me his chair and fetch me a clean jigger from the bar.

I plopped into a chair and looked at Smith, his black eyes as deep as the pits of hell. "I was figuring on Adam being here tonight."

Soapy scowled. "The bastard won't show around me ever again. He was doing legal work for me on a mining claim I was securing. He inserted his name rather than mine in the contracts and now owns the property that should be mine."

My mouth gaped. "That's what the son of a bitch did to me."

"We know," interjected John L. Bowers, drawing a scowl from Smith. "The Lord works in mysterious ways," the reverend continued, "and our prayers have been answered."

Nodding, Soapy replied with a sinister grin as his compatriot put a clean jigger in front of me. "Tell me what happened, Lomax." He uncorked a bottle of whiskey and filled my glass.

Downing the liquor in a gulp, I started my tale of signing what I thought was a claim extension when it was instead a bill of sale to him. "He defrauded me out of my mining interests, saying he was repaying my hundred and twenty-five dollars when I signed a document selling my land to him for that amount."

Soapy growled as he refilled my jigger. "I saw it. I was

there. And he did the same thing to me. Property that should've been mine is now his."

"I went to his new office this morning to get my documents," I continued, "but he just laughed at me, saying I should've followed his legal advice and read the documents before I signed." I gulped the next jigger of liquor. "I told him to make things right."

Smith pushed the whiskey bottle my way. "Drink what you want. Sounds like you need it. What did Adam say?"

"Nothing. He pulled a sawed-off shotgun from a desk drawer—"

"That's good information," Soapy said to the reverend.

"—and pointed it at my gut, ordering me to scat before I had a bellyache I'd never get over." Furious at recalling my meeting with Noose Neck, I had another beverage and then another, ignoring my two-drink limit with Soapy's shady circle of friends. They commiserated with me and agreed I had been wronged, encouraging me to drown my sorrows in whiskey. A kind fellow provided a second jigger so I might down one while Soapy filled the other.

I lost count of the drinks and grew drowsy, the room began to spin in my head, the conversation becoming garbled. At one point, it seemed several men assisted me from my chair and outside as they walked me somewhere. Vaguely I recalled my friends helping me up some stairs, then shouting and a loud explosion. After that, I went blank. When my senses came back together, I found myself flat on a sticky rug. I pushed myself to my hands and knees and realized my boots and socks were missing. Standing up, I saw everything as a blur, confused by the location and the lump on the floor a footstep away. Stumbling around, I spotted a narrow shaft of moonlight coming through a cracked door. I staggered that direction, nudged the door open and stepped on the landing at the top of an exterior staircase. Grasping the wooden railing, I wobbled down the steps. I tottered into the empty street, realizing I stood at the corner of Harrison and Main and turning toward Tabor's. In my bare feet, I stumbled home and fished for the key in my pants pocket. It was gone! I pounded on the door. "Pete,

Pete," I called, my throat parched and my voice raspy as the penned mules across the street mocked me with their brays. Holding onto the coffin to steady myself, I looked through the front window and saw my helper emerging from the back room, a candle in his hand. As the tiny ball of light near me, I cried, "Pete, it's me, Lomax."

When he unlocked the store, I released the casket and stumbled inside, Pete quickly shutting the door behind me. Looking at me, he held the candle in front of me, lifting and lowering it. "Damnation, you're covered in blood. What happened, Lomax?"

I shrugged. "I have no idea."

"Did you kill Adam Scheisse?"

"I can't remember. After a few drinks, things got hazy. I may've been to Noose Neck's office, but it was dark and I couldn't see much."

"This doesn't look good, Lomax. I never thought you'd do it."

"I don't know that I did," I replied, as confused as a Baptist at a Methodist baptism.

"Get in the back. I'll fetch a jug of water and a washbasin to clean you. Then you're gonna need to hide out until we can figure out what happened and what to do."

Stumbling to the storeroom, I sat on a crate and leaned forward, resting my elbows on my knees and my face in my palms, which were still sticky. Pete placed the candle down, lit a lamp, poured water in the washbasin and dipped a rag in the liquid to wash my hands and face.

"You need to change clothes because I can't scrub all the blood out of them." He paused and looked at my feet. "Damnation, Lomax, where are your shoes and socks?"

I leaned over and slapped my ankles, my fingers rubbing my flesh. Pete was right, the new boots I'd wrangled from Tabor had disappeared, but I vaguely recalled missing them before I left the upstairs office, but my memories were so confusing, nothing made sense, except one thing: If my footwear had been stolen, so had my money. Other than what Horace Tabor owed me for the last week, I was dead broke. Everything I'd won and made in Denver plus every cent I'd hoarded in Leadville had disappeared.

Pete left with the candle and returned with work pants and shirt from the store. He pulled a spare pair of drawers and socks from my saddlebags and tossed them to me. "Change your clothes quick, so I can hide the bloody ones. And put on your old boots."

As ordered, I removed my gun belt and revolver, stripped off the stained clothes and put on their replacements, then my socks and boots. Pete grabbed the bloodied garments and shoved them in a mailbag, tightening the cord quickly. He poured the pink-stained water in the slop jar we kept in the room for when nature called.

Beyond the window glass, the day lightened and my senses sharpened. "Where am I gonna hide, Pete?"

"Here under the mail sacks," he replied, "though you may have to stay here until we close and can figure this out." Pete began yanking mailbags from the stack until I could wade to the far wall beneath the window. He pitched me my canteen and a tin of crackers. "There's water and something to eat if you get hungry, but I'm gonna bury you under these mail sacks."

I clawed my way through canvas bags to the wall, pushed four away to give me room to lie down and situate my water and crackers. No sooner had I done that, Pete piled the bags over and around me, hiding me inside a canvas cocoon. My heart and my head throbbed, and I drifted off to sleep, not knowing how long I had slept in my dark womb, until I detected three voices, one I didn't identify and the other two I recognized as Pete's and Augusta's.

"Marshal, that doesn't sound like something Lomax would do," Augusta said. "He's not that mean."

"He's not that smart either, if it's true he courted Susan B. Anthony. That aside, I'd never seen a bloodier carcass than the lawyer's. Both barrels from a sawed-off shotgun at close range," the lawman replied.

From the description, it sounded like an assassination Shotgun Jake Townsend might have pulled off, though I didn't claw my way from under the mailbags to make the accusation.

"Here, marshal, is where Lomax and I bunk, sleeping on the mail sacks."

"How do you explain the smears of blood I found on the door jamb and the coffin outside?" the lawman asked.

I held my breath, fearing the slightest movement might reveal my hiding place. Then I felt something sliding along my leg. I gritted my teeth. A mouse was crawling inside my pants.

"Can't say, marshal. Someone banged on the entry a couple hours before dawn this morning, but I thought nothing of it as it happens often, a drunk or a customer mad he didn't get his mail. That's all I heard other than the incessant braying of the mules across the street."

The mouse kept wiggling as it inched up my leg, tickling me. I squelched a chuckle.

Augusta added, "Lomax had a key. He could've let himself in, marshal."

After a brief silence, someone started kicking the mailbags.

The rodent moved another inch up my calf, then scratched at me with his tiny claws. I didn't know whether to laugh or cry.

"You want me to un-pile the mail sacks so you can check them? There's forty-three at last count, and I've got to keep them in sequence so we sort them in the order they arrived."

The mouse bit at a sliver of my flesh. I suppressed the flinch that would have put me on the trapdoor of a scaffold for murdering a worthless lawyer. I gritted my teeth harder, and squished my face to stifle any movement or noise, but I flinched at the mixture of pain from the bite and the itch from the tickle. Did my reaction tip off the lawman?

The long quiet alarmed me, but I had to admit Pete was an able poker player when I was the ante. I doubted I was as good an ante as he was a bluffer, not with a mouse working up my pants and nibbling at my flesh along the way.

Finally, the marshal spoke. "Is that Lomax's saddle, carbine and saddlebags?"

The rodent squirmed past my knee.

"They're his," Pete acknowledged. "Take them, if you want. I don't care to keep a murderer's belongings here."

Inching my hand to my calf I thumped my middle

finger against the intruder, and he scurried down my pants so fast that I almost screamed out with the agony of a squelched laugh. I smothered the cascading chuckle in my throat.

"No one's proved he's a murderer," Augusta interjected. "I bet that lawyer swindled him. I never did trust Adam Scheisse."

"That's no reason to kill anyone," the marshal replied.

The mouse evacuated my pants, and I nearly wet myself from the tension of stifling the laughter.

"Can you prove he did it, marshal?" Augusta asked.

"Can't prove anything yet, ma'am, but I've got fifty or more witnesses from Billy Nye's place last night, saying he was threatening Adam Scheisse's life from the time he entered the saloon until the fellows helped him leave."

"What fellows?" Pete asked.

"Jeff Smith and his friends. They said the last they saw he was staggering toward the Merchants and Mechanics Bank."

"What do you want us to do, marshal?" Pete asked.

"Send word if Lomax returns, so I can jail him before he murders someone else."

"I'll be glad to," Pete answered as I heard the lawman leave the room.

After a brief silence, Augusta fretted. "We've only been open two hours, but the marshal's already the third man to inquire about Lomax this morning. The fellow that tried to buy our soap supply came by looking for him and then a reverend, saying he was available to get Lomax right with God before his hanging. You don't think they'll hang him, do you, Pete?"

"Not if they can't catch him," Pete said.

"Where is he?" she asked.

"Probably hiding until dark so he can escape Leadville. Now we need to return to work. Keep the new help out of here so they don't pilfer Lomax's belongings."

With that, they left the room, the door slamming shut, which I took as Pete's signal they were gone. I slept on and off the rest of the day, trying to clear my head from the hangover muddle. I nibbled on crackers and washed the wafers down with occasional sips of water. While I waited hot and sweaty under the mail sacks, I considered how to escape. Heading back to Denver was out as I was known there. Too, I needed to flee Colorado as fast as possible. I vetoed heading north, as I was tired of frigid winters. South remained my best option. I'd follow the Arkansas River between the mountain ranges toward Granite and turn southeast to Trinidad, then head into New Mexico Territory. I knew little of the region, but figured it was warmer and hoped the folks were decent. While I had no idea what I'd do in the territory, I bet New Mexicans weren't as corrupt as the lawyer they accused me of shooting.

Since I needed to move fast, I had to steal a horse, another crime that might get me hanged, but if I took one off the street the owner would soon miss him and more men would search for me. About mid-afternoon I heard the door open and close firmly.

"Lomax, it's me, Pete. You doing okay?"

"It's warm under here and mice keep pestering me," I rasped. "Been trying to figure how to leave town tonight, but stealing a horse will just draw more attention to me."

"I'll give it thought," he responded.

"Another thing, Pete, whoever stole my money took the key to the store. Horace may want a new lock to be on the safe side."

"Okay, I'll tell him after you're gone, but you've gotta leave tonight. And don't be mule-headed about trying to prove you didn't do it."

"That's it, Pete. A mule. I'll steal a mule from the stable across the street. They're bringing so many to town to work the diggings, they won't miss one."

"Good thinking, Lomax. I'll be back when we close. Rest as much as you can because you'll face a long night." He shut the door firmly. I sweated and slept until closing.

Pete came in once he sent Augusta home and locked up the store. He dug me out of the mailbags. It was good to see light, even if it was the fading glow of a dying day, and to breathe without the weight of mail sacks atop me. Pete brought over the wash basin and let me sponge myself off with a rag. He opened me a tin of peaches to eat. I attacked the fruit like a wild animal and drained the syrup from the can. When darkness finally draped Leadville, we never lit a candle or a lamp so no one might spot me through the window. I packed my saddlebags with my few belongings and added cans of peaches and apricots plus the tin of crackers. I carried my saddlebags and carbine to the front door, then retrieved my saddle, saddle blanket and bedroll.

After that we waited for midnight, Pete offering to saddle my mule as long as I stole it first. We agreed, sitting on the floor on either side of the door, whispering so that no one passing by overheard. About the time I thought I should go steal a mule, I detected voices on the walk outside.

"Do you hear that?" I whispered.

"Could be thieves."

We both crouched at our posts, me sliding my carbine to Pete. "If they get inside, wait until they close the door and coldcock them with this." I pulled my pistol out and waited, figuring they'd break the glass or bust the door down. They did neither as I caught the metallic sound of a key being inserted in the lock, then twisting the catch free. As the door parted, two figures slipped in, pushing the door shut behind them. At that moment, I stood up and smashed the butt of my pistol against one man's head as Pete slammed the carbine stock into the other's. Both men collapsed without so much as a groan, the only sound being the clink of the key hitting the floor. We pulled both from the doorway.

"You steal your mule," Pete said, handing me my carbine. I picked up my bridle, opened the door and scurried across the street to the livery corral where three dozen mules mingled. I opened the gate and slipped in, weaving among the animals until I found one that didn't shy away from me or the bridle. After slipping the bridle on him, I climbed atop him to ensure he didn't buck and he wasn't too stubborn to guide. He met my criteria. Dismounting, I led him to the entrance, unlatched it and flung it open, leading my mount out and letting the other animals meander wherever they wanted. Freeing the mules would disguise my theft as the work of a prankster. Leading my mule back across the street where Pete had carried my rigging and waited, I gave him the reins and my carbine.

"You know who those two burglars were?" Pete whispered.

"No idea."

"It's that fellow Smith, the one they call Soapy, and the reverend that came by to get you right with God. I'll drag them out of the store, but I found the key they stole from you."

"Now Horace won't have to change the locks," I replied. "Saddle my mule and I'll pull them from the store." I ran inside, grabbed Smith by his legs and yanked him out by the display coffin. I lifted him erect and pushed him into the casket, propping him up against the sides. Next I dragged out the Reverend Bowers and leaned his torso against wall beside the coffin. I patted him for his Bible, but didn't find it, so I tried linked his hands together like he was praying.

By the time I finished arranging the would-be thieves, Pete had my saddled mule and put my saddlebags, bedroll, canteen and carbine in place. I shook Pete's hand and thanked him, then mounted and headed south out of town. I never saw Pete again, nor the Tabors, though I read about them in the papers on occasion. Tabor became fabulously wealthy from the Little Pittsburg mine that arose from the Rische and Hook claim. Barely months after I left, he was proclaimed the Silver King of Colorado. That wealth carried him to statewide political office, becoming lieutenant governor the next year and after that serving a three-month appointment as a U.S. Senator. Augusta's cooking wasn't tasty enough to keep her around, however, and he divorced her. Instead of courting Miss Susan B. Anthony, who was still available, Horace married the voluptuous Baby Doe McCourt, a union that scandalized Colorado. The controversial marriage cost Tabor his political career as he subsequently mounted three unsuccessful campaigns for governor. Some say the second marriage also drained his fortune as he squandered his money on impressing his new wife and died broke, as did Baby Doe. Augusta, though, took her share of the divorce settlement and led a prosperous Denver life until her death.

As I rode away from Leadville, I prided myself in having put Jefferson Randolph "Soapy" Smith the Second in his coffin. I never expected to see him again, but when I did two decades later in Alaska, I had the honor of repeating the deed.

Chapter Fourteen

From Colorado I escaped to New Mexico Territory and later to Arizona Territory, picking up experience at differing jobs, whatever I could make a living at, including cowboying, rustling cats, tending bar and even owning a Tombstone saloon, which I named the Stubborn Mule for the animal that carried me away from my Leadville troubles. In all those years, I avoided Colorado as much as I could for fear I'd be arrested for a murder I couldn't remember. Early on when I was in Lincoln County, New Mexico Territory, I saw a wanted poster with my name on it. Lake County was offering $500 for my capture, though I thought the amount too small for a man of my accomplishments and the county should pay *me* three or four times that much for the valuable public service I had rendered to Leadville by ridding it of a crooked lawyer. But Colorado didn't see it that way.

For years, I looked over my shoulder, worried that my humanitarian deed might catch up with me, but after my time in Tombstone when I created more enemies than I could keep up with, both my conscience and my concern over being caught lessened. After an unfortunate 1896 misunderstanding that angered the Texas Rangers and some crooked gamblers with a pugilistic bent, I found myself in the middle of 1897 in San Francisco, a city I had wanted to visit since hearing of my father's stay there during the California Gold Rush. Despite the financial panic the year before, I'd come into a windfall that's best left unexplained except to say that Wells Fargo should've kept better track of their strongboxes. Finders keepers is what I always heard, and I didn't see any point in countering that adage.

Any way I wound up with almost $3,500 in San Francisco and a new dedication to making sure that I hung onto the money longer than was my habit, usually losing it through rotten luck or occasionally through fraud. I possessed cash that had just dropped into my lap or, more precisely, fallen off a Wells Fargo baggage cart at the train depot, and I desired to experience the life of a robber baron so I checked into the Palace Hotel, which took up a whole San Francisco block bounded by New Montgomery, Market, Annie and Jessie Streets. As I entered the hotel a fellow in a fancy blue cap, jacket and trousers tried to grab my suitcase, but I fought him off since that's where I had deposited my Wells Fargo earnings. Had he been adorned with a badge, gun belt and nightstick, I would've thought him a policeman, but I later learned the Palace Hotel called him and others like him an "attaché." He grimaced when I didn't turn over my bag, but he opened the door for me and wished me a pleasant day anyway as I entered the most amazing space I'd ever seen. Standing in the entry court, I found a circular drive where two horse-drawn carriages were unloading passengers surrounded by attachés, who were grabbing their baggage and escorting the arrivals to the front desk. Looking up, I saw seven stories of white-columned balconies crowned with a glass skylight that flooded the room with sunlight. Men and women promenaded in fancier clothes than I wore, giving me a glimpse of the fine life that I had never known, except for those times I'd stayed in a bawdy house with other amenities. The hotel boasted luxurious rooms and suites, any of which would've been beyond my normal budget, but thanks to Wells Fargo's oversight, I had increased my holdings substantially. After recovering from the sudden shock of such elegance, I marched through the courtyard over inlaid tile floors to the magnificent mahogany front desk with three clerks helping the newcomers in their fancy attire while the attachés hovered over them like a swarm of bees. Behind the desk stood a huge panel of cubby holes for keys and mail to each of the hotel's 755 rooms. Atop the mail slots, which would've made my sorting at Tabor's much easier, sat a key-wound clock with gold hands, numerals and trim.

When the previous guests marched off, I moved toward the counter, but an attaché sitting on a bench along the side wall jumped up and rushed over to steal my carpetbag from me. I fought him off and stepped up to the desk, dropping my bag by my feet and slapping the bell with my palm even though clerk stood right in front of me.

"May I help you, sir?"

"I want a room, if you'll tell me your prices."

"Rooms start at five dollars a day going up to twenty-two dollars a night for a suite. I'd be happy to suggest alternative lodging, sir, as you don't look like you can afford our rates."

Bending to retrieve my bag, I knew the attendant thought I was leaving, but I plopped the case on the counter, loosened the latch and pulled out a stack of bills. "I'll take a suite, paying four days in advance," I announced as I counted out $88 and slapped the cash before him.

"Yes, sir," the clerk said with newfound respect.

"How'd you make your money, if I might ask that and your name?"

"Railroading," I answered, "and I'm H.H. Lomax, formerly of Cane Hill, Arkansas."

"Welcome to the Palace Hotel, Mr. Lomax. Pardon my questioning your resources, sir, but most of our residents dress more formally."

"And I can appreciate that, though I prefer not to flaunt my wealth. It reduces the chances a ne'er-do-well will try to take advantage of me like these uniformed young men that keep trying to steal my carpetbag."

The desk clerk laughed. "Those are Palace employees, here to help you carry your bags to your room and do any other tasks you might require."

"Can he shoe my horse?" I asked.

"No, sir, but he can find a blacksmith for you and take your mount there for shoeing. Would you like to arrange that, Mr. Lomax?"

"I was just spoofing you. I'm afoot."

"You'll discover our rooms to be most palatial, Mr. Lomax. Each guest room is equipped with an electric call button to summon an attaché for every wish and whim. Every room is elegantly furnished with a bay window overlooking the city or the bay."

"I'm impressed," I admitted. "Just point the way to the stairs."

"No need for that, Mr. Lomax. Use one of our rising rooms." My newfound desk friend slapped the bell and instantly an attaché ran to my side, grabbing my carpet-bag before I could stop him. "Take Mr. Lomax to Room 729, but show him the amenities first."

I put my hand on my revolver in case the attaché ran away with my money, but he was a cordial fellow, show-ing me a restaurant with clean linens and sparkling silver and glasses on each table, a billiards room with six pool tables, a reading area with plush chairs and sofas. As we passed an end table in the reading room, the young man grabbed two newspapers, then pointed me to a side wall where another attaché stood in an open double door. I went that direction, and my helper followed. I paused outside the wide entry because I could see the small redwood-paneled room led nowhere.

"Go on in," he instructed.

I hesitated again, figuring the moment I stepped in-side his partner would shut the door and then the fellow would run off with my carpetbag and money.

"Please go ahead," he implored me.

Not caring to make a scene, I walked in, looking over my shoulder to make sure he followed. He did. Once he entered, his partner lifted a lever and the metal grate doors closed. He twisted another lever and the room lurched and climbed the wall.

"The miracle of hydraulics," the operator informed me. "With elevators the sky's the limit for buildings a hundred stories or more."

I'd listened to tales before, but I didn't believe this one. Moments later without me having to climb a single step, the rising room arrived at the seventh floor and the operator opened the door, my personal attaché leading me out of the elevator along the hallway that overlooked everything below. Always scared of heights, I stayed closer to the wall as we reached my room.

My attaché unlocked the door, pushed it open and handed me the key. I marched inside, him tailing me like my shadow. He placed my case on the bed and the two newspapers on the table by a plush reading chair. "Care for me to unpack your bag?"

I stood stunned in such a luxurious room. I sat on the mattress and never felt a softer spot. Not even Mattie Silks' mattress compared to this one. It sure beat sleeping on the ground on a cattle trail or on Leadville mailbags.

"Would you like me to unpack your bag?" my attaché asked again.

"I'll manage."

He smiled and pointed to a black button on the wall. "Just push that if you need anything and someone will be up to assist you." He held out his hand, palm up.

I grabbed it and shook it vigorously. "Thank you," I said.

"A tip?" he replied. "Customarily residents give attachés a tip."

Surprised, I couldn't think of a tip for an instant. Finally, it came to me. "An apple a day keeps the doctor away."

My attaché frowned, spun about and marched out, huffing as he slammed the door. Though I wasn't sure what I had done to offend the fellow, I realized I had much to learn about living like a silver king when money was no object. My next lesson in the high life came at supper when I went to the dining room and was shown to an expensive table with more eating utensils than I'd ever seen. I ordered from a menu I didn't understand and had a delightful dinner. When it was time to pay, I was reaching into my pocket when the waiter asked if I was staying at the Palace. I nodded and he requested my room key.

"You can just sign your room for the meal," he informed me.

"What? I don't pay?" I stammered as I showed him my key.

"Not until you check out," he said. "You are Mr. Lomax are you not, the railroad king?"

I thrust out my chest in pride. "That's me."

The waiter handed me the bill. "Sign your name and write Room 729 on it and you will settle your account when you check out."

Doing what I was told, I finished and handed the pencil and paper to him, as I heard a noisy horde out in the lobby. "Can I sign any room number?"

My waiter laughed. "Rich and a sense of humor," he said. "At least your wealth hasn't corrupted you yet." He pulled my chair out as I stood and started to my suite, though I was amused by the swarm of men and women following a couple toward the registration desk. Like me, the man carried his own suitcase and resisted efforts by an attaché to assist him with the load, which weighted his shoulder as he marched across the inlaid tile floor, half carrying, half sliding his baggage. Everybody shouted questions, wanting to know about the Klondike and the couple's plans. While some of the mob appeared to be newspaper reporters scribbling notes on folded paper, most were regular folks. As the strapping man approached the desk ahead of the wiry woman with a tanned face, I studied them and decided they were dressed shabbier than me. I wondered if the desk clerk would recommend a lower-priced hotel to them.

As an attaché scrambled by, I grabbed his arm. "What's going on?"

"Haven't you heard about the *Excelsior*?"

"The *Excelsior*?"

"A steamer that arrived from Alaska Territory carrying more gold and millionaires than any civilian ship in history, so they say."

"They don't look rich," I said, pointing to the couple.

The attaché grinned. "That's Tom Lippy and his wife Salome. There's two hundred pounds of gold in his suitcase and his Yukon mining claim is worth millions more." He yanked his arm from mine. "I need to see if I can help him and get a nice tip."

"An apple a day keeps the doctor away," I called after him. "A stitch in time saves nine."

The attachés weren't interested in my tips. I figured they were trying to steal our suitcases instead.

People threw questions at the husband and wife like I tossed tips at attachés. They were shouting about gold, where to find it, the quickest way to get to the Klondike, what kind of equipment they needed, and on and on. As I stood there watching, I calculated what that bag Lippy was toting amounted to. If it was two hundred pounds with sixteen ounces to the pound, that came out to 3,200 ounces of gold, which fluctuated at around twenty dollars an ounce. That meant Lippy's suitcase was worth $64,000. My $3,500, thank you Wells Fargo, paled by comparison. At that moment, I was bitten by the gold bug again, determined this time not to let some crooked lawyer steal my claim. I had yet to spend a full night in a Palace Hotel bed, but I had already decided I should live out my life in such luxury with soft mattresses, clean linens on dinner tables, fancy meals, rising rooms instead of stairs and the other benefits my prior existence had never afforded me out West.

While everyone else was throwing questions at Mr. and Mrs. Lippy, the hotel staff remained as courteous as a salesman trying to meet his quota. Somehow money always bought courtesies that weren't accorded to regular people in threadbare clothing. I made a mistake in watching the Lippy circus because as soon as the couple got their key and started for the rising room, the reporters and the curious trailed after them, as many as could crowd on the hydraulic ride and going up with them to my floor. The swarm was intent on following the pair into their room. Perhaps they had invited them up to celebrate their newfound wealth. Whatever the case, the line for the elevator extended halfway across the lobby. I decided I'd take the stairs, an idea shared by other members of the horde. I followed them to the staircase and walked up, taking my time and saving my breath while fifty or more men and two women bolted past me.

When I reached my floor, I was winded and the

hallway was teeming with the nosy crowd. Best I could determine, the Lippy couple roomed in Suite 733, at least that's where folks were clamoring and begging for a meeting. News gatherers wanted more facts, others sought grubstakes and some promoted investment opportunities. I'd seen a circus as a kid, ducked Yankee lead in the Battle of Prairie Grove, ridden in Buffalo Bill's Wild West show, dodged Sioux arrows at the Little Bighorn and even heard a Democrat tell the truth once, but I'd never seen such a commotion as this. I wasn't the only one bitten by the gold bug. I fought my way through the throng to get to my room, then unlocked it, slid in before anyone else could join me and fastened the door.

Plopping into the plush chair, I picked up the papers from the table and searched for stories on the *Excelsior.* On page seven of the *San Francisco Call,* I found a lengthy story, though it was less enthusiastic than the tip-craving attaché's account. The headline announced, "Gold from the Yukon River" and said the *Excelsior* delivered to the San Francisco wharf a half million dollars in gold dust. The fact that caught my attention was the statement that forty passengers disembarked from the *Excelsior* and not a one carried less than three thousand dollars apiece from Dawson City in the Yukon Territory of Canada. Now that wasn't Wells Fargo money, but it was close. Another observation that struck me was the sentence that said gold camp saloons bringing in less than two thousand dollars a day had a poor day. I'd run a saloon in Tombstone and knew it could be lucrative, but I understood it wasn't as rewarding as having a paying mining claim. Still, it gave me options.

The *San Francisco Chronicle* played the story on the front page, listing the fifteen richest passengers to step off the steamer. The Alaska Commercial Company brought back a quarter million dollars in gold dust while my Palace Hotel neighbor T.S. Lippy had $65,000. Others on the list were: F.G.H. Bowker, $90,000; Louis Rhodes, $25,000; Albert Crook and Alex Orr, $20,000 each; James McMann and U Galbraith, $15,000 apiece; and J.O. Hentwood, J. La Du, J. Fox, John Marks, Barnard

Anderson, Henry Cook, J. Urnmerger and Fred Lendesser, all $10,000. The newspaper account began, "A story rivaling in intensity of interest that told of the fabulous wealth of Monte Cristo was related by the passengers of the little steamer *Excelsior*, which arrived from St Michaels, Alaska, yesterday. Millions upon millions of virgin gold await the fortunate miner who has the hardihood and courage to penetrate the unknown depths of the Yukon district."

The more I read, the more intrigued I became, but it was hard to concentrate on the newspaper for the noise and clamoring outside my door from the curious trying to get the attention of Tom and Salome Lippy. Unable to stand the clamor anymore, I left for a while. Grabbing cash from my suitcase, I tucked the money in my pocket and the bag under my bed, then slipped to the door, unlatching it and squeezing into the hallway, locking it behind me and wedging my way through the pressed bodies to the stairwell, then raced down the steps as people still climbed them in hopes of meeting the Lippy couple.

Downstairs I asked one of the attachés directions to the wharf where the *Excelsior* had docked, hoping to see the treasure ship for myself. I found it and a crowd of the curious like me, inspecting the steamer with the tales of riches running rampant, such as passengers carting off wheel barrows of gold dust and nuggets and others going straight to the smelter to have their gold processed into bars for easier handling. The pier buzzed with gossip and rumors about the fortune to anyone who beat the rush to the Klondike, which was said to be richer than King Solomon's mines. I wondered if Solomon were still alive, whether or not he would head for the Yukon or be satisfied with the wealth he had already accrued, assuming he didn't have a crooked lawyer swindling him out of his claim. I listened to the exaggerations and speculations as we inspected the steamer with its center black smokestack, its two masts midway between the stack and the opposite ends of the boat. I lingered around the docks, then started back to the hotel, taking my time over the hilly streets of San Francisco, hoping that the crowd had cleared outside my room. Walking into the Palace, I passed the registration desk and looked up at my floor, seeing a smattering of people, but not nearly as many as before. As I headed for the rising room, the attendant called me. "Mr. Lomax, Mr. Lomax," he cried. "I have something for you. A gentleman left a card for you."

Not understanding who might know I was at the Palace, I hastened my pace in case a titan of mining, railroading or shipping had gotten word of my stay and my newfound wealth. When I took the card and inspected it, I caught my breath. It read: DAYLE LYMOINE, SPECIAL INVESTIGATOR, WELLS FARGO & COMPANY.

"Mr. Lymoine went to your room to see if you were in," the clerk advised me, "but there were just too many folks up there to handle his business. He left his card and said he'd catch you later."

I gulped. Catch me later? What did Lymoine know? "Thank you. I wasn't expecting him today."

The clerk smiled. "And let me apologize for the commotion on your floor, but it's not every day we have a guest arrive with two hundred pounds of gold in his suitcase. Anyway, the attachés are clearing the floor. This evening hotel staff will prohibit those without a key from accessing your floor."

Finders might not be keepers after all, I thought as I took the calling card toward the rising room, where the attendant made me show him my key before he lifted me to my floor. When I reached my stop, a herd of people waited to get on, the attachés driving them into the hydraulic lift as I got off. I saw the floor had been cleared and marched to my door. Taking out my key, I caught a noise from down the hallway.

"Psssst, pssst."

I turned and spotted a man sticking his head out of the room, reminding me of a prairie dog peeking out of a burrow. It was Tom Lippy. I pointed at my chest. "Me?" I whispered.

He nodded and motioned for me to approach.

Looking both ways and seeing nobody, I slipped toward him. When I reached his room, he opened the door and pulled me inside, closing it behind him. I saw his wife standing by the bay window, an odd look on her face, either bewilderment or awe.

Grabbing my hand, he shook it firmly. "I'm Tom Lippy. Everybody's pestering me, wanting things from me. Worst of all, they know our room number. Salome fears they'll bust in on us. Would you swap rooms with us without telling the staff? There's money in it for you."

With Wells Fargo looking for me, I liked the idea, but I wanted to spend one night like a king on a Palace mattress. "I'm paid up for four nights. Give me eighty-eight bucks and advice on the Klondike, and I'll do it, but I'm slipping out in the morning as something's come up that requires me to leave without telling the hotel staff."

"Even better," Lippy said. "It's difficult being rich, people wanting something from you, attachés here with their hands out expecting you to tip them."

I nodded. "I tell them 'an apple a day keeps the doctor away'."

Lippy guffawed. "That's the funniest one yet, fellow. Next time they ask for a tip I'll give them that advice rather than money for their assistance."

That was when I realized a tip was paying them cash for their help. I was learning something every day, but before completing the deal with Lippy I demanded more information on the Yukon. "Before we swap, tell me all you can about the Klondike."

Lippy gestured toward a chair, and I sat.

"What's the best way to get there the fastest?"

"There's no good route this late in the season as winter'll freeze things up before you arrive. Winter is hell," he said, then laughed. "That's a contradiction in words, but it's true for the Yukon." Lippy said he and his wife had traveled the water route 5,000 miles from Dawson on the Yukon River to St. Michael Bay and then on the Pacific all the way to San Francisco. "You'll not reach Dawson City before the Yukon freezes. The seas can be rough. I was seasick for a thousand or more miles, wanted to die. Another option is to go from here to Juneau and then change ships for the final hundred-plus miles to Skagway or Dyea, then it's five or six hundred more miles overland and river to Dawson City, a tough go in horrible weather. Whichever route you take, you'll sail the Pacific for days so take a bundle of newspapers, as many as you can get."

"To read?"

"No, so you'll have something to puke in when you get seasick because every bucket on the ship will be in used by others throwing their guts up."

"That's good to know," I said.

"Another thing you must understand," Lippy continued, "is that you should only go if you're physically and financially strong. It is not an easy undertaking. It is filled with difficulties and trials you can barely imagine. You've never been cold until you've endured a winter in the Yukon, where the Mounties are not letting anyone enter the district unless they bring almost a ton of supplies. I've a list I'll give you, but you must manage those provisions and transport them to Dawson City."

After offering an hour of instruction, he gave me the list of necessary supplies and eighty-eight dollars. Then I carried two of their bags to my room, where I pulled my suitcase from under the bed and grabbed my newspapers, taking them to their suite. When no hotel staff were looking, I gave Salome my key, picked up two more of their bags and followed her to my room. We slipped in unseen, and she gave me her key to their room. Once I got back to Lippy's room, I held the door open for him, and he tugged his bag of gold to my suite. That was the last time I ever saw him or his wife.

I enjoyed the night in the Palace, taking a hot bath without having to heat water, using the toilet without having to go outside to empty it, sleeping on a bed as soft as an angel's wings. It angered me that my stay was being shortened by an inquisitive Wells Fargo man. To shield myself from the investigator, I gave myself an alias, figuring I'd use names of men I hated most during my years since leaving home. Jesse James stood at the top of my unlikeable list so I decided I'd go by Jesse and take the last name of Murphy for Lawrence G. Murphy, the Lincoln County, New Mexico Territory, responsible for so many of my troubles after I escaped Leadville.

After a relaxing night's sleep, I got up, dressed and slipped out into the hallway about six o'clock in the morning and slid into the San Francisco fog. I or should I say Jesse Murphy, found a cheap hotel where I spent ten days for the same price a single night cost me at the Palace. The press took to calling the urge to go to the Yukon "Klondicitus" and symptoms of the disease were everywhere in newspaper ads and signs in stores: "Alaska or bust—all for sale;" "Going to Alaska—best paying saloon on street for a man who wants to stay;" "Will deed my ranch for a stake for Alaska;" and "Poultry business for sale on account of going to Alaska." I spent the next ten days preparing for the trip, bribing a clerk at the Pacific Coast Steamship Company a hundred dollars just to buy a $300 ticket to get me passage on the steamer *Umatilla* to Juneau. I purchased the supplies on Lippy's list and more so I was prepared for Alaska, even buying me new clothes, a money belt and arms to give myself the proper look and the needed protection for heading into a rough-and-tumble country. At 10:30 on the Sunday morning of July 25, the *Umatilla* pushed back from the Broadway wharf and started the journey north to Alaska. I or at least Jesse Murphy, was among 400 passengers on board with over 800 tons of supplies, three of those tons belonging to Jesse Murphy. Despite stormy waters, I never got seasick and didn't have to use the papers to vomit in. Those newspapers earned me my first bonanza when I reached my final destination, Skagway as it turned out.

Chapter Fifteen

I lost track of the days as the *Umatilla* plowed north the fifteen hundred-plus miles to Juneau. Half the passengers suffered from seasickness and threw up much of the way, hanging over the rails and feeding the fish or staying in their rooms and moaning in their misery before reaching the Gulf of Alaska. We entered the Inside Passage where the seas calmed, and we steamed into spectacular country with gigantic tree-covered mountains to our east standing sentinel over the bluest waters imaginable and striking, fertile islands to our west. Occasionally, we saw humpback whales blowing and then their tails when they dove back into the depths.

While many passengers fought seasickness and boredom, my biggest problem was eating the meals, generally a liquid concoction thicker than a broth but thinner than a soup and smelling of fish. My greatest challenge remained remembering that I was now Jesse Murphy instead of H.H. Lomax. As we neared Juneau, passengers organized for the trek to Dawson City, agreeing it made sense to form companies of men to work together. I avoided making any partnership as I was better provisioned than most with my Wells Fargo windfall. I didn't care to make any commitments until I inspected the lay of the land and what it took to get to the Klondike. The third day out of San Francisco, a handsome fellow my age approached me and introduced himself as Roger Meredith.

"My name's H. errr ... Jesse Murphy," I stammered.

"I'm glad to meet you, H.R. Jesse Murphy,"

"Just call me Jesse."

Meredith nodded. "Okay, Jesse, I'm a thespian. How about you?"

"Raised Baptist," I replied, "though I've slipped in recent years."

My new friend laughed. "I'm not talking religion, Jesse, but the theater, the stage, drama, tragedy, comedy, Shakespeare, Gilbert and Sullivan—"

Recalling the line the old Leadville prospector quoted me years earlier, I blurted out, "Bell, book, and candle shall not drive me back, when gold and silver becks me to come on."

Meredith inspected me with his blue eyes and grinned. "From the third act of Shakespeare's King John. I can tell you are a well-read man for a back-sliding Baptist. Have you formed a partnership or joined a company yet, Jesse?"

I looked over my shoulder to see who had walked up, then realized I was Jesse. "Not yet. I'm not sure I want to start for Dawson City with winter approaching. I spent a winter in Leadville, Colorado, and would've frozen to death without a room."

"Ah, Leadville," Meredith mused. "I played Hamlet in the Tabor Opera House, one of the grandest venues I've ever performed in, even stayed in the Tabor Grand Hotel during our run. Magnificent facilities, though the air is thin in the high altitudes, increasing the difficulties in projecting your lines during a performance."

Sighing, I wondered if I might've owned an opera house or a grand hotel had Noose Neck not swindled me out of my mining claim. I stood there thinking what might have been.

"You look pensive," Meredith said.

I didn't think I looked like a pencil, but I didn't live in the make-believe world of Roger Meredith. "Just a lot on my mind."

"Look, Jesse, men on this steamer are partnering up and forming companies. I'm not going to the Yukon to pull gold from the earth. I'll take it from the miners' pockets. It's easier than digging in the dirt." Meredith showed me his palms. "You don't see calluses, do you?"

"Not a one."

"And I don't intend to rub a single blister on my hands grubbing for gold when these Argonauts can willingly give me money from their wallets."

"You running a shell game or three-card monte, Roger?"

"No, sir, I plan to establish the Alaska Theatrical Company in Skagway, entertain the vagabonds crazed with gold fever. I need a partner, and you look like one who knows the long odds at finding paydirt and is shrewd enough to make money in other ways."

Pondering his offer, I questioned whether to get involved with a man I'd just met, and an actor to boot. But I had three tons of provisions, and I couldn't abandon them at our destination while I explored routes to Dawson City because my supplies would be pilfered. Having a partner, at least temporarily, who was interested in gold by other means might be what I needed.

Meredith studied me, my hesitation worrying him. "I've got eight trunks of costumes and props to open my theater, Jesse. I intend to earn my bonanza without sticking a shovel in the ground, which will freeze solid by the time any of our shipmates reach the Klondike. I'm planning on staking my claim in Skagway or maybe Dyea, whichever looks the most promising."

I nodded. "I'll go in with you, Roger, for a week, then reconsider if our partnership continues."

Meredith grabbed my hand and pumped it. "Any man that knows Shakespeare is worth having as a partner, even if he is a Baptist. I take it you don't drink."

Shrugging and smirking, I said, "My religion didn't take real good as I imbibe now and then, and once owned a saloon for a spell back in Tombstone."

My new partner rubbed his chin. "Did you know Wyatt Earp and Doc Holliday?"

"Holliday pulled a tooth of mine. And the Earps needed a few more nooses hanging from their family tree."

He laughed, and we teamed up for the journey. As we had visited many of the same places throughout the West, him performing and me surviving, we discovered several common acquaintances or locations we had been. My actor friend was medium height and build, with a pale complexion and graying eyebrows and hair. His distinguished nose separated blue eyes that sparkled like the azure ocean waters over which we steamed. I paid five dollars to his roommate to swap rooms, and I bunked with Meredith the rest of the way to Juneau and even felt comfortable leaving my suitcase, which still held what money I couldn't fit in my money belt, with him. Unlike the reputation of his profession, the actor seemed as honest a fellow as I had ever been around. We passed our time visiting or re-reading the newspapers I had brought.

At Juneau we disembarked, me supervising the unloading of our provisions and trunks while Meredith arranged for a smaller ship to take us up Lynn Canal that led to Skagway and Dyea, our dropping off point for our Yukon adventure. We booked passage on the second ship out of Juneau, costing us half what we had paid in San Francisco to reach Juneau for a hundred-mile trip that was one-fifteenth the distance covered by the *Umatilla*. Our new steamer, the *Sly Fox*, was half the size of the *Umatilla* and lucky to stay afloat. After inspecting it, I thought it should've been called the *Leaky Box* as it had seen better days. I bribed six of the crew five dollars apiece to put Meredith's and my goods in the hold last, figuring they would be the first unloaded at our destination. When we shoved off from the dock in Juneau, the *Sly Fox* pushed me toward religion because I prayed for deliverance on my knees, so rickety was the ship that I feared never reaching our next port without me swimming or drowning.

The *Sly Fox* traveled half as fast as our first steamer, and that was when she was moving. I lost count of the number of times the ship stalled in the water until the crew made repairs and got the tub going again. While we sat dead in the sea and adrift, four other boats passed us in the race for the Yukon. We didn't know whether we would disembark in Dyea or Skagway as the captain would make that determination based on the time and tides when we arrived. Having been a land creature my entire life, I never considered tides, but as I listened to the ship's passengers, I learned we were sailing over a fjord, a long and narrow steep-sided inlet carved by a glacier or a slow-moving wall of ice. In such a constricted channel as Lynn Canal, the regular rise and fall of the ocean was exaggerated with Skagway tides rising twenty-five feet on some days. I found much of the talk amusing and irrelevant until the captain announced our steamer would disembark first at Skagway, which had but a single dock, still under construction. The *Sly Fox* captain cursed Billy and Ben Moore, the father and son who had homesteaded a hundred and sixty acres of land at the river's mouth and founded the town a decade earlier, anticipating a gold discovery in the Yukon. When that occurred Skagway stood as the doorway to the Klondike, and the Moore family stood to grow rich. Besides their log cabin, the Moores had established a sawmill to cut the lumber everyone would need when the rush hit. The captain begrudged the Moores for their foresight a decade earlier and for the exorbitant rates they now charged to use the unfinished dock. While a bigger steamer, one that had passed us the day before, was docked there, two other steamers anchored in the bay like the *Sly Fox*, offloading passengers and cargo onto boats and barges. Stampeders and freight were ferried to the shore, where everything was unloaded on the mud flats as the tide receded. It was up to the passengers to then tote their own provisions and supplies from the muck to dry ground before the next incoming tide.

"Bet you're glad you have a partner now," Meredith noted.

I nodded, "But I wish he had more muscle."

"Jesse," he said, causing me to glance over my shoulder until I remembered that was my new name, "I've moved the toughest audiences in the world, the frontiersmen of the American West, to laughter and tears with the sound of my voice. Moving our baggage will be less challenging."

Pointing to his hands, I asked, "What about calluses?"

"I'll risk it."

As the *Sly Fox* neared Skagway, we retrieved from our room our simple belongings, my suitcase with my money, new carbine, gun belt, and canvas bag with my change of clothes, comb, and razor. Then we marched to the Skagway side of the steamer as the crew lowered into the water one boat for passengers and another for cargo. One officer took the names of the people that were disembarking and the number of containers they had loaded in the hold, then passed the information to the sailors below. The seamen used the mast derricks to raise the crates and trunks from the ship's innards as a barge approached from shore.

As we waited for our boat, I stared at the confusion beyond the shoreline. Skagway was wedged between the mountain peaks and the mouth of the Skagway River west of town. From the boat I made out three or maybe four wooden structures, everything else being canvas tents. From afar, the gray canvas looked like tombstones in a massive cemetery with the residents scurrying among the markers as if they were seeking the grave of a long-deceased relative. The temperature was pleasant and the skies overhead were as blue as the waters beneath us.

When I wasn't inspecting the town, I looked behind me as they hoisted crates and trunks in cargo nets over the side and loaded the flatboat that took the first freight ashore. Finally, the officer called our names, and Meredith and I squeezed into the skiff that delivered us to shore. We set foot on dry land and waited for the flatboat to arrive. When it did, the crew offloaded the freight on the beach. We were lucky as a half dozen of my crates and three of Meredith's trunks arrived on the first skiff. By the time they unloaded and started it back to the *Sly Fox*, the tide had receded a foot. My partner and I carried our belongings another ten yards from the water's edge so we kept everything together and avoid theft. We placed my suitcase, my bundle of newspapers and canvass sack between two of his trunks and then stacked boxes atop them so no one would steal my money.

Men from town with horses or dogs came out and offered to assist. We told them we didn't need help, but they responded that would change once the tide rolled out. I didn't understand it at the moment, but as the bay receded, the flat boats with our gear landed farther and farther from us, and we had to wade through the muck to reach our belongings and carry it to dry land. Meredith and I alternated these trips, one of us staying with our provisions while the other slogged through the mud to get the next crate or trunk. By the time we found our last load, the tide had receded a hundred yards. At that point, we realized the men with the horses had been right. We hired one to skid Roger's last trunk and three of my crates up from the water's edge. Faced with carrying all our goods into town, we hired another local with a wagon to transport our goods to town.

"Where do you want your stuff delivered?" asked our freighter. "You got a place?"

Roger Meredith and I looked at each other, shrugging. "What do you suggest?" I asked.

"File on a city plot," our guide said.

Though I wasn't interested in buying land until I determined what I planned to do, I looked at Meredith, then our new acquaintance. "I'm not sure I'll be staying."

"Buy it today for five dollars, then sell it tomorrow for a profit," the fellow replied. "At least you'll have a place to set up a tent and leave your things. And plots don't cost anything other than the five-dollar filing fee for now."

"Who do we need to see?" Meredith asked.

"I'm as good as any," he answered. "Frank Reid's my name. I surveyed the town and laid out the streets. We started with three thousand lots, most of them fifty by one hundred feet in size and have sold a sixth of them so you have plenty to choose from."

"You have any on a main street corner where we can build an opera house?" Meredith inquired. "We want two adjoining lots."

"We do?" I asked. "Remember, our partnership's only good for a week until I decide what I'm gonna do."

My partner nodded. "If you head for Dawson City, I'll purchase your lot." He turned to our hand. "Let's load up the wagon and find our new home."

Reid drove his rig over and helped us stack our gear in the back until he saw my bundle of newspapers as I grabbed them. "I'll buy those papers for a dollar apiece," he offered.

I was ready to sell them, but Meredith grabbed my arm. "Don't do it. I smell potential money here."

"Why do you need them? Outhouse use?" my partner asked.

"Reading material and news are scarce around here without newspapers and telegraph," Reid answered.

"And that's why we brought them," my partner responded.

"I carried them to puke in, if I got seasick," I informed him.

"Our intent was to bring news north to Alaska," Meredith replied.

Reid looked as confused as me. "How's that?"

"Dramatic readings of newspaper stories from the states. You, Mr. Reid, are looking at Roger Meredith, thespian extraordinaire, an actor who can bring to life the words of the great bard William Shakespeare or of the common newspaperman from San Francisco. Tomorrow, once we get situated and identify a hall for a proper reading, I will perform the news."

"There's no hall," Reid replied.

"Then I'll find the biggest tent in town and sell admission for Skagway to hear reports from the San Francisco papers." He pushed the bundle against my chest, then whispered to me. "Guard these with your life."

"What?" I asked, questioning that any lying newspaper anywhere was worth my life.

"I will make enough cash with these newspapers to grubstake us, assuming you're still my partner."

While I questioned Meredith's sanity, I went along with it, especially if it would save me cash. I grabbed my suitcase and stuffed as many papers as I fit inside, then the rest in one of my partner's trunks. Reid loaded the last two on the wagon and secured the cargo with ropes. He motioned for us to take a seat on the rig. Once we were aboard, he checked the freight a final time and squeezed in beside us, taking the reins and rattling his team into motion. We started toward the tent city, Reid pointing out stakes that represented streets and the markers that separated the individual lots among all the tents and commotion that was Skagway.

"The avenues run east and west, starting with First Avenue. We're on State Street and one block to the east is Broadway, both running north" Reid explained.

As we crossed Fourth, I pointed to a wooden structure built halfway across the road.

"What survey allowed that?" I asked, pointing to the clapboard building.

Reid cleared his throat. "That is a temporary anomaly."

"Looks like a building to me," I replied, uncertain what he meant by anomaly.

"To maximize plots for sale, we had to survey the land and plot it regardless of existing buildings. That's Captain Moore's bunkhouse."

"Is that the Moore that established Skagway?" Meredith asked.

"That's the one," Reid answered.

"Shouldn't he be selling us plots?" my partner asked.

Reid laughed. "Things are moving too fast for him to keep up, what with land sales, wharf construction, lumber milling. We'll let the lawyers work it out once the boom's over."

"Lawyers cost me a fortune in Leadville and a saloon in Tombstone," I informed Reid. "Letting the lawyers work it out is the same as letting the crooks settle everything."

Shrugging, Reid maneuvered the team and wagon around the bunkhouse and down State Street toward Sixth, where he turned east, heading for Broadway. He pulled up at the intersection and pointed to the vacant land at the corner. "I've got two plots side-by-side here at one of the best intersections in town. Buying both lots will give you a hundred-foot frontage on both streets. You won't find a better deal than that."

Without consulting me, Meredith said, "We'll take it. Jesse here will pay you."

"What?" I said, turning to my partner.

"I don't have the cash, Jesse, but—"

"Then don't be spending my money."

"—but I'll have it in a couple days. I'll repay you with interest before our agreement expires, I promise."

If Meredith didn't have the money then, I doubted he

would make enough to reimburse me within a week. The gold was in Dawson City, not on a hundred-foot-square piece of real estate at the corner of Broadway and Sixth in Skagway, Alaska Territory.

"A wise choice," Reid informed us as he drove the wagon onto our property-to-be. "I'll unload and then return with the filing documents, assuming you pay cash up front."

"We can," my actor friend proclaimed.

Just I can, I thought to myself as we climbed from the wagon and removed out trunks and supplies, positioning them in the center of our two plots. I kept a close eye on my suitcase with my valuable newspapers and cash inside.

"Wells Fargo doesn't come this far north do they, Frank?" I asked as we unloaded a crate together.

"That's a strange question, Jesse. Why do you ask?"

"Curious mostly, though I had profitable dealings with them back in the states," I answered as I thought about Dayle Lymoine's calling card in my suitcase with my valuables. I prayed the special investigator was still searching for H.H. Lomax in California rather than following Jesse Murphy to Alaska.

After we emptied the wagon and Reid drove away to get the paperwork, I turned to my partner. "How are you going to pay me back with interest, Roger?"

"By reading your newspapers," he responded confidently. "Just wait until tomorrow."

I didn't believe it, but had too little time to argue as I needed to find the crate with the canvas tent I had secured and set it up so we'd have shelter for a few days until we decided our plan. Spotting Frank Reid returning with his wagon, Meredith asked me for the funds he'd spent on our behalf. I grumbled as I took ten dollars from my money belt. "Make sure the property is in both of our names," I demanded.

"I was thinking one plot in my name and one in yours," he countered. "Since it's my money, I'll take the corner lot, and you can have the inside lot."

"If that's what you want, that's how I'll do it, partner."

After I found the tent, I staked it out as Meredith handled the purchase. True to his word, he gave me the corner lot. As darkness didn't set in until almost ten o'clock, we had time to finish setting up our shelter, organize what gear we needed and secure what we didn't, never wasting a nail. When we pulled a nail from a crate, we saved it because who knew if you could find nails in Skagway or how much a pound would cost if you did. Because everything was scarce, men overpaid for what they took for granted back in the states. That was how Roger Meredith used my newspapers to repay me and grubstake his theater.

Come morning when daylight broke around five o'clock, Roger rose and told me he would make his money, provided I loaned him another ten dollars. I removed the bills out of my money belt and gave them to him, then turned over and rested until mid-morning when he returned.

"We're set," Meredith announced. "Come one o'clock, I've rented the town's biggest saloon, a huge tent over on Third Avenue and will do dramatic readings for two hours from one of your papers. You, Jesse, can even collect the money for me, so there's no question you're getting a fair shake. How many newspapers did you bring?

I remembered I'd bought copies of the *Call,* the *Chronicle,* and the *Examiner* each day from my night in the Palace Hotel until I boarded the *Umatilla* ten days later. "I brought at least thirty."

"Wonderful, Jesse. I can drag these readings out for a month if necessary. All we need to do now is hire someone for a dollar to watch our things while we're gone."

I got up from my bedroll and opened my suitcase, taking out a paper and offering it to my partner. He looked at it and said it would do as I got dressed. While he went searching for a trustworthy fellow to guard our belongings, I slipped outside with my bag and pried the lid off one crate. I removed a sack of sugar so I could slip my valise inside and nail the box shut again.

Around noon, Meredith brought back an old codger that appeared too weak to fight off a thief and too decrepit to catch one if he took something. He looked as if he should be sitting in a rocking chair on the front porch of some veterans home, but we left our valuables, save the July 22nd copy of the *San Francisco Chronicle*, with the puny fossil, who seemed way too frail to have made the trip to Skagway, much less continue to Dawson City. I called him General Charlie.

As we walked away from our property, Meredith promoted in a deep baritone voice his upcoming reading. "Gentlemen, gentlemen," he cried, "come hear the latest news from the *San Francisco Chronicle*, just arrived in Skagway in the last twenty-four hours. See Roger Meredith, the world's greatest thespian, read the news with the drama of the great bard William Shakespeare himself. Only a dollar to find out what's going on in the world. Reading begins at one o'clock at the biggest tent on Third Avenue. Enjoy drinks at the bar while you listen, but it'll cost you a dollar to enter."

For forty-five minutes we marched along Broadway and State streets with Meredith promoting his upcoming performance. At a quarter until one, we reached the tented saloon and walked inside, my partner reminding the proprietor of the rental agreement that all patrons could finish their drinks, but had to pay a dollar to stay past one o'clock until three. Some grumbled and left, while others paid and took up seats. Meredith stationed me at the door flap and I collected bills and silver from the line of men that snaked outside the saloon. So many wanted to hear the reading that the saloon owner stacked tables on top of one another and pushed them to the side so more people could squeeze in and listen.

At one o'clock, Meredith climbed atop an empty barrel with my paper in his hand and read, his voice taking a theatrical tone as he pronounced stories from the newspaper, its front page devoted to the Klondike Gold Rush. His expression was so powerful it was if God were reading the newspaper, even such mundane items as a list of supplies Yukon stampeders—as they were being called—needed, drawing cheers and hisses from the crowd.

"The ordinary outfit for the Juneau route will cost the prospector eighty dollars at least. From those who have gone over the trail, it has been learned that the following items are absolutely essential for the journey: Fifty pounds of flour, one-half pound of baking powder, fifteen pounds of dried fruit, twenty pounds of bacon, thirty-five pounds of beans, ten pounds of sugar, three pounds of coffee, one pound of salt, one-half pound of pepper, one pound of desiccated onions, matches, butter, milk, rice, corn meal, and such other articles of food as the pocket of the adventurer will permit."

Meredith read about the gunboat *Bennington* inspecting Pearl Harbor to tighten the nation's hold on Hawaii and about mails only going once a month to the mines in the Yukon, drawing jeers from his listeners. He reported on six workers, including four women, dying in the loading room after an explosion at the Winchester factory in New Haven, Connecticut, and on an Oakland man who hiccoughed for forty-eight straight hours. And he dramatized items from the personals section like the one addressed to C.C.: "Am heartbroken and will go to Alaska if you don't let me hear from you at once; this is dead earnest and the last call; silence will mean that you have given me your farewell. J.W." The distraught crowd could not decide whether to cheer or hiss the personal ad.

Meredith read for two hours, and I collected $263 by the end of his recitation, which earned a stirring round of cheers and applause. He concluded his performance with a bow and announced he would perform from another newspaper tomorrow at the same time. My partner had been right. Money was to be made in Skagway, 500 miles away from the diggings in Dawson City. Yet, the lure of gold still called me. Before I decided whether to continue our partnership after a week, I had to explore the possibilities for making it to the Klondike.

Chapter Sixteen

A good actor might make hundreds of dollars a day reading newspapers, but a good prospector stood the chance of making thousands of bucks daily. The thought of such riches stuck in my craw, my wanderlust for wealth forcing me to explore the options for getting to the gold diggings. Though I wasn't in as bad a condition as General Charlie, I wasn't as young as I once was. While the idea of being wealthy still intrigued me after my single night in the Palace Hotel, climbing Alaskan peaks and suffering through a winter trek to get to Dawson City made me wonder if it was worth it, especially if I froze on the trail or became a meal for a grizzly bear.

From my talk with Tom Lippy in San Francisco and what I had overheard on the *Sly Fox* during the trip up Lynn Canal, the first aim was to reach Canada's Bennett Lake, which fed into the Yukon River, navigable much of the way to Dawson City until it froze over and provided an icy road to the diggings. Reaching Bennett Lake required the stampeders, as we were now being called, to conquer White Pass from Skagway or Chilkoot Pass from Dyea on up Lynn Canal. While the Chilkoot Pass route was thirty-three miles long, twelve miles shorter than the White Pass Trail, it was much steeper, making it impossible for animals to traverse. The White Pass route was forty-five miles long, but could accommodate horses and mules for much of the way, but the path narrowed to only two feet at the trail's upper reaches.

The morning after Meredith's first reading, Frank Reid dropped by to drop off copies of the deeds to our city plots. After he gave us the papers and I confirmed that my partner had given me the corner lot, I started assaulting Reid with questions about the preferred route.

Reid studied me, shaking his head. "It doesn't matter," he answered. "Whichever trail you take, you wish you'd taken the other one. One miner told me, 'There ain't no choice. One's hell and the other's damnation.' Do you realize what's involved?"

I shrugged.

"You're nothing more than a pack animal over treacherous trails, one slip and you can fall to your death down sheer mountainsides. And you don't climb it just once, you must do it time after time after time because the Canadian Mounties won't let you in Canada without your ton of provisions. Besides, Jesse, you don't look like you have the mettle for it."

"I'm not made of iron, if that's what you mean," I replied.

Reid elaborated on the challenge. "I've done ciphering on what it takes to meet the Canadian requirements to enter the Yukon. You need two thousand pounds of supplies and equipment. If you can't afford a horse or a sled you can pull that load on, you have to carry it on your back. A strong man can manage sixty-five pounds. That means he has to make thirty or more round trips of ninety miles simply to get his belongings over the mountains. That comes to over twenty-five-hundred miles you walk, Jesse, before you start the trek to Dawson City another five hundred miles away. You know how long that takes?"

"A month?"

"Three months minimum, assuming you didn't break your leg, back or noggin and assuming you didn't slide off a mountain ledge to your death."

"Don't sugarcoat it for me, Frank."

He laughed.

"Being my partner's not that bad, Jesse," Meredith offered.

"I'd intend to check it out for myself. Anywhere I can buy a horse?"

"Not for less than fifty dollars," Reid replied, "but I'll rent you mine for ten bucks a day if you want to ride out and see for yourself. There's a camp five miles out of town where several of the boys are staging their goods for the hike. It's called 'Liarsville' because a few newspapermen hang around there, asking stampeders about the trail, rather than climbing it themselves. They're saying and printing it's not difficult because they never climbed it."

My partner nodded. "It'd be easier running a drinking establishment, Jesse. All you have to climb over in a saloon is an occasional drunk passed out on the floor."

"I need to see it for myself," I insisted.

Reid extended his open hand. "Give me ten bucks for the first day, and I'll fetch my horse if you don't believe me."

"You're wasting money," Meredith told me. "Stay here this afternoon and help me collect admissions at my reading. We'll make a killing and you won't have to climb any mountains." He pointed to north to the imposing peaks. "Look at that, will you? You don't want to spend months going back and forth with supplies before you start on a five-hundred mile trek to Dawson City where nothing's certain." He stamped his boots. "This is a sure thing."

"I've come this far so I need to go a bit farther, even if it's only to Liarsville." I fished ten dollars out of my money belt.

Reid noticed my grubstake. "Don't flash around your cash outside of town and be sure you take your revolver with plenty of ammunition."

"Fetch your horse," I said, "and I'll grab my weapons."

Reid returned 30 minutes later and gave me the reins. I mounted and rode north out of town, following the trail across shallows in the Skagway River. Tents, stacks of supplies, and exhausted stampeders dreaming of the Yukon, if not the hard work to get there, peppered each side of the road. I reached Liarsville in an hour and saw even more tarp-covered provisions and equipment stacked along the road and around the camp, which was nothing but three primitive log cabins and dozens of tents, with a hundred men milling about. I'd never seen such lifeless eyes in fellows as when I dismounted.

"You willing to sell your horse?" one asked.

"He's not mine," I replied.

"All the more reason to sell him," he replied.

"How many trips you made up and back?" I asked.

He sighed. "Nine so far and I ain't moved half my goods yet. Sure you won't sell your horse?"

"I'm certain," I answered, deciding not to tie my horse, but lead him around by the reins, as I studied the stampeders and determined if I wanted to join them. They were a tired looking bunch, save for three that had the sordid look of vultures. I took them to be newspapermen.

One of them wore a stained white shirt with garters on the sleeve. He carried a pencil and a folded square of paper in his hand, approaching me with liquor on his breath. "You heading up the trail, too, buster?"

"Thinking about it."

"It's a cake walk," the newspaperman said.

"The hell it is," interjected a nearby stampeder with slumped shoulders and tattered clothes. "Ask him how many times he's been to the peak and back."

Turning to the newspaper man, I fired a question at him. "How many trips have you made to White Pass and back?"

He mumbled something I didn't catch.

"Nine?" I asked.

"None," my slump-shouldered friend answered for him. "He and the others of his bastard breed sit on their asses here and mine information from us for their stories that draw more fools in search of our fortunes. These newspaper jackasses don't care to work for a living. All they want to do is ask questions and scribble their notes when they're not drinking their liquor." The fellow spat at the newsman's feet, spun around and marched off.

"Is that true?"

The writer stared at me glassy eyed, like he never answered questions on his own. Maybe he wasn't smart enough or sober enough to respond to queries. He raised his nose in the air. "I stand behind the First Amendment and freedom of the press!"

Uncertain what he was referring to, I asked him another question. "How many trips does it take a man to ferry his supplies over the pass?"

The newsman shrugged. "I don't know."

"More than thirty," I told him. "How many miles will those thirty trips cover?" I paused as he stared blankly at me. "Over twenty-five hundred miles," I informed him.

"I'll be damned," the newspaperman answered. "I never thought of that." He uncorked his bottle and took a swig of liquor, then wiped his sleeve across his mouth. "Back to protecting the First Amendment," he said, turning and walking away.

My slump-shouldered pal got up from the crate he was sitting on and came over, slapping me on the shoulder and scratching his whiskers. "They're the stupidest and laziest breed of man I ever saw, them newspapermen. Don't let what you read in any account fool you, friend. It's a tough climb, places where the trail's barely two feet wide, shards of rocks that are as sharp as razors, drops of a couple hundred feet along mountain rims. I wish I'd gone the Chilkoot route. It's a tougher climb, but it's miles shorter to Bennett Lake. I ain't trying to scare you off, but you can't believe that son of a bitch news dog because he's never hiked past Liarsville, much less with seventy-five pounds on his back."

I shook his hand. "Obliged for the information, fellow. I'll check out Chilkoot." Mounting Reid's horse, I turned him around and started back to Skagway, debating all the way whether or not the men paying to hear that great Shakespearean actor Roger Meredith read from the San Francisco newspapers knew most of what they heard was lies or fairy tales made up by vagabonds too lazy to climb the peaks and write about reality.

When I got back to town, it was supper time. I rode to my plot and found Meredith boiling a pot of coffee over a fire he'd started outside our tent. "Welcome home, prodigal son," he called. "You missed another fine reading by yours truly, this time of the *Call* of July 17th."

"Lies, lies, all of it lies," I answered as I dismounted.

"Indeed not, good sir, as my dramatic reading was perhaps the greatest of my career."

"Not your performance, but anything written by a newspaperman. Lies, lies, all of it."

"I must disagree, Jesse, as I have read in the very newspapers you blaspheme reviews of my performances that were truer than God's words."

Crossing my arms over my chest and cocking my head, I asked, "Were all your reviews good?"

Meredith shouted, "Lies, lies, lies, all of it lies!" He grinned. "Well, are you going to Dawson City by White Pass?"

"I'll check out the Chilkoot route."

" 'And if you rattle on about mountains'," my partner countered, " 'then let them throw millions of acres over us. It will be so high a peak that it scrapes against heaven and makes Mount Ossa look like a wart.' See? I can talk crazy as well as you." Meredith bent at the waist for his bow. "From *Hamlet*, Act Five, Scene One."

"You're insane. From the book of Jesse Murphy, Chapter One, Verse One."

Meredith rose and shoved his hand in his pants pocket, pulling out a wad of money. "More than two hundred dollars again today, Jesse. Here's where the gold is, not over a mountain high, nor across a lake frozen, nor through a forest primeval. It is here on the streets of Skagway where men are thirsty not only for liquor and women but also for entertainment that will bring a few minutes of joy and escape from their hard lives as packhorses over the mountains high and as miners of the icebound earth."

"I'll ride over to Dyea tomorrow and check out the Chilkoot trail," I announced.

"No you won't," came a voice from behind me.

I turned around to see Frank Reid approaching.

"Glad you're back, Jesse, because I need my horse. The ride to Dyea is too long and tiring for my horse. Your best bet is to take a boat that ferries men and goods between here and there. Chilkoot's a shorter trail, but the final ascent is twenty-seven hundred feet over the last two-and-a-half miles. And you make that climb thirty or more times, Jesse. Just getting your supplies and equipment from here to Dyea'll cost you a dollar a pound at least."

"I'll decide if it's worth it. There are too damn many newspaper reporters on the White Pass trail."

"Last I heard," Reid say, "there were only three at Liarsville."

"Like I was saying, too damn many."

"Be at the shore at dawn in the morning to catch the first boat you can. Once you land in Dyea, it's ten miles up the trail to reach a thousand-foot elevation. When you arrive at that point, you'll be able to see Chilkoot ahead of you. It's an imposing sight. The last two miles to the summit, you climb a grade I'd say was at least thirty percent, though I've never surveyed it. It'll take you a full day or better to climb the final thousand feet. You don't look as if you've got the grit for that two times, much less thirty."

Meredith stepped toward me. "There's easier money to be made in Skagway, Jesse, without all that climbing and pack-horsing. With my theater talents and your saloon experience, we can make our fortunes right here."

The gold bug had bitten me too strong not to explore the Dyea option, intimidating as it sounded. A life of ease once I made my fortune in gold offset the hardships of making that fortune in the first place. I liked the idea of sudden wealth rather than accumulating a gradual fortune through steady and profitable work.

"I must see for myself," I insisted.

Come dawn, I arose and dressed, my partner getting up with me and asking me to reconsider my trip to Dyea as he needed me to collect admissions for his next reading. Only after I visited Dyea would I gain confidence in my decision, I told him. Further, I let Roger know I held him accountable for our property in my absence, and he assured me that General Charlie was looking after things, including my money. My partner gave me six leftover biscuits from supper and knotted them in a kerchief for me to carry with me. I took the gift, stuffed it in my shirt, then snugged up my gun belt and strolled to the shore. There I found a boatman willing to take me and a dozen other passengers to Dyea.

We reached our destination mid-morning, and Dyea was even less inspiring than Skagway, a collection of tents by the dozens and seven or eight wooden structures, most owned by Tlingits, a band of Indians that lived along the southeastern Alaska coasts. The Tlingits were a hardy people, the men often hiring out to carry loads that would've staggered us stampeders. The shoreline outside Dyea was littered with stacks of supplies and equipment bound for Dawson City on the backs of men strong enough to navigate the trail. The more I looked at the piles of materials necessary to make the Klondike trek, the more I realized Frank Reid and Roger Meredith were right. There was easier money in Skagway saloons, selling drinks and recreation rather than trying to climb either the Chilkoot or White Pass trails.

Even so, I disembarked at Dyea as two steamers unloaded their passengers and freight onto smaller boats. I walked from the beach through the tent city north of town until I could see the Chilkoot Mountains in the distance, if not the summit. The tallest peak I saw loomed like a foreboding tombstone with my name written on it. I reversed course back through town to the shoreline where I killed time awaiting a boat to return me to Skagway. On the Dyea beach guarding his and his partners' gear, I met a young man named for a capital in Europe. It was Jack Paris or Jack Madrid or something like that, and he proclaimed he was a writer, but it looked to me he was more of a reader, resting on the tarp-covered provisions and devouring a copy of *The Origin of the Species*, a book I was unfamiliar with but one that fascinated Jack. Curly brown hair spilled out of his woolen cap as he looked up from his volume, gauging me with his gray eyes. We exchanged introductions and Jack felt obliged to explain himself.

"I'm guarding the gear for my partners and me while they arrange for the journey to Dawson City."

"Looking for gold are you?" I asked as my attention alternated between Jack and a caged dog that someone had left in the mudflats exposed by the receding tide.

"If I find it," he replied, "but mostly I'm after adventure, things I can write about and support myself."

"Another one of those that wants to make a living doing no work," I replied, "like the newspapermen at Liarsville."

"Liarsville?"

"North of Skagway where the news hounds write about the misfortunes of others."

"I'd report for a newspaper if they'd pay me."

"You should aspire to something higher, like town drunk," I suggested.

"I take it, Jesse, that you loathe writers."

"When they lie and steal, I do."

"Lie?"

"When I can't believe what I read in the newspapers, that's a lie."

"And stealing?"

"When they take the stories of others and write them as their own for profit."

"But if they didn't, who would, Jesse?"

I stuck my hand inside my shirt and pulled out the kerchief that held biscuits. "Care for one?" I offered, first grabbing the biggest one, then letting Jack choose his own. He closed his book, sat up on the edge of his gear and selected one. I returned the remaining biscuits to my top and stood beside Jack, nibbling on the manna with my attention bouncing from Jack to the caged dog a third of the way out on the mudflats.

"What's the story of that dog?" I asked Jack.

Swallowing a bite of biscuit, he looked at me as if I was crazy. "Don't know."

"He won't survive long if his owner doesn't return before high tide," I responded.

He shrugged, and we finished our biscuits, then visited for a half hour. While men scurried around us, guarding their gear or moving their supplies, no one went near the dog. Finally, I couldn't stand it, fearing his owner might not return before the tide reached him. "I'm gonna free that dog," I told Jack, who reclined on his mountain of provisions, picked up his book and resumed reading.

I marched out through the muck, the animal beginning to growl and snarl as I approached. He leaned back in his wooden cage and lunged forward, his nose poking between the slats.

"Easy, boy," I said. "I don't want you to drown." As I neared the slatted pen, I realized the dog was bigger up close than he appeared from afar. He had the pudginess of a St. Bernard, but he was no purebred, likely a mix with some herding collie. As I stepped up to the cage, he snapped at me. I put my hands on the corners of the crate and rocked it, then tried to lift it, letting it settle back in the mud, estimating the enclosure and dog weighed a hundred and fifty or more pounds. Studying the shoreline, I spotted no one concerned about the dog or heading toward me. I had a moment of doubt, whether I should rescue him or leave him for his owner to save or bury. Though I wanted to free him, I could not guarantee by his disposition that he wouldn't attack me. I decided if I saved the dog and no one showed up, I would take him to Skagway where he would be a better guard than General Charlie.

"Easy, boy," I repeated, sticking my hand inside my shirt and pulling out the kerchief with the remaining biscuits. I unknotted the fabric and picked out the smallest biscuit, deciding to minimize my losses if he tried to bite me. Bending, I slipped the food between slats in the cage. The canine snatched it away, devouring it greedily. I offered him a second biscuit. He yanked it from between my fingers so fast that I checked ensure all my digits remained.

For a moment I considered whether or not taking a dog in Alaska was as serious a crime as stealing a horse or steer in Texas. I decided not, since Alaskans likely had more sense than the average Texan. But before I unlatched the cage, I vowed to buy the dog, leaving a dollar wedged in the door if he didn't attack me. I tucked the two remaining biscuits back in my shirt and took a breath as I unlatched the gate and slowly lowered it. The dog burst out and bolted ten feet from me before turning around and staring. Uncertain if he planned to attack, I extracted another biscuit from my shirt and dropped it to the ground at my feet. The enormous dog approached warily, watching me, then dropping his head and grabbing the biscuit. I leaned down enough to stroke his ears. "Easy, boy," I said.

When he finished the biscuit, he raised his head and wagged his tail. I petted him a minute and rubbed his fur, then bent and lifted the cage gate, holding it with my knee while I fished a dollar out of my money belt. I put the dollar at the corner of the cage and clamped it in place when I latched the door. Taking my final biscuit and extending my hand, I offered it to my new watchdog. He leaned forward and took it gently from me. As I marched back to Jack, I pondered what to call my dog, uncertain of an appropriate name. Since my new friend was a writer, I figured I'd ask his help in christening my canine.

As I approached the gear where Jack rested, the youth closed his book and sat up, shaking his head from side to side. "You not only saved the dog, you stole him, Jesse."

"No, sir, buster," I answered. "I left a dollar for his owner, but I need a name for him."

"Why don't you call him Jack in my honor?"

"I'm not sure you're honorable, Jack."

He grinned. "At least I didn't steal a dog."

"I told you I paid a buck for him," I defended myself, then paused. "That's it. I'll call him 'Buck' and you can write a story about him."

Jack nodded. "Buck? I like it. Only two letters off from Jack." He put his book down and scratched his chin. "Develop a tale about a dog?" he asked himself. "I like that idea, Jesse."

"I intend to do actual work, Jack, not just push a pencil across paper."

"Mind if I call my dog 'Buck,' too?"

"Why not? That would honor my dog. Of course, my Buck is real."

Jack laughed, "But my Buck will outlive yours when I finish my story. This'll give me something to chronicle on the way to Dawson City, make notes on the dogs I encounter."

I spent another hour conversing with Jack, talking him out of a twelve-foot strand of cord so I could make a leash for Buck. Around supper time a Tlingit rowed his canoe up to the edge of the water, which had reached the spot where Buck's cage had been abandoned. The slatted crate floated on the waves. I said goodbye to Jack and never saw him again, then walked to the canoe and negotiated with the fellow to carry me and Buck back to

Skagway. We agreed on the price of three dollars for the both of us, but he started to check if any other men on the beach wanted to go to Skagway, but I caught his arm and told him I'd pay six dollars if he just took me and my dog alone. He nodded, and I gave him an extra three dollars.

After that, I lifted Buck up and carried him to the canoe, easing him into place. Then I helped our guide slide the vessel back into the inlet, and we returned to Skagway, arriving about dark. Getting out of the canoe, I carried Buck to dry land, tied the cord around his neck so I wouldn't lose him in the hubbub along the shore as another steamer offloaded men and supplies onto the beach, even in the darkness. I walked down Broadway to our property and surprised Meredith with my premature return.

"I didn't expect you back today," Roger said. "Does this mean you're giving up the trip to Dawson City?"

"It does."

"So we're partners?"

"We are."

He pointed to my dog. "Who's your new friend?"

"Buck. We can use him to guard camp when you're doing your performances."

"Another day of readings and it'll be a good start on paying to construct our building. I've talked to Frank Reid about getting workers to build our saloon and opera house. We've got to move quickly to get it built while there's still lumber and carpenters to do the work."

As of that moment, Roger Meredith and I had a partnership that we knew would make us wealthy. And although I didn't know it that first night, I had acquired a dog that could talk!

Chapter Seventeen

I rested well that night knowing I'd not be climbing the White Pass trail or the Chilkoot route thirty or more times just for the opportunity to crawl another five hundred miles in winter to Dawson City for an even slimmer chance of finding enough gold to put me up in the Palace Hotel for the rest of my life. I prayed Dayle Lymoine didn't catch up with me and reclaim my Wells Fargo windfall and the fortune it promised to generate from my partnership with Roger Meredith, who slept across from me on his bedroll, while Buck stood guard outside our tent.

About sunrise, I detected this voice coming from somewhere indistinct. It was low at first, and I was emerging from a deep slumber. Gradually, I came to my senses enough to understand the message. "I'm hungry. Feed me." I turned over on my bedding with my back to Meredith, who was drawing irregular breaths. "I'm hungry. Feed me," the voice repeated five times until I'd had enough. "Get your own damn breakfast, Roger."

My partner snorted and pulled the covers higher with me believing I'd put an end to his annoying request so early in the morning.

Moments later the muffled voice called again. "I'm hungry. Feed me."

"Leave me alone, Roger," I ordered.

"I'm Buck, not Roger."

I sat up from my covers, tugging at my ears. "What the hell?"

"I'm Buck. I'm hungry. Feed me."

I threw back the bedding and crawled on my hands and knees to the tent flap, untied it and stuck my head out. There sat Buck on his hind legs, staring at me. He leaned forward and licked my cheek.

"Did you say something, Buck?"

He ignored the question, slobbering on my jaw.

"Okay, okay. I'll fetch breakfast, Buck. Give me time to dress." I retreated to my bedroll. As I arose, Buck spoke again.

"Thank you, Jesse. I'm hungry."

I grabbed my shirt and shoved an arm in a sleeve as I slipped over to my partner, who hid under his covers. "Roger," I whispered, toeing him with my sock.

He rolled over in bed and shoved himself up. "What is it?"

"You won't believe this, but Buck can talk."

My partner shook his head and groaned. "You woke me to tell me that? That's the dumbest thing you've ever said, your dog talking. What have you been drinking?"

"I swear it's true, Roger. He told me he was hungry and to feed him. Even called me Jesse. I couldn't believe it either."

"You must've been dreaming, Jesse."

"It may sound crazy, Roger, but I'm telling you the truth. Perhaps we can get him to read the newspapers and earn us even more money."

"Hell, Jesse, feed him and leave me be. I've another reading this afternoon and want to rest." He grabbed the covers and yanked them over his head.

I finished buttoning my shirt and as I was putting on my pants, the muffled voice came again. "Hurry, Jesse. I'm hungry."

"Did you hear that, Roger? Buck was talking to me"

"You're crazy," he cried. "Now leave me be."

I tugged on my britches, pulled on my boots and fastened my gun belt around my waist. I barged past the tent flaps and headed out to converse with Buck, leaving the flaps open to annoy Roger since he didn't believe the dog was talking to me. Uncertain what to feed Buck, I led him to the shoreline where he found dead salmon marooned on the mud flats when the tide receded.

"Okay, Buck," I said as we strolled along the beach, "let's talk, tell me where you learned to speak English." He never answered, likely mad that I had waited so long to take him out for breakfast or too intent on finding food to respond to my silly questions. "You ever thought about acting on stage, Buck? My partner is an actor. Him and a talking dog could make us rich." Buck ignored me, even when his stomach was full, and we were returning to our lot.

When I got back to the tent, I left Buck outside and ducked inside to find Roger shaving over a mirror and washbasin. He ignored me, so I figured he was still mad that I awoke him. Finishing his shave, he grabbed a towel and swathed his face in it as he stepped to the entry.

That's when Buck spoke again. "Thanks for breakfast, Jesse."

I leaped toward Roger and yanked the cloth from his face. "Did you catch that?"

"What, Jesse?"

"Buck, that's what. He thanked me for breakfast."

"Have you gone mad, Jesse Murphy? You're telling me your dog can talk, is that right?"

"He did, Roger. I swear I'm not crazy."

"I didn't hear a thing."

"You must be deaf, Roger." I marched out to my dog, grabbing him by the ear and tugging him toward my partner. "Talk to him, Buck. Tell Roger I'm sane."

My dog looked up at me, then at Roger, but stood wordlessly between us.

"Yeah, Buck, say something," Roger implored him.

My big dog silently wagged his tail as I patted his head.

"I'll make it easy on you, Buck," Roger continued. "What surrounds a tree trunk? Can you say 'bark'?"

Content and panting, Buck lowered himself to his haunches.

"How about this, Buck?" my partner went on. "What covers the top of a house?"

Buck sat there.

"Can you say 'woof,' Buck?" Roger asked.

By not answering the question, Buck proved Roger's point. Maybe I was loony, but I knew my dog spoke.

"Okay, Jesse," my partner concluded. "Whatever you heard, it wasn't Buck talking, okay?"

I shrugged.

"Promise me you won't disclose your dog talks, and I'll vow not to tell folks you're crazy. We need each other to realize our fortunes here. Are you fine with that, partner?"

"I'm not crazy," I insisted.

"I know that, Jesse, but I don't want anyone thinking you are. That'd kill business, and we stand to make a fortune, providing liquid refreshment and entertainment for the stampeders. Will you agree with that?"

I nodded, and we shook hands, our partnership secure, though Roger doubted my sanity, and I questioned his hearing. While we didn't bring up the topic again for several days even though Buck kept speaking to me in the morning or in the evening, always when Roger was around, though my partner made no sign of hearing the dog's English, Buck's vocabulary much greater than "bark" and "woof." I let it slide as construction began on our building a week after I returned from Dyea. The biggest dispute was what to call our business.

"I like the Stubborn Mule Saloon and Grand Opera House," I suggested.

"Stubborn Mule?"

"It was the name of my first saloon in Tombstone," I answered.

"Not classy enough. The name must attract a crowd."

"How about the Talking Dog Saloon and Grand Opera House? That'll attract a crowd."

"Of crazy people," Meredith replied.

"You come up with a name."

"What about the Gold Nugget Saloon and Opera House?" he suggested.

"Our customers can't spell 'nugget.' We need something simpler?"

"Gold Dust Saloon and Opera House?"

For a moment I mulled it over and decided that was a better tag than most. "I'll ask Buck if he likes it first," I responded.

"Fine, let's go see," Roger said, as we stepped out of our tent.

"Here, Buck," I called, and he ran over between us for me to pet his head.

"Now ask him."

"For our saloon—"

"And opera house," Roger interrupted.

"—and opera house, do you like the name Gold Dust Saloon and Opera House?"

Then in that unmistakable rasp, Buck answered, "Feed me. I'm hungry."

I glanced at my partner. "Did you hear that?"

Meredith nodded.

"Gold Dust is a wonderful name," Buck answered again.

Delighted that my partner had at last heard my dog, I grinned. "How do you explain that, Roger?"

"Ventriloquism!" he announced, crossing his arms over his chest and grinning.

"Ven what?"

"Ventriloquism, where you talk without moving your lips."

I slapped my palm against my forehead. "Not only can Buck talk, but he can do so without moving his lips. What a dog!"

Meredith slammed his hand against *his* forehead. "Not the dog, Jesse, but me. I'm the ventriloquist." He squeezed his lips together and looked me straight in the eyes. "Feed me. I'm hungry," he said without so much as a quiver from his lips or cheeks.

"So it was you speaking?"

He nodded. "Just funning you."

"I could've sworn Buck was talking."

Roger grinned. "I can imitate voices, too. It's something you pick up when you're an actor. It comes in handy on stage in the footlights."

"Promise me one thing. You won't ever fool me with your voice again."

Meredith slapped me on the back. "Agreed, Jesse Murphy, as long as you promise no secrets between us."

I nodded, deciding that me being H.H. Lomax instead of Jesse Murphy didn't count as a secret as I'd been Murphy ever since we met. "We're in this together."

Our partnership blossomed in the coming weeks as we supervised construction of our saloon and opera house, seldom leaving our property except to buy supplies or give a dramatic newspaper reading, though attendance tapered off and we had to reduce admission to fifty cents and later to two bits, especially after Skagway claimed its first newspapers and had boys peddling the broadsheets on the streets. My partner managed our affairs well and signed the building contracts, placing orders for the bar, backbar, gambling equipment, tables, and chairs for the saloon and for the benches, curtains, backdrops, and lighting for the stage. He contracted for a regular supply of whiskey and beer and got the supplier to throw in the mugs and glasses free.

I supervised the construction, working with Frank Reid, who recommended the best carpenters and laborers in town, and I paid the bills from my Wells Fargo inheritance. Reid desired to help Skagway thrive into a community that outlived the boom of the gold rush. Ours was not the only building going up. Dozens more took shape and rose along the streets Reid had plotted. The sound of hammers and saws, curses, and shouts echoed through Skagway as men erected structures, cut trees, dug up stumps, drove pilings for wharfs and graded roads as August gave way to September and the following months. The days shortened and the air chilled as fall fell over Skagway with frigid rains, sleet and snow. Even so, work continued. Ships from the states docked at two wharves, with two more being built and unloaded tons of goods and supplies plus stampeders who had gotten a late start, but carried the same dream as their predecessors of striking it rich along the Yukon.

The Gold Dust took shape on the northeast corner of Sixth and Broadway, thanks to my partner who met ships at the docks, bargaining for loads of lumber, shingles, and hardware to build our drinking and drama emporium. His haggling even secured us the first piano to arrive in Skagway, though it was useless until we found someone to play it. Gradually, our dream came together despite the frigid weather, the limited daylight, and the rain, sleet and later snow that turned the streets into a quagmire of mud, ice, and despair, especially for those living in a tent. By the time the conditions turned on us with precipitation, our saloon and opera house had a roof, and we abandoned our canvas shelter for our unfinished building. I had expected to sell my mining hardware at a handsome profit to ill-equipped latecomers, but the prices fell as many others had inspected the routes to the Klondike and had given up on making the trek, deciding to exchange their equipment for return fare to the states. Prices dropped so much that what had cost $10 in San Francisco or Seattle was going for $5 or less in Skagway. One outfit that had paid $27 dollars apiece for two canoes in Seattle sold them both for $3.50 in Skagway after realizing they must tote the boats up Chilkoot or White Pass. Men that had brought horses and mules to Skagway found the pack animals a liability because the owners had to purchase hay and oats for them. While the horses and mules carried heavier loads than the men, they also had to carry the fodder necessary for their survival. Some men were so crazed by the possibility of gold that they ignored their starved draft animals and worked them until they played out, a segment of the White Pass trail becoming known as Dead Horse Gulch. Argonauts who made the trip up and down White Pass swore that some horses committed suicide by jumping off cliffs to avoid the abuse and starvation. Not only did numerous pack animals die, but also many men. The more I saw, the gladder I grew that we stood poised to make our fortunes with drinks and drama in a warm Skagway building.

With our two lots, we had a hundred-foot frontage on both streets and opted to have our entrance on Broadway as that sounded to the actor more fitting than Sixth, though it meant our alley was on the side rather than at the back of our building. The two-story structure took up four-fifths of our lot, leaving space along the alley for deliveries, and a small shed for horses if we ever purchased any. My saloon occupied the south side of our building with a second floor overhead where my partner and I built a bedroom apiece. At the end of the bar we included a small room where we put our wood stove to cook our meals and a table where we could eat or manage our ledger books. Beyond it we added a storeroom for our supplies of liquor and other needs. The theater occupied the north half of our edifice, two stories high, with three boxes accessible from the saloon stairs. The boxes overlooked the stage at the east end of the room. We even installed sliding partitions that could close off the saloon from the theater for those instances when a traveling preacher might want to shut out the drinking and rail against the sin that was taking place on the other side of the temporary barrier. Roger Meredith was full of ideas as his theatrical dream took shape.

Once the stage and dressing rooms were finished, Roger and I carried his trunks backstage and unpacked them. He had dozens of costumes and props, everything from fancy wigs and beards to swords and flintlock pistols. He arranged copies of scripts and books on a shelf, picking up one and talking to it. "So there you are," he said. "I've been wondering what happened to you." He held up the book for me to examine. I had seen the author's name somewhere before, but forgot where.

"This is *Descent of Man and Selection in Relation to Sex*, published in 1871 by Charles Darwin. You know about him? He wrote *On the Origin of Species*."

The title intrigued me, even if I didn't understand it. "I recall a young fellow I met in Dyea reading that *Origin* book."

"He was a smart man if he was."

"Jack Madrid or Paris or something similar was his name. He was there when I rescued Buck. Said he might write a dog story one day."

Meredith patted the book. "Darwin explores the species, dogs, men, cats and monkeys."

"What about the sex part?" I asked.

"It's not what you think, Jesse."

"It never is," I replied.

"You should read it. You might learn about the evolution of men and women and their roles in society."

"I was more intrigued by the sex part, but it sounds like Darwin pulled the fun out of it. Am I right?"

Meredith shrugged. "Let me read you a passage from Part Two, see if you'd be interested." He flipped through the book, coming to a page he had bent the corner and marked with a pencil. " 'The chief distinction in the intellectual powers of the two sexes is shown by man's attaining to a higher eminence, in whatever he takes up, than can woman—whether requiring deep thought, reason, or imagination, or merely the use of the senses and hands. If two lists were made of the most eminent men and women in poetry, painting, sculpture, music (inclusive both of composition and performance), history, science, and philosophy, with half-a-dozen names under each subject, the two lists would not bear comparison. We may also infer … that if men are capable of a decided pre-eminence over women in many subjects, the average of mental power in man must be above that of woman'." He looked up from his book at me. "What do you think, Jesse?"

I swallowed hard. "I'm glad Miss Susan B. Anthony isn't here. She'd wallop you up beside the head and I'd be looking for a new partner before she was through."

"Those suffragists don't know what they're talking about. This is Darwin writing, one of the intellectual greats of our century. Darwin wrote that when men chose tools and weapons from the beginning of history while women opted for family and home, the fellows made themselves superior to women."

"Nobody's superior to Miss Susan B. Anthony, in her mind at least," I replied.

"How come you know so much about Susan B. Anthony? Do you wear bloomers?"

"I dined with her years ago in Colorado when she was making stump speeches promoting the vote for women. She gave a powerful speech, but never smiled once."

Meredith closed his book and placed it on the shelf with his scripts. Turning to face me, he scratched his chin. "I'd never suspected you of being friends with Susan B. Anthony."

"Can't say for sure she had any friends, her disposition

being sour and political, but she could give a speech. She might've converted me if she'd ever smiled, but she was tart as a boxcar full of lemons." Then I had a question for my partner. "Will you be hiring any women to perform in your plays?"

"I will," he replied and grinned. "Unless you'll let me put you in dress, wig, and rouge, assuming you can act and don't mind kissing a fellow actor when the script calls for it."

I almost spit out my teeth. "I'd rather kiss Miss Susan B. Anthony than you."

"We'll hire actresses."

"Now by actresses, do you mean women who perform on a stage or on a mattress?"

"Both," he replied.

"We're not building rooms for any mattress matrimony," I said.

"Precisely," Meredith answered. "We don't want our establishment's reputation tarnished by bed-bouncing. The actresses can solicit on our premises, but must do their calico cavorting at their own places. At the Gold Dust we'll offer liquor and clothed entertainment. If actresses want to do business here, they can as long as they sell drinks for us. When a fellow buys drinks, we give him whiskey and her colored water. She gets twenty-five percent of the price and we keep the rest. Are you agreed?"

I nodded. It sounded like the best option as I had previously worked in brothels. If you ran a decent house, the laundry bill alone ate your profits.

As we left the dressing room and emerged onto the stage to the ovation of pounding hammers, grinding saws and grumbling carpenters, Meredith stopped center stage and looked around. "We'll be ready to open in another week. I must confirm our liquor supplies will arrive in time, find a piano player for the grand opening and hire more thespians."

"You mean actresses?"

"And actors, Jesse. I cannot carry a whole play alone, though opening night I will merely give a free reading of the latest newspaper we can get from the states and finish with dramatic interpretations of the bard's greatest soliloquies."

"As long as we have liquor and a piano player, you can't miss."

Over the next few days, I watched the finishing touches go on the Gold Dust, including the painted sign identifying our venture over the Broadway entrance and the temporary sign in the front window announcing: OPENING SOON. In my spare time, I took Buck for a walk, keeping him on a leash so he wouldn't splash mud on pedestrians in his exuberance. I had canvas socks made to slip over his paws, so he could walk in the muck without dirtying his feet and tracking mud back in our place when we returned. Buck wore his footwear proudly and never resisted when I put them on or off.

My aim in those walks was to check out the competition. Seventh Street to the north between State and Broadway had shaped up as the red-light district, though other saloons and dance halls had rooms upstairs for the illicit activities. Our greatest and closest competition came from Clancy's Saloon and Music Hall and the Red Onion, whose owners periodically peeked in our front windows to gauge our progress. I occasionally visited Clancy's on the southwest corner of State and Seventh Street or the Red Onion and buy a jigger of watered-down whiskey while I studied their business. One day in Clancy's, I noticed the owner Frank Clancy pointing me out to a tall gentleman wearing a dark hat, thick long coat and heavy boots. The fellow with a handlebar mustache and narrow, black eyes inspected me and nodded to Clancy as he tipped a glass of whiskey. I thought nothing of it at the time, finishing my drink and heading back to the Gold Dust.

Three days later as I stocked the back bar with bottles of whiskey and the carpenters cleaned up for the grand opening, Buck trotted around the counter and snarled. His growl confused me as he was accustomed to the workmen, so I turned and spotted the fellow from Clancy's Saloon. The man shut the door and started toward the bar and me.

"We're not open yet," I informed him. "Day after tomorrow'll be the grand opening. Come back then."

He shook his head. "That don't matter," he said, striding toward me with a smug grin.

"I'm not serving you any whiskey," I advised my uninvited guest.

"You're not serving anybody any whiskey today, tomorrow, the next day, or any day after that," he said, unbuttoning his winter overcoat.

"And why's that?"

"It's against the law."

"What's against the law?"

"Bringing liquor into the district."

"There's a dozen or more saloons in town. I've drunk whiskey at Clancy's and the Red Onion."

He nodded. "I saw you in Clancy's the other day." He pulled back the lapel on his coat, showing me the badge of a deputy U.S. marshal. "It's against the law to bring liquor into Alaska Territory so the Gold Dust Saloon and Grand Opera House is closed before it ever opens."

Chapter Eighteen

I stood stunned, not believing what I was hearing. "Roger," I shouted. "We've got a problem." Buck growled at the visitor until I called his name and pointed to the end of the bar.

Meredith poked his head out from the stage. "What's the matter?"

"We're being closed."

"We haven't even opened yet. By who?"

"By the law."

Meredith walked down the stage steps. "I didn't know there was law in Skagway."

The lawman stepped toward my partner. "I'm Deputy U.S. Marshal Sylvester Taylor of the Sitka District. My authority is split between Skagway and Dyea. Don't even have an office here. Operate out of my hotel room in the Occidental."

Approaching the lawman, the thespian extended his hand. "Glad to meet you, deputy. I'm Roger Meredith and Jesse Murphy's my partner."

"I know who you both are," Taylor replied.

My dog growled again. "Hush," I ordered Buck, though I agreed with his sentiment.

Releasing Taylor's fingers, Meredith gave a wide sweep of his arm toward the stage. "Now tell me, deputy, what's at issue here preventing us from opening this grand emporium?"

"Liquor," the lawman replied. "You can't bring it into Alaska."

Meredith rubbed his chin. "Maybe I heard that on the boat up from San Francisco, but remind me why liquor's illegal."

"We don't want it falling into the hands of the Indians, the Tlingits, and other natives to these parts of Alaska."

My partner nodded. "A noble goal, deputy, but why is it I see other Skagway establishments serving whiskey, beer and even wine?"

Taylor gazed at the workers, then at Roger. "Can we visit in private?"

"Absolutely, sir." Meredith pointed to our office. "Why don't we step inside?"

We headed to the entry, Buck growling as we passed and Taylor kicking at him with his muddy boot, slinging specks of muck on the bar, but missing my dog. As we entered the office, Taylor marched to the door on the opposite wall and looked into the storeroom, nodding and turning around to the table and taking a seat without being invited to sit.

"From the looks of your supplies, you've invested in a lot in illicit liquor," the lawman noted, "but we can work out an agreement, gentlemen."

Meredith nodded, "We're law-abiding citizens trying to meet the needs of the stampeders, entertain them before they fight the elements all the way to the Klondike. What, pray tell, must we do, deputy, to stay within your law?"

Taylor smiled, tapping his trigger finger on our table. "Promise not to sell liquor to any Indian that enters your place."

"Why, deputy, we are more than willing to go along with such a request for such a noble goal. We would never want to start an innocent Indian on the road to drunkenness, when we can fully devote our efforts to so many white men. So, you have our solid promise that we will not sell liquor in any form to the Indians. Would you like me to put that into writing for you?"

"Not necessary, Roger," he answered, still tapping his finger on the table. "But there's just one more thing."

Meredith smiled. "Of course, deputy, there always is."

"You and Jesse must pay me twelve dollars a week to

look the other way."

"Would you like to put that in writing, marshal?" I asked.

Both Taylor and Meredith glared at me.

"Forgive him, deputy," Roger apologized. "Jesse's attempts at humor often fall flat."

The lawman grunted at me. "The law's serious business."

I wasn't sure if extortion was the law, but it was costly commerce. I shrugged and smiled, "A joke?"

"Why, deputy," Roger continued, "I can't tell you how delighted we are that you'll have an interest in the Gold Dust. We'll both rest easier knowing you'll protect us from the criminals that always try to take advantage of an honest endeavor like ours."

I wished I'd had a newspaper to puke in as he was sickening me with his fawning over this crooked lawman.

"Glad you see the benefits, Roger."

Meredith smiled. "And let us give you payment in advance, deputy, assuming you understand that this covers the first week we open. We owe you nothing until a week after that date."

"I can live with that," the deputy replied. "Payment due every seven days."

"Splendid," my partner replied. "Now Jesse, pay the gentleman."

Shaking my head, I dug into my pocket and pulled out my roll of money, counting out twelve dollars for the marshal. I offered the bills to Taylor, who grabbed and counted them to confirm I hadn't shorted him.

"Now we'd like a receipt," Roger said.

Both men laughed as they shook hands."

"Wait a minute," I said. "What's so funny? You asking for a receipt is no different than me suggesting we put it in writing, Roger."

"It's in the delivery, Jesse, something a thespian can finesse that mere mortals can't."

I could only shake my head, never before realizing that actors thought themselves above the rest of us.

"Yeah," Taylor said. "Roger was funny. You were insulting."

Meredith slapped the lawman on the back as he arose.

"Let's celebrate with a drink, deputy. You'll be our first customer, though we'll be picking up the tab any time you need to wet your whistle." My partner put his arm around the deputy's shoulder, and they marched out of the office like long-lost brothers. "Fix our new friend a jigger of premium whiskey, Jesse, will you?"

For an instant, I stood stunned, my only joy being in Buck growling at Taylor as he passed. I followed them, slipping behind the bar while they stood in front.

"Give him our best liquor," Roger commanded.

Gritting my teeth, I remained steaming mad at Meredith's sudden friendship with the corrupt lawman. I took a jigger from the stack I had so carefully spent my morning arranging, held it up to the lamp light and grabbed a towel from the counter, and wiped the glass of any smudge. As I lowered it, I tossed the cloth on the back bar and screened the glass from our patron. I spat in the jigger and set it aside, grabbing a bottle of our most expensive liquor, uncorking it and pouring the amber liquid into the glass. To stir the whiskey and my spittle, I stuck in and retrieved my finger from my nose, then swirled it around in the concoction before turning and offering it to Taylor. He downed the whiskey and let out a long breath.

"That's quality stuff," he said. "Better than Clancy's liquor."

Roger grinned. "Only the best for our newfound friend," he said, slapping him on the back again.

"Care for another?" I asked. "I have a nose for good liquor."

"Absolutely," the deputy answered, slamming the jigger on the counter.

"Deputy," Roger said, turning his back away from the bar. "Let me show you around the place."

"Don't have time for a tour, Roger, but show me what you're proudest of while Jesse pours me another drink." Taylor turned his back to me, and my partner pointed out the only piano in Skagway, the largest stage in town and plenty of room for gambling, dancing, theatrical performances.

As he looked across the room, I spat in his glass and slid my finger in my nose, poured his liquor and stirred the drink. Roger glanced over his shoulder and chuckled when he saw what I was doing. "Here's your whiskey, deputy, with my special touch."

Taylor twisted about and downed the jigger. "I'm gonna enjoy our partnership, fellows."

"And I'm delighted to serve you, deputy."

"Return for our grand opening," Roger said. "I'll see Jesse gives you special treatment on your drinks."

"I'll be back," Taylor said, turning and marching out the exit, Buck growling in his wake.

The moment the door closed, Roger turned to me. "I saw what you did to that son-of-a-bitch's drink. Keep it up every chance you get."

I sighed. "I thought you'd taken to him like a boy to a puppy."

"Can't stand the bastard, him extorting us. The difference is, I'm a better actor than you!"

At that point I gained more respect for my partner. That admiration grew the night before our opening, when we boosted ourselves up onto the bar, poured us a jigger of our best liquor and looked over the saloon and stage, hoping they teemed with customers the next evening. While our piano player practiced on the ivories, we talked about our plans, what Roger called his philosophy of business.

"I don't know how you ran your Tombstone saloon, the Stubborn Jackass, wasn't it?"

"Mule," I corrected.

"We can either play it straight or crooked. Straight's always best for return customers. We don't cheat them, and they come back for more drinks and shows. Boomtowns always go bust. Since you're running the saloon, did you ever cut your liquor in Tombstone?"

"Maybe a little," I admitted.

"How little?" my partner asked.

"A lot."

"How often?"

"All the time."

"What did you cut it with? Water?"

I twisted my head from side to side. "Water was scarce in Tombstone, though I occasionally used it when I could afford it, but mostly turpentine, vinegar, a little coal oil, rattlesnake venom, trough water when no one was looking, things like that."

Roger answered with a sigh of relief. "I'm glad you didn't say horse piss."

I sighed.

"Don't tell me you did, Jesse."

"Never once did I cut my liquor with horse pee," I replied, "though I did leave buckets of such at the back doors of competing saloons to start rumors. It's amazing the number of stories a single bucket of horse urine behind a competitor's place can spawn."

"I don't want any of that in Skagway, Jesse, not a bit. Our customers get straight whiskey or beer so they're served what they bought. And no spitting in drinks or mixing it with your nose-picking finger, except for one patron, Deputy Marshal Sylvester Taylor. Since he's expecting free drinks, do whatever you want."

"What about the girls' drinks?"

"They get tea or colored water, but they know it up front. And we don't stiff them on their cut per drink. We'll build our reputation on fair dealings. There's enough crooked dealing in Skagway as is."

I nodded. "Lot of men scared away from Chilkoot and White Pass are trying to survive. You and I both know they're always looking for easy marks."

"Right now it's just thieves, conmen, and bunco artists, but those things lead to killing and lawlessness. Fact is, I hear some of the more decent businessmen about town are meeting tomorrow night to organize and fight the corruption."

"That'll be hard when the law is crooked," I replied.

"Yes, sir, and I want to keep Buck in and around the saloon. I noticed how he growled at Deputy Taylor. He saw Taylor for the crook he was from the beginning."

"Yep, Buck is an excellent judge of a man's character." I poured us a second drink.

"I don't know what to expect for business tomorrow or

if we've got enough help. You and another bartender may cover it, but we could need more, depending on our hours."

"I've hired a faro dealer and a poker dealer, and I'll tell them to play straight and how we share the splits," I announced.

"Your three plus my piano player and my assistant will give us five workers. If it goes well, we'll have to hire more plus players for stage productions."

"What about saloon girls?"

"We'll visit with them when they come in. Explain how we'll split their drink purchases and allow them to dance for a fee. They'll have to go to their cribs for any bedspring waltzes. One thing I'm worried about is my newspaper reading. The new paper's already cut into my attendance and profit."

When we finished the conversation, we shook hands and slid off the bar, telling the piano player we were closing. He left us, and we locked up the Gold Dust for the last time before it opened for business. We climbed the stairs, Buck following me into my room. I had a restless night, uncertain what to expect for our grand opening.

Come morning, I arose after a fitful night's sleep and took Buck in his canvas stockings outside into the chilly breeze and visited the outhouse we had built in the corner of our property along the alley. We stepped back to the front of the building and marched down the plank boardwalk, me looking at the community that was waking up for a new day. Though it had been ten weeks since my arrival, I couldn't believe how Skagway had grown, more than a hundred buildings dotting the town site along with twice that many tents scattered among the muddy streets, stumps, and occasional trees still standing. Though we were far from the states, the four completed wharves now handled huge loads of freight and passengers daily as latecomers arrived with gold on their mind.

I took Buck back in and put firewood in the stove in the saloon half of the room, starting a blaze to help cut the chill. Come evening, if the place filled up, the body heat would keep everyone warm. If not, we might go broke supplying the stoves with wood throughout the winter. As opening time neared, I returned to my room, put on a fresh pair of trousers and a starched white shirt I'd bought at one of the mercantiles for the occasion. I strapped on my gun belt to be on the safe side. My partner joined me in the costume of a medieval nobleman, a touch he had never used for his previous readings. Our piano player, bartender, and card dealers arrived at noon to help us make final preparations. As we scurried to finish our last chores, we noticed men lining up outside the window.

"That's a good sign," Roger observed.

I looked at the customers and responded. "Deputy Taylor's in the line."

"That's bad news. I wonder what that skunk wants."

"A free drink," I replied.

"Give him the Jesse Murphy special, will you?"

I nodded. "With pleasure."

By one o'clock the column extended to the end of the block so we opened the door and welcomed our first customers as the piano player banged out a new style of music called "Ragtime" that was said to be the rage back in the states. My partner greeted everyone and announced he would read in half an hour from the Sunday, October 10th edition of the *San Francisco Chronicle*.

Deputy Marshal Taylor barreled toward the bar and demanded a drink of our hired bartender. I waved him aside. "I'll handle this for the deputy. Nothing's too good for our fine lawman."

"That's decent of you, Jesse, but I must confirm you're not serving any Indians. I'd hate to close you down."

"That would disappoint me too, deputy, especially since we have invested so much in opening this place up." Turning my back on the lawman, I made up his special drink and sat it on the bar in front of him. "Enjoy. Let me know when you need another."

Taylor downed the concoction and smacked his lips. "You pour a fine whiskey, Jesse, for such a dumb bartender."

"Why, thank you marshal. Your confidence warms me all the way from my toes to my nose. And knowing you are protecting our fine community from corruption and the lawless gives me great faith in the future of Skagway."

"Just doing my duty," Taylor responded. "Now give me another drink, another of your Jesse specials."

"My pleasure," I replied and made him four more drinks before he left the bar to wander among the saloon's growing and noisy crowd as my partner began his dramatic reading from the *San Francisco Chronicle*.

Roger started with a report of rising tensions between the United States and Spain. "All social intercourse between the American minister at Madrid and the Spanish officials and the diplomatic corps have been suspended for more than a year," Roger intoned, looking silly on stage reading the news dressed like a medieval nobleman. He next proclaimed the headlines of another *Chronicle* story, "Streams lined with pure gold; the wonderful richness of Klondike creeks; winter yield placed at twenty millions." The hopeful millionaires cheered the report, until Roger read another headline, "Food very short in Dawson City." The crowed hissed and booed the announcement. I liked the idea of gold-lined streams, though the report was likely pure bunk from the imagination of one of the lazy newspapermen at Liarsville, but the food shortage sounded serious since it was only October and the full brunt of the winter was still to fall on the Yukon Territory.

Roger read a headline that brought the chatter and celebration to a standstill. "Going to the Klondike," Roger proclaimed, "to end his life." The noise fell and everyone looked to the stage, even Buck, who was wandering among the customers. My thespian partner gave a few more details from a sub-headline, "The member of an alleged Hawaiian suicide club who drew the fatal card." Roger paused to study his audience, then continued. "Hawaii has a suicide club, says a Honolulu paper brought by the steamer *Miowera* today. It is situated in Hilo, and there are thirteen members, some of whom live In Honolulu. All the names are known but withheld by the press. The club meets once a year at Hilo. Not a member is over twenty-five years old, and all are of the fast set.

"On the thirteenth day of the month thirteen months after their last meeting they assemble to decide who shall be the next. Thirteen ballots are placed in a hat numbered from one to thirteen. The poor fool who draws number thirteen is doomed. A drawing has just taken place, and a popular young Hilo blood, well known in Honolulu and recently visiting there was condemned to die by drawing the fatal thirteenth ballot. He became so distraught over the horror of the situation that he has told the story to his friends in Honolulu. He is, however, determined to destroy himself according to his oath and has avoided the police, who are on the track of his associates, by a hasty departure for the Klondike with baggage but with no money except to pay his fare."

Roger paused, surveying his quiet audience, then finished the story. "The manner of his self-destruction is not yet known to himself, but going to the Klondike without money in winter is a sure-enough suicide as it is." For dramatic effect, my thespian friend threw aside the newspaper, then lifted his arm toward the nearest coal oil lamp and froze for a moment, milking the silence of the awed crowd even more.

"To be, or not to be, that is the question: Whether 'tis nobler in the mind to suffer the slings and arrows of outrageous fortune, or to take arms against a sea of troubles, and by opposing end them: to die, to sleep; no more; and by a sleep, to say we end the heartache, and the thousand natural shocks that Flesh is heir to? 'Tis a consummation devoutly to be wished. To die, to sleep, perchance to dream; aye, there's the rub, for in that sleep of death, what dreams may come, when we have shuffled off this mortal coil, must give us pause." Roger continued with his dramatic performance and more men stepped to the bar ordering a beer or a whiskey.

One fellow banged his fist on the bar. "Give me a whiskey," he complained in a squeaky voice. "Damn the stage actor, damn Shakespeare, and damn Hamlet." He downed his drink as the saloon noise picked up, then sobbed, demanding a refill. Barely over five-and-a-half feet tall and a hundred and fifty pounds, something seemed vaguely familiar about him with his wild bushy black beard, his dark intimidating eyes and his larcenous lips. Biscuit crumbs were scattered in his whiskers like flecks of gold dust. Buck ambled by, glaring and growling at my customer. "Buck," I called, "behave yourself." Somewhere I had encountered this fellow before, but I couldn't place him. Was it in Tombstone or Lincoln, or in Deadwood or Denver, or Abilene, Fort Worth, Bismarck, or Waco? Something about him piqued my memory. I offered him two more drinks, then demanded he pay before I poured another. He shoved his hand in his pocket and extracted payment, plopping it on the bar, then spun around and marched to the faro layout to try his luck at bucking the tiger.

As I was swamped with other customers, I paid the fellow no more attention while up on stage, Roger finished his recitation, saying his soliloquy came from Act 3, Scene 1 of *Hamlet*. He announced he would next perform Mark Anthony's funeral oration from Act 3 of *Julius Caesar* and conclude with Portia's quality-of-mercy plea from Act 4 of *The Merchant of Venice*. "After that," Roger informed his growing audience, "the piano music will resume."

The crowed answered with rousing cheers, surprising Meredith with their enthusiasm for Ragtime over Shakespeare. Me and the other bartender stayed so busy, I no longer heard Roger's performances over the crowd and didn't realize he finished until the piano player started pounded out more tunes. By then a scattering of women had joined the festivities, dancing with exuberant stampeders as Roger meandered among them, taking each aside and explaining how they had to follow the house rules to ply their trade in the Gold Dust.

As the short afternoon devolved into an early twilight, Deputy Marshal Sylvester Taylor returned to the bar, his arm around the fellow with biscuit crumbs in his beard. "What do you think, Jeff?"

"We can make a killing," he answered.

The deputy looked at me. "Give me the usual, Jesse, and one for my friend and put it on my account."

"You don't have an account, deputy."

"I know," he replied, "but my friend's drinking under

my arrangement tonight. He leaves on a steamer in the morning for the states. I want to give him a good sendoff."

Nodding that I understood, I feared our profits would be further undercut by the graft of the lawman demanding free drinks for his friends in the coming months. The saloon was too crowded for me to risk spitting in his drink and stirring the concoction with my finger. Roger insisted we avoid the rumors that could harm out business. I poured both men drinks and sat them on the bar in front of them.

Taylor downed his jigger, pursed his lips and cocked his head at me. "What's a matter with this whiskey? It's not as good as your usual."

"We ran out of the quality stuff, so many customers."

"Well, Jesse, you set aside some of the better liquor for me and my friends when I need it," Taylor ordered.

His bearded buddy swigged his drink and pushed it toward me for more.

"Twenty-five cents for a refill," I said.

The deputy shook his head. "No charge, Jesse, as Jeff's my guest."

I hesitated.

The marshal pointed to one of our dark-skinned customers at the bar. "Is that an Indian I see? It'd be a shame for me to have to close you down for breaking territorial regulations."

"The drink's on the house," I answered.

"There's a lot of money to be made in Skagway," Taylor's guest said as he downed his free whiskey.

I knew biscuit beard planned to dig those funds out of gullible miners rather than the stubborn earth.

The fellow shoved his jigger at me. "Give me another."

"I haven't seen this much potential since Leadville."

At the mention of Leadville, my hand quivered as I refilled his glass, spilling some.

"Careful, Jesse, don't waste Jeff's drink."

Jeff! Leadville! Now it fell into place as my mind linked the present to the past like a brakeman hooking railroad cars together. This was Jefferson Randolph Smith the Second, his beard wild and unruly unlike the last time I saw him after coldcocking him when he tried to rob the Tabor store in Leadville the night after Noose Neck died. I then realized the wisdom in going by the alias Jesse Murphy rather than H.H. Lomax. I steadied my hand and refilled Taylor's glass, then took a towel and wiped up the mess I had made.

"Yes sir, marshal, there's a lot of money for the taking in Skagway."

I agreed, especially if Soapy didn't have to pay for any Gold Dust drinks.

"We can both profit, Jeff, to my way of thinking."

Smith nodded. "Give me time to gather my men together, so they can drift into town in small numbers. First thing we'll want to do is establish a welcoming committee and start our own place to draw customers."

Taylor smiled. "I have a feeling we'll do just fine once you get things arranged."

"That's the plan, marshal."

I refilled their jiggers and they took a last drink and slapped each other on the shoulders.

"I've got a steamer to catch in the morning," Smith said, "but I'll be back in January."

"I can't wait," Taylor responded, as they turned and walked out of the Gold Dust.

Chapter Nineteen

As fall gave way to winter, the days grew even shorter and the temperatures colder, but still the adventurers came with visions in their heads of gold in their pockets. Roger Meredith and I were filling our wallets with the profits from the Gold Dust. Our reputation for running a clean operation had put us in good standing with the decent men of Skagway who were trying to keep the place respectable and honest despite the crooked Deputy Marshal Sylvester Taylor, who dropped by daily when he was in Skagway to make certain we weren't serving drinks to Indians. Finding no violations, he always insisted on a jigger or more of whiskey, always complimenting me on pouring the best liquor around.

"I can pick good whiskey," I said, pointing my stirring finger at his nose as he lifted a jigger and swallowed another cut of our profits.

Taylor also stopped in every Monday to collect his weekly payoff of twelve dollars. Roger considered it the cost of doing business, but insisted I mix Taylor my special drink anytime I served him. I was more than obliged to accommodate my partner in serving the two-legged, badge-toting leech.

Other local businesses, not just the saloons, brothels and gambling dens, were being fleeced by Taylor, so the proprietors organized to counter Taylor's corruption. Roger Meredith and I received invitations to join the group and fight to keep Skagway from being overrun with crooks, confidence men, bunco artists, thieves, swindlers, and ne'er-do-wells. We were the only saloon operators other than Frank Clancy to earn membership in the assembly, which came to call itself the Committee of One Hundred and One.

In addition to fighting the corruption, the organization planned for Skagway's growth and future. The community leaders talked of a railroad from Skagway over White Pass into Canada, securing investors and surveying a route to take the misery out of getting over the mountain range and into the Promised Land. They took to calling their dream the White Pass & Yukon Railway. Based on what I'd heard of the treacherous path, I didn't see how they could bridge the chasms between Skagway and White Pass, but such was the allure of gold that men would try. The WP&YR imported surveying teams and hired construction crews for the work they projected to take two years. Some of their schemes sounded as if they came from the imaginations of the newspapermen clustered at Liarsville and lying about the route they had never traveled.

As Skagway exploded with dreams, people and crooks, the Committee of One Hundred and One created a public safety committee dedicated to maintaining the law and order that the federal deputy marshal ignored in favor of lining his pocket with other men's profits. By December 1897, the Committee of One Hundred and One, variously called the Citizens Committee or the Merchants Committee, had established a city council and certain rules that fell beneath the deputy marshal's jurisdiction and gave members a feeling that they were keeping Skagway's reputation respectable so their businesses might prosper. The first city council included Frank Clancy, who as proprietor of Clancy's Saloon and Music Hall remained a direct competitor of ours. Even though Clancy was a committee member and councilman, I doubted I could trust him as he had identified me to the deputy marshal and, in my mind at least, started the weekly payoffs that we had to make to the federal lawman. My partner was less worried about Clancy, saying as long as we ran a straight business we had nothing to fear from the committee or Clancy, other than the regular payouts to Taylor.

Being a pessimist by nature, I fretted not only over Clancy and Taylor, but also Jeff Smith when he returned and Dayle Lymoine, the San Francisco special investigator whose card I still kept. Maybe my conscious bothered me for investing the Wells Fargo windfall in Skagway, but Wells Fargo agents were like Pinkerton men, never giving up until they caught their man.

By December the Gold Dust was booming, the drinks and gambling providing fair entertainment at a fair price, the saloon girls attracting customers and boosting sales when they weren't waltzing with fellows on our dance floor or on mattresses in their rooms. Roger by then had brought together a troupe of actors and actresses who put on a new show every six weeks, fluctuating between Shakespearean plays, American melodramas and comedies to keep the stampeders returning for more. Two dozen ladies worked our place, Ella Wilson being the most striking, a mulatto with a creamy brown skin, long black hair, brown eyes, and perfect white teeth peeking out from behind the friendliest smile you could imagine. She claimed to be from Louisiana, though you never knew as women in her profession often lied to protect their kin back home from the shame of her occupation,. Her slight southern accent gave credence to her claim, however. For all her beauty, her single flaw became her choice in men, not always leaving the place with trustworthy customers. She called every man "mister" and even went to church when local services began that fall.

"Good evening, Mr. Murphy," she would say, then curtsy when she came in for work.

"You're looking fine tonight, Miss Wilson," I would answer, reciprocating her manners. "I'd say you're cuter than a speckled pup in a red wagon."

She would bat her thick eyelashes at me and say, "Mr. Murphy, your flattery will make me blush if you're not careful." She danced with the men for a dime a song, and if she liked the fellow, she'd take him to her crib on Holly Street for further amusement. Sometimes she'd take three or four men back to her place in one evening and at other times none, but she always had a smile on her lips. And when she spoke, she purred with an irresistible voice. We had more girls working our saloon than I could keep up with by name, but Roger managed them and I enjoyed their looks without ever taking in the fruit of their loins as my partner insisted on propriety to keep the Gold Dust's reputation above that of the other local saloons. By then, though, we had enough business that I no longer tended bar unless Marshal Taylor visited for his special drink. We hired six other bartenders. Business thrived and my pockets, though not lined with cash from gold finds, were flush with the money from others still hoping to make it to Dawson City.

In December, though, I noticed the arrival of a handful of men with soft hands and jaundiced eyes. They were not men seeking to make money from climbing the Chilkoot or White Pass trails, but men like Roger and me, hoping to profit from the men focused only on gold. They would come into the Gold Dust individually or in pairs, maybe having a drink, but sizing up our customers and convincing them to leave, either telling them of a saloon with better chances to win wagers at the gaming tables or advising them of a surefire money-making scheme. One day, I saw a man I might never have recognized had I not seen Soapy Smith weeks earlier. He was a tall, handsome gentleman with a guileless face devoid of larceny. Though he called himself "Professor," I remembered him as a preacher back in Leadville. The Reverend John Bowers was now calling himself Professor John Bowers, retired. He wore a fraternal pin that changed from day to day and knew each order's secret handshake that confirmed fraternal brotherhood, even when untrue. If Skagway newcomers belonged to the Masons, Freemasons, Oddfellows, Woodmen of the World, Fraternal Mystic Legion, Granite League, Independent Order of Mechanics, Knights of the Globe, Independent Workmen of America, Ancient Order of Pyramids, Mystic Workers of the World, Order of the Golden Chain, Pythians, or dozens more such groups,

Bowers had a pin, a handshake, and a spiel that convinced the newcomer to trust his newfound fraternal brother. As a grip man for his glad-handing, Bowers steered each "brother" to an ally to cheat, drug or rob the fellow of his money and his Skagway innocence.

Another evening I recognized George Wilder, the real estate speculator that worked with Soapy Smith in Leadville. Wilder specialized in land transactions, selling property he didn't own, inflating prices of plots he had title to and sometimes robbing newcomers straight out. On occasion he walked on crutches to the piers when new arrivals disembarked from the steamers, hoping to convince a naïve cheechacko, as newcomers were called, he had been injured and needed to sell his cabin at a cut-rate price for fare back to the states. When he showed a newcomer the place, the dupe, and Wilder encountered a shotgun-wielding confederate that robbed both men of their wallets. Wilder got his back, but the dupe did not.

While Skagway had always attracted scoundrels willing to scam the unwary, they had been lone wolves. Now dozens were arriving at the wharves, and they reminded me of the Leadville associates that hung around Jeff Smith in Bill Nye's Saloon, an untrustworthy a bunch as I had ever known. I worried that since I had recognized a few of Soapy's men, one of them might recognize me as H.H. Lomax. I hid in our office or in my room whenever I saw Bowers or Wilder in the Gold Dust. Anyone could be a shill for Soapy, anyone except Roger and Buck. I trusted them. I only half trusted the men and women I had been around since opening the saloon and joining the Committee of One Hundred and One. But recent arrivals, I suspected of larceny.

On the last night of 1897 we held a New Year's celebration that drew as big a crowed as we ever had in the Gold Dust, thanks to my partner organizing a stage performance of dancing girls who showed more leg than was our custom. I was enjoying the flashes of calf and occasional thigh when a fellow approached me, cocked his head and stared.

"May I help you?"

"Ye be the owner of this place?" he asked in an Irish brogue.

"I be one of them."

"Be it true ye be the one that calls hisself Jesse Murphy?"

Before answering, I studied the man, taking in his ruddy face, freckled nose, hazel eyes, brown hair, and bushy eyebrows. His rumpled coat covered his waist so I could not tell if he carried a pistol. I couldn't remember seeing him before, but I had traveled near and far over the years and prayed my past wasn't catching up to me. Finally, I nodded. "I be Jesse Murphy."

"That be a lie," my new acquaintance said, shaking his head with vigor.

I froze, studying my accuser, taking in his worn work boots, his wrinkled pants and his wide-eyed gaze over that freckled nose. Was this Dayle Lymoine, the Wells Fargo agent whose card I kept? Had he followed me from San Francisco? He was not what I had expected in a Wells Fargo special investigator, not with his rumpled clothes and his naïve eyes. Or, was this one of Soapy's men trying to unmask my alias? "Sure I'm Jesse Murphy," I argued.

"You be not Jesse Murphy," he insisted.

"Why not?"

He laughed. "Because I be Jesse Murphy, 'ere from the green isle."

I was looking at myself in another man's flesh and blood. I didn't like what I saw, though I was glad he had nothing to do with Wells Fargo.

"Ye be from Ireland?" he asked.

"Arkansas."

"I not be familiar with that part of Ireland. Ye not be sounding Irish. I be from County Cork."

"Tell you what, Jesse. Why don't you celebrate Ireland and the New Year with a trip to the bar, free drinks on me?"

"Ye be meaning it, Jesse?" he asked, his wide eyes expanding until they looked the size of wash tubs.

"Nothing's too good for a fellow Irishman named Jesse Murphy," I informed him as I threw my arm around his shoulder and steered him through the throng to the bar. "Give my friend as many drinks as he wants on the house," I instructed the three bartenders struggling to keep up with the customers' thirst for liquor to celebrate a proper New Year's Eve.

My namesake thanked me a dozen times, grabbing my hand and pushing it up and down like he was working a pump handle to get water from a dry well.

"Enjoy," I offered as I slipped away from the bar and wandered among the celebrating throng, keeping my hand in my britches pocket so no pickpocket might steal my money roll thick with saloon profits, most of which I hid in my mattress.

At midnight we welcomed 1898 in with shouts and hugs, everyone who hadn't gotten rich in the previous year knowing they would find wealth in the coming twelve months. Several of the girls wandered about, giving free kisses to the customers that had bought dances. The mulatto girl Ella Wilson worked her way through the crowd to me and threw her arms around me. "Well, Mr. Murphy, here's to a happy and prosperous New Year to you in eighteen ninety-eight." She pecked my cheek with an innocent kiss.

"And to you, too, Miss Wilson. What are your plans for the New Year?"

"I've been saving my money and to return to the states, give up this life forever. I've got over three thousand dollars," she said.

"Shush," I said. "Don't speak so loudly of your earnings, not in this group when you can't trust a soul."

"I trust you, Mr. Murphy."

"But we never know who might be listening. Do you keep it in your room?"

She nodded. "I have nowhere else to put it. I don't trust the banks."

Buck wormed his way between us, and Ella bent down to pet my dog.

I looked around and studied the packed saloon. I wanted to talk with her alone and didn't consider it appropriate to take her into the saloon office or upstairs to my room as Roger might think I was partaking of the merchandise. "Let's go for a walk and visit," I offered.

Ella glanced up from Buck and smiled. "We can go to my place, Mr. Murphy."

"I don't want people talking, Miss Wilson."

She laughed. "Talk's cheap in my profession. Doesn't matter where we go, other girls will talk."

"Let's walk to the wharves, if you can manage the cold."

"I live in Skagway, don't I? Let me get my coat." She turned and worked her way through the crowd.

"Come on, Buck," I said, "let's go to the office and get my coat and your socks." I led my dog past the bar and into the room, where I fetched my coat and slid the stockings over Buck's feet. As soon as I put the first one on, he realized we were going outside and licked my cheek. Much as I loved Buck, I preferred Ella's innocent kiss.

After attending my dog, I slipped my coat on and exited the room, working my way through the crowd to the front door where Ella Wilson awaited me, bundled up like a Christmas present in warm wrapping paper. I opened the door for her and we stepped outside, accompanied by Buck, and turned south toward the piers. Like Skagway, the docks had sprouted by magic in the bay, the pilings extending out into Lynn Canal for hundreds of yards. Moore's Wharf, the one owned by the town founder, hugged the east side of the fiord, then came the pier operated by Alaska Southern. The Juneau and Seattle wharves, so named for the towns their steamships served, completed Skagway's dock facilities.

As we walked and talked, our breath exhaled clouds of vapor in the brisk night air. Gunshots punctuated the darkness as several New Year's celebrants wasted ammunition. We strode down Broadway toward the bay and turned on Second Avenue to State Street, where the foot of the Juneau Wharf began. We climbed the steps and strolled along the planked walk. I laughed as we ambled above the mud flats where I had first landed in Skagway.

"What's funny, Mr. Murphy?"

"Just recalling my arrival in town and carrying my supplies and gear through the mudflats. An unpleasant experience, Miss Wilson."

"I've never seen a town grow so fast," she answered.

"Nor attract so many desperate men, Miss Wilson. That's what I wanted to discuss with you, but only when our conversation remained private."

The night air chilled even more as we walked out over the waters, stopping halfway to the end of the pier. I looked around to make sure no one was close enough to overhear us and called my dog who kept exploring. "Here, Buck," I cried and he returned, sitting on the wooden decking at our feet. I turned to Ella. "Don't mention your money to anyone, not even me, Miss Wilson. It's not safe to keep it in your room when other people might find out."

We both moved toward the wooden railing and rested our hands there as we looked out over the water, which rippled in the soft moonlight peeking between fluffy clouds.

"I have no idea what else to do with it," she said, "because I don't trust the banks or the stores that offer storage in their safes. I'd rather keep it where it's secure with me."

"That's not safe. I'd hate for you to lose your money or get hurt."

"You're my guardian angel, Mr. Murphy."

"I'm no angel, Miss Wilson, but your safety concerns me."

"Six months from now at the end of June, I plan to return to Louisiana," she answered. "I should have five thousand dollars saved up by then. That's good money for a bayou girl who can barely read or write."

"Sounds like you can count cash at least, and that's more important than reading or writing."

"Somehow I've managed, and when I return to the bayous, I expect my earnings will be enough to live out the rest of my life in comfort. I can join the Women's Christian Temperance Union and pretend I've led a pure existence."

I thought back to my oldest sister, Constance Louise Lomax, who had left home before I was eleven and disappeared until I ran across her running a brothel in Deadwood, Dakota Territory, in 1876. By the time the territory became two states thirteen years later, Constance was one of the most respected women in the new state of South Dakota. "My sister ran a house in Deadwood," I confided to Ella.

"Is that why you've always been so decent to me?"

"It seemed the right thing to do."

"Thank you," she replied, patting my hand with hers on the wooden railing. "I wish all men were like you."

"They're not, Miss Wilson, and that's something I wanted to discuss with you. You've left the Gold Dust with some of the hardest men in Skagway."

Ella snickered and patted my fingers. "Oh, Mr. Murphy, isn't that my job?"

I stammered. "No, I mean rough men, hard cases, men that would think no more of slapping you around than they would of kicking my dog."

"They're all the same to me, Mr. Murphy."

"Not to me. There are dangerous men out there, ones that would slit your throat for that much money. Don't be telling anyone, not even me, how much you've got or that you'll be leaving Skagway as soon as you save five thousand dollars. It's too risky."

Ella stood silently patting my hand, staring across the waters to the mountains on the west side of the bay. She grabbed my fingers and squeezed them as she shivered in the frigid air. "I'm cold," she said. "Perhaps I should get back to my place."

"You want to go home instead of the Gold Dust?"

"I'm giving myself the night off, unless you'd like to join me, Mr. Murphy, at no charge."

Squeezing her hand, I shook my head. "The offer's tempting, but I promised my partner I'd not take advantage of our girls."

"I suspected you would refuse, Mr. Murphy, but I wanted to offer."

"Come on, Buck," I called, "time to return home." We retreated along the pier to the landing, then strolled up State to her crib on Holly, chatting on inconsequential topics.

At her front door, she kissed me on the cheek again. "You're welcome inside, Mr. Murphy."

"I'm flattered," I answered, "but I promised Roger I wouldn't."

She leaned my way and whispered in my ear. "I knew you wouldn't, and I know I can trust you. The money's in my clothes trunk."

Pulling myself from her, I looked in her dark eyes that I could just make out in the moonlight. "I wish you hadn't told me."

She took her key from her coat pocket, unlocked the entry, and slipped inside. "I had to tell someone and you're trustworthy."

"Thank you," I said, taking the knob and closing the door before I gave into her charms.

Five months later I was left to wonder how our lives might have changed had I accepted her invitation and spent the night with her, though I had done the proper thing at the time.

When I returned to the Gold Dust, the saloon bulged with revelers, most waiting for the final showing of the dancing girls before ending the festivities after a successful start to 1898. Roger Meredith found me before the last show was to begin.

"Where have you been, Jesse?"

"Ella Wilson and I took a stroll, spending time on the Juneau Wharf to talk."

"You sure it was merely talking."

"Nothing more. She wanted to visit about things I feared others would overhear."

Meredith leaned into me and whispered, "About retiring by summer and returning to Louisiana once she's got five thousand dollars?"

I nodded. "Did she tell you where she kept the money?"

"Fortunately, not. Did she you?"

Pursing my lips, I nodded again.

"She always favored you between the two of us, but she's so innocent about things, even in what she does. I worry for her."

"I'll protect her from unsavory men whenever I can."

And I did, except for one man—Soapy Smith.

That became the biggest regret of my time in Alaska!

Chapter Twenty

On the second day of the New Year, after his hangover had cleared from all the free Gold Dust liquor, Deputy Marshal Sylvester Taylor stopped by the saloon to collect his weekly payoff. He barged past the bartenders into our office where Roger Meredith and I were counting our receipts over the last two days. Taylor looked at the money on our table and licked his lips.

"You know what today is, don't you?" he asked, then answered his own question. "Collection day, though I must inform you there's been a change."

"Our cost is going up?" Roger guessed, pushing himself back from his desk.

The lawman nodded. "An additional three dollars a week."

"That's a twenty-five percent increase. Isn't that steep?"

Taylor pointed at the table. "Looks like you can handle it."

"These are once-a-year receipts, deputy. You saw the crowd on New Year's Eve."

"I did and I spotted Tlingits in here drinking firewater. I ought to arrest you and take you to jail in Sitka." He looked at me. "Both of you."

"Fifteen dollars it is," Roger said, counting out the bills and handing them across the table to the lawman.

"I'd love to fix you a couple drinks before you go," I offered.

"Not today, Jesse. I'm behind on my collections."

"We've got a new whiskey brand in, one you'll enjoy."

"Oh, yeah! What's it called?"

"Old Horse Piss," I answered.

Taylor laughed. "Save it for the Indians." He spun around and marched out.

"Bastard," Roger said when the lawman closed the door. "The Merchants Committee is tiring of his corruption," he told me, "and have written letters to the president, but the territorial commissioner looks the other way. The deputy's paid from a cut of the fines and fees, so he extorts us and the other honest businesses for more. Decent folks are fed up with it."

I agreed, but there wasn't much we could do, not with Taylor's boss in Sitka and no one even at the highest levels listening to us. Our only option was to wait.

A week later, the deputy marshal returned, barging into our office like before, but this time with another man he introduced as James Rowan. "Fellows," Taylor announced, "Jim will be deputy in my absence."

"Where're you going?" Roger asked.

"Taking prisoners to Sitka, meeting with my boss, government business."

I grimaced, knowing now we'd be making two payments a week, one for fifteen dollars to Taylor and another as yet unspecified amount to Jim Rowan. "Glad to meet you," I said with as much enthusiasm as a man standing on the gallows trapdoor.

"Obliged," he answered.

After Roger and I shook the new deputy's hand, Taylor excused him.

"Wait outside, will you, Jim? I've got a personal matter to handle with these gentlemen."

"Sure thing, Sylvester."

Once the door closed the lawman demanded his fifteen dollars.

"You'll split this with Jim, right, deputy?" Roger asked.

Taylor scoffed. "He's on his own, though I better not hear of him getting more than me."

"How 'bout a jigger of O-H-P, deputy?" I asked.

"O-H-P?"

"Old Horse Piss."

"I thought I told you to use that on the Indians."

"You told me I can't sell liquor to them?"

"Then give it to them." Taylor smiled and left us scratching our heads over the dent he was making in our profits.

Later that afternoon deputy marshal Jim Rowan returned and requested to meet us. We took him in our office and gritted our teeth, wondering what his bribe would cost us.

"Boys," Rowan said, "I know Taylor is extorting money from you."

"Where'd you hear that?" Roger asked.

Rowan grinned. "You need not play coy with me. I've seen how he works, and I'm here to assure you I don't operate that way. I'm serving because I didn't want another crook continuing the extortion. I've got a wife with a baby on the way in a few weeks, and I want Skagway to be a decent place to raise my son or daughter. I don't cotton to crooked lawmen. They damage a town worse than crooks."

A soft breeze could've blown me and my partner down, so shocked were we by Rowan's integrity. "You're a godsend," Roger said. "He ordered us not to pay you more than him."

Rowan nodded. "I'm not surprised. What's he taking from you?"

"Fifteen dollars a week and all the whiskey he can drink when he's thirsty," Roger informed him.

"And he's plenty thirsty, except when I offer him some O-H-P."

"O-H-P?"

"Old Horse Piss," I answered. "It's top quality Kentucky bourbon. They say if you hold the bottle up to the sunlight you'll spot a tint of blue from the bluegrass those Kentucky racehorses graze on."

Rowan laughed. "I'll leave that for Sylvester because I won't be taking your money." He paused. "Or, drinking your liquor for that matter."

When he left, we watched him step out past the bar, stopping a moment to pet Buck before exiting the saloon. We felt optimistic about the direction Skagway was heading, at least that night until our clientele was tainted by the arrival of Jefferson Randolph Smith the Second, just back from his trip to the states.

It was a slow evening, half the customers we normally had, the girls mingling among the men, begging for business and drinks when on most nights they had to turn offers away. Even Buck seemed tired, lying in the corner, his tail wagging to the beat of the piano music, which was slower than usual. Soapy marched in like he owned the place or at least expected to in a matter of weeks and studied our saloon and opera house. Shortly, Professor John Bowers and George Wilder, the land speculator and manipulator, joined him. They took a table and motioned for a bartender to bring them over a bottle and glasses. I moved to the side of the room and stood by the wall, studying them, wondering what they were up to but fearful of getting too close in case they remembered our Leadville acquaintance and the charge of murder that still hung over my head. I damn sure didn't want a noose around my neck because of something that had happened two decades earlier, though the details still escaped me.

When I got the chance, I found my partner and pulled him to a corner to point out the larcenous trio. "See the table with the fellow with the untamed beard?"

Meredith nodded. "What of it?"

"The bearded devil is Jefferson Randolph Smith the Second, sometimes called 'Soapy.' He's a sure-thing man, a confidence man not to be trusted. The taller dapper fellow, he's John L. Bowers, sometimes calls himself a reverend but now claims he's a retired professor. He's a glad hander, a grip man who funnels suckers to Soapy's gang that then swindles or robs them. The third fellow is George Wilder. He specializes in land sales, fraudulent transactions, selling land on which he lacks title. That's the three that I recognize, but they are like the tip of the iceberg. Where there's Soapy, there's dozens more doing his dirty deeds."

Roger frowned. "How come you know so much about them, Jesse?"

"I had dealings that soured with them a long time ago in a place I don't care to discuss. A crooked lawyer died, and I was accused of killing him."

My partner swallowed hard and cocked his head at me. "Did you do it?"

Shrugging, I lifted my hands in exasperation. "I remember nothing from that night, other than waking up the next morning and finding a body on the floor. Maybe I did, maybe I didn't. I'd been drinking and the lawyer had swindled me out of a mining claim."

Roger whistled. "What do we do? Run them out?"

"We can't create a stir or he might recognize me. Keep an eye on him and anybody that sits at his table. Warn our dealers not to make any arrangements with him, especially the faro dealer. Soapy loves to buck the tiger, it's his weakness but he also loves to hire card mechanics on the side that'll cheat his marks out of their money. Inform our dealers I'll fire anyone that makes a side deal with him. If Soapy gambles here, it'll damage ours and the Gold Dust's reputation. Beyond that, I plan to stay as far away from him and his stable of crooks as I can. I don't want the murder charge coming back to haunt me."

Roger looked at me and grinned. "I never realized you had such a mean streak in you."

"Let's just say that my partnership with Noose Neck, that's what I called him, soured over a misunderstanding. You understand, don't you, *partner*?"

Meredith froze, his face as motionless as a marble statue's until I smiled. He released a deep breath. "You had me worried for a minute."

"Try to screen me from Soapy and his boys."

The actor nodded and kept his word. Unfortunately, my dog had made no such agreement. Roger marched over to the piano and ordered our musician to play a livelier tune, more Ragtime. The player banged out one of those ragged tunes with an irregular rhythm that reverberated through the saloon and theater, disrupting Buck's rest. His tail quit wagging, his ears popped up and he shook his head, getting to his feet and ambling among the tables toward me until he reached Soapy's table in the middle of the room. Buck stopped, growled at our unwanted customer, and spat out a sharp bark, something he'd only done to Deputy Taylor. He barked again, then snarled.

Soapy shoved himself up from his chair, his hand going to the revolver at his waist. I bolted across the room. "Stop," I cried, "that's my dog." I charged between tables, yanking my pistol from my holster to discourage Soapy from firing his.

Buck growled again, crouched and prepared to lunge at Smith. Bowers and Wilder pushed themselves away from the table, overturning their chairs as they jumped to their feet. Soapy swung his pistol toward Buck, as I got there.

"No, Buck," I screamed as I lunged for him, grabbing his ear and yanking him toward the bar. He yelped, twisted his head and freed himself from my grip. "Get," I commanded, pointing him to the office door. Buck growled a last time, tucked his tail between his legs and left.

I shoved my gun back in my holster when I saw out of the corner of my eye that Soapy had returned his to its nest. "Sorry, gentlemen," I said, trying to screen my face from them as I shooed Buck away. "I'll have the bartender send over a bottle of our best."

Smith scowled. "It better not be the Old Horse Piss that Marshal Taylor's mentioned."

"That's a joke," I answered, walking past Soapy until he grabbed my arm and turned me about, staring at my face with those dark malevolent eyes. I avoided his direct gaze, looking instead at the cracker crumbs on his beard.

"Don't I know you from somewhere?" he asked.

"Marshal Taylor introduced us on your last visit to Skagway."

Soapy released my arm and scratched his beard, likely prospecting for crumbs, then shook his head. "That's not it. I remember that, but I've seen you elsewhere."

"I don't travel that much."

"You get around enough to be in Skagway. I know we've met somewhere else in another mining town." He shrugged to his friends. "John, George, do you recognize this fellow?"

Bowers and Wilder examined me with their gazes.

"There's something familiar about him," Bowers said.

"I'd never remember a face like that," Wilder added. "It'd cause nightmares."

"Don't provoke him with insults," Soapy ordered.

I turned to Smith. "I can handle it," I said, "but don't insult or provoke my dog."

"We didn't," Soapy shot back. "We were sitting here, minding our own affairs when he started growling."

"As long as you mind your own business, Mr. Smith, you won't have any problems in the Gold Dust."

"That's right," Roger said from behind me. He pushed me aside, motioning for me to move on, then stepping to the edge of the table. "I'm Roger Meredith, the proprietor with my partner, who's fetching you a bottle of whiskey as I speak."

I started for the bar to get the liquor as Meredith continued.

"We run an honest place, no crooked gamblers, no sure-thing men," Roger told them. "You're welcome here as long as you follow our rules. If not, find another saloon and opera house for your business."

Soapy shrugged. "We do business wherever we like, but I'm not sure we care for this place. Where's our bottle of whiskey?"

At the bar I took a cheap bottle of liquor from the bartender, then toted it over to Soapy's table. Roger grabbed the bottle by the neck and placed it in the middle of their table.

"Like we promised, here's your free whiskey."

Bowers grabbed the bottle. "Let's take our liquor and go, Jeff." He pushed his chair back to stand as Wilder arose. At that moment, though, Ella Wilson sashayed past us, her shapely figure, her bronzed flesh, her dark eyes and her inviting lips drawing Soapy's attention.

"No, fellows," Soapy countered, "I'm enjoying the view here."

Bowers and Wilder reclaimed their seats as the professor uncorked the bottle and filled his own jigger before passing the whiskey to Soapy, who took a healthy swig from the bottle, then filled his glass and passed the drink to Wilder.

"You're welcome here as long as you follow our rules,"

Roger reiterated before turning and walking to the piano player, requesting a slower song to ease the tension. As the music slowed, I led Buck into the office and left him there, shutting the door on him to avoid any more trouble with Soapy and his minions.

I slipped over to Ella Wilson without Soapy's men noticing, catching her in a far corner. "Miss Wilson," I said, "I'm obliged to warn you about untrustworthy men. You should avoid those at the table that spooked Buck. They're as mean as they come."

"I've seen worse," she said.

"Avoid the one with the unruly beard for sure. Rumor has it a dozen rats are nesting in those whiskers."

"Mr. Murphy," she said, "you're such a devil with your words."

"I want you to avoid those men and anyone associated with them. They're trouble."

She smiled. "Thank you, Mr. Murphy, for watching out for me. Now it's back to work, if I can find a customer willing to buy some drinks or me."

"Don't endanger yourself simply to get back to Louisiana on schedule."

Ella batted her eyes at me. "I'm ready to put this life behind me. The faster I work, the sooner I get home." She offered me so angelic a smile that I forgot her trade and wondered how any man might hurt such an innocent young woman, even in a rough place like Skagway.

A clean-shaven adventurer approached and asked for a dance. Taking his arm, she led him to the dance floor in front of the stage. I wandered around the saloon, checking that nothing untoward was occurring. While I stayed away from Soapy's table so he or his men would not recognize me as H.H. Lomax, I observed them as much as possible. Once the bottle was empty, Bowers and Wilder got up and exited, though Jeff Smith remained. While I eyed him, he ogled every move that Ella Wilson made. His fixation bothered me, especially when Ella left the place with a customer and Soapy arose and strode out the door behind them.

As he exited, I dashed to the office, barging in and

grabbing the cord I used for a leash on Buck, who jumped up to welcome me. I put the length around his neck and pointed him toward the front door, not even taking time to grab my coat as I chased after my quarry.

I saw Smith at the end of the block, turning on Holly where Ella lived. When I reached the corner, I angled for Ella's place, where Soapy stood outside leaning at her window, looking inside. "Sic him," I said to Buck, releasing the leash and my dog lunging toward Jefferson Randolph Smith the Second. Then I yelled, "Watch out. My dog got away." Several men on the walks scurried to get out of the way as Buck darted past.

Soapy spun around and heard Buck's howl and footfall. I witnessed a blur of movement and the space outside Ella's window stood vacant as Smith bolted down the street.

"Here, Buck," I cried. "Come back, Buck. Here, boy; come here boy." In a moment, I welcomed a dark shadow approaching me, panting from the exertion. Buck stopped in front of me, and I bent to pet him and retrieve the mud-splattered leash. "Let's return home," I told him as we headed back toward the Gold Dust.

When we reached the saloon, I tied him to a hitching rack and went inside, returning with a bucket of water and a rag to clean the mud from his legs and paws. I hadn't taken the time to put on his canvas socks, so he was dirtier than usual. In the jaundiced light seeping from the saloon window, I untied him, led him onto the planks and washed his feet with the clean rag. When I was certain he would not track up the saloon like our customers, I escorted him inside and gave him the run of the place as usual.

I expected to see Soapy and his gang back the next night, but they never showed up, nor did they for the following week. Their absence left me happy for Ella Wilson's sake, though rumor had it Smith found the mulatto most attractive and planned to dance with her one day. But pleasure never came before business with Soapy, and he spent his other nights checking out competing saloons, identifying those most accommodating to his scams, since the Gold Dust was off his list. Shortly, we had dealers who had worked at the other saloons seeking a table at our place to ply their trade. Each told of being fired and replaced by a dealer with connections to Jeff Smith, who then used the new dealers to fleece unsuspecting arrivals and marks in Skagway. The problem was, you never knew for certain if their stories were true, or they were trying to gain a job to swindle Gold Dust customers on Smith's behalf.

Beginning that January, the influx of Smith's gang became noticeable with shell games and three-card monte operations on the street corners. Soapy's associates applied for bartending jobs at all the saloons and started intimidating the prostitutes with threats unless they paid protection money. Nothing seemed what it was or had been. Smith's men built two clapboard cabins near the wharves and identified them with vivid signs labeled GENERAL INFORMATION BUREAU, so they were among the first so-called businesses that newcomers spotted on arriving in Skagway. A man in a starched shirt, coat, and tie greeted the new arrivals, offering information about conditions on the White Pass and Chilkoot trails, the costs of portage for the required supplies and gear, and honest businesses in town to gamble, dine or stay. All those stores, of course, were paying protection money to Soapy's minions and providing an environment for cons, swindles and outright theft and intimidation of the newcomers. The manager at the information bureaus referred men to the sham telegraph office downtown where newcomers sent word to worried loved ones back home that they had reached their first destination safely. Any recent arrival who availed himself of such services received an answering telegram the next day with a sob story about some calamity striking home and requesting that money be wired to their folks. While Skagway was running electrical wires through the city from a generating plant by the bay, telegraph service was months away and Soapy's men simply pocketed the funds intended for the needy kin back home.

Besides giving out false information and steering newcomers to crooked vendors, the bureau managers also collected facts and figures on new arrivals, helping cull from the herd those with limited resources and those wealthy enough to merit swindling. Those managers would hook the newcomer up with a fellow member of a fraternal order or with a trustworthy confidant guaranteed to help the cheechacko navigate the corrupt currents of Skagway, though not without losing his money.

By that time, Skagway had competing newspapers in the *Daily Alaskan* and the weekly *Skagway News* with reporters meeting passengers as they disembarked to gather news of the states, everything ranging from national politics to the growing tensions between the United States and Spain. Newspaperman William Saportas of the *Daily Alaskan* sought information for his paper and for his editor, J. Allen Hornsby, to share with Soapy's minions. Saportas greeted and interviewed new arrivals, gaining their confidence and eliciting facts about their wealth, how long they planned to remain in Skagway, and where they intended to stay. He referred new passengers destined for Dawson City to a packing and portage business run by his brother, who advertised in the *Daily Alaskan*, a publication that printed favorable stories about Jefferson Randolph Smith the Second, whether it be his benevolence or good deed of the day, none of which was likely true. I never observed those benevolent acts. The web of deceit Soapy wove in the first weeks of 1898 so complicated the interactions in Skagway that we no longer knew who we could trust or believe.

Everything Smith touched, even second hand, tainted everyone involved. I wished I hadn't called off Buck the night I followed him to Ella Wilson's crib because it might have saved Skagway a lot of heartache, especially her. As Soapy got into a routine, he dropped by the Gold Dust once a week when he needed a woman. And, he favored Ella. The first evening I watched her leave with him, I felt my stomach knot in anger and fear. I had warned her, but never stopped her from leaving with him as I didn't want to risk him recognizing me from Leadville.

The next evening she came to work in the Gold Dust after spending the night with Soapy, I invited her into the office and asked her to sit for a visit. She seemed a harder woman than I'd seen in our past conversations, not the same one that had greeted me as Mr. Murphy and kissed me on the cheek.

"It's about Mr. Smith, isn't it?"

Nodding, I answered. "He's evil, Ella."

She looked at me, her eyes widening. "That's the first time you've ever called me anything but Miss Wilson."

"I'm worried about you. Your relationship with Soapy will end badly."

She stood. "Jesse—can I call you Jesse?"

I nodded.

"Jesse, the fact is that Mr. Smith pays me double what I make from four clients a night. I'm using him like he's using me. If he'd do that every day from now through the end of next month, I could leave for Louisiana by the end of March. Even at this rate, I should be able to leave the first rather than the last of June. As long as he doesn't slip my grasp, I can depart four weeks earlier than before. I want to put this behind me."

Pursing my lips and grimacing with the frustration of knowing I would never change her mind, I simply nodded.

"Thank you, Jesse, for watching out for me. May I go?"

"He's got a wife in St. Louis. They've been married twelve years."

"Many of my customers have wives, Jesse. May I go?"

"Sure, Ella, but be careful whatever you do."

Though she remained as gorgeous leaving the room as she had been when she entered, I never again looked upon her as beautiful. Something had changed, whether in me or her or both, but I was never as disappointed in a person as I was in Ella Wilson that day.

My hope bounced back the next afternoon when Deputy Marshal Jim Rowan stopped by to visit with me and Roger Meredith. He asked us a single question: Would we testify against Sylvester Taylor for malfeasance if he reported to his superior in Sitka all the corruption that Taylor had fostered in Skagway? We both agreed without hesitation.

"I'm leaving for Sitka in three days on February first. I've got a dozen people willing to testify. Once I get him, I'll go after Soapy, though right now all I want is to see my baby born before I leave."

At that moment both Roger and I shared a renewed optimism about Skagway's future. We wished him well with his impending fatherhood and his trip to Sitka. That was the last time we saw Jim Rowan alive. At two o'clock in the morning on the last day of January, Rowan died after a shootout at the Peoples' Theater, a rival opera house and bar down the street from the Gold Dust. Rowan expired two hours after his son's birth.

Chapter Twenty-one

The killing of the honest deputy marshal threw Skagway into an uproar. Reports said People's Theater bartender Ed Fay had defended himself against a drunk named Andy McGrath and accidentally shot Jim Rowan when he thought the lawman was in cahoots with his inebriated patron. Since Roger Meredith and I along with several members of the Committee of One Hundred and One knew about Rowan's scheduled visit to Sitka with the goods on the crooked Sylvester Taylor, most men in the know figured it was a murder orchestrated by Taylor and Jefferson Randolph Smith the Second. Such speculation increased when Fay scurried to Soapy and his gang for protection.

When committee members met in the Union Church later the day of the killing, everyone wanted to know what connections Fay had to Taylor and Smith. The question that nobody stated but hovered over the group like a low-hanging dark cloud was who had tipped off the other side. I sat in the meeting listening and gauging the possibilities. I studied Frank Clancy, proprietor of Clancy's Saloon and a competitor I had distrusted from the beginning. Another possibility was J. Allan Hornsby, editor of the *Daily Alaskan*, which most of us believed took payoffs from Soapy for favorable coverage.

Even as we debated how to bring justice to Jim Rowan's killer, Hornsby heightened those suspicions by praising the conman. "Jeff Smith has promised fifty dollars to a widow's fund for Mrs. Rowan," he announced. "Please join Jeff in contributing to this worthwhile fund for the widow of one of our upstanding citizens, unfortunately taken from us."

Major John F.A. Strong, who conducted the session, was the rival editor of the *Skagway News*, scowled at his competitor and gaveled for quiet. "The issue is what to do about Ed Fay."

Most of us glared at Hornsby for mentioning Soapy, but Frank Clancy chimed in.

"I'll match that fifty dollars and encourage everyone else here to do so," he called.

"The question is what to do with Ed Fay," Strong reminded the group.

"Hang him," shouted several men.

"Arrest him and try him before a jury of his peers," answered others.

"This," intoned Major Strong as he waved his gavel in the air, "is a crime that will damage Skagway's reputation if we don't handle it right."

The heated argument over the best strategy, not only for justice but also for the future of Skagway, raged for three hours. Those who argued for a lynching said it was the only way to guarantee justice, considering the lawlessness of the principal deputy charged with enforcing the laws. The opposition countered that a hanging damaged Skagway's reputation far worse and damaged prospects for future prosperity and respect. Those wanting a trial contended that a jury verdict was the only guarantee of true justice, but the opponents argued the murderer would get away with it like all the little swindles and big thefts that went unpunished.

With Sylvester Taylor out of town, supposedly chasing crooks up the White Pass trail, Rowan had been the only available law. With him dead, the community's two opposing forces lined up not only for and against lynching Fay but also favoring or opposing Jeff Smith. After three hours of contentious debate, Strong adjourned the meeting to resume the next day.

When we gathered again the following afternoon, nothing had been settled other than Soapy Smith, accompanied by some of his thugs, came to speak to the committee and defend his actions in shielding the murderer from harm. "Every man is entitled to due process under our laws," Smith pleaded. "We must avoid vigilante justice in Skagway, in Alaska, anywhere."

"What we need," countered an opponent, "is Ed Fay decorating the end of a rope."

"And Soapy decorating the end of another rope," shouted one of Smith's many enemies, "after what you've done to Skagway."

"The name's Jeff Smith," Soapy growled, staring the man down with his dark eyes burning like the fires of hell, then resuming his plea. "We don't want Skagway known for lawlessness."

At first Soapy's defense of the rule of law surprised me until I realized he hated the Committee of One Hundred and One because it opposed his ways and might turn vigilante against him and his allies. Calmly he argued his case, promising to turn Ed Fay over to the proper authorities including this committee, provided he received assurances no harm or intimidation would befall the accused. Nobody offered such a promise, not with feelings burning so hot. After all, a decent man who wanted to clean up Skagway for posterity was dead, barely hours after he had held his son for the first and only time in his life.

Chairman Strong appointed twelve men to an impromptu jury to rule on the fate of Ed Fay, but Soapy and his dozen henchmen, including Bowers and Wilder, by their stern lips and narrow eyes telegraphed that such jurors would be held accountable for the wrong decision.

The outcome weighed in the balance for two more hours until one of Soapy's accomplices rushed in with a note and shoved it in the crime boss's hand. After perusing the missive, Smith held the sheet up in the air and announced that he had sent a courier to the marshal's office in Sitka, seeking protection for Ed Fay until a proper trial could be conducted. The message not only granted that request but also indicated the marshal was deputizing as many of Jeff Smith's men as needed to safely deliver the prisoner to Sitka's jail.

Though some of us doubted the authenticity of the marshal's orders since it took more than two days for a round trip to Sitka, neither I nor anyone else challenged Smith or requested to inspect the order. Soapy had used the law—or his own duplicity—to outfox the committee. The murdering Ed Fay was spirited out of town the next day and Jim Rowan, who tried to do right by Skagway, was buried the day after that with the Reverend Robert M. Dickey presiding over the funeral as the deceased's wife stood dressed in black by the grave, sobbing as the preacher recalled Rowan's inherent decency. The widow held to her bosom the son that Rowan had known but for mere minutes. More than two hundred men and women braved the bitter weather to honor Rowan at his burial, nodding at the kind words heaped upon the dead lawman. Neither Soapy nor any of his known cohorts attended the internment. Never was there a sadder day in the history of Skagway than on that occasion.

Whether Rowan's death was an accident as Fay and his adherents claimed or a planned execution at the behest of Soapy Smith, everyone remained edgy, uncertain who to trust, even among members of the Committee of One Hundred and One. Suspicions and animosities lingered between those trying to make Skagway a respectable city and others seeking to profit from its boomtown youth. With Soapy's tentacles extending into so many businesses in hidden and insidious ways, few spoke about the corruption for fear word might filter back to Smith's gang.

The evening of Rowan's burial, I handled business in the Gold Dust when I heard Buck growl. Turning around, I spotted Jeff Smith entering the saloon and studying our place. I led my dog to the office and shut the door, observing Soapy strolling about. I knew he was seeking Ella Wilson, but she had left earlier with another customer. Not finding her, Soapy strode to the faro table and started betting wildly on the cards.

Faro stood as the Gold Dust's and other saloons' most popular game because it was simple to learn, moved fast and accommodated as many players as could crowd around the faro layout. The dealer shuffled a single deck of cards and placed it face up in a dealing box which exposed the top card. The bettors set their wagers atop representations on the layout of the thirteen card denominations, regardless of the four suits. With a fresh deck, the dealer removed the top pasteboard or "soda card" and exposed the second card, which won for the dealer. When he removed that card, he revealed the second denomination which won for the bettors. Bets placed on denominations other than those two cards could ride or be moved before the next round. The dealer went through the deck a pair at a time, called "turns," until he got to the final three pasteboards, where the players had the chance to "call the turn" or bet on the exact order of the remaining trio of cards. Besides the regular bets, a gambler could "copper" a wager by putting a six-sided token atop any ante and reversing the outcome so he won on the dealer's card. Other variations allowed players to bet on high or low cards or even multiple cards on the same turn. To help bettors keep up with the cards remaining in the deck, a "casekeeper" assisted the dealer by recording each exposed card on an abacus-like device at the dealer's side.

What made the game popular was the one-to-one payoff, a dollar back for every dollar bet. On the final three cards, the player's odds were five-to-one, though the payoff was only four-to-one, giving the house a slight edge. The house's other advantage came when two cards of the same denomination showed up on the same turn. When such a pairing occurred, the dealer claimed half of the bets placed on that denomination. Despite the relative good odds for the bettors, Smith was the poorest faro player I ever saw.

Ella Wilson saved Soapy a hundred or more dollars when she returned from her previous rendezvous. He looked up from the table, the scowl on his bearded face softening as he saw her gliding toward him. She answered with a soft, seductive smile, considering him easy money. I viewed him as a threat to her savings at best and her life at worst. As she moved to the faro table, I blocked her advance.

"A fellow was in earlier looking for you," I lied. "He said he'd return in a few minutes and was willing to spend the night."

Ella shook her head. "You don't want me leaving with Mr. Smith, do you?"

"Is he here?" I asked, playing dumb.

"You know he is." She rolled her eyes.

"Have him buy you drinks before you go," I offered, trying to stall.

"No, sir. What he saves on liquor he spends on me. The more he spends on me, the sooner I return to Louisiana."

"Ella," came a voice from behind me.

I turned to see Jeff Smith approaching.

"I'm available, if you're interested, Mr. Smith." Ella batted her eyes at him.

"You're the only reason I come into the Gold Dust. This is the worst saloon in town." He said, staring at me. "I'm embarrassed to be seen in this dump."

"Well, here you are," I countered. "You don't look embarrassed, though you should be humiliated for all the money you lose at my faro table."

Soapy cocked his head at me, his evil eyes focusing on my face, and scratched his beard. "I've seen you somewhere before, and it's been plaguing me. You ever been to Colorado?"

"Been lots of places."

"It'll come to me one day," he said, turning his gaze from me to Ella. "Right now I intend to escort my lady to her place." He offered her an arm, and she slid hers in his, marching out together.

Disappointed that Ella ignored my warnings, I watched her strut out with that cocky little bantam rooster. The only thing that would've lifted my spirits was if Soapy had left with Miss Susan B. Anthony. Then *he* would be in danger. For Ella's sake, I vowed I'd torment Smith any way possible until he quit hiring her. I figured to do it not only at our faro table but also at the saloons where he had planted crooked dealers. After explaining to my partner my plan, I told our faro dealer to keep rigged decks stacked with back-to-back cards of the same denomination so the house odds on splits improved when Soapy played at our place. I wasn't sure how to attack him at his own faro tables until events almost 4,000 miles away disrupted life in Skagway.

After the middle of February, word reached town that the battleship *USS Maine* had been blown up in Havana Harbor by the dastardly Spaniards, not that most of us knew where Havana was or even Spain. The *Skagway News* and the *Daily Alaskan* reported on the naval catastrophe, claiming that three-quarters of the crew of 355 had died in the attack. Of the ninety-four survivors, only sixteen had escaped without injury. Every American flag in Skagway the next day flew from a pole or hung from the buildings lining the streets. If we could've found a Spaniard or a Cuban, we would've hanged him as well to show our patriotism. I started spreading the rumor that Soapy Smith was a Spaniard and needed punishment for his mother country's depredation, but nobody believed me. My ability to spread gossip had declined since the days of Shotgun Jake Townsend back in Denver. Other citizens disseminated believable tittle-tattle as talk of war between Spain and the United States echoed up Lynn Canal. The most serious rumor came that Spain planned to invade Alaska, starting at Skagway and then claiming Klondike gold to finance the war that was sure to come. That grated us Americans, though we overlooked that the Yukon gold was in Canada, not the states or its territories, so hot burned the fever of conflict and the fear of invasion by the Spanish army and navy.

Every day we looked toward the bay, half expecting to see Spanish warships anchoring to demolish our fair city with their naval guns. After the navy pulverized the place, we expected soldiers to invade our shores and subjugate us to the king of Spain. But the only ships docking each day were freighters unloading supplies or steamers dropping off more adventurers, all hoping to realize the gold dust of their dreams somewhere between Skagway and Dawson City. The rumors became unbearable, and finally one man stepped forward to defend our town. That man was Jefferson Randolph Smith the Second.

Barely had the tensions peaked than Soapy announced he was organizing a company of volunteers to protect the city until called upon by the government to join the battle against the Spaniards. I first got word of his plan from my partner.

I responded, "That's a great idea, him raising a company of volunteers and heading off to Havana to fight the Spaniards."

Meredith shook his head. "You're too naïve, Jesse."

"What do you mean?"

"He has no intention of going off to fight. He wants to raise a private army to intimidate the honest folks of Skagway."

That made more sense to me than Soapy's patriotism as he thought only of himself.

"I tell you, Jesse, the committee is skittish about what he plans to do, once he has a hundred armed men following his orders. It doesn't bode well for Skagway's future or reputation."

"What's the committee gonna do?"

My partner shrugged. "Not much we can do, save watch him. If they try to stop it, they'll look unpatriotic, as if they're spitting on the watery grave of our brave heroes."

"Like everything else Soapy's involved in, nothing good will come out of it," I answered.

Sure enough, I was right. Within days of announcing his plans, Soapy opened a recruitment office out of what he called "Jeff Smith's Parlor," a long, narrow building he rented from Frank Clancy at 317 Holly Street. After his announcement, men lined up outside the Parlor to enlist. Most of those initial recruits were shills, who quickly passed through and were admitted to the militia company without further ado. Those that were genuine volunteers with no connections to Soapy or his organization endured a more rigorous recruitment, going through a mental check, a physical examination and a test to see if they might be used by the gang for nefarious rather than patriotic duties.

A week after the recruiting began, my namesake Jesse Murphy came into the saloon, his face as long as a kid's whose dog had been run over by a locomotive. He saw me and headed my direction. "Can ye spare a drink on the house?" he asked. "I've been swindled, and I'm broke."

Motioning for him to follow me, I stepped by the bar and grabbed a bottle of cheap whiskey before escorting him back in my office, Buck trailing us both. I closed the door, pointed at a chair and plopped the bottle on the table in front of him.

"Ye be having a glass?"

I shook my head. "The bottle's all yours."

"Glory be to ye," he said, uncorking the whiskey and taking a full swig.

"Now tell me what happened, one Jesse to another."

After finishing a second sip, he re-corked his liquor and began his tale of patriotic fervor to avenge the battleship *Maine*. He had gone to Jeff Smith's Parlor and signed the paperwork, pending his physical, then was sent to a second building where a doctor awaited. "I be thinking now he wasn't a doctor," my namesake continued. Murphy explained how he had undressed in one room and entered another where the doctor closed the door for privacy, proceeding to prod, poke and pinch his body before deciding Murphy was unfit for duty with the Skagway volunteers. When Murphy returned to his dressing room, he found his clothes rifled and his money gone.

"I be protesting that I be robbed, and the doctor be saying that I be knowing of Skagway's thievery, and that I should be showing more care with my money."

"Did you report it to Deputy Marshal Sylvester Taylor?"

"I be going to the marshal's room in the Occidental Hotel. He be telling me there be nothing he can do. I be broke."

Taking a minute to mull over his predicament, I finally replied. "Would you like a job?"

"I be needing money bad."

"I want you to spy for me, keep an eye on Soapy. Can you do that?"

"What information be ye wanting?"

"I plan to scam Smith, and I need help."

"I be willing to assist ye as Soapy be the one behind this swindling."

"Good, Jesse. I want to visit with my partner today, but you come back tomorrow, and I'll give you specific instructions on what to do."

"Ye be counting on me," he answered.

Reaching into my pocket, I pulled out a dollar and offered him. "This'll buy food until then. Then we'll get Soapy."

My namesake pointed to the bottle.

"Take it, but when you start working for me, I don't want any drinking during the day when you're on my time."

"I be thanking ye," he said, taking his whiskey and departing.

After he left, I told Buck to follow me, and we went out into the saloon where business boomed and girls danced on stage to the Ragtime beat of the piano. I found Roger and asked him to accompany me outside to talk over matters away from sinister ears. We grabbed our coats, and I put the stockings on my dog so he could go with us.

Exiting our saloon and opera house, we marched down Broadway toward the bay. I explained my concerns about Ella Wilson seeing Soapy and told him how the Irishman named Jesse Murphy had been robbed trying to serve his new country. I suggested if we couldn't beat Soapy Smith and his gang head-on, we should try subterfuge. As a more faithful member of the Committee of One Hundred and One, Roger agreed because the members were getting nervous with Soapy organizing his own militia. I indicated I planned to have our faro dealers use rigged decks anytime Smith played at our table. Also, I informed him of the job offer to my namesake.

"Doing what?" Roger asked.

"Spying on Soapy and his men, just watching, seeing if there's a way, to scam them."

As we walked, we spotted professor Bowers on the opposite side of the street. "Watch this," Roger said, as he nudged me in the ribs. We kept walking and without looking back, my partner cried out, "Hey, professor," in a perfect imitation of Soapy's voice, "wait for me at the bar in the Gold Dust." The impersonation was so good that Buck growled at my partner. We turned the corner, peeped around the building and saw Bowers looking up and down the street, scratching his head and starting toward the Gold Dust. We both laughed.

"I think we can damage old Soapsuds," Roger grinned. "So, put Murphy to work in the morning. We'll see what happens. Now, let's return to the saloon and check on the professor."

We scurried back to our place and sure enough found Bowers waiting at the bar.

"Should I use my voice to send him home?" Roger asked.

"No," I replied, "I'll handle this, but hang around and watch." On the plank walk, I bent and removed the stockings from Buck's legs.

Entering our saloon, I led Buck to the office where I closed the door on him and retreated behind the counter where I asked my bartender about business. He informed things were busy as I walked to the end of the bar. I glanced at Bowers, stepped past him, then turned and approached.

"You're Professor Bowers, correct?"

He nodded.

"I ran into Jeff Smith on the Broadway and he said he decided not to stop here after all."

"And why not?" the professor said, studying me intensely.

I leaned over the bar. "He encountered Ella Wilson and wanted to go for a ride, but told me you'd pay the thirty-three dollars he owed at the faro table."

"You expect me to believe that?" he replied, studying me even more intently.

Laughing, I tapped the counter with my finger. "You know what kind of faro player he is, don't you?"

Bowers shrugged because I'd pegged Soapy. "He carried enough money to pay you."

"Maybe so," I replied, "but he was saving it for Ella, left with her, mad about his losses."

The professor sighed. "Jeff's a sure-thing man until it comes to faro." He slipped his hand in his pocket and pulled out thirty-three dollars, offering the cash to me, then yanking his fingers back when I reached for it. "You look oddly familiar, like I've seen you in the past."

"Likely here in the Gold Dust. I'm here most of the time."

"No, somewhere before Skagway," Bowers replied, putting the money on the bar and pushing it to me. "It'll come to me. Jeff's been saying the same thing, and now I think he's right. We have met somewhere else."

"I don't remember being swindled by either of you," I lied, "here in Skagway or anywhere else, professor."

Bowers laughed. "Before that, I was a reverend. Maybe I saved your soul in an earlier mining town. The boomtowns need religion the most."

"And honesty," I added.

The professor looked at me and nodded. "It'll come to me where I've seen you before."

"Probably church somewhere, reverend."

Bowers tipped his hat and shook his head. "Not church, but somewhere. One day I'll remember." He turned and walked out of the saloon.

As he exited onto the street, I hoped he'd never recall our Leadville encounter. When the professor disappeared, Roger strode over and slapped me on the back. "My voice fooled him."

"And made us thirty-three dollars richer," I responded, holding up the bills, then placing them back on the bar and counting them. I cursed when I realized Bowers had shorted me five bucks. "Make that twenty-eight dollars."

Roger laughed. "It don't matter. We'll put the other Jesse Murphy to work and figure out how to take more of Soapy's money."

Chapter Twenty-two

Despite his Irishness, the second Jesse Murphy proved an excellent spy. He followed the conmen around Skagway as they fleeced the newcomers or cheechackos. Some fell for the telegraph con, others lost sure-thing poker games or three-card monte swindle, several had their pockets picked and a handful were outright robbed when they didn't fall for any of the other tricks Soapy's men employed.

After a week of tailing various members of the gang, Murphy met with Roger and me to discuss his observations once they had latched on to a mark, many going to locations operated by Soapy and others to saloons where Soapy paid dealers to cheat the newcomers. My namesake pretended to be drunk, something he'd had experience at, and watched what happened at the poker tables or the faro layouts.

"I be stumped. Ye be having any ideas short of robbing the thieves?" Murphy asked.

Roger shrugged. "I'm out of ideas."

"Faro is Soapy's weakness and our opening into his pocketbook," I said. "Is it correct his men steer some of their marks to faro tables?"

"That be true," Murphy replied.

"Faro's our best chance, as long as we don't get greedy," I said.

"How?" Roger asked.

"When we know they've hooked a faro mark, one of us will follow him to the saloon and join the betting. Place a small bet or two on the layout, but pay attention to the mark's bets. When he wagers, follow his lead, anteing only half of his bet, but wagering opposite bet. If he bets to win, bet the same card to lose. If he bets to lose, wager to win."

Roger and Jesse grinned.

"Ye be having a streak of larceny in ye," Murphy noted.

"I do what I can."

My partner scratched his head. "They'll recognize us and catch onto our intent before long. How will we avoid that?"

"You're the expert," I answered.

"Huh?"

"Theatrics," I explained. "We'll use your wigs, beards and even your costumes to change our appearance. We'll do one a day in different saloons."

Roger cocked his head at me. "You think he'll call in the militia on us now that he's in charge of the volunteers? The committee's worried about that."

"If we play our cards right, Soapy'll never know the difference, and we'll make money on the side, take a little out of his pocket for a change."

"Ye be counting me in," Murphy answered, "after them be robbing me while I be trying to do me patriotic duty and protect these shores from the Spanish."

I nodded. "We'll start tomorrow. Jesse'll identify the mark, and I'll do the betting."

Come the next day, my namesake and I ambled to the docks mid-morning to watch a steamship disembarking passengers from Seattle. Murphy pointed out the six grip men stationed to greet new arrivals and steer them to the location best suited for swindling them. Professor Bowers was one of the welcoming party. Jesse and I separated so as not to be too obvious. While he worked his way among the new passengers, I sat on a tree stump near the end of the wharf, pulled out my pocketknife, picked up a stick and began to whittle.

I sat close enough to the pier to hear snatches of conversations. Conmen warned their marks that they couldn't be too careful in Skagway because of unscrupulous men waiting to take their money. Soapy's hands steered their new acquaintances toward Merchant's Exchange, the telegraph office, the Cut Rate Ticket Office, Reliable Packers and the Information Bureau, all fronts for Jeff Smith, as honest places where a man could do business without being swindled.

After a half hour, Murphy walked off the pier two dozen paces behind Professor Bowers who had met a fraternal brother and was steering him along Broadway, carrying on the most amiable conversation you could imagine, reassuring his new acquaintance what a fine and safe city Skagway was.

I pulled down my hat and continued whittling as the two men passed.

"And," Bowers said, so focused on his quarry that he never looked my direction, "we have a deputy federal marshal here. His name is Sylvester Taylor. He's as straight an honest a lawman as you'll find anywhere, and a close friend of mine. If you have any trouble here in Skagway, you just let me know. I'll introduce you to him to get matters straightened out."

Bowers and his mark marched on. I kept whittling until my namesake walked by, then I tossed the twig aside, folded up my pocketknife and followed about ten paces behind him all the way to Clancy's Saloon. When I eased inside, Bowers and his victim stood by the faro layout. The dupe exchanged his cash for chips to play. As he did, Bowers slipped away from the table and turned for the door, stopping as he reached me.

"Creede," he announced.

I shrugged. "What are you talking about?"

"Creede's where I first met you," Bowers said, "eight years ago when the silver came in and started another Colorado boom."

"You're mistaking me for someone else, professor. I don't remember being in Colorado," I lied, hoping he had forgotten the Leadville boom.

Bowers shook his head. "There's something about that sneaky face of yours that's familiar. Jeff told me he didn't owe you any thirty-three dollars the last time I was in your place. You conned me, Murphy."

"It's the other way around, professor. You shorted me

five dollars of what I said Soapy owed."

"You're a crook," he said, glancing from me to the faro layout and bolting for the door. "We'll settle this later, I gotta run." He sped past a dozen customers and raced outside before his quarry was taken for his money and turned to Bowers for help.

Hurrying to the gambling table, I squeezed in between two customers on the opposite end of the layout from the dupe, hoping the dealer carried him another hand so I could see where the fellow had placed his money before the house slammed the hammer on him. I exchanged a hundred dollars for chips and waited for the turn which came up a queen and a trey. The dupe kissed the tip of his forefinger, then touched the hundred-dollar stack of chips on the ace. I put a dollar bet on the king and placed fifty dollars on the ace, grabbing a copper token and stacking it atop my wager. The dealer scowled at me, giving me confidence that this turn was the one that would sink the fellow's hopes. Sure enough when the dealer revealed the next card, an ace showed up and the dealer claimed his quarry's hundred dollars, but owed me fifty as I had coppered the card to lose. I grabbed my chips and the matching stack the dealer shoved my way.

I played two turns without shadowing the prey, who looked around for Bowers. "Where's the professor?" he asked. Prior to the third turn, he added another stack of chips worth a hundred dollars on the ace. Evidently, Bowers had told him the aces were winners. I pressed my luck, putting seventy-five on the same denomination, again coppering the bet. Sure enough, the dealer's card was an ace, and he took the dupe's money as well as another man's foolish bet. The dealer begrudgingly counted out my winnings and handed them to me.

I shoved all the chips back at him. "Cash me in before my luck changes."

The dealer glared at me and counted out my original hundred-dollar investment plus the additional hundred and twenty-five dollars I'd won betting the opposite of the dupe. When I had my cash, I marched for the door, but Frank Clancy cut me off.

"What are you doing here, Jesse?"

"Playing faro," I responded.

"You were lucky."

"Yeah, but your mark there was unlucky. Guess it sort of evens out."

Clancy crossed his arms over his broad chest. "I don't want you playing in my saloon anymore. Stick to your own place if you want to play. I'd hate for you to run into a streak of poor luck, a streak so bad you could get killed."

I pondered the threat a moment and smiled. "If I inform the Committee of One Hundred and One you're in cahoots with Soapy Smith and his gang, they won't like it."

Now Clancy studied me. He knew I had him, but he refused to admit it. "What are you talking about?"

"The agreement you've got with Smith so his men can bring dupes here to get fleeced by your dealers. What's your cut of the take, Frank?"

"Have you gone crazy, Jesse?"

"Nope. If you kick me out, I'll go tell Major Strong at the *Skagway News* about the connection to Soapy. Gossip has it that Jeff Smith's Parlor is a building you're renting to him. We'll see if he prints the story and boots you from the committee. The *Daily Alaskan* can't print enough stories of Soapy aiding widows and orphans or feeding stray dogs to offset such news."

Clancy grinned. "Maybe you're right, Murphy. You come over anytime to play faro."

"Thank you, Frank. I knew you were an understanding man."

I marched out of Clancy's confident that I had buffaloed the saloon owner, but worrying that Bowers was narrowing in on having met me in Colorado nearly two decades earlier. That concerned me, especially if he connected me to Leadville and Noose Neck's death.

Over the following four weeks Murphy, Meredith and I cleared almost three thousand dollars playing faro in other saloons. We were getting wealthy without having to march across Canada to Dawson City or dig in the frozen ground or deal with crooked lawyers. We tried to hit one competing saloon a day, alternating our disguises, our clothes and our hats to hide our scheme and drain as much of Soapy's ill-gotten gains as we could from his pocket to ours. One day I wore a miner's rough attire, a ragged slouch hat that came down to my eyebrows and a mustache that Roger fitted beneath my nose with spirit gum. To make the disguise even better, I sprinkled my outfit with cheap whiskey and doused more on my face like barbers used tonic water. I carried a half empty liquor bottle filled with tea and marched down to the wharves.

I waited by the pier and followed one of Soapy's men and his quarry to the Red Onion Saloon, a popular joint with the horny crowd because rooms upstairs were reserved for women plying their trade. The place was decent, though not nearly as well furnished as our establishment. When I stepped up to the table next to the shill, I plopped my liquor bottle on the layout, but the dealer chastised me.

"Remove your bottle if you want to play."

I lifted the liquor, took a swig and then shoved the bottle in the waist of my work pants. "I'm here to win. Can you change sixty-three dollars and seventeen cents into chips?"

Looking at me like I was sure-thing money, he nodded. "All but the seventeen cents."

I counted out my cash and offered it to the dealer, who replaced it with chips. Then I started mirroring the dupe's every bet, just betting for his winners to lose and his losers to win.

At one point the dealer looked up at me and shook his head. "Is your mustache supposed to be up?" he asked.

I nodded like a drunk, though I was uncertain where he was headed.

"Well," he continued, "it's up and down."

Grimacing, I reached for my fake whiskers, which angled down across my lips. The liquor I had splashed on my face must have acted as a solvent and released the grip of my fake mustache. I lifted the corner and pushed it back in place, hoping it would stick long enough for me to win another turn and escape.

"I've seen hundreds of drunks before," the dealer said, "but I've never seen a drunk mustache. What's your name, fellow?"

"H. err jes err," I mumbled for words until a name from the past tumbled from my brain and past my tongue. "Jake Townsend," I managed.

Two men at the table gasped. One wearing a red cap asked in astonishment, "You wouldn't be Shotgun Jake Townsend, would you?"

His hatless pal with a receding hairline and thinning hair grimaced. "Some say he was the meanest killer on the frontier. I was in Leadville when he blasted an honest lawyer in the back with a shotgun."

"I never heard of such," I said.

"Oh, yeah," said Thinning Hair, "a scatter gun is good for bird hunts and assassinations."

"Not a shotgun," I corrected, "but an honest lawyer. I never heard of such."

"Are you him?" Red Cap asked.

"I'm not a lawyer."

"No, are you Shotgun Jake Townsend?"

Turning to the dealer, I pressed my mustache, hoping it stayed in place, then and wagged my head side to side. "I'm not Shotgun. Cash me in, dealer." I pushed my chips toward him.

Realizing this drunk with the inebriated mustache was about to take his money and leave before he had a chance to regain it for the house, the dealer pleaded with me to stay. "Don't leave, Townsend. You've been on a decent run. Why break your luck?"

"I've been running for years from the stains that murderer splattered on my good name. I thought I'd escaped his legacy in Alaska, but I was wrong."

"We meant nothing by it," said Red Cap. "We didn't want to get on Shotgun's bad side."

"It's not your fault, fellow," I replied, "but a man tires of living down a reputation that's not his." I turned to the dealer. "Now give me my money before I go fetch my shotgun."

Everyone gasped and stepped back from the table.

Nodding, I said, "Just funning you boys. It's a joke."

The crowd relaxed, but none moved closer to the table until the dealer pushed me my cash, which I grabbed, then backed away from the layout, pulling the whiskey from my pants and sliding the cash in my pocket. I lifted the bottle to my lips as I retreated from the Red Onion so I could hold my fragile mustache in place until I got outside. I ran down the mushy street toward the Gold Dust, checking behind me several times to be sure no one was following. Even if I was not being tailed, my Leadville past was gaining on me, partly due to coincidence and partly because of my carelessness in bringing up Shotgun Jake after almost twenty years. I wondered how many men Townsend had killed in the interim.

I scurried into the Gold Dust, ran through the saloon and backstage to the dressing room where I pulled the cash from my pocket, placed the whiskey bottle on the table. Next I ripped off the loose mustache, shucked my clothes and slouch hat, then found a pitcher of water and dabbed a cloth in it so I could remove the aroma of liquor from my body. Roger Meredith burst into the room, Buck jogging after him.

"What's the matter, Jesse?" he asked.

"My mustache fell off at the Red Onion and a name came up from my past. We must lie low for a spell, avoid the faro games."

"You sound scared, Jesse."

"There's things you don't know about me, things I can't explain."

"We've all got a past, Jess. You've played square with me as a partner, so I'll take your word for it."

"Thanks, Roger. Have you seen my twin today?"

"Last I saw him he was headed toward the wharf to look for whatever suckers Soapy's men had hooked."

"When he returns, we need to inform him to stay low for a spell." I pointed to the clothes on the floor. "Can you slip these out and into a stove to burn so no one will find them?"

Roger nodded, bent and wadded them into a ball and left the dressing room as I put on my regular clothes. Once dressed, I petted Buck. He wagged his tail and licked my hand. We enjoyed each other's company because I could trust him.

Roger returned a few minutes later with Jesse Murphy. "Tell him what you told me."

I explained to my namesake that we needed to end our scheme for a spell and not play any more faro with dealers that shilled for Smith. Jesse grinned with relief. "Every day made me more nervous. I was thinking of quitting."

"Why?"

"I be followed. A stranger be offering me a dozen cookie cookies, and I be taking them to be decent mannered. I be not liking cookies so I be tossing them aside. A stray dog eats them up. Next day I be coming by the very place where I be discarding the cookies and the dog be dead. I be thinking someone tried to be poisoning me."

Roger looked at me. "Sounds like something Soapy would do."

"That's what I was thinking."

"I be scared," Murphy replied. "Ye be paying me my money, and I be looking for new work. I be hearing a railroad's coming and be needing workers."

Roger paced around the dressing room. "That's the rumor among the committee. The White Pass and Yukon Railway is being formed to go from the wharves in Skagway to Bennett Lake in Canada. They'll need laborers. It'll do away with all the hardships of packing supplies over the mountains once it's built."

"That be safer than taking on Soapy Smith," Murphy said.

"You've made back more than you lost from the doctor's exam, have you not?"

"That be true, but it be doing me no good if I'm dead and buried."

"We understand, Jesse," Roger said. "Return tomorrow and we'll have your last payment. We're grateful for what you did."

Murphy left the room, but returned immediately, looking scared and pale.

"What is it, Jesse?" I asked.

"He be out there in the saloon."

"Who?" Roger asked.

"Soapy Smith. He be wanting to see both of you."

Roger looked at me. "Don't accept any cookies from him."

Nodding, I laughed. "Thanks, partner."

"I be going," Murphy answered. "I be seeing you to-morrow if you still be alive, the both of you." He scurried out of the dressing room.

Roger and I eyed each other, uncertain what to do.

"Let me handle this alone, Roger? My foray into the Red Onion likely caused this."

"I'll keep a revolver handy."

I slapped at my belt. "Mine's ready, and I'm taking Buck with me. We'll visit in the office and decide things there."

Drawing a deep breath, I patted my dog's head. "Come on boy, let's go meet the devil and see what he wants." Buck followed me out of the dressing room and down the hall to the stage steps that led into the saloon. I spotted Soapy standing by our faro layout, though he wasn't betting this time.

He acknowledged me with a slight nod, scowling at Buck.

Approaching him, I looked around the room for his woman. Stopping in front of him, I hesitated, but Buck greeted the criminal with a growl that showed his loathing for Soapy. Then I spoke. "I don't know where Ella is."

"I'm here to see you and Meredith."

"Did you bring any poisoned cookies?"

The response stunned Soapy for a moment, but I the surprised look on his face confirmed our suspicions.

"Get your partner and let's visit in your office."

I pointed to Buck. "He's my partner. Roger's busy. Take it or leave it."

Soapy hesitated.

Buck growled.

Deciding to give Soapy incentive to meet on my terms, I informed Soapy where Roger was. "Right now, he has a rifle pointed at your back. If I lift my arm, he'll shoot you."

"And if he does, my men'll kill you and burn this place to the ground."

"Maybe so, but you won't be around to enjoy the fire."

Buck snarled at Soapy.

"Easy, Buck," I said. "Jeff is trying to make friends." I raised my arm, but Soapy grabbed it.

"Okay, let's visit in your office, you, me and the dog."

"Buck won't tell anyone, I promise you." I motioned

for him to head that way. He started, and Buck and I followed, my dog growling the total time.

We marched in the room and shut the door. I pointed Buck to the corner and the dog loped over and laid down, staring at Soapy, who took a seat. I sat in the chair on the opposite side of the table, my hand sliding to my side where I could pull my revolver if I needed it.

"What do you want, Jeff?"

"I heard Shotgun Jake Townsend was in Skagway in disguise. Any truth to that?"

"Who?"

"Don't toy with me, Jesse. Folks saw him run into your place after he left the Red Onion. He's working for you, isn't he?."

"What makes you think that?"

Soapy leaned forward in his chair. "For the last month, you've had your men tailing our marks and honing in on our winnings, taking money out of our pockets."

I put both hands on the table. "My men never dealt a card. Your hacks showed the cards, controlled the chips and managed the casekeeper. We played by the rules of the game. You should know them by now as much money as you've lost at faro here and every other saloon in Skagway."

"I'm willing to let bygones be bygones, Jesse, if you introduce me to Townsend. He's got some talents I can use here in the militia. I am captain of the Skagway Guards."

For a moment, I studied Smith in disbelief that a character I made up twenty years earlier had come back to life thousands of miles away from where he had never existed in the first place. "No deal, Jeff. He's my ace in the hole against you."

"He can be bought, Jesse."

"Says who?"

"All of Denver knows it. Somebody hired him to kill Mattie Silks and Cort Thomson years ago, but that fat madam outbid her enemy, and he didn't shoot her or her lazy lover. When I find him, I can damn sure pay him more for a killing than you can."

"Good luck finding him, Soapy."

"Don't call me that."

"Sure thing, Soapy."

Smith stood up from his chair. "Once I find him, Jesse, you're the first one I'm having him kill because somewhere I know I met you and when I figure it out, I'll get you with or without Townsend." He turned for the door, Buck jumping up and nipping at his ankle until I called him to my side.

I feared the circle —or was it a noose—of deceit was closing around me in Skagway. Needing more help than I could muster, I decided to do something I'd rarely done since leaving home. Come Sunday, I planned to attend church.

Chapter Twenty-three

While I had been in the Union Church before when the Committee of One Hundred and One met to discuss business or to consider the fate of the murdering Ed Fay, I had never attended a service there. After men of the various denominations arrived in late 1897 to wring all the sin and fun out of Skagway, they agreed to put aside their religious differences and share a single building—Union Church—until they had the resources to construct their individual houses of worship. Once they picked enough pockets of churchgoers by passing the plate, they would build their own sanctuaries so their religious tenets remained unsoiled by sharing the same pews and offering plates. After Union Church opened toward the end of 1897, Sunday services followed a set morning schedule: Roman Catholic mass at seven each Sunday and Episcopalians at eleven. Afternoon worship started with Baptists at one, Universal Sunday School at two, Methodists at three and Presbyterians at seven-thirty. Being raised a Baptist had never fully taken with me, but I opted for the Baptist service, though I would've switched denominations if I knew of one that might smite Soapy Smith and his gang quicker than the others.

As time neared for my sermon, I put the stockings on Buck's legs and told Roger I was taking my dog for a walk. My partner waved me off. He was preparing for an afternoon dramatic reading of Shakespeare since newspaper recitations were no longer profitable because the

Skagway News and the *Daily Alaskan* had filled the void for news, even if most of it was lies, especially from the *Alaskan*. After I loosely knotted a rope around Buck's neck for a leash, we strolled south along Broadway to Fifth, turned west and crossed State Street where the church stood on the south side of the street. As the previous service was letting out, I thanked God I considered myself Baptist rather than Episcopalian as they had endured a two-hour rite. Even so, those departing were all smiles and courteous as they emerged, including some I recognized as Gold Dust patrons. The biggest shock came when Ella Wilson exited, looking as saintly as a virgin, her smile genuine, unlike the seductive visage she presented in the saloon.

When she saw me, she looked as surprised as me. "Well, Jesse," she said, "I didn't expect to see you here." She paused. "And I know you're thinking the same thing."

I missed the days when we addressed each other as Mr. Murphy and Miss Wilson. "I figured I needed religion, Ella."

"It does our souls good," she replied, bending to pet Buck on the head.

"I'm sure I need it much more than you," I offered.

She looked up at me with a sweetest expression. "Why, Jesse, that's the kindest thing anyone's ever said to me. None of the pious women I worshipped with would have said that."

She took my hand, and we moved from the church entry toward the corner, so not to block the exiting Episcopalians and the entering Baptists.

"I worry for your safety, Ella, taking up with Soapy."

"Mr. Smith hates that name," she replied.

"He's told me as much. That's why I call him that."

"As for my wellbeing, I can take care of myself. As for my future, it's locked in my trunk. I'll return to Louisiana by the end of May, perhaps earlier."

"Why not leave tomorrow?"

"I'm still shy of my target, Jesse, though you might help me make five hundred more dollars real quick."

Nothing I could do was worth that much money, I thought, and her statement stumped me. "How's that?"

"Mr. Smith's been asking about a friend of yours, a fellow called Jake Townsend, who's rumored to be in Skagway. Jeff said he'd give me five hundred dollars to find him."

I felt my neck and cheeks burn with rage. "Townsend's a dangerous man, just like Soapy. The difference is Townsend has reformed. He wants to be left alone, like he never existed."

"Mr. Smith says there's money in it for Townsend."

Shaking my head, I answered, "And for you! Much as I care for you, Ella, I'll not betray a friend like Jake or even you. The longer you're around Soapy, the riskier it becomes."

"Three months, maybe four at most, Jesse, and I'm returning to Louisiana." She smiled. "Don't let me make you late for church."

I nodded, lifted her fingers to my face and kissed the back of her hand. "And you take care of yourself."

She curtsied. "You're such a gentleman, Jesse."

"And you're always a lady to me."

As Ella walked away, I watched her turn the corner on State Street, then led Buck to the church door, where I bent and removed his stockings so he wouldn't soil the church floors. I shook the mud off the socks and inserted them in my coat pocket, leading Buck inside and taking a seat at the end of the back pew so my dog could rest on the floor. A dozen Gold Dust customers marched by, three greeting me, the remainder ignoring me.

When the sermon started, the preacher gave a stem-winder, attacking every sin I had ever heard of plus a few new to me. He lamented the breed of men that came to Skagway to prey on others, never mentioning Soapy but decrying the recent arrival of Shotgun Jake Townsend, insisting such murderers were the scourge of a growing community. He especially assailed the fornication in Skagway, but unlike many preachers who condemned whoring, he offered a way out, saying his congregation would pay the passage for any soiled dove that desired to return to her home and start a fresh and Godly life. I doubted the Episcopalian cleric had made such an offer, but I wanted to inform Ella that the Baptist reverend offered to cover the freight on sending her to

Louisiana. The preacher envisioned a Skagway free of harlots and, as a result, a better place for families. His words and sentiment carried power, though I wasn't sure that his message was practical, Skagway being overrun with men and too few women for marriage prospects. Even so, the preacher was a commanding talker, almost as polished with language as Miss Susan B. Anthony from my Leadville days, which had caught up with me in Skagway and forced me to church. When the spiritual leader asked us to pray, I beseeched God to protect Ella as much as me from the evil that walked the local streets in the human form of Jefferson Randolph Smith the Second. The reverend invited all who had not accepted Jesus as Lord and Savior to come forward and submit themselves for baptism. For all his preaching eloquence, he convinced no takers, because nobody cared to be baptized in February in the Skagway River. I wondered if the Methodists in the following service might have more luck since they sprinkled rather than dunked.

Next we sang *Shall We Gather at the River?*, the lyrics I vaguely recalled from church services back in Cane Hill, Arkansas, then a newer, unfamiliar song *When the Role Is Called Up Yonder*. Never being musical, I mouthed what words I knew, never singing above a whisper, figuring God would listen if he wanted or ignore me if he didn't. Some fellows, though, crooned with abandon even though their musical talents were so lacking that even I recognized it. Despite their inferior musical abilities, those men enjoyed singing the most. With the hymns completed the preacher passed the collection plate. While I rarely gave, having not been in church in years and not having tithed any portion of the San Francisco godsend from Wells Fargo, I was moved to donate to the Baptists in Skagway. If I offered enough, I hoped to convince God to protect to Ella Wilson. I reached in my britches pocket and pulled out my wad of money, peeling off fifty dollars that I added to wicker basket when it reached me.

We ended the service singing *Amazing Grace*, then exited for the Sunday school crowd, the preacher greeting us at the door as we departed. He shook my free hand as I left with Buck on the leash. Instead of releasing my fingers, he squeezed tighter and put his other arm around my shoulder. "You look troubled, my son."

The reverend appeared half my age with innocent eyes that had not seen all that I had in the previous decades. I didn't know what to say.

"Tell me your worries," he implored.

"I'm worried for a young woman that needs saving."

"Perhaps I can help her," he offered.

"She's not your kind."

"Is she a harlot?"

"Not only that, she's Episcopalian."

The preacher laughed. "We all pray to the same God. Share her name, and I will pray for her."

"She goes by Ella, but I don't want to tell you more."

He smiled and patted me on the shoulder. "God will know for whom I pray."

"Thank you," I said as Buck and I stepped through the door into the frigid air and cold-heartedness that was Skagway. I slipped the canvas stockings over Bucks legs, and we returned to the Gold Dust.

Having just heard a sermon, I didn't care to listen to Roger Meredith's dramatic soliloquies from Shakespeare, so I walked around town, the streets humming with activity, even on a Sunday afternoon. In the seven months since I had arrived to find a city of tents beyond the bay's mudflats, Skagway had grown into a fine town with dozens of buildings. By my count the community now claimed more than two dozen saloons, a bowling alley, twenty mercantiles, nineteen hotels and fifteen restaurants plus eight tobacco stores, seven groceries, six meat markets, four bakeries, two barbershops, two bathhouses, a laundry, two newspapers, four blacksmiths, a livery stable, two hardware businesses and two furniture stores. Among the professions, Skagway boasted offices for six doctors, two dentists and, unfortunately, five attorneys. With five real estate dealers, three builders, an architect, and three painters, more structures were being constructed, even in the cold months since it was not such a harsh winter as it was up into the mountains. The water from the bay helped moderate the temperatures so that the snow and ice did not present a daily challenge as much as the mush and mud that everyone had to navigate. Men and a growing number of women meandered through the streets, going to church, making their purchases or falling for the entreaties of Soapy's men, intent on cheating decent folks. I'd always heard you couldn't swindle an honest man, just a greedy one. But Smith's minions had devised so many schemes involving so many actors, and that's how I viewed his henchmen, that a decent fellow might easily fall for one. The performances of Soapy's actors surpassed anything that my partner did on stage, whether he was giving dramatic readings of San Francisco newspapers or the soliloquies of Shakespeare. I walked to the piers, stopping between the Moore Wharf and the Alaska Southern Wharf to admire the White Pass & Yukon Railway office that was going up, confirming that talk of a railroad over the mountains was more than wishful gossip.

From there I let Buck choose where he wanted to go, and he pranced west on Second Avenue toward the Juneau Wharf where Ella Wilson and I had visited on New Year's Day. I stood at the foot of the dock, then turned north up State Street, where I encountered my namesake. Jesse Murphy waved at me and ran over to confirm that he had taken work with the railroad. In his Irish brogue he told me he thought hauling ties, laying rails, blasting rock and traversing cliffs was safer than challenging Smith and his gang, though he had enjoyed scamming Soapy at faro and recouping with interest the money he had lost in the phony militia physical. I told Murphy I'd offer him a dozen cookies if I had any, but he snickered and said he wasn't taking free food from anybody since his last edible gift had poisoned a dog. After looking down the street at the stray dogs, he admitted poisoning a few more might do Skagway some good. We shook hands and went our separate ways.

Buck and I returned to the Gold Dust. Barely had I removed the dog's stockings and stepped inside, than Roger Meredith approached me, still in a cloak and tights from his reading. "It true you've been to church?" he asked.

"Ella told you, did she? What of it?"

"You don't seem the type," Roger responded.

"I surprise myself sometimes."

"Something's worrying you, isn't it?"

"Somehow I've got this feeling Soapy's working against me."

"He's working against everyone." Ready to change the topic, I inspected Roger from head to foot. "I wouldn't wear such garb when I wasn't on stage."

Roger laughed. "The performance was one of my best. I'm sorry you missed it."

Pointing at my dog, I blamed him. "Buck said he'd heard enough Shakespeare for a spell—you know he can talk, don't you?—so I took him to church, then a walk. You seen Ella?"

"A minute ago. She's around here somewhere."

"Go change your clothes before a drunk thinks you're one of the gals available for bedding." I turned and spotted Ella across the room. She started toward me.

"Good sermon?" she asked.

"The preacher identified sins I'd never thought of before," I responded. "Best of all, I learned the preacher's offering free passage for any woman of your type back to the states!"

Her lips tightening, Ella balled her fists and planted them on her hips. "What do you mean by any woman of my type?"

Grimacing, I realized my choice of words had been insulting. "Episcopalian?" I replied.

Ella's stern gaze cracked like melting ice. She laughed, throwing her arms around me and kissing me on the cheek. "Even for your faults, Jesse, you mean well," she told me. "And, come May or June, I'll take your Baptist friends up on their offer."

"That's a few months away," I said.

"Maybe so, but in less than a year I'll have set aside my money," she replied.

"Shhhh," I said. "Don't say such where people might overhear. You could get killed."

She smiled. "In the time I've been here, no girl like

me—" she hesitated, "—no Episcopalian has been killed or beaten. This is as safe a place as I've ever plied my trade, Jesse."

"How much do you lack reaching your goal? I'm doing well enough to make up the difference, if you'll get out of Skagway."

"That's so sweet, Jesse, but I've got to do this my way, no charity, save whatever fare the Baptists will pay for this Episcopalian to return to leave." She pecked my cheek again with a kiss. "I best return to work, recruiting I call it like Mr. Smith calls the enlisting his militia." She turned and flitted among the men whose money would ultimately secure her future in Louisiana.

The next afternoon I found myself in Union Church again, though not for another sermon. The Committee of One Hundred and One had called a special meeting to discuss unspecified matters germane to the future of Skagway and its reputation. Behind the pulpit where the Baptist preacher had stood the day before, Major John F.A. Strong banged the gavel to open the session. Immediately, the attendees shouted and argued, taking up where they had left off with the Ed Fay charges in the wake of Deputy Rowan's murder. In the weeks since Rowan's burial, Strong reported that thefts and robberies had doubled and crooks conducted their business with impunity.

"If it's so bad why haven't I been reading about it in your paper?" a citizen cried.

"I keep a list at my desk of every incident," Strong began. "All of you are welcome to come by the *Skagway News* and view it. I don't print it because Skagway gets hit over the head enough by the Seattle, Portland and San Francisco papers as being a lawless community. I see no reason to print such stories and give them more fodder to demean Skagway. As for my competitor, I can't say why the *Daily Alaskan* or its editor J. Allen Hornsby and reporter Billy Saportas publish only favorable articles about Soapy Smith instead of the truth."

Everybody in the room knew Smith bribed Hornsby for flattering articles at the expense of the truth, but that didn't keep Hornsby from responding. He jumped up from his pew and waved his arms over his head. "I will not stand for such slander as the *Alaskan* wears the cloak of truth in its coverage. I, too, will not defile the name of this good town by printing every minor dispute that arises between our citizens." Several booed and heckled as Hornsby finished his harangue and sat after his valiant defense of lies.

Strong banged the pulpit with his gavel. "Let's move on to other items and we shall return to this before we adjourn," he announced, then updated the committee on the legal matters affecting the ownership of city lots.

As I understood it, Alaska was a district rather than an American territory without the lawful foundation upon which a territory is organized. The governing authority was a U.S. Commissioner who made decisions that would otherwise be handled by county or territorial governments. Consequently, when Roger and I purchased our lot, we only had to pay five dollars for a filing fee to the commissioner's office instead of buying the land from the founding Moore family who had settled and homesteaded part of the town a decade before the gold rush. Ownership of the property was headed to the federal courts for resolution, which might take years. That explained why Moore's bunkhouse still stood in the middle of State Street. Strong said that the committee had agreed with Moore to skid the offending bunkhouse to an undisputed acre of his land as soon as the streets dried up enough to accomplish the task.

Major Strong also announced that the White Pass & Yukon Railway planned to lay tracks starting in the summer, drawing cheers from everyone, until he indicated the rails would be laid down the middle of Broadway. Those of us with businesses on the street jumped to our feet and protested the damage to our trade, the danger to our patrons, especially those from saloons who often left too drunk to cross the street much less step over iron rails, and the fire hazard to the whole town with a WP&YR locomotive spewing cinders and sparks near the wooden buildings that made up Skagway. The commotion raged for half an hour over what would be best for the railroad we agreed we needed, though few of us agreed on the route it should take. When the dispute flared at its hottest, another noisy disturbance arose outside. Committee members at the back of the church exited to the street, then rushed back in. "You've gotta see this."

Everyone bolted from our chairs and raced out the door like WP&YR sparks had set the Union Church ablaze. We scrambled outdoors and looked toward State Street where a band made up of musicians from saloons tied to Soapy Smith marched down the street playing *The Battle Hymn of the Republic.* Behind the musicians on a white horse rode Soapy Smith himself in front of a hundred men with weapons propped on their right shoulders, marching in step as best they could down the center of the mushy street. As Soapy approached Fifth Avenue, he glared at the committee members standing outside the church. He fixed his gaze on us and never moved his head until he crossed Fifth. His ragtag troops in unmatched uniforms and carrying varied rifles and shotguns watched us with hateful eyes as well.

"Isn't their drill reassuring," cried *Alaskan* editor Hornsby. "The Spanish will never take Skagway, not from the Skagway militia."

"Hip hip hooray for the U-S-A," shouted saloon owner and Smith ally Frank Clancy.

The rest of us stood stunned at the challenge from the most crooked man in Skagway and perhaps in all of North America. Our worries grew even more when Deputy Sylvester Taylor brought up the rear of the parade atop his black gelding. He, too, looked the committee's way. Instead of glaring at us, he smiled and tipped his hat before riding on.

After the procession passed our intersection, I retreated inside with the rest of the committee. Hornsby, Clancy and a few of their allies were invigorated by the display while the implied threat chastened most of us. Everyone against Soapy Smith now understood the challenge facing Skagway.

Strong ended the railroad discussion and returned to the original topic of how to counter the corruption, specifically Soapy Smith. "Gentlemen," he said, "this afternoon we saw what we face, did we not?"

"Indeed, I did," cried Hornsby. "A glorious future for Skagway when we have a patriot such as Jefferson Smith protecting our fair town from the Spanish."

"Shut up," cried my partner. "If you're so enthralled, why don't you go join the volunteers or leave so the rest of us can decide what to do?"

"Leave him be," answered Clancy. "He's as much right to be here as you."

"Order," cried Strong. "As designated head of the committee, I intend to send word to the U.S. Commissioner for protection."

"Troops aren't needed," Hornsby cried, "we've got our own militia."

"That," said Strong, "is exactly why we need federal soldiers."

Clancy and Hornsby argued against the move, but they and their few allies were outvoted by a five-to-one margin.

Strong announced, "I'll ask Josias M. Tanner to accompany me to Dyea or Sitka, whichever it takes so we can be assured that law and order will come to Skagway. This meeting is adjourned." With that, he banged the gavel, took it and his papers and started down the aisle for the front door.

Hornsby stood up to challenge Strong, but thought better of it when his rival lifted the gavel to his chest, ready to answer any demand with a thumping. Most of us filed out of the building, angered at what we had seen and certain the tensions portended violence. On the way back to the saloon, Roger told me Si Tanner, as he was called, was a good choice to deliver the message as he was a former lawman from Iowa who had run barges in and out of Skagway before going to work for the White Pass & Yukon Railway.

True to his word, Strong and Tanner delivered the request and eight days after the meeting adjourned, a company of U.S. troops arrived at the Alaska Southern Wharf and disembarked. The soldiers marched through town and bivouacked on the outskirts in their tents. The next day, they patrolled the streets of Skagway, closing saloons and gambling halls. They shuttered the Gold Dust first, accusing us of serving alcohol to Tlingits. After Roger and I locked up the saloon and walked the streets, we realized the troops had been selective in which saloons they closed. Frank Clancy's saloon remained open as did Jeff Smith's Parlor and four more affiliated with Soapy.

"Damnation," muttered my partner. "How far does Soapy's influence reach in Alaska?"

"I wish I knew," I answered.

Our faith in the army and the U.S. Commissioner weakened even more when we saw Soapy escorting the captain in charge of the troops for a Skagway tour. As Soapy passed the two of us, he aimed his finger our way and informed the officer in a stage whisper. "There's two of the crookedest men in Alaska. Murphy and Meredith are their names, though Murphy is using an alias. I've seen that bastard somewhere before, if I can ever place him."

We stood there glaring back at a legitimate officer of the U.S. military and a self-appointed captain with a grudge against every honest or semi-honest man in Skagway.

"What are we gonna do, Jesse?" Roger asked me.

"I've been in many scrapes before, partner, and something always comes through."

"Perhaps we should sell the place and get out of here."

"I don't run," I said, thinking for an instant and then continuing, "unless I have to."

"I'm not so sure that this isn't the time to skedaddle."

"No, we need to wait."

"Why wait?"

"We don't want to lose our fortune in the saloon."

"It's better to lose a fortune than your life."

"Let's wait until it warms up."

"Why stay until summer?" he wanted to know.

"Graves are easier to dig then."

Chapter Twenty-four

With the militia parade and the visit by U.S. troops, Soapy Smith showed he controlled Skagway with influence none of us could counter, at least directly. The soldiers left after three days, and everything resumed as it had been, save that people grew even more suspicious of each other, never certain who was on Soapy's payroll and who was not. For all the fear he created, you never read about it in the newspapers. He paid the *Daily Alaskan* to run stories about him, and every issue featured an account of his benevolence, how he donated to the church, or gave to widows and orphans, or tried to find homes for the stray dogs that roamed the streets. In the *Alaskan*, Jeff Smith became as great a philanthropist as Andrew Carnegie. The *Skagway News* mentioned him as little as possible because when he wasn't threatening to sue the paper if something amiss appeared on its pages, he was bullying the editor with promises to burn the place down. If arson took a single building, it might consume every structure in Skagway.

As March inched toward April and a glorious Alaskan spring, the Committee of One Hundred and One met on the sly, keeping Smith's sympathizers at bay by convening in small clusters and then having a representative from each meet together to discuss a strategy without Soapy knowing in advance. The first action the committee took was posting handbills around town warning ne'er-do-wells to do well or get out of Skagway. Roger and I passed out flyers, tacked them elsewhere and read them to illiterates who might otherwise miss the message. The dated posters marked "Skagway, Alaska" were simple and to the point:

WARNING!

A word to the wise should be sufficient! All Confidence, Bunco and Sure-thing Men, and all other objectionable characters are notified to leave Skagway and White Pass Road Immediately. And to remain Away. Failure to comply with this warning will be followed by prompt action.

101

Barely had those notices appeared than Soapy called a town meeting with an ad in the *Alaskan*:

ANNOUNCEMENT

The business interests of Skagway propose to put a stop to the lawless acts of many newcomers. We hereby summon all good citizens to a meeting at which these matters will be discussed. Come one, Come all! Immediate action will be taken for relief. Let this be a warning to those cheechackos who are disgracing our city! The meeting will be held at the meeting hall at 8 p.m. sharp. (signed) Jefferson R. Smith, chairman.

At that gathering Soapy attracted his regulars as well as those naïve to Skagway and its politics. By vote of the group, they created a Law and Order Society, which he headed. He announced that unlike the rival committee, his organization boasted members totaling 317, the same number as the address on Jeff Smith's Parlor in an unsubtle message to those supporting true law and order in Skagway.

Two mornings after that evening meeting, the decent folks of Skagway awoke to find a rival handbill plastered all over town, even on the homes of Committee of One Hundred and One members, answering that group's original warning. The placards announced:

ANSWER TO WARNING

The body of men styling themselves 101 are hereby notified that any overt act committed by them will be promptly met by the Law-abiding Citizens of Skagway and each member and HIS PROPERTY will be held responsible for any unlawful act on their part and the

Law and Order Society consisting of 317 citizens will see Justice is dealt out to its full extent as no Blackmailers or Vigilantes will be tolerated.

THE COMMITTEE

Some townsmen thought it was pure bluster, but those fellows had never been around Jefferson Randolph Smith the Second for long. I figured the only person mean enough to take on Soapy and his gang was Miss Susan B. Anthony, but she was somewhere back east still worried over suffrage and lesser matters than life and death or Skagway's survival.

The very Saturday night Soapy's handbills appeared at our door, Ella told me she wasn't feeling well, woman problems she said, and asked me to accompany her to her crib. I agreed, checking that my revolver was loaded and retrieving my carbine as I started carrying it whenever I left the saloon. I called Buck and put on his canvas stockings and stepped out onto the mushy streets. Halfway to her place, Buck growled, but I thought nothing of it other than perhaps he had sniffed another dog as strays roamed throughout town. I saw Ella to her door and gave her time to light a lamp and lock up. When she signaled me at the window that everything was okay, I retraced my steps, reaching the corner at Broadway when Buck growled and snarled.

"There's the son-of-a-bitch," came a muffled voice. "Get him!"

I spun around, encircled by five or more men. Falling to the ground, I landed in the muck, as gunfire erupted all around me. I yanked my carbine to my shoulder and fired in front of me, then rolled over and shot in the opposite direction, then to both sides as fast as I levered cartridges in and out of my long gun.

Growling and snarling as I'd never heard him before, Buck lunged ahead, leaping for one gunman and grabbing his arm, yanking him off the walk into the street.

"Get this damn dog off of me," cried a squeaky voice that I recognized as Soapy's.

The bullets quit splattering in the muck around me and whizzed over my head toward Buck, who bit and tugged my screaming assassin deeper into the grime. The terrified man fired a shot. In the flash I discerned the bearded face of Soapy Smith.

Buck yelped and loosened his grip enough for my assailant to yank his arm free and jump to his feet as four other men surrounded him. Two fired shots in Buck, who yelped weakly. I aimed my carbine at Soapy and squeezed the trigger, ready to put him in his grave, but the metallic click told me my carbine was empty.

"Let's get out of here," called a voice that sounded like that of professor Bowers.

Suddenly, the men scattered like quail as I yanked my pistol from the scabbard and emptied it in their direction. I knew I'd missed, but I'd put a scare in them. I jumped up and raced to Buck, who sprawled in the mud whimpering. "Bastards," I screamed at my assailants as I shoved my revolver back in my holster. I placed my carbine atop Buck and picked him up, cradling him and my weapon in my arms as I stumbled to the saloon. At the door I kicked it with my foot until someone came and opened up. I barged inside, staggering into the light and heat. Roger rushed to me, confused at what he saw.

"Have you been wallowing with the hogs?" he asked, confusing Buck's muddy carcass for a hog.

"It's Buck, dammit. He's been shot," I cried, dropping to my knees and rolling him onto the floor, my carbine tumbling on the planks beside him. "Get a doctor." I looked at him and his eyes closed once, then fluttered open and shut forever after that. "It's too late," I said.

"Somebody get the marshal," Roger ordered, then studied at me. "I'm sorry, Jesse."

"Don't anybody touch Buck," I screamed. The patrons remaining in the saloon backed away as I got up and retrieved my carbine, taking it to the bar where I dropped it and unbuckled my gun belt, placing it beside the long weapon. The bartender brought me a basin of water to wash my hands and face. I removed my coat and took a bar towel from the barkeep and dipped it in the chilly liquid, rinsing the mud and grit from my fingers and palm, then I washed my cheeks with the damp cloth.

Roger ran upstairs to my room and returned with a clean shirt and britches as I undressed in the middle of the saloon for everyone to see. I was down to my long johns when Deputy Marshal Sylvester Taylor entered.

"What happened, Murphy?" the lawman inquired.

"You know," I responded.

"I don't. That's why I asked."

"Soapy Smith and his men ambushed me."

"Now that's impossible," Taylor replied.

"How so?" I responded in disbelief.

"Jeff's been in my room the past two hours until your fellow ran over saying you'd been shot. By the looks of you, he was wrong. I don't see any blood, just mud." He laughed.

I lifted my fist and shook it in his face. "Were you one of them, deputy?"

Taylor snorted, offering me a sneer and a few words. "One of who?"

"One of the men that ambushed me."

"If I'd been shooting, Murphy, you'd be dead." the lawman smirked.

"Did you kill, Buck?"

"Buck?"

"My dog." I pointed at the carcass on the floor.

Taylor marched over and toed the lifeless form with his muddy boot. "Appears to be a suicide."

"Then you're not doing a thing about any of this?"

"I don't investigate dog deaths," Taylor shot back. "The streets are filled with strays."

"What about shootings on the streets of Skagway?"

"When a witness comes forward to verify your claim, then I'll look into it. Until then for all I know, you tripped and fell in the mud, discharging your gun and killing your own dog." Taylor tossed me a parting laugh and started for the door, then stopped and turned around, lifting his finger and pointing it at my nose. "Why don't you run to your Hundred and One Committee and have them look into the shooting?" He snickered and exited, leaving everyone stunned.

My partner stepped beside me and patted my shoulder. "Perhaps it's time to sell out."

Wagging my head from side to side, I disagreed. "I'm not letting that scoundrel scare me out of Skagway, not while I'm making good, honest money for a change."

"You can't spend your profits when you're dead," Roger responded. "If the law won't protect us, what are we going to do? Start our own gang?"

"Not when we bring in the right ally, one so mean they'd cower in their boots."

"Who are you talking about?"

"Miss Susan B. Anthony," I declared.

"The suffragist? Isn't she against drinking and gambling and whoring and fighting, everything that makes us men?"

I nodded. "She could lecture them to death, spewing words faster than they could dodge them. I'd give even odds, matching her against Soapy, Taylor and their associates. Miss Anthony could speak from our very stage and set the world right. She's spoken in saloons before."

Shaking his head, Roger replied, "I'm not interested in healing anything but Skagway."

"You got any better ideas, partner?"

"I'll mull it over."

"You do that," I said. "I have a burial to prepare for." Stepping to the bar, I picked up the basin of water I had used to clean myself and toted it to Buck. Dropping to my knees I washed the mud and blood off of his fur, biting my lip and dabbing at my moist eyes. One of the ladies squatted down and helped as the piano player tapped out *Amazing Grace* on the ivories. Roger headed upstairs to his room and returned with a worn wool blanket. Once I finished cleaning him up, I swaddled Buck in Roger's cover and then carried the bundle to the end of the bar where I placed my dead dog.

"Come daylight, I'll bury him in the cemetery," I announced, as several patrons marched by and petted my dog through the shroud. I started for the stairs, desperate for rest.

"Would you care for company?" one of the ladies asked. "On the house."

"Thank you, dear," I replied, "but I just need to be alone for a spell."

She took my hand and patted it. "I understand," she answered, releasing my fingers.

I headed up the steps, sad and angry over losing Buck, and wondering if Ella Wilson had set me up for the ambush by feigning her malady. At the head of the stairs, I stopped, turned about and retraced my path, looking for the gal that had offered to comfort me.

As I approached, she smiled. "Change your mind?"

"No, ma'am" I replied, "but you might do me a favor. Would you run over to Ella's place and make sure she's okay? She wasn't feeling well, so I want you to check on her, see what's wrong and if we need to take her to a doctor."

"I can do that."

"Thank you," I said, reaching in my pocket for a dollar and giving it to her. "That's for your time. As soon as you return, come up and let me know what you found out."

She grabbed her coat, then left the saloon. I retreated to my room and waited. The space felt empty and lonely since Buck always slept at the end of my bed. I returned to the bar, picked up my dog and carried him upstairs, placing him on the floor at the foot of my bed so we would have a final night together. A half hour later my messenger came in and informed me Ella was okay except that she was suffering from what women her age endured once a month. Ella may not have lied about feeling poorly, but I questioned whether she used the malady to set me up. Perhaps Soapy had offered her more money to betray me, hastening her return to Louisiana.

"I described the ambush," my emissary informed me. "Ella was horrified, said she'd heard shots, but was too scared to look for fear a stray bullet might hit her. I told her about Buck and your plans to bury him in the cemetery tomorrow. She wants to attend."

"Thank you," I said.

"The offer's still open if it'll help you."

"I appreciate it, dear, but good night." After she closed the door, I debated whether or not Ella had betrayed me to Jefferson Randolph Smith the Second, who sullied every person he touched. And, much as it repulsed me, Soapy had touched Ella Wilson more than I could stomach. I tossed and turned in bed before I finally dozed off.

After a fretful sleep, I awoke, dressed and carried Buck back downstairs where Roger and several of the saloon's help waited, including the piano player, three bartenders, three performers and five ladies who entertained our customers. As I conveyed Buck outside, the others followed me, three of them grabbing shovels that Roger had left by the door. He locked up the place, and we marched north up Broadway to the cemetery where we had buried Deputy Marshal Jim Rowan. I picked a spot beneath a spruce tree on the west side of the graveyard and placed Buck on the ground, took a shovel and started a grave. Roger and the other men alternated digging with me. After thirty minutes, we had excavated a satisfactory plot. I stuck my spade in the mound of fresh dirt and stepped out of the hole, looking around and seeing Ella Wilson, dressed in black and looking at me with sad eyes. "I'm sorry," she mouthed without saying the words, confusing me even more. Was she apologizing for losing my dog or for setting up the ambush?

Turning away from her, I dropped to my knees, picked up Buck and lowered him into the grave. Then I stood up, uncertain what to say or do next. He was, after all, a dog, not a human like the murdered Deputy Rowan, but still he was a good and faithful animal. Ella broke the awkward silence, stepping forward and reciting the Twenty-third Psalm. As she started, others that knew the scripture joined in, me too as my mother had forced me to learn it as a child. We recited it together:

"The Lord is my shepherd; I shall not want. He maketh me to lie down in green pastures; he leadeth me beside the still waters. He restoreth my soul; he leadeth me in the paths of righteousness for his name's sake.

"Yea, though I walk through the valley of the shadow of death, I will fear no evil; for thou art with me; thy rod and thy staff they comfort me.

"Though preparest a table before me in the presence of mine enemies; thou annointest my head with oil; my cup runneth over.

"Surely goodness and mercy shall follow me all the days of my life; and I will dwell in the house of the Lord forever."

We said amen in unison. Nothing else was spoken as nothing else required words. I pondered the statement about a table being prepared in the presence of my enemies because I had plenty of foes in Skagway now and I damn sure didn't care to dine with them. I wondered if Ella Wilson was one of those antagonists. Everyone walked over and shook my hand or patted my shoulders, save for Ella, who held back. I informed the others that I would cover Buck, and they could return to the saloon. A couple men grabbed the two extra shovels, and I used the third to fill the grave. After the mourners departed, Ella edged toward me as I dumped scoops of soil over my dead dog. When the others stepped beyond hearing range, Ella spoke.

"I'm sorry, Jesse. I skipped church today just to tell you that and that I had nothing to do with the shooting."

I kept shoveling, uncertain if I believed her.

"Trust me, I was not involved in it."

"In what? The shooting? I know you didn't shoot at me, but did you lead me into a trap, Ella? Did you lie about feeling poorly to lure me onto the street?"

"No, Jesse, I didn't lie. I can show you the bloody rags at my place to prove it's my time. All I want is to return to Louisiana, and live out my time in peace and quiet."

Shrugging, I replied, "Should I believe you or not, Ella?"

"I've never lied to you, Jesse. I swear that's the God's honest truth."

Since I was living under an alias, I could not say I had never lied to her so I remained silent, uncertain whether or not to believe her."

"What's next, Jesse? I'd prefer to stay at the Gold Dust as you and Roger have been decent to me from the beginning, but I can take my wares elsewhere, if that's what you want. It may delay my returning home, but I'll do it if you or Roger say so."

I hesitated, uncertain how to answer. "Take it up with Roger whether you stay or go." I lifted my trigger finger and pointed it at her nose. "This I will demand, though. Tell

Soapy never to set foot in the Gold Dust again. Same goes for his men. They taint everything they touch, you included."

Ella hung her head and whispered. "The taint will disappear once I get home and folks don't know my past. I'll talk to Roger." She turned and walked to town.

I resumed mounding dirt over Buck, doubtful I would ever believe her again. Trust was like virginity, once you lost it you never regained it. When I returned to the Gold Dust, everyone kept their distance, giving me time to grieve —or fume—over losing my dog. That afternoon, Roger caught me and said Ella inquired if she should look for work elsewhere.

"She says you blame her for the ambush and Buck's death."

Shrugging, I told him I was as confused as a teetotaler in a brewery. "As long as Soapy never sets foot in the Gold Dust again, I couldn't care less whether or not she works here."

"She's created no problems with the other girls or customers so I'm fine with it, provided you don't mind, Jesse. I say she can stay."

"Your call," I answered.

"I'll tell her she can remain as long as Soapy stays away. She can meet him on her own."

"Fine by me. I'm going to church later to see if I can pray Buck into heaven."

"Don't you mean yourself?" Roger answered.

I shrugged, uncertain what to believe.

That afternoon I headed for the one o'clock Baptist service at the Union Church, carrying my carbine into the meeting room. The preacher spoke of the growing town animosities and the need for the hand of the Prince of Peace. I figured Skagway had so many problems that the Prince of Peace needed to use both hands with a revolver in each to clean up the evil that had infected the town. After the service, the reverend caught me at the door and offered his condolences for Buck, saying he remembered how docile my dog had been at the last sermon.

"He was a good dog and trustworthy friend," I said.

"And you're a good man," he answered.

"You're Baptist, aren't you, reverend?"

He nodded.

"You're forgetting I run a saloon, sell liquor and let loose women wander about."

"I know, but you and Roger Meredith run an honest place rather than a front for swindlers like so many saloons. If men must sin, let them do it in a safe place like yours." He pointed at my carbine. "It's a shame a man has to carry a long weapon to church, but God has a plan for you in Skagway."

"Thank you, preacher," I said, eager to get out on the street because I was uncomfortable with the pastor's words as I figured God had more important worries than me and much better men to handle His bidding.

When I returned to the saloon, I remained despondent and did something I had avoided since arriving in Skagway. I sat at a table with my back to the wall and drank my troubles away on that Sunday evening. I remember little other than Roger and someone else guiding me upstairs to bed that night. When I awoke, I had a terrible headache and lay in bed almost until noon before I rose. As my guardians had not undressed me other than my boots, I pulled them on and headed downstairs. That's when I learned how lucky I had been as Roger greeted me with stark news.

"You were fortunate, Jesse. There was a murder last night and rumor has it Soapy and his men were behind it."

I held up my hand and squeezed my eyes shut, the noise, the light and the news exploding in my head. Moving over to the table where I had drunk myself into oblivion, I sat down rested my elbows on the table, my face in my hands. Roger joined me. "Talk softly," I instructed him.

Roger whispered that a man named Sam Roberts, said to be one of Soapy's men, had taken a bullet at point-blank range as he returned to his cabin last night. Two rumors circulated as possible motives. The first was that he had been skimming money for himself from Soapy's gambling operations. The second was that Roberts aimed to take over Smith's ventures and send the conman to jail once he reported to the law that he had witnessed Soapy ambushing me. Problem was, so the story went, he made the accusation to that paragon of legal virtue,

Deputy Marshal Sylvester Taylor. Either way, Roberts wound up dead.

After that, the bad news kept coming. Two nights later a local merchant who belonged to the Committee of One Hundred and One was robbed and beaten outside his home and threatened with violence to his family if he identified his assailants. The next night a cheechacko was held up and assaulted on one wharf, then tossed into the bay, his body washing ashore the following morning. No one even knew his name, and he was buried in an anonymous grave near where Buck lay.

Skagway remained tense for the following three weeks, uncertain what to expect next. I stayed in the Gold Dust as much as possible, only going out when I had to and then using Roger's beards and mustaches to disguise myself when I went out, always carrying my carbine with my revolver. I never saw Soapy, but a few that did told me he was wearing a bandage on his left hand and arm. They said he claimed he sprained his wrist in a fall, but most suspected it was from a dog bite in fighting off Buck the night I was ambushed.

On the first Sunday of April, three weeks after my last church visit, tragedy struck with an avalanche that buried as many as a hundred stampeders twenty miles up the Chilkoot Trail from Dyea. The mountain snowpack had given way and covered men in up to thirty feet of snow. Skagway volunteers raced there to help, including Soapy Smith, who finagled an appointment as assistant to the coroner and took a handful of his Skagway militia to assist.

The *Daily Alaskan* touted Smith's benevolence in leading men to find survivors and recover bodies and praised him for the foresight in creating the Skagway volunteers even if the unit never fought the Spanish. While that was what the paper said, many locals returned from the rescue disgusted that Soapy's confederates were robbing the dead of their cash, rings and valuables and claiming the deceased's recovered supplies for militia use. Most of us came to believe Soapy would rob his own mother to the day she died and then slander her memory for not leaving him an inheritance.

Chapter Twenty-five

As long as Jeff Smith and his men focused on plundering the tragic dead of the Chilkoot trail avalanche, the living of Skagway enjoyed a brief reprieve from the mischief of his gang of thieves, swindlers, bunco artists and murderers. In his absence the Committee of One Hundred and One met twice, pleased that the town now had thriving businesses, but frustrated that no legal authority possessed the strength or willingness to take on Smith, whose crime threatened the community's growth and reputation. Part of the reason was the vast expanse of Alaska that federal authorities had to manage, but the biggest problem remained that Soapy bribed officials to look the other way just like he paid off the *Daily Alaskan* editor for favorable coverage.

While Soapy and most of his gang plundered the Chilkoot avalanche, Ella Wilson worked in the Gold Dust, spending time with strange men, but missing Soapy, not so much for himself but for his wallet which provided her double or more the going rate, drawing Ella ever closer to her Louisiana home. Unlike many of the girls, she never took a drink other than the tea we served as her whiskey when clients were paying, and she avoided the laudanum that the working girls sometimes acquired through their jobs.

On a slow night in his absence, I invited Ella to join me at a table so we could talk. We both sat stiffly in our chairs, knowing that the ambush that had killed Buck had raised a wall of suspicion between us. I always wondered if she had set me up, and she knew I distrusted her principal lover, whether or not she had been involved.

"Why don't you leave for home, Ella, before Soapy returns?"

"I don't have all my money," she argued.

"You must be nearing your goal. Get out of town now. Soapy's more fond of money than he is of you."

She clenched her jaw. "You never have liked Jeff, never seen his soft side."

"He's a greedy killer, Ella."

"That's a lie," she shot back. "Folks are telling stories about his supposed misdeeds, but he's told me they're all lies. Don't you ever read the *Daily Alaskan*? That's the Jeff I see."

"I encountered him in Colorado years ago, but not so long ago that I can't see his sordid past repeating itself here. He's using you like he uses everybody else."

She shot up from her chair. "I'm not listening to this anymore. He pays me well, better than any other man in Alaska."

"No matter how much he pays, he will always take more from you, Ella. He's a sure-thing man. Everyone knows that."

She turned away. "Don't badmouth Jeff anymore, Jesse. I won't stand for it." Ella grabbed her coat and marched outside into the darkness.

That was the last extended conversation I had with Ella Wilson. Though she plied her trade in the Gold Dust, after that we nodded or only greeted each other with a word or two, no more. Of all the things Jeff Smith touched and tainted, Ella Wilson was the prettiest and the saddest.

When Soapy, his left hand still bandaged from Buck's attack, and his men returned from plundering the Chilkoot deceased, he strutted around town like a bantam rooster, waving a letter from the Executive Mansion for everyone to see. He acted as if it was a personal missive from President William McKinley himself, thanking "Capt. Jeff R. Smith," for offering the services of his militia to help the nation defeat the Spanish. In reality, the response came not from the President but from John Addison Porter, the president's secretary, who advised

Captain Smith that his offer was being referred to the Secretary of War for consideration should additional volunteers be needed to whip the Spaniards. To Soapy, the letter confirmed his rank, and he instructed folks to address him as "captain" henceforth. Then he had the response framed and hung in Jeff Smith's Parlor for all to read. Most of those that heard of the letter speculated that Soapy's battlefield strategy would be to come down from the hills after the battle, shoot the wounded and then plunder the belongings of the dead soldiers, Spanish and American.

As spring bloomed by the end of April, arrivals picked up at the wharves as new waves of gold seekers arrived to start the journey over White Pass to Dawson City. By then those of us who had been around for a while were called "sourdoughs" because we had seen reality. Still the cheechackos came with wide eyes and visions of riches, many of them having their dreams dashed by Soapy's band of cheats who swindled them minutes after their disembarkation.

When Deputy Marshal Sylvester Taylor dropped by for his weekly payoff, I always asked him for any developments on finding the would-be assassins who ambushed me. He said he'd never investigated the incident, since no one died.

"Buck did," I reminded him.

"Dog suicide!"

"What about the murder of Sam Roberts? Any progress there?"

"Nope," he answered, "but that's no business of yours." I gave him his extortion money, and he counted it to make sure I hadn't shorted him. He smiled when he saw it was all there and waved the bills at my nose. "I'm planning on building a house, starting in June. No longer will I have to office and live out of my room at the Occidental."

"Hell, marshal, you could build a mansion from all the bribes we paid you or buy up all the property Soapy owns."

"Jeff doesn't own a single plot of land in Skagway to my knowledge."

"Not even Jeff's Parlor?"

"Clancy owns the land and the building, plus most other properties folks think belong to Jeff. He doesn't invest in things he can't carry off if he has to get out of town quick."

"Is this the Frank Clancy that's on the Committee of One Hundred and One?"

He grinned at me. "Yep, that's the one. Just count your blessings I didn't close your saloon like Jeff and Frank demanded."

"Why not?"

Taylor waved the money at me again. "The Gold Dust remains the only place that Soapy didn't demand a cut of my take. He loathes you so much that he thinks even your money's dirty. Besides that, you always paid me on time and never shorted me, like others tried."

"Are you saying crooks value honesty?"

The deputy stifled a chuckle, then cocked his head at me. "I'm the law, Jesse, but you might say that. See you next week."

"Why are you admitting this about Clancy and Soapy?"

"Jesse," he replied, "you're too dumb to make anything of it." He turned and walked out of my office.

"You're forgetting your drink, deputy," I called after him, scurrying up from my chair and giving chase to the bar, motioning my bartender aside. I took a jigger and held it up to the light, then grabbed a towel and wiped it clean. With my back to him, I spit in the glass, poured him a mediocre whiskey, shoved my finger in my nose, then mixed the concoction with that finger. Turning around, I put the jigger on the counter in front of him.

Taylor grabbed it, downed it, then let out a deep sigh. "You pour a mean glass of whiskey, Jesse."

"Why thank you, deputy. I try to put a little bit of me in every one of your drinks."

"I'm obliged," he replied.

"Want another? There's more where that came from."

He waved my offer away. "No, I'm behind on collections. Wish everyone was as faithful as you about paying."

My bartender looked at me and shook his head. "He'll shoot you if he ever finds out."

"It's an art," I answered.

"Fixing his whiskey?"

"No, not getting shot!"

Later that afternoon, I caught my partner's attention and signaled for him to see me in our office. "We've got to talk," I said.

Roger joined me. I closed the door, and we both took our chairs. "Have you been attending meetings of the committee?" I asked.

"Sort of," he nodded. "Everyone's jumpy and afraid to meet in numbers, just a few of us leaders get together, then spread the word around."

"Does Frank Clancy attend those meetings?"

"Every one of them."

"Sylvester Taylor as much as admitted today that Clancy and Soapy are in cahoots. The way I'm reading it, Soapy gets a cut of everything as does Clancy, who owns the properties folks think belong to Smith."

Roger whistled. "The son of a bitch."

"I'd say two sons of bitches and throw the deputy marshal in with them. Anything that Clancy hears gets back to Soapy and Taylor."

My partner laughed. "That's funny because we've been talking more about Taylor's lawlessness than Soapy's. Until we get him replaced, there's little we can do."

"I'd put Hornsby in the same pigeonhole as Clancy, so I figure he's another river of information flowing to Smith and possibly Taylor."

Roger bit his lip, his eyelids narrowing as he thought. "We've had our suspicions, but this confirms it about Clancy. Will you go with me tomorrow to visit Major Strong at the *Skagway News* and tell him yourself? I want it to come from you."

"Sure I will, anything that'll help get rid of Soapy."

Mid-morning the next day, Roger and I walked to the newspaper, weaving among the horses and wagons that traversed the streets sticky with the mud and muck from an overnight rain. Strong greeted us and invited us into his office with the clatter of the typesetting machine echoing through the wooden building. We took our seats across the desk from the major.

"I suppose you've realized the value of advertising in the *News* and have come to buy a month's worth of promotions," he offered, leaning back in his chair.

"Wish it were so, Major," Roger said, "but Jesse's got information that confirms our suspicions." He turned to me.

I detailed my conversation with the deputy marshal and the concerns that meeting raised. "Anything said in front of Clancy and likely Hornsby—"

"The lowest form of newspaper man, that Hornsby is," Strong interjected.

"—and probably others is reported to Soapy. He and his gang of three hundred and seventeen know everything you're doing," I concluded.

Strong slapped his desk. "Dammit, I should've known and taken action before now."

"What should we do?" Roger asked.

The editor pondered the question, then sighed. "We can't meet as a body of the whole anymore. Even in smaller groups, our comments and plans are unlikely confidential. I'll call a special meeting of six others I can trust, if you two will join us."

We both nodded.

"I'll want you to tell them what you've told me, Jesse. Can you do that?"

"Anything to get rid of Soapy."

"Now," the major asked, "where can we meet inconspicuously. Too many places around Skagway have ears."

"We could gather on a wharf after dark," Roger offered.

"Sound carries over the water. Too much of a risk. We need a place where people come and go frequently."

"The Gold Dust would work," I offered.

"Our office is too small for nine men," my partner noted.

"We could meet backstage, Roger. You could have the piano player bang out some Ragtime and offer a few free drinks. That'd keep the place noisy."

Strong grimaced. "Some men I'm inviting don't care to be seen entering a saloon."

"You have any better ideas?" I asked.

The committee head shrugged. "Reckon not. It'll need to be after dark. This late in April that means ten o'clock or after."

"Let's make it ten-thirty tomorrow night," Strong said, standing up. "You sure you fellows don't want a month of *News* advertisement for the Gold Dust? It'll do wonders for your business."

"And for yours," I said, before Roger could answer. "Get back to us once we rid Skagway of Soapy, then we'll buy a month of ads."

The next night at the appointed time, Strong and the six others he invited, including Si Tanner, slipped into our saloon individually. I showed them backstage to the prop and costume room where we had arranged chairs in a circle. After the last guest arrived, Roger announced a round of free drinks in the saloon, then joined us as the pianist banged out a Ragtime tune.

With the din of whiskey-oiled voices and music at its most raucous in the background, Strong explained the need for the secrecy and asked me to repeat to his confidants what I had learned from the deputy marshal. I repeated my story for the attendees, who were more merchant than mercenary in their outlook. They were not men who had made their way in a wild land with brawn, but rather by brain.

Major Strong summed up our predicament. "The dilemma we face is that we need the law to step in, but the law is in league with the lawless. We can't tell how far the tentacles of the lawless reach. If we take the law into our own hands, we are no better than the lawlessness we are trying to end."

"Sometimes you have to take a stand," Tanner noted. "Now's that time."

The others gave half-hearted nods, knowing Tanner was right but fearing the consequences.

I listened, but grew annoyed as the conversation skirted the obvious. Finally, I spoke. "Soapy tried to assassinate me. I don't think any of you have had that experience."

One fellow shook his head. "I'm Alex McLain. Soapy's men sandbagged me in front of my house and robbed me, beat me bad. I know fear, and I fear they'll learn of this meeting."

"Everyone's afraid," I answered, "but if the law won't put him in jail, we need to kill him plain and simple. That's all that will save Skagway."

The attendees grimaced and defended inaction, hoping for a new deputy marshal or divine intervention. They said more on the committee should be included in such a decision, but they no longer knew who to trust.

"I've got a wife and kids," McLain offered. "I can't risk this without knowing that the support is there for us."

"But we can't share this with everyone," Tanner said, "or our adversaries will get wise to our plans."

Strong studied us, then spoke. "Let's start small, each of you meet with one other member you can trust and let's see if we can expand our circle of confidants and gain strength in greater numbers. We'll meet once a week to gauge progress. Maybe the law will right itself before we must act."

"If it doesn't," Tanner said, "we should develop a plan to handle this on our own."

Strong and the others nodded, though none of us had a solution. "Us nine will be the governing subcommittee. Are we agreed?" The men nodded and Strong adjourned the meeting, the participants slipping out individually past the revelers and back to their homes.

The subcommittee met four more times, taking us to the end of May. Everyone, though, remained too scared to act or pull the trigger on the nefarious crooks and their activities. Some members were so terrified as the first of June arrived that they believed getting rid of Soapy would only make matters worse, his gang breaking up into smaller groups and intimidating even more residents and Skagway arrivals passing through on the way to the Dawson City.

The only major decision the group made was to add Frank Reid, the surveyor, as he was fearless and reputed to be a good man with a gun. Reid, Tanner and I were the only subcommittee members ever involved in gunfights. The more we discussed the problem, the more complicated the others made it when the only answer was to kill Soapy Smith and then take our chances with whatever followed. Even Roger was getting nervous when it appeared a showdown was inevitable.

As we approached June, I considered resigning from the subcommittee, frustrated with the indecision. The clandestine meetings had gone on for so long that word had likely slipped to Soapy of our discussions. Though Roger kept attending, I gave up, figuring one of Alaska's glaciers might reach Cane Hill, Arkansas, before the group decided anything worthwhile. Major Strong and his trustworthy subcommittee members met backstage with Roger one night when I remained out front, keeping an eye on the saloon and making sure the piano player banged out loud Ragtime.

As I wandered among the tables, I glanced at the door and saw Soapy Smith standing there with Ella Wilson. I pulled my revolver and started for them, ready to shoot the conman whether or not the subcommittee backstage agreed. I had warned him to stay away from the Gold Dust. Now the bastard was trespassing. As I strode toward him, gun pointed at his chest, Ella stepped between us.

"Get out, Soapy," I yelled.

"It's Captain," he shouted.

"Then get out, *Captain* Soapy. You're not welcome here."

He sneered. "I know your committee's been meeting for weeks, planning to run me out of town, but I'm staying. You and your bunch should pack up and go."

I cocked my revolver.

"No," cried Ella, stepping toward me.

As she did, Soapy backed away into the darkness. "I'll see you at your place in a few minutes, Ella," he called, disappearing in the night.

Lowering my gun, I released the hammer and shoved it in my holster.

"I'm leaving day after tomorrow," she announced. "Finally going home to Louisiana."

"Don't tell, Soapy."

She smiled, "Jeff bought my steamer ticket."

"You'd been safer letting the Baptist preacher pay your fare. I hope things work out for you in Louisiana."

"Thanks, Jesse," she replied, then frowned. "Jeff wanted

me to deliver you a message, two words and three initials. He said you'd understand what he was talking about."

"Tell me."

"*Leadville* and *murder* were the two words. The three initials were H-H-L."

My blood turned colder than a White Pass winter. He had connected me to Noose Neck's murder and the initials told me he now remembered who I was.

"It made no sense to me," Ella continued, "but I promised him I'd deliver the message."

"I know what he's trying to tell me."

She smiled. "Good. I'll let him know, but I want to advise you I won't be back in the Gold Dust. Tomorrow I'll pack and the next day leave for Louisiana. Tell Roger I enjoyed working for him and you. Both of you treated me decent and paid me fair. I wouldn't be going home without the two of you and Jeff."

"Good luck, Miss Wilson," I replied with the formality of the days before she took up with Jefferson Randolph Smith the Second.

She stepped toward me and pecked my cheek with an innocent kiss. She turned and strode out of the saloon, disappearing into the darkness just like Captain Soapy. I said a silent prayer that she and me too, for that matter, might escape Skagway and Soapy's clutches. Now that he recalled my name and my past, he would likely inform the deputy marshal to arrest me or kill me himself to collect the five-hundred-dollar reward posted after I escaped Colorado two decades earlier. I wondered if it was time for me to leave Skagway as well, perhaps join Ella Wilson on the steamship sailing to the states.

I was still in a daze when Major Strong and other members of his committee concluded their meeting and slipped from backstage to return to their homes and the warm beds with their wives. After Roger saw the major off, he walked over to me, his smile evolving into a frown.

"You don't look so good, Jesse. Have you've seen a ghost?"

"Soapy came to the door with Ella, saying he's aware of the meetings going on."

Roger's faced paled. "Even now, someone's feeding

315

him details of our discussions."

"It appears so."

"Dammit," Roger cursed. "Is there no way to escape his evil?"

"Besides that, Ella's leaving in two days, returning to Louisiana."

"Isn't that what you've been wanting."

I nodded. "But she informed Soapy, and he bought her steamer ticket. Ella's in danger."

"With as many folks as know about their liaisons, he'd be foolish to rob or hurt her," Roger offered.

"He'd just have his men do it for him."

"Surely he's not that brazen."

"Who'd stop him, Roger? The law won't, nor will the committee members. They believe they can talk the problem to death."

Roger patted me on the back. "You're seeing too many boogeymen, Jesse. Get some rest and we'll visit in the morning."

"There's more," I admitted.

"What else?"

"Soapy has figured out where we met. He knows my past, Roger."

"We all have a past, Jesse."

"But not one that'll get you hung."

Roger whistled, then laughed. "I've given stage performances that should've gotten me hanged, they were so bad."

"This is no play-acting, Roger. I'm heading to think and sleep it off."

"And you haven't even been drinking. Do you need to take a bottle with you?"

Waving the offer away, I started up the stairs and undressed for bed. On this night, I truly missed Buck as the dog had been as dependable a friend as I'd had in Skagway, giving his life to save mine. I thought about the church sermons I'd heard over the years praising sacrifice as a Godly virtue. Maybe if those lessons had taken, I'd slept better that evening, but I worried about Ella's safety and my Skagway future. I rolled around on the mattress like a Mexican jumping bean and finally arose, no more rested than if I hadn't dozed any. I dressed and headed downstairs mid-morning where a small but noisy crowd of customers were buzzing with gossip.

As I walked past the bar, our bartender motioned for me to approach. "Boss," he said, "there's a commotion at the mulatto gal's crib."

Not waiting for another word, I dashed across the saloon, flung open the door and ran up Broadway to Ella's place. Turning on Holly Street, I saw a throng of men clumping around her front door.

I realized that Ella had been robbed.

Worst of all, I knew Miss Wilson was dead!

Chapter Twenty-six

I shoved my way through the crowd, worming between the throng of men and the few terrified women of her profession standing with wide eyes and their hands over their gaping mouths, knowing that it could've been them instead of Ella. I pushed between two burly spectators, who threatened to thrash me for my poor manners.

"She worked at the Gold Dust for me," I announced and the pair begrudgingly parted, letting me slide to the door. Inside I saw Sylvester Taylor bent over an open trunk, the hiding place for Ella's five thousand dollars.

When Taylor straightened up and moved aside, I spotted Ella's body. Her killer had stuffed her in the trunk, her left arm and shoulder draped over the side, her head hanging at an odd angle outside the chest. Even on her brown flesh I detected the bruises where someone had strangled her and likely broken her neck. I wanted to throw up.

The lawman spotted me. "Did you do this, Jesse?"

"You know better than that. If Soapy didn't do it, he hired whoever did."

"That's impossible," Taylor answered. "Jeff was with me all night in my room at the Occidental."

"You're lying, deputy. Soapy came to the Gold Dust with Ella, and she left with him. He was the last one to see her alive."

"Jeff spent his night visiting with me in my place, telling me some interesting stories about a murder in Leadville, Colorado. You know anything of that, *Jesse?*"

By the way he said my alias, I realized Skagway's sinister element knew my real identity. "What I remember from Leadville is hearing Miss Susan B. Anthony lecture on what sons of bitches men are."

"Are you sure you're not the son of a bitch that killed Ella Wilson?"

"I was in the Gold Dust last night."

"No one reported seeing you after eleven o'clock or midnight."

"I went to bed early."

"Or, you slipped out to rob and kill her. That's what I'll be investigating, *Jesse*. And don't you leave Skagway until my investigation's done. Hell, *Jesse*, there may even be reward money out for you in Colorado. Now, git!" Taylor stepped toward me.

I retreated from the crib, squeezing my way through the crowd.

At the crib entrance, Taylor ordered the spectators to back away. "There's nothing to see. Clear out so the undertaker can do his business when he gets here."

Walking from Ella's place, I rethought my actions or inactions from the previous night. I should've shot Soapy and saved both Ella's life and the Committee of One Hundred and One's time in deciding what to do about Jeff Smith and the crimes he spawned. I moved in a daze back to the saloon, encountering Roger at the front door.

"Is it true? About Ella?"

Nodding, I answered, "Somebody strangled her, likely broke her neck."

"Dammit, it just gets worse."

"Yep, and on top of that, Taylor knows of my past. Soapy told him."

"If you need to leave town, I'll buy out your share of the Gold Dust."

"I'm not leaving until Ella's death is avenged," I said, moving beyond him and barging into the saloon. I stepped to the bar and pointed to a bottle of our finest whiskey.

The bartender brought it to me. "Are the rumors true about Ella, boss?"

"She's dead."

"I'm sorry," he said as he placed the liquor in front of me. "I'll get you a glass."

"Don't need one." I grabbed the container by the neck and took it to a table near the back so I could sit and watch the front door, prepared to shoot Soapy on sight if he dared return to the Gold Dust. Taking my seat, I uncorked the whiskey and swallowed big, letting the liquid slide down my throat as if it could wash away the memories of the past twelve hours. At first I planned to get drunk, but then thought otherwise to keep my senses sharp should I need to defend myself against Soapy, his gang or Taylor since they understood my secret.

For three or more hours I just sat there stewing in regret, occasionally tipping the bottle to my lips without imbibing. Anybody that came near my table, including Roger, I waved away. "Leave me alone," I told them. Roger approached me a couple more times, then left to run an errand when I advised him I didn't want to talk. By mid-afternoon my stomach grumbled from hunger, and I realized I needed food, but I lingered in the saloon. While debating whether to find an eatery or grab a tin of crackers from a grocer, a woman whose best years were behind her ambled in and headed straight for the bar. The matron had a familiar look. For a moment, I feared she was Miss Susan B. Anthony who had returned to torment me or to avenge some past wrong I'd done to her just by being a man. But if it was her, she had grown up and out since our Leadville acquaintance. I shivered at the thought of her and considered draining the liquor bottle after all, especially when the bartender pointed to me and this matron started my way. I'd seen her somewhere before, but didn't care to renew my acquaintance, not today, not after losing Ella. The woman charged at me like a runaway freight wagon. If she hadn't found the brakes, I'd have died a horrible death in the collision.

She braked at the table's edge opposite me, plopped her huge purse down, leaned over and placed her hands on either side of her bag, which was large enough to carry a revolver and a Gatling gun or two. This woman studied me as if she was removing my clothes, then shook her head and spoke. "Good afternoon, Mr. Murph—" she started, then stopped. "Well I'll be damned if it isn't H.H. Lomax," she said in a voice much too loud for my comfort.

I shot up from the chair and slapped at the revolver at my waist as she shoved her hand in her purse. Then I realized I was staring at Mattie Silks, several years older and many pounds heavier than when I had last seen her in Denver. "It's Jesse Murphy," I replied. "You must have me confused for someone else."

Mattie winked at me as she slid her revolver back in her bag. "My apologies, Mr. Murphy. Do you have a place we might visit in private over a business proposition?"

I looked past her at all the eyes staring at us. Though not worried about their prying gaze, I feared eavesdropping ears might pick up my actual name. "Let's step in my office." I pointed to the door at the end of the bar. She picked up her purse and started that way. Grabbing the whiskey bottle by the neck, I followed her, picking up two jiggers as I marched inside the office behind her. As soon as I closed the entry, she dropped her bag on the table and threw her arms around me, giving me a healthy hug.

"It is Lomax, isn't it?" she asked as she broke her grip and stepped away to inspect me.

I sat the liquor bottle and two glasses on my desk. "Between you and me, yes, Mattie, but the rest of Skagway needn't find out."

"You remember me, do you?"

"Mattie Silks, how could I forget. You and Cort Thomson. Is the leech with you?"

She laughed and shook her head. "No, I left him managing our ranch back in Colorado."

"Chasing cattle rather than skirts for a change, is he?"

Mattie grinned. "I finally broke him of the habit. Threatened to shoot him if he didn't."

"I can have Shotgun Jake Townsend do it for you, if you like. Word is, he's in town."

Shaking her head, she declined my offer. "I never got to thank you for taking him off our trail. Didn't hear much of him after you left Denver. Is it true you murdered a lawyer over in Leadville? That's the rumor that circulated around

Denver months after you left, though the killing sounded more like a Shotgun Jake Townsend murder."

"You can't believe those wild stories," I replied, ready to change the subject. "Is Lupe still with you? She was my favorite."

"Funny thing about Lupe," Mattie replied. "Around the time you left she had a secret benefactor that gave her a thousand dollars. That gift along with everything she saved allowed her to quit and open a Denver orphanage, something she'd always dreamed of doing. There's not a Mexican, man or woman, more respected in Denver than Lupe now."

"I'm glad to know that. Lupe and I shared a few secrets during my brief stay in Denver. What brings you to Skagway?"

"Business in Denver and Colorado as a whole is not what it used to be, now that we're civilized. I was trying to profit on one last boom before I gave up the trade and settled down with Cort on the ranch. I think another twenty thousand dollars would leave us well set for the rest of our lives, and I would never make that much as quick as I needed in Colorado. Before I open a house, I'm looking for an honest saloon where my girls can show their wares safely."

"Why start with the Gold Dust?"

"I didn't," she replied. "Each saloon I visited had ties to that bastard Soapy Smith, and I'm certain he knows I'm in town now. The Gold Dust was one of only three I found untainted by him."

"You got word they murdered one of our local girls last night, did you not?"

"Strangled," Mattie replied.

I nodded.

"Did you know her?"

"She worked here. A decent girl, she was leaving town tomorrow with her savings, five thousand dollars I was told. I'm certain Soapy murdered her for the money."

"The bastard," Mattie replied. "I'm not surprised. Six years ago in Denver, Cort witnessed Soapy and four of his gang surround Cliff Sparks and shoot him dead. My Cort testified against Soapy, who's held a grudge against us both ever since. Soapy devised a cunning plan that his barber overheard and told Cort. All his men carried identical guns, surrounded their prey and shot him so that the authorities could never tell with certainty which man and gun killed the victim. The courts called it 'reasonable doubt'."

Recalling my own attempted assassination, I swallowed hard. "Soapy tried to ambush me a few weeks back. Same setup. They surrounded me and shot to kill. My dog saved me."

"You be careful because Soapy never forgets a grudge."

"Same for you, Mattie."

"Don't worry, Lomax—"

"Remember it's Jesse, not Lomax."

Mattie smiled. "Worry for yourself, Jesse, as I carry my protection in my purse, and I don't go out after the dark anymore. I'm staying at the Occidental Hotel and my room is next to the deputy marshal's. He apparently uses it as his office as well."

I frowned and shook my head.

"What's the matter?"

"Sylvester Taylor's in Soapy's pocket, doing his bidding. When Soapy tried to ambush me, Taylor claimed Smith was with him the whole time. This morning when I told the deputy that Soapy was behind the murder of the working girl, he claimed Soapy was with him all night."

"I'll be careful," she assured me.

My stomach growled loud enough for Mattie to hear. "I've had nothing to eat since last evening," I explained. "I'll treat you to a meal if you want to sit and visit for a spell."

"That'd be wonderful, *Jesse.*"

"Let's drink to our Denver days." I uncorked the bottle and filled two jiggers. We drank to each other's good health and longevity.

When we finished, I stepped to the corner to grab my carbine, figuring Soapy would be twice as angry with me, knowing I was escorting another of his enemies around town. After I informed the bartender I'd be out dining with Miss Mattie Silks, I offered her my free arm and we marched out of the Gold Dust together, confident that with luck, we could conquer Skagway. We were wrong.

We dined at a restaurant, talking of old times in Denver and how much the city had changed as it became civilized. Mattie missed the wilder days because they were more profitable in her profession. She was hoping for one last ride on a boomtown merry-go-round until she discovered how deeply Soapy Smith was entrenched in Skagway. We visited for a couple hours, Mattie's enthusiasm for Alaska diminishing the more she learned about the corruption. Ella Wilson's death disturbed her because Mattie understood Soapy held to a grudge as tight as a tick to a mutt. After we finished eating, I walked Mattie around Skagway, showing her the saloons, brothels and cribs that would be her competition. She took heart that none of the establishments were a fancy brothel like she had built in Denver, but could not shake her fears of Soapy.

"I need to think about it," she said. "I don't care to spend the money for a high-end house if Soapy can break me by his intimidation."

"He killed Ella," I reminded her.

"I won't let him get that close to me."

After showing her Skagway, I escorted her to the Occidental Hotel and up the stairs to her room. "I've never visited the Occidental before," I admitted.

"It's not bad. The mattresses are thick, but the walls are thin so it can be noisy, especially if there's bedsprings a bouncing next door."

At the head of the stairs, I spotted the sign on the first door designating the marshal's office. Mattie stopped at the next room, extracted her key from her purse and unlocked her entry. "I felt safe rooming next to the law," Mattie admitted, "but I'm not so certain anymore."

"Don't leave your room after dark."

Mattie gave me a plump-cheeked smile. "You're welcome to stay and visit for a spell."

"I need to get back to the Gold Dust before my partner thinks something's happened to me, as I seldom venture out on the streets at night now after the assassination attempt."

"Once I've thought things over, I'll come by tomorrow afternoon. I could open a place here or try Dawson City, though I'm unsure how the Canadian Mounties view my work."

"Good to see you again, Mattie, and please keep my name a secret."

She smiled. "Sure thing, *Jesse!*"

I descended the stairs and out the front of the Occidental as Deputy Marshal Sylvester Taylor stepped on the plank walk for the door. He scowled at me.

"What are you doing here?" he demanded.

"Checking if you'd arrested anybody for Ella Wilson's murder. Soapy Smith was with her before she died, I'm telling you."

The lawman shook his head. "Soapy was with me all evening. You best stay out of my business, Jesse or whoever you are. Who's to say it wasn't you that killed her?"

"You know who murdered her, deputy, you know."

The lawman strode into the Occidental, slamming the door behind him.

I returned to the Gold Dust, checking over my shoulder several times to determine if I was being followed. While I felt I was being tailed, I never identified who the tracker was. When I stepped back inside my saloon, Roger came over and hugged me.

"I feared something had happened to you since I couldn't find you."

"Visiting with an old friend from Denver, Mattie Silks."

"The well-known madam?"

"That's her. She's thinking of opening a fancy house in Skagway, though she has a history with Soapy Smith. Mattie said she'd drop by tomorrow afternoon and tell me her decision."

"She knows of Ella's murder?"

"She does, and I ran into Deputy Taylor, but he told me to mind my own business."

"As long as Taylor's handling it, her murderer will go free."

"Not if I can help it," I said.

"Don't try anything on your own without informing me or the committee first. At least then we'll know when to search for your body."

"Thanks for your confidence in my success, partner."

"Nobody's beaten Soapy yet."

"Don't bet against Mattie," I responded. "If she locates

here, we'll have an ally with more balls than the men on the committee."

We tended our business until after midnight, then retired to bed. I had had a pair of fitful nights of rest the last two days and expected to sleep until noon, then rise and meet Mattie to learn of her decision. Barely had the dawn light softened the darkness engulfing Skagway than a banging on my doorway woke me. I grabbed my pistol and pointed it at the entry. "Who is it?"

"Boss," cried my early bartender, "it's a woman demanding to see you, the one you met yesterday."

"Hold your horses," I answered, putting down my revolver. "Let me get decent, and I'll see her downstairs."

"No," came Mattie's voice. "I want to visit in your room. It's safer."

"Hold on," I said, fumbling to light a lamp, then yanking my pants on and grabbing my shirt and buttoning it. I stepped barefooted to the door, cracking it. The moment I did, Mattie pushed past the bartender and barged in, wearing a fancy yellow silk dress and matching head ware. Beneath the wide brim of her hat, I saw unbridled terror in her face, her eyes afloat with fear. She slammed the door as she entered.

"They're planning to kill me," she said, "and you, too." She marched over and sat on the bed. "I'm leaving on the first steamship back to the states, Seattle or San Francisco, I don't care."

"Calm down, Mattie. Tell me what's scared you."

"Last night loud voices awakened me, liquor talk it sounded like, from the deputy's office. I recognized Soapy's squeaky voice and the marshal's. There was a man called Bowers there and a fourth man whose name I didn't catch."

"Go on," I said.

"They talked first of splitting the thirty-eight hundred dollars they'd taken from the mulatto whore as they called her. Soapy said it was the easiest money he'd ever made."

Anger coursed through my veins because he spoke so callously about Ella. Too, she had at least five thousand bucks or she would not have booked passage from Skagway. Soapy was cheating his fellow crooks by skimming money off the top before splitting with them.

Mattie continued, talking so fast, she had to stop and take deep breaths before resuming her tale. "Then Soapy said I'd been snooping around town, trying to move in on the whore business. He said he planned to have me followed and murdered, strangled like the dead girl. The deputy laughed, saying he didn't need to have me tailed since I was rooming next door, that they could even do it right then. I got my pistol from my purse and waited, but Soapy said people had seen him enter the hotel, and he wanted no more attention drawn to him so soon after he'd killed the mulatto whore. He said they'd attack me in a day or two. I'm leaving today."

"You said they mentioned killing me."

Mattie nodded. "They spent more time talking about you than anybody else, and you will not believe what they said."

"Go on," I implored her.

"It goes back to Leadville as Soapy explained it to the deputy. You had title to a valuable mining claim, and Soapy bribed a lawyer, a fellow named Adam Scheisse, to have you sign papers transferring your ownership to Soapy. The lawyer, though, double-crossed Soapy and transferred the mining property to himself."

Remembering the fraud, I gritted my teeth and nodded. "Now it makes sense."

"Vowing revenge, Soapy ambushed the lawyer in his office, shooting him in the back with a shotgun. Sometime later, you joined Soapy's men for drinks. They drugged your drink and carried you to the lawyer's office, leaving you on the floor with the shotgun by your side to frame you for the murder."

The awful Leadville memories, the encounter with Miss Susan B. Anthony, losing my mule Ciaha, the fraud that cost me a fortune and the death of Noose Neck, flowed back to me. I rubbed my eyes in disbelief. Why hadn't I figured it out before? Soapy's wickedness remained boundless.

"Damn him to hell," I said.

Mattie nodded. "I understood Soapy was evil, but I never realized the depth of his depravity until now. That's why I'm leaving town quick as I can."

"Why did you stop here first instead of getting to the wharves?"

"I didn't owe Jesse Murphy a thing," she replied, "but I was indebted to H.H. Lomax for saving my Cort from assassination and then buying off Shotgun Jake Townsend from killing us both. Now we're even."

While that had all been a lie two decades ago, that fib had saved Mattie's life in Skagway and mine, if I played my cards right. "Now I owe it to you to get you on a steamship for the states." I tucked my shirt in, tugged on my books and wrapped my gun belt around my waist. I looked at my carbine in the corner and passed it up, deciding to take one of the double-barreled shotguns we kept under the bar for rowdy customers. Grabbing my hat and coat, I opened the door for Mattie, who tromped down the stairs, me following in her wake. At the foot of the steps, I inquired, "Where are your bags?"

"I left them in the hotel as I didn't want anyone to realize I was leaving. I put money on my bed to cover my stay. Never will I go back to that room or return to Skagway once I escape."

Stopping at the bar, I asked the barkeep to give me a shotgun and a handful of shells, which I tucked in my pocket. "Are you ready?"

Mattie nodded and tugged her hat over her forehead to help screen her face from curious eyes, though few people roamed the streets so early. We marched to the wharves, spotting two steamships at the Seattle Wharf. "Looks like I'm going to Seattle," she said.

"You got enough money for the passage?"

She patted her purse. "When I travel I always carry plenty of bullets and lots of cash so I can make my own way. It's something I've learned in my business."

We walked up the pier steps and headed down the wharf toward the dock office where Mattie inquired about the next departing ship for Seattle. She arrived at the perfect time as the *SS Farallon* was scheduled to depart at one-thirty that afternoon. She paid her fare while I guarded her back, patting the short shotgun so any attackers understood I meant business. Completing her purchase, Mattie turned around and said she could board. I escorted her to the gangway that led up to the steamship's deck.

"Do you need me to stay with you?"

"I should be safe once I get aboard," she said. "Thank you for what you did years ago for me and Cort and for what you've done for me in Skagway."

"Glad to help, Mattie, but would you do me a favor?"

Looking around to make certain no one was within hearing distance, she said, "Sure, Lomax, whatever you need."

"If you see Lupe when you get back to Denver, tell her that I send my regards and am proud of what she did."

"She'd love that," Mattie replied. "I'll run by her orphanage to deliver your message."

"Thank you," I answered.

"And I'll do something else for you. I'll stir up nasty feelings against Soapy."

"How you gonna do that, Mattie?"

"Skagway gets the Seattle and San Francisco papers I've noticed. Just wait. You'll see. how I've learned to play the press." She smiled and hugged me. "You be careful, Lomax, and get Soapy if you can."

I watched her climb the gangway to the *Farallon's* deck. She looked at Skagway a last time and waved to me. I signaled back, then started down the pier for the Gold Dust. I never encountered Mattie Silks again, but eight days later another steamship arrived from Seattle, carrying her gift that prolonged my life long enough for me to get revenge with Jefferson Randolph Smith the Second.

Chapter Twenty-seven

Knowing I was a marked man in the days following Mattie's departure, I stayed around the Gold Dust, except for the few hours it took to attend Ella Wilson's funeral. I always wore my pistol and carried my sawed-off shotgun. Our customers understood they should duck if Soapy or any of his known men entered, as the conman had put out word that he'd pay a pretty penny to anyone that killed me. Now that he knew who I was, he could've turned me over to Deputy Marshal Sylvester Taylor on the bogus Leadville murder charge, but he craved to see me dead in Skagway. I remained tense in the week and a day after Mattie departed so when Roger Meredith barged into the saloon shouting "Look at this!" and waving a newspaper in the air, I lifted my shotgun and aimed it at his gut before realizing it was my partner.

"You've got to read this," cried my partner. "It's last Saturday's *Seattle Times*." He threw the broadsheet on the table in front of me.

I placed my scattergun beside it, but Roger moved the barrel so it didn't point to his midsection.

"Read it," he commanded.

Picking up the paper, I scanned the stacked headlines aloud, "Conspired to Murder; A Terrible Tale of Crime Comes from Skagway. What a Mrs. Silks Says: Marshal Taylor, 'Soapy' Smith and Two Toughs Said to be Running the Town and Murdering at Will—Awful Condition of Affairs."

I looked up at Roger and whistled.

"Read it," he ordered.

I lifted the paper and started the most amazing article I'd ever seen in a newspaper.

"If the story told by Mrs. Mattie Silks, a passenger who arrived in Seattle from Skagway on the steamer Farallon *this morning, be true it is time something was done by the United States Government to straighten out the lawless condition of affairs at Skagway. According to Mrs. Silks' story, Deputy United States Marshal Taylor of Skagway is a consort of murderers, a consort with them in crime, and 'Soapy' Smith has taken to murdering people for their money. Briefly told, Mrs. Silks' story is as follows:*

"On the evening of May 28th Ella Wilson, a mulatto prostitute, was strangled to death and robbed in her house on one of the principal streets of Skagway. A large trunk in her room, which was supposed to contain her money, was found broken open. It was the only thing in her room that was molested.

"Deputy United States Marshal Taylor took charge of the body and began an 'investigation' to discover the perpetrator of the deed. Mrs. Silks says that she occupied a room in the Occidental Hotel in Skagway, and adjoining her room was the office of the Deputy United States Marshal. The only partition separating the rooms was one of thin boards. The night after the murder, she says she heard Marshal Taylor, 'Soapy' Smith and two others, being well-known crooks, talking in Taylor's office while they were dividing up $3,800. She says she gathered from their conversation that the money was what had been taken from Ella Wilson and that the murder had been committed at the instigation of 'Soapy' Smith.

"But that was not all. Mrs. Silks says that while she sat in her room, she heard this outfit plan to strangle her to death in the same way in which Ella Wilson had been served and to assassinate an upstanding saloon owner. After hearing this plan, Mrs. Silks came to the conclusion that Skagway had become too hot to hold her and she immediately took her departure on the first boat.

"One of the passengers who came down on the Farallon *said this morning to a reporter for* The Times: *'The*

condition of affairs at Skagway is a disgrace to civilized government. The United States officials make no pretense at enforcing the law. They are making money hand over fist, and any sort of crime can be committed as long as the officials of the United States get their share of the loot. The only law that is respected is the rifle or the revolver, and unless something is done pretty soon, Skagway will be absolutely unsafe for any man to venture into who values his life.'"

Glancing up at Roger, I shook my head. "Mattie said she intended to provide us cover, but I never realized she meant this."

"You're the saloon owner she's referring to, aren't you?"

"That's what she told me." I pointed to the shotgun. "That's why I've been carrying this around ever since she left."

"This will stir the pot in Skagway," Roger said, "and I intend to see that everyone in town knows about this piece."

"How's that?"

"I'm visiting Major Strong to ask him to call a special meeting of the committee, every member, including Soapy's spies, so that everyone will hear what the Seattle paper is saying. I'll demand he reprint the story in the *Skagway News*. And for the illiterates that might miss the printed account, I'll give dramatic readings this evening."

"Why would anyone attend your reading?"

"Free beer," he said. "I don't care if it depletes our profits for June, I'll draw a crowd and seek justice for Ella and Skagway."

Doubtful his scheme would succeed as Soapy always bribed or strong-armed his way out of binds, I shrugged. "Whatever you think, but I doubt it'll change anything."

"It might help you live to be an old man," he countered. "Soapy's threatened you. If everyone in Skagway knows about his intimidation, he might reconsider killing you, at least for a while."

I slapped Roger on the back. "Thanks, partner, for looking out for me."

"You're welcome, Jesse or whatever your name is. I will visit Strong at the *News* office."

My partner grabbed the newspaper, folded it up and slid it under his arm, then strode out of the Gold Dust on a mission. I went in the storeroom and counted four kegs of beer, plenty for Roger's planned performances. The normal morning lull in business gave way to a hurried afternoon as customers came in and asked for free beer. I refused their requests, surprised how they had found out about the offer so soon, at least until Roger returned. He explained he had given dimes to a dozen news boys to promote the giveaway starting that evening *after* the first dramatic reading. Roger advised the bartenders to be prepared and told me he planned a surprise for me during his second performance.

Besides that, Strong had agreed to reprint the *Seattle Times* story in the next edition of the *Skagway News* and to call a special meeting of all members of the Committee of One Hundred and One for that afternoon at three o'clock at Union Church. "I want you to speak at the meeting, confirming what Mattie Silks told you before she left, Jesse, but volunteer nothing until I ask you to talk." He paused. "Bring your shotgun."

"I don't go anywhere without it anymore," I answered.

"Good. It might come in handy."

From then until mid-afternoon I turned away men wanting their free beers, telling them to return in the evening when Roger Meredith would give his greatest performance ever. As the committee meeting approached, I checked the load in my pistol and grabbed a handful of shotgun shells which I jammed in my pocket. Roger and I marched out of the saloon for the church as other members converged on the site. As I entered the building, I recalled meeting Ella Wilson outside as she left the Episcopalian service. I bit my lip at the remembrance as she deserved a better fate than she received in Skagway. I sat in the front pew with my sawed-off shotgun lying across my lap, glancing over my shoulder at the sound of anyone approaching. With the arrival of each committee member, I wondered if he was a Soapy sympathizer. I knew J. Allen Hornsby and William Saportas of the *Daily Alaskan* fell into that camp along with Frank Clancy, whose saloon, dancehall and brothel holdings made him a natural ally with the criminal kingpin.

I recognized most of the attendees as regular merchants or professionals, but a handful were new, likely shills of Soapy. I saw Professor John Bowers and George Wilder enter as spies for their boss. With their arrival, I twisted in my seat so I could watch them and the podium.

Precisely at three o'clock, Major John F.A. Strong stepped to the front and called the meeting to order, apologizing for the short notice, but emphasizing the necessity of the gathering in light of new information from the states, details of which cast a pall over Skagway, its reputation and its future. With that, the major recognized Roger Meredith.

Taking a deep breath, my partner arose and pulled a folded newspaper from beneath his arm. "Gentlemen," he announced, "I have in my hand a copy of the Saturday June fourth edition of the *Seattle Times* with a disturbing story that should concern us all."

"The *Seattle Times*," cried Hornsby, "is a rag that publishes lies to slander Skagway and the wonderful people that call it home. I move we adjourn and ignore its fabrications."

"I second the motion," shouted Frank Clancy, as a dozen men clapped their approval.

Strong banged the podium with his gavel. "The motion is overruled as the chair first recognized Roger Meredith."

Hornsby, Clancy, Bowers, Wilder and their allies booed and hissed at Strong's ruling until Josias M. Tanner stood up, facing the crowd with a Winchester cradled in his arms.

"Order, everyone, order," Strong shouted, then pointed his gavel at Roger. "Please proceed, Mr. Meredith."

The actor cleared his throat and lifted the paper in the air. "This edition of the *Times* arrived at the Seattle Wharf today with a disturbing story that you should hear." As Soapy's allies murmured, other audience members leaned forward in their pews to listen.

"I read this as printed," he announced and started giving a dramatic interpretation of the article. When he finished, Roger folded the newspaper, slapped his palm with it. "Soapy killed Ella Watson and planned to kill

Mrs. Silks and a local saloon owner, my partner, Jesse Murphy." He paused, then asked, "What say you to that?"

"Disgusting," offered one of Soapy's opponents.

"Lies," shouted editor Hornsby above everyone else, "just like I knew it would be. You can't believe anything from the *Seattle Times*."

"More truth in it than in your *Daily Alaskan*," Strong challenged from the front.

Disagreeable arguments filled the room as the men showed their allegiances, most for Skagway, a few for Soapy Smith.

"Mattie Silks is nothing but a jaded old whore past her prime," Clancy shouted. "She came to my place to hone in on my business. I sent her packing, and she left angry, vowing revenge that she couldn't just waltz into Skagway and take over."

Roger pointed his finger at Clancy. "I suspected she would have her doubters, Frank, so I brought my partner to explain a conversation he had with Mattie before she fled Skagway. Jesse, please share with the others your discussion with her."

Several in the crowd booed me when I arose, but their displeasure fell quiet when I put the shotgun in the crook of my arm and turned so the barrel pointed their direction. I explained that a terrified Mattie had come to me after overhearing the conversation, sharing what Soapy and Taylor had said. She confirmed that Soapy murdered Ella and planned to kill her and me.

"You can't believe a vindictive whore," Clancy shouted.

"Is it true, Jesse—if that's even your actual name—that you murdered a lawyer in Leadville?" Hornsby screamed.

"That's a lie," I shouted back.

"Order, order," cried Strong. "No more outbursts."

As the noise lessened, I stepped toward my pew, but instead of sitting I stood with my back to the wall where I could watch my enemies.

"The question is what do we do next?" Strong continued. "Such lawlessness will hurt Skagway if we let it continue."

"You're not the law," bellowed Clancy.

"Neither is Deputy Taylor," Tanner interjected. "That's the problem."

Most in the crowd agreed with the statement, though Soapy's supporters objected, pointing their fingers and shaking their fists at their opponents. I expected a brawl to break out as Strong pounded the gavel on the podium and demanded order.

As the room quieted and the men settled in their seats, the major asked, "What should we do?"

"Nothing," Clancy screeched. "This committee is a toothless tiger."

Roger Meredith shot up from his seat and impersonated Soapy's high-pitched voice. "Even a toothless tiger has claws, Frank," Roger said in such a perfect imitation that the crook's allies stopped and his enemies looked over their shoulders. Then my partner resumed in his regular voice. "I requested this meeting to inform the leading citizens of Skagway as well as Soapy's ruffians that infiltrate all our gatherings. I'm not requesting anything other than to make sure the community knows what it faces. To ensure everyone learns of the threat, I'm offering free beer to anyone that comes to my dramatic readings of the article this evening."

Clancy bounced from his seat and down the aisle toward Roger. "Not if I get that paper from you, you won't."

I jumped from the wall toward the podium, cocking the hammers on my shotgun and waving it at Clancy. "You touch my partner, Frank, and you'll be splattered across this room."

"If he misses," Tanner added, his Winchester at his shoulder and pointed at Clancy's head, "I won't."

Halting abruptly, our rival saloon owner glared at me, then Tanner and back to me. "You gonna shoot me in the back like you did the Leadville lawyer."

"Nope, Frank, because I want to see the look on your face when I send you to hell."

He eased away.

"It's time we adjourned this meeting before someone gets hurt," Strong announced, banging the gavel.

Clancy, Hornsby, Bowers, Wilder and their cohorts burst from their seats and out the door, leaving everyone else to sort out what had happened during Mattie Silks' visit. As soon as Soapy's shills departed, I gently released the two hammers on my shotgun and lowered the barrel to the floor. Tanner removed his rifle from his shoulder. When the crowd cleared, save for the major, Tanner, Roger and me, Strong coughed and asked if we'd done any good.

"I'm hoping it buys time for my partner. If something happens to Jesse, then everyone'll know who did it. Whether the law has the integrity and gumption to follow through with charges is another question."

The four of us exited the building together and had barely walked half a block before a committee member approached with word that Soapy's men were trying to buy for ten times its cost every copy of the *Seattle Times* they could find in town and destroy the offending paper. Strong thanked our ally for the information, then laughed as the man marched away. "I bought three copies and stored them in different places."

"I have five copies beside this one," Roger told us. "Nothing will stop my performance this evening, perhaps the best dramatic reading in the history of theater."

"Most of Skagway will be there, what with free beer as an incentive," Strong observed.

"And when I see Jesse safely to the Gold Dust," Roger announced, "I'm going to go buy me a new suit, see if I can find Soapy's clothier and purchase one in his style."

Shaking my head, I said, "Actors are crazy."

Roger snickered. "Just wait, partner. Before I'm done, you'll be giving me rave reviews for tonight's performance, well the second, third and fourth readings at least."

Strong abandoned us for his newspaper office as Roger and I marched to the Gold Dust, where customers lined up the walk waiting for free beer. Roger announced that the giveaway would start after the first reading at six o'clock. Once the free beer flowed, another three dramatic readings would follow on the hour, beginning at seven o'clock. He suggested that the men bring a tin cup or their own mug because we didn't have enough glassware to accommodate the expected crowd.

Once he saw me safely inside, Roger left to purchase his new outfit, which struck me as an odd matter to attend to on such a worrisome day, especially since the offer of free beer might wipe out our June profits, but I accepted that actors were just one step away from the insane asylum, even if they were as decent as Roger Meredith. The saloon became so crowded with men just standing around and not buying anything, the bartenders and I shooed them out, telling them we would re-open just before six o'clock. Roger returned at five o'clock, worming his way through the crowd at the door and carrying his new duds across the empty room and backstage rather than upstairs to his room. I thought when he re-appeared he would be attired in his new duds, but instead he came out in a toga with a gold crown on his head, explaining it was his Julius Caesar costume for when he did Shakespeare. While I found it odd to wear what the Romans wore for the newspaper reading, I'd never been to Seattle and maybe that's how they dressed.

"Keep your shotgun handy," Roger told me, "in case I need protection. But I want to warn you, I'm doing the first reading, but I've invited someone special to give the last three recitations. Don't shoot him, okay?"

"Who is it?"

"I can't say, just promise me you won't shoot him or let anyone else do so."

Silently, I stood there as confused as a suffragist in a voting booth.

"Give me your word, Jesse, that you won't kill whoever comes on stage for the reading."

Shrugging, I nodded my agreement, then helped the bartenders roll out the beer kegs as I figured we'd drain them all by the size of the crowd gathering outside. Roger visited with the piano player, telling him what music he wanted and when. At five-thirty Roger let the working girls in, instructing them not to leave with any customers until after the second show at least and ordering them not to accept customer offers for drinks as the barkeeps would be too busy to keep up with their cut. But Roger offered them as many free beers as they desired.

At a quarter of six we opened the saloon and the men streamed in, most laughing at Roger's costume and advising him he was the ugliest girl they'd ever seen in the Gold Dust. Another customer, who already had downed too many drinks elsewhere, asked if he could escort Roger home after the performance. Our customers crowded in tighter than even at our New Year's Eve celebration. Right at six o'clock, the pianist played a classical song, barely audible above the din, then Roger appeared in shafts of illumination from two footlights. I worked my way to the foot of the stage and turned to face the audience, my shotgun at the ready in case a Soapy crony tried to end the show before it got started.

"Good evening, ladies and gentlemen," Roger cried as the spectators hushed each other for quiet. "Let me welcome you to this dramatic reading from the *Seattle Times*, which has brought to our attention disquieting information about our fine city of Skagway. I appear tonight as Julius Caesar, whose ambitions and corruption led to his own demise to the greater benefit of Rome and the Roman Empire."

The crowd fell silent as Roger continued.

"We as residents of Skagway have decisions to make if we are to prosper in a city free of taint and fraud, just as the Romans did."

Now I was no scholar in theater or literature, but I took it that my partner was calling for Soapy's assassination.

"Friends, cheechackos and sourdoughs, lend me your ears," Roger called as he pulled a copy of the *Times* from under his toga. He unfolded the paper and with a voice like God Himself read the news account with its accusations against Smith and Taylor and their brigands. With every breath, he added power to the words by his inflection, pauses and emphasis. The audience stared in slack-jawed awe at the intensity of his performance. When he completed the article, he bowed and the crowd clapped, yelled and whistled their approval. Then he stepped to the edge of the stage and inspected the crowd, his blue eyes sparkling.

"I am honored by your applause, but I need your help. Though unnamed in the story I just read, the saloon owner that Soapy Smith has threatened is none other than my partner, Jesse Murphy, who stands below me at the foot of this stage. Wave your shotgun at them, Jesse."

Lifting the scattergun over my head with one hand, I waved at them with the other as if I knew what the hell Roger was doing.

"Jesse must carry his sawed-off shotgun with him everywhere he goes because of these threats from Soapy Smith and his gang, including Deputy Marshal Taylor."

The crowd booed and hissed.

"I do not care to lose my partner because he's a fine man and good for Skagway, running as honest a saloon as you'll find on the continent, unlike Jeff Smith's Parlor and other local drinking establishments. You don't get clipped or swindled or robbed in our place." He let the men nod their agreement. "You like free beer, do you not gentlemen?"

The crowd cheered.

"Has any other saloon ever offered you free beer in Skagway?"

"No," the men shouted in unison.

"Then thank Jesse Murphy standing here before you. It was Jesse's suggestion, the free beer. Now if something happens to him as Soapy has threatened, according to the lovely and honorable Mattie Silks, you'll never get another free beer in Skagway ever. This wasn't my idea to give our beer away and cut into our profits, it was Jesse Murphy's and that just shows you the decency of my partner. Don't you agree?"

The freeloaders clapped and cheered. I felt like the corpse at a funeral, all these wonderful things being said about me, even if most were false.

"Now can I ask you to do me a favor?"

"Yeah," they cried out.

"If you see anyone threatening or attempting to shoot Jesse, please step in and shoot his attacker in the name of humanity and free beer now and forever in Skagway."

The audience celebrated the loudest yet.

"At seven o'clock we will have the second of four readings. I have asked a special guest to analyze the newspaper article so I can get out of this ridiculous costume and enjoy a beer if any remains. We started the evening with four kegs and if there's a drop of beer left in any of them by the time we're done, I'll consider the night a failure and you'll have insulted the generosity of one of Skagway's most honorable citizens, Jesse Murphy. Let's hear it for my partner."

A roar swept across the saloon and opera house, men pretending they were cheering me, though in reality, they were celebrating free beer. At that point, Roger announced what everyone wanted to hear. "Gentlemen, enjoy your beers." Instantly, the crowd turned from the stage and pressed toward the bar. I feared the more petite girls might get trampled in the rush. As I watched the stampede, Roger squatted down and patted me on the shoulder. "Remember, Jesse, don't shoot the guest performer when he takes the stage."

"Who is it?" I asked.

He ignored me, standing up and walking offstage to the dressing room. Soon men crowded around me, slapping me on the back, thanking me for the free beer and promising to protect me. If I even survived all the thank yous, my shoulders would be black and blue come morning. The hour dragged by slowly until just before seven o'clock when the pianist punched out the same classical tune as before to announce the impending performance. I took my place at the foot of the stage, shotgun in hand, ready for anything. Or at least I thought I was ready for everything.

I studied the crowd as the guest performer stepped into the footlights. I saw the audience flinch and heard the members gasp. Spinning around, I had the shock of my life. At the front of the stage just a few feet away and staring at me with a copy of the *Seattle Times* in his hand stood Soapy Smith!

Soapy Smith! I couldn't believe it. What had my partner done to me?

I cocked the hammers on my shotgun, ready to dispatch Jefferson Randolph Smith the Second to hell.

Chapter Twenty-eight

After an instant of stunned silence, the crowd booed as Soapy strode to the very edge of the stage, towering over me and staring at me with blue eyes. His gaze confused me because. Soapy's eyes were as black as his soul, not blue like this pair.

Soapy, studying me without moving his lips, said, "Don't shoot, Jesse; it's me, Roger."

I couldn't believe it. My partner had dressed in his new black suit, shirt and tie, then added a black wig and unruly beard beneath a black hat, standing there like Skagway's biggest crook. I shook my head, clearing it of the cobwebs of confusion.

"Don't shoot, Jesse; it's me, Roger," he repeated without moving his lips.

Releasing the hammers, lowered the shotgun and nodded. "Glad you told me."

"Don't let any of them shoot me, either," he said, his lips motionless.

Nodding, I turned around and studied the crowd as the pretend Soapy spoke behind me in a high-pitched voice that matched conman's squeaky speech precisely.

"Some terrible things were said about me from this stage earlier tonight by Roger Meredith. Even if he is one of the world's greatest theatrical performers and Skagway is lucky to have his talents for our enjoyment, he lied, just as this Seattle newspaper wrote falsehoods about me." My partner pulled the paper from his coat pocket and waved it at the hissing crowd. Unfolding it, he prepared to read it in Soapy's squeaky voice.

Still the spectators answered with catcalls.

The phony Soapy shook the paper at them. "Be quiet for the truth," he cried and spoke the first sentence, then the second. "Deputy United States Marshal Taylor of Skagway is a consort of murderers, a consort with them in crime, and 'Soapy' Smith has taken to murdering people for their money." He paused, then winked at the crowd. "It's true," drawing more catcalls.

"Go to hell," a man near me yelled.

"I've been there," the imitator shot back, "and plan on returning."

"Soon," shouted another skeptic.

My phony Soapy stared him down and continued the story, talking of Ella's murder and the cash stolen from her trunk. He then read about Mattie Silks overhearing him and his cohorts splitting up the money. "The night after the murder," Roger continued, "Mattie Silks says she heard Marshal Taylor, Soapy Smith and two others being well-known crooks talking in Taylor's office while they were dividing up thirty-eight hundred dollars."

Soapy stared at the crowd and shook the paper at them. "That's a lie," he screamed. "It wasn't thirty-eight hundred dollars, it was five thousand dollars. I took twelve hundred right off the top and into my pocket." My partner winked at his audience. "I don't rob just you; I steal from my partners because they're even stupider than you."

As the others booed, one angry spectator threw a mug at Soapy, though it missed and shattered on the stage behind him. I hoped it was his own glass rather than one of the saloon's.

My favorite actor continued reading the article and came to another passage that he emphasized. "But that was not all. Mrs. Silks says that while she sat in her room, she heard this outfit intended to strangle her to death in the same way in which Ella Wilson had been served and to assassinate an upstanding saloon owner." He looked down at me. "That's the son of a bitch I planned to kill. Tried it once, but missed, killing his dog instead."

The audience derided the impersonator even louder, almost as if they valued Buck more than Ella.

"Now I don't know when I can shoot him, since he's offering free beer to you imbeciles."

Though he drew more threatening taunts from the throng, Roger continued his imitation.

" 'The condition of affairs at Skagway is a disgrace to civilized government,' " he smirked, "but not to me because it's making me rich. 'The United States officials make no pretense at enforcing the law,' because I am the law in Skagway. 'They are making money hand over fist, and any sort of crime can be committed as long as the officials of the United States get their share of the loot.' That's true as I run Skagway. 'The only law that is respected is the rifle or the revolver, and unless something is done pretty soon, Skagway will be absolutely unsafe for any man to venture into who values his life.' That's another lie because the town will always be safe for me and my gang."

Again everyone booed, but Roger continued Soapy's warped reading.

"Thank you, each one of you, for your support," he cried, "and remember I'll be back in an hour for the next reading. Until then, enjoy all the beer you can drink, compliments of Jesse Murphy, who is to honesty in Skagway what I am to thievery." With that, Roger's Soapy took a bow and exited into the backstage shadows, drawing a chorus of boos and insults.

I stood amazed at Roger's duplicity, the audience believing he was Soapy. Either he was that good an actor or the beer was having its desired effect. As the customers moved to the bar for refills, I slipped to the dressing room, opening the door and shaking my head at Roger.

"How was that for acting?" he laughed.

"Amazing," I answered.

"When you cocked the hammer on your shotgun, I feared it was my last performance."

"I was ready to shoot you and never realized it was you until I saw your blue eyes."

"Remember I'll perform again at eight and nine."

"Why're you doing this, Roger?"

"If the committee won't take action, then I needed to do something to protect you. By the time I'm done portraying Soapy, he'll have even more enemies than he's got now. You'll have more friends, men that'll watch your back in hopes of more free beer. Besides that, it's too much trouble and expense to bury you."

"Always thinking of yourself, huh, Roger?"

He grinned. "What are partners for? Now you take your shotgun out and keep an eye on the crowd. I don't want Soapy or any of his gang shooting me before the night's over."

"Me neither," I answered, patting my shotgun. "It's too much trouble and expense to bury you, huh, partner?"

We both laughed, and I left, mingling with the crowd. If any of Soapy's men slipped into the Gold Dust, I never detected them. The free beer held the freeloaders like a magnet in the place, though once the alcohol ran out, who knew what might happen? By the next dramatic performance the saloon was more packed than earlier, stifling with the heat of so many crowded together. Some passed out from the beer or the warmth, but when the final keg was drained twenty minutes before the last show many loyal customers staggered out into the cool night air. Roger gave his final reading to a crowd a third the size of the first, but that was fine as many customers with dulled senses departed, complaining about what a son of a bitch Soapy was. On top of that, numerous folks who didn't know who I was before the readings now protected my back, hoping to get free drinks later. I joined Roger backstage after the last performance and watched him remove his wig and beard, then add his new suit, tie and shirt to the other costumes in his wardrobe. We agreed the evening was a success.

Our business took a hit over the next three days until we could get our next shipment of beer in from the states. While there was a local brewery by then in Skagway, Frank Clancy soaked up its entire production to squeeze other saloons. The following morning, deputy Sylvester Taylor dropped by, catching me and Roger in our office. He barged in, pointing his finger at my nose.

"What the hell happened here last night?" he demanded.

"Early for your bribe, are you, deputy?" I challenged.

"You should've been here," Roger added.

"That's right," I said, "because Soapy Smith stood on stage and admitted to murdering Ella Wilson. By the way, deputy, how's that investigation coming along?"

"That's another lie about Soapy," Taylor replied. "He was—"

"He was with you all night," I interrupted. "Well, there were hundreds of men in here last night who believe he was in the Gold Dust from seven to nine."

"That's a damned lie," the deputy sputtered.

"Try telling that to those that enjoyed his talks," I shot back.

"You can't convince them they didn't see what they saw with their own eyes," Roger added. "Soapy Smith stood on our stage reading from the *Seattle Times*. You should've been here, Taylor. Soapy must've been drunk because he admitted killing Ella, even admitting he skimmed twelve-hundred dollars off the top of the take before splitting thirty-eight hundred with you, Bowers and Wilder."

"It's a lie, dammit," he replied. "I know because I was with Soapy the whole night."

I shook my head. "You sure spend a lot of nights with Soapy, deputy. Is something unnatural going on between you and him?"

Taylor's face reddened, his eyes bugged out and the veins in his neck bulged and throbbed in anger.

Before Taylor could respond, Roger broke in. "If I remember correctly, Taylor, it's called buggery, a crime against nature."

"All lies, like everything else spewing from both of your mouths."

"Maybe so, but gossip such as that could get you removed from office," Roger countered.

"Not only that, deputy," I added, "we'll invite Soapy back to our stage to confirm such unnatural acts on another free beer night. It won't matter if it's true or false because your reputation will be stained forever once that happens."

"It'd be an imposter," Taylor said, pointing at Roger. "Likely the actor."

Roger scoffed. "I could never play such a vile character."

Taylor patted the revolver at his side. "I ought to shoot you both."

Patting the sawed-off shotgun on the table in front of me, I said, "I've got a better chance of hitting you with my scattergun than you do one of us with your pistol."

The deputy moved his hand away from his sidearm. "I'm doubling what you owe me each week to thirty dollars. I'll be back tomorrow to collect."

Roger shook his head. "No you won't, deputy. You're dropping your bribe to nothing or we'll spread rumors tonight about you and Soapy spending so much time together in your hotel room."

"It's my office," he shot back.

Grinning, I nodded. "That won't look good. Skagway folks can accept your corruption, but I don't think they'll be as forgiving when word gets out of your sins against nature."

Taylor stammered, realizing he was caught over an empty beer barrel.

"Here's the understanding, deputy," Roger said. "No more payments to you or anybody else and no attempt to shut us down, is that clear? No speculation that I was the Soapy Smith imposter. As long as you keep that agreement, we won't gossip about your warped relationship with Soapy."

I clarified the arrangement. "The deal's off if you arrest me over what you may have heard I did in Leadville, Colorado. Understood?"

Taylor bobbed his head meekly.

"The moment you break any of those conditions," Roger reiterated, "that's when we put out word about you and Soapy."

I'd seen whipped puppies that cowered less than he did. He nodded his agreement again.

"Should we shake on it to confirm our deal?" I asked.

"Not necessary," he replied.

"Well," I said. "It's been a pleasure doing business with you for a change, deputy. Care for one of my special drinks?"

"Not today," Taylor answered, his shoulders slumping.

"I promise you a booger of a drink, if you'll let me do one last jigger for old time's sake!"

The deputy waved my suggestion away, turned and marched out the door. We stepped to the exit and watched him stride past the bar and depart from our business. "I wonder if he'll ever return," my partner mused.

"We should've demanded repayment of everything he's extorted from us."

"No," Roger replied, "we're pressing our luck as it is because we made a new enemy." Meredith's assessment was correct, but he had done such a wonderful job of defiling Soapy that even Jefferson Randolph Smith the Second had to repair his sullied reputation for the rest of June. The *Daily Alaskan* helped, mentioning his stellar deeds in supporting widows, donating to churches, saving stray dogs and waving the grand old American flag to support the nation's war against the Spaniards all the way from Cuba in the Caribbean, where the Rough Riders and other troops had landed to await battle, to the Philippines in the Pacific where Admiral George Dewey had whipped the Spanish fleet.

With July Fourth just weeks away, Captain Jeff Smith of the Skagway militia decided he must participate in the day's parade and activities to prove he was a patriot above everything else. Planned by the city's Commerce Committee, made up of businessmen and merchants from the Committee of One Hundred and One, the celebration promised a parade, patriotic speeches, athletic contests, concert with dance and fireworks.

The planning committee ignored Smith's initial request to participate in the parade, but Soapy eventually prevailed, either by threat or by promising to stop his shady endeavors until after the celebration. While the committee hesitated to approve his entry, Soapy sweetened the deal by promising a float displaying the bald eagle he had acquired that very month. Whatever the case, the committee approved his participation as long as he brought up the end of the procession in the fourth division, as they named it. Eager to improve his reputation after Roger's devastating stage impersonation, Soapy agreed to the committee's demands. Those days leading up to the Independence Day celebration were among the most carefree and pleasant of my stay in Skagway. The weather was perfect, save for the occasional showers, and the town donned the colors of red, white and blue, as buildings wore flags and stars and bunting and stripes and lanterns in American colors. It brought a lump to your throat if you were a U.S. citizen, though I'm not sure it did much for the Canadians who called Skagway home.

The whole community bonded over the patriotism, especially in this time of war, even if we weren't officially part of the United States. With each steamship arriving from the states came more goods and supplies and, most importantly, more females. Many were wives of men who had established businesses in town, others were women looking for husbands and a handful sought brief monetary encounters with men. We had gotten so accustomed to a community with few women of proper values that we had to remind ourselves to tip our hats at the ladies and watch our language as we walked the streets. In addition to women, Skagway now boasted a telephone line to Dyea, our competitor for economic superiority along Lynn Canal. Everything was going grandly with swindles and robberies on the decline and the future of Skagway on the rise, except for the lingering taint of Soapy Smith and his gang.

"You think the good times will last?" Roger asked me the evening of the third.

Raising my shotgun, I answered. "Nope. That's why I'm still carrying this."

When July Fourth arrived, the entire town turned out as participants and spectators at the events. The festivities began with the parade at one o'clock. My partner and I agreed to close the Gold Dust so even the piano player could watch the patriotic procession. We stood outside our saloon on the plank walk as the city band led the parade's first division, including aging members of the Grand Army of the Republic. As those old soldiers passed, I wondered if any of those Yankees had fought against my older brothers during the war. Then followed a children's float representing the Goddess of Liberty; a cavalcade of ladies; a float by City Brewery; the gentlemen's cavalcade; and a selection of men and women in costumes of red, white and blue. Every group drew appreciative applause and cheers.

A minute later, the second division approached, again receiving a great tumult from the spectators as members of various clubs, societies and secret orders marched by, tipping their hats and fezzes as they passed. Next came a merchant's float; a line of men's and women's bicyclists; a *Skagway News* float; and finally the paper's news boys association with all the kids that sold papers on the corner. Everyone cheered this section of the parade as well.

After a fifty-yard break in the procession, third division stepped forward, led by officers and employees of the White Pass & Yukon Railway, which was making progress in reaching the peaks impeding the rush to Dawson City. Next passed floats of the trades and mechanics group and of the *Daily Alaskan*, where the crooked J. Allen Hornsby stood waving at the crowd. A column of the Independent Newsboy's Association, as the *Alaskan* called its paper peddlers, marched by grinning and waving at the crowd. Bringing up the rear of this section came patriotic Indians identified by a banner as Chilkat, Pyramid, Harbor and Haines Mission Indian Tribes. This whole division drew great cheers, especially the Indians whose patriotic fever was acknowledged.

After another gap in the procession, the fourth group advanced with Captain Jeff Smith riding a mottled white horse, smiling and brandishing a sword he had secured from somewhere. Behind him marched a hundred and twenty of Soapy's cronies, playing soldier boys with mismatched rifles and uniforms in name only. The only common identifier they wore were red, white and blue ribbons, identifying them as members of the First Regiment of Alaska Militia. As the captain reached the Gold Dust, he saw me and guided his horse in my direction, stopping within spitting distance and pointing his saber at my nose.

"You're gonna die, Lomax," he said, using my real name to my face.

"Greetings to you, too, Captain Soapy, on this patriotic day," I answered.

"I'm not Captain Soapy."

"And I'm not Lomax, whoever that is."

"It don't matter who you are. You'll not live to the next Independence Day."

He yanked the reins on his horse and rejoined his troops.

Looking at the surrounding folks, I shrugged. "Don't know who this Lomax character is." I watched Soapy's thugs march by and realized his section of the parade drew only modest applause and feeble cheers. The folks of Skagway understood his role in the death of Ella Wilson and had no intention of lauding him. Following the captain's men came a wagon driven by Professor John Bowers and George Wilder. In the back was the caged bald eagle that had likely earned Jeff Smith his place in the procession. The eagle sat on its perch, staring at the people staring at him. Even the national bird drew faint cheers because of his link to Jeff Smith.

As the parade advanced toward the bay, we spectators fell in line behind it, heading to the Seattle Wharf to listen to patriotic speeches of local and district dignitaries. Once the speakers had settled in their places at the head of the wharf, I grimaced when I saw that Soapy weasel his way into a seat with the special guests, though he was never introduced and didn't speak. More than one orator expressed the dream of Alaska one day becoming a star on the American flag, while others voiced support for the nation's war against the Spanish. After an hour of more stirring talks on America than I'd ever heard at one time, the celebration moved to the dry flats between the Seattle and Skagway wharves for the athletic competitions. We watched foot races, sack races, horse races, bicycle races, ladies races and canoe races. Besides the tug of war, my favorite event was the fat men's race, which required every contestant to step on the scales and prove he weighed over two hundred pounds. A dozen men passed the weigh-in and Roger and I bet a dollar on our favorites, me taking the thinnest fellow in the contest and my partner placing his hopes on the fattest. The first-place winner received a keg of beer and the second-place finisher earned a ham. Roger's fat man won by two lengths. As I was paying off my partner, I felt a hand on my shoulder.

"Care to make another bet?" asked a squeaky voice.

I spun around to see Soapy Smith staring at me.

"You've been spreading lies about me, Lomax," he scowled.

"It's Murphy, Captain Soapy."

"You and I both know what happened in Leadville."

I nodded. "You killed the lawyer then set me up to take the blame. Every bone in your body is crooked, Soapy."

He shook his head. "Care to make that bet with me?"

"You're a sure-thing man, isn't that what you call yourself? I don't gamble with your type."

"I bet you a hundred dollars you're not alive by the end of July, twenty-seven days away, Lomax."

"You missed me the last time you ambushed me."

"I won't miss the next time," he shot back.

"Too bad Buck didn't give you rabies, Captain Soapy. How's the hand?"

"Shut up, Lomax!"

Shaking my head, I wagged my finger in front of Soapy's nose. "It's Murphy, Jesse Murphy. Pester me anymore, Soapy, and I'll tell the town of all the buggery between you and the deputy marshal."

Soapy hesitated, uncertainty awash in his dark eyes over the stunning accusation.

"Another thing Mattie told me from overhearing you and Taylor was the unnatural acts you and the deputy were doing each night," I lied.

"Bitch," he cried. "When I return to Denver, I'll settle scores with her and Cort for good."

"No, you won't, Soapy, because you're not leaving town alive. The noose is closing around your neck."

"There aren't enough men with guts in Skagway to scare me away."

"Maybe not," I replied, lifting my sawed-off shotgun and patting it on the barrel, "but it doesn't take men with guts, just a blast from this to take care of you."

352

Soapy narrowed his dark eyes. "If you so much as touch a hair on my head, my men'll swoop down and kill you on the spot."

"If their aim's as bad as yours, I'll live a long and happy life." I wagged the shotgun at him instead of my finger.

As I did, Bowers and Wilder approached.

"Come on, Jeff," Bowers said. "Let's enjoy the celebration. We'll get this bastard later. It's a shame we didn't get him years ago in Leadville and saved us all a lot of trouble."

I grinned at Bowers. "There's nothing lower than a man pretending to be a preacher."

"I'm a professor," he answered.

"You were a reverend in Leadville. There's a special place in hell for a man that proclaims the word of God to defraud others."

"Come on, Jeff," Bowers said, grabbing his arm. "Let's find your horse and head back to the Parlor. Don't let him ruin your celebration."

Wilder took Soapy's other arm, and they yanked him away.

I watched them disappear in the crowd, then lowered my shotgun.

"Damn," said Roger. "I didn't think you had that much grit in you, Jesse or Lomax or whatever the hell your name is."

"I've been threatened by meaner folks than him. I'm still here. Most of them aren't."

"Who else have you stood up to?"

"How about Jesse James or Billy the Kid? Even Doc Holliday and Wyatt Earp as well as Johnny Ringo and Wild Bill and General Custer himself. And then there's the meanest varmint I ever encountered."

"Who might that be? A Democrat or a Republican?"

"Miss Susan B. Anthony."

"The suffragist?"

"That's the one. Encountered her in Leadville and lived to tell the tale."

"Leadville must've been a tough place."

"It started many of my problems and it's the reason I

kept moving over the years, so my past wouldn't catch up with me. But now, I'm thinking of settling down in Skagway, once we get rid of Soapy."

Roger slapped me on the back. "Let's go and re-open the saloon, see if we can recover our losses over the free beer from last month." He paused and looked me in the face. "You're a damn good liar when the situation calls for it, facing down those legends."

"I wasn't lying," I replied, knowing Roger still didn't believe me.

We returned to the Gold Dust and did a solid evening of business, even though we missed the fireworks over the bay. The real fireworks that changed Skagway forever started four days later, and I helped set them off.

Chapter Twenty-nine

Stretching my arms as I walked down the staircase from my room after a good night's sleep, I reached the bar as the door flew open and Roger Meredith barged in. "Glad you're up, Jesse. Trouble's brewing."

"What is it?"

"Can't say. Fetch your revolver and your shotgun. You may need them."

Reversing course, I bounded up the stairs and into my room, fastening my gun belt around my waist, grabbing the sawed-off scattergun, pulling my hat from a peg and yanking it over my head. I raced to the ground floor and out the front door where I found Roger standing on the plank walk. "What's going on?"

"There's a special meeting you need to attend."

"The full committee?"

"No, only the dozen we can trust. There was a robbery this morning at Soapy's Parlor."

"Nothing new about that."

"This one's different. It's the first fellow of the season to return from Dawson City. His poke was stolen, almost three thousand dollars in gold dust and nuggets swiped. Our commerce will die if word gets out that a man and his gold are not safe in Skagway. We've got to stop this."

Roger and I jogged toward the Union Church, as men I recognized as merchants and business owners approached the building. We marched inside and found a handful of others on the pews up front, Major Strong marching back and forth in front, wringing his hands as newcomers filed down the aisle.

Strong stopped and lifted his right hand, counting us with his forefinger. "That's all of us. Would one of you lock up so we can get this meeting going before any of Jeff Smith's men find out?"

Behind me I heard the door shut and the lock click as I took a seat between Frank Reid and Josias M. "Si" Tanner. I recognized the other men in the room save the one sitting on the front row, a wool cap clenched in his hand as he looked over his shoulder at us. With everyone seated, Strong introduced John D. Stewart, who stood up, grimacing as he twisted his cap in his hands.

"Mr. Stewart is the first man to reach Skagway from Dawson City after the season's thaw," the major began. "He arrived with three thousand dollars of gold dust and nuggets, the culmination of backbreaking work in frigid conditions, only to have his poke stolen by Soapy Smith's men. We either address this crime, or our city will suffer when word reaches Dawson City that folks and their gold are unsafe here." We nodded our agreement. Strong pointed to the victim. "I'll let him tell what happened."

Stewart cleared his throat and licked his lips, shifted his weight from foot to foot and sighed. "Eighteen months of work gone in eighteen seconds," he told us, "and the law doesn't care." The victim explained his arrived the previous day, taking a room at the Hotel Mondamin and splurging for a bath, haircut, and shave, then buying a new suit and dining at the hotel with actual porcelain plates and silver pieces rather than the tinware he had grown accustomed to in the Yukon. After a good night's sleep, he was enticed to Jeff Smith's Parlor at the invitation of Professor John Bowers and George Wilder, who plied him with drinks as they sought news from the Klondike. Stewart admitted during the conversation that he bragged about the eighty-seven dollars cash and the gold in his poke.

"Bowers and Wilder congratulated me on my good luck, and invited me back of the saloon to see a caged eagle as it was close to feeding time. I followed them outside where a half dozen other guys watched as a man yanked a live hen from a canvas sack, opened the cage door and shoved the terrified chicken in. The raptor tore into that bird, ripping its head off with his beak and talons, then devouring it. As we crowded closer for a better view, a big fellow in work clothes squeezed in behind me and pushed me toward the cage. I stumbled and fell, others falling atop me before helping me up. When I got up, everyone was dusting me off and distracting me before I realized my poke was missing. I looked and saw the huge guy dashing off with my money. I screamed and gave chase, but one of the fellows tripped me. They scrambled to help me up, holding me and checking I was okay. By the time they released me, the robber had escaped with my gold. Eighteen months of work gone in eighteen seconds."

The rest of us looked at one another, shaking our heads, but not surprised at the latest chapter in Soapy Smith's shady history.

"Tell them what happened next," Strong instructed.

"I visited the deputy marshal in his hotel, telling him the whole story. He just laughed, saying the only solution was for me to return to the Klondike, dig up more gold, and take better care not to lose it next time. Is that how the law works in Skagway?"

No one answered, as we understood the authorities favored the lawless in our fair city.

"Thank you, Mr. Stewart," the major answered. "Please be seated while we discuss what to do about this outrage."

"We know Soapy's behind this," I offered. "The only answer is to kill the son of a bitch."

"That's easy for you to say," Strong replied, "because you're heeled. Most of us don't carry revolvers, much less a sawed-off shotgun. We've never been in scrapes with guns."

Most of the men nodded to each other.

"How many of you have been involved in shooting difficulties?" Strong asked.

I raised my hand as did Frank Reid, Si Tanner and one other attendee.

"We're outgunned," Strong noted. "What are we gonna do?"

Tanner stood up, stretching his long frame and tugging at his mustache. He surveyed the room, then spoke. "If the deputy marshal won't investigate, we should call Dyea, as there's a new United States commissioner there, Charles Sehlbrede."

Strong shrugged. "The last one looked the other way while Taylor extorted us."

"Maybe Sehlbrede's cut from honest cloth, maybe not, but we start with him to do it legal. You can make the call, Major, as a representative of committee or the *News*. He might take your call before someone else's."

"I'll do it," Strong replied. "Are we adjourned now?"

Tanner shook his head. "Next we demand that Soapy returns the gold and inform him his lawless days are over in Skagway."

Strong paled at the comment and several shook their heads, squirming in their seats. "We're not fighting men," said one.

"Some time we all have to fight for what's right," Tanner answered.

"I appoint you new head of the law and order committee," Strong said. "Handle it, Si."

Tanner nodded. "I'll do it as long as somebody takes the message to Soapy that he's been summoned to meet with me and the committee."

The men looked at one another, then at their shoes as they pursed their lips and avoided Tanner's gaze.

"I'll do it," I volunteered.

Reid raised his arm. "I'll go with Murphy."

"Thank you both," Tanner replied. "Major, you make your telephone call to Dyea. I need two more men here as witnesses if Soapy shows up."

As Frank and I arose, Tanner shook our hands. He pulled his pocket watch from his vest and checked the time. "It's ten-thirty. I'll wait here until noon for him. Tell him if he's not here to answer charges, we'll find him."

I grinned. "Maybe you should go in our place, Si."

He laughed. "Explain whatever suits you as long as you make the point."

Reid and I marched down the aisle to the exit, unlocked the door and emerged into the late morning sun as other committee members scurried out behind us. I didn't expect for a single one to stay with Tanner until we returned as we headed to Smith's place, hoping to find him there.

Reaching his saloon, I strode inside, my shotgun at the ready and Frank Reid right behind me. Soapy stood at the bar, drinking, and laughing with Bowers and Wilder.

"You boys are in the wrong saloon," Soapy said with that squeaky, annoying voice.

"Not today," I replied. "The law and order committee instructed us to deliver a message. Your men robbed a stampeder of three thousand dollars in gold dust and nuggets. You're to meet with the committee before noon today in Union Church and bring the money back or explain yourself. If you don't, we'll turn this over to the authorities."

Soapy smirked. "I'm the law in Skagway, not you, not the law and order committee, not the deputy marshal."

"Not anymore, Jeff," Reid answered. "Things are changing and you're finished here."

"Be there or reap the whirlwind," I said. "And come alone."

Soapy cocked his chin at me. "Whirlwind my ass! You fellows don't scare me, especially you, Lomax."

"We'll see you there or we'll find you later," I replied as I backed out.

Reid retreated with me, shutting the door as he cleared the exit and running down the street, turning the corner toward Union Church. "What was that about, him calling you Lomax?"

"It was an alias I lived under years ago in Colorado where I first encountered the bastard."

"You should've killed him then and saved us all a lot of trouble."

"I wish I had," I admitted.

When we got back to the building, we found Tanner and Roger visiting with Stewart. "Well, this is more than I was expecting," I said, turning to my partner. "I'm glad you stayed, though I doubt you'll have anything to worry about, as Soapy won't show up."

I was wrong. Thirty minutes later Jefferson Randolph Smith the Second appeared in the door, carrying a Winchester in one hand and a bottle of whiskey in the other. He marched toward us, taking a swig of liquor. He scowled as he neared. "This is a tough-looking crew."

Tanner answered, pointing at the victim, "You know Jesse Murphy, Roger Meredith, Frank Reid and myself, but this is John Stewart, who was robbed of his Klondike gold behind your saloon this morning. As chairman of the law and order committee, I'm ordering you to produce his gold."

"Nothing was stolen," Soapy answered.

"It damn sure was," Stewart shot back.

"The robbery occurred on your property by men in your employ, Jeff," Tanner said. "You're responsible for it, and I'm ordering you to reimburse Mr. Stewart for the theft."

"You don't have any authority, and he lost it in a game of chance," Soapy scowled.

"That's a lie," Stewart cried.

"What game?" Tanner demanded.

"Who knows? I wasn't there, and I'm not paying a thing."

Tanner crossed his arms over his chest. "You better listen, Jeff, to what I'm gonna tell you. Your reign of thievery and fraud is over in Skagway. This isn't a mining camp anymore, but a city and the citizens are fed up with you tainting its name."

Soapy suckled on the bottle and spat the liquor on the floor. "Do your damndest, boys."

I'd always heard growing up it was a sin to spit in church. I decided at that moment God would have his revenge on Soapy.

Smith didn't care. "Do your damndest, boys," he repeated, spun around and marched out of the building, slamming the door behind him.

"It's about what I expected from Soapy," Tanner said.

"What of my gold?" Stewart asked.

"Give us time," Tanner responded, turning to Reid. "Once the major reaches the commissioner, we'll decide what to do next. Stewart, you can come with me and Frank."

"Roger and I'll be at the Gold Dust," I said. "Keep us posted."

We exited the building going our separate directions. Roger and I arrived at the saloon at noon, but passed it up and stepped into an eatery on the opposite side of the street. We didn't say much, listening instead to the conversations of those around us, all gossiping that the vigilantes would challenge Soapy and his gang, finally putting an end to the lawlessness.

After lunch we returned to the Gold Dust and I sat at a table with my back to the wall, watching the entrance for trouble in case Soapy or his men came after me. Every entering customer had caught the tension in the air and realized something big was developing in Skagway, though none of us could predict exactly what. The one thing that kept gnawing at me was the need to cull Soapy from his herd of thugs, so we were not outnumbered by his gang. That weighed on me, so I motioned for the bartender to bring over a bottle of whiskey and a jigger. Over the coming hours I nursed on two jiggers of liquor, taking enough to calm my nerves, but not so much as to impair my judgment. I took in the door, the room, and the stage, my gaze lingering there until a smile wormed its way across my lips as I thought through a scheme to separate Soapy from his henchmen. I was pleased with my plan, then bored with the waiting as the time crawled along like an Alaskan glacier.

Ten minutes before four o'clock, Frank Reid raced in the front door and surveyed the saloon. I stood up and waved. The moment he saw me, Reid rushed over. "Commissioner Sehlbrede caught a boat from Dyea. He's in town, wanting to meet with a few of us. Find Roger and join us at Union Church."

As he spun around and left, I downed a final jigger of whiskey, grabbed my shotgun and found my partner backstage, polishing costume boots. "The United States commissioner is in town and wants to meet us."

Roger dropped his boot and rag and tailed me out of the saloon. "Think anything'll come of this? I'm not up to gunplay."

"What's worrying me is separating Soapy from his herd, so we're not outnumbered if shooting starts."

"You got any ideas?"

"As a matter of fact, I do, Roger. And, you'll play your biggest role yet."

My partner gulped. "What do you have in mind?"

We reached Union Church and opened the door, "I'll tell you later."

"Lock it, Jesse," called Tanner.

I obliged, then marched with Roger to the front, Tanner giving our names to Commissioner Sehlbrede, who studied us with no-nonsense eyes and nodded when we sat. We covered with the commissioner the same ground we had gone over with Stewart earlier in the morning, explaining the crime, the deputy's refusal to do anything about it and the meeting Tanner, Reid, Stewart, Roger and I had later with the indignant Soapy Smith.

Sehlbrede listened attentively, sitting in a chair in front of us, his elbows propped on the arms as he rested his chin on his fists. He nodded occasionally. When everyone finished, he stood. "I intend to relieve Taylor of his duties and place him under house arrest for dereliction of duty and corruption. I am appointing as acting deputy Si Tanner, who can appoint two others as deputies. It's time to clean up this mess."

We applauded the commissioner and his decision.

Tanner turned to me and Reid. "You two can handle a gun so I'm deputizing you both."

"You three lawmen will now accompany me to the deputy's office and relieve him of his badge," Sehlbrede said. "Once that's done, find Mr. Smith and give him the opportunity to return the gold. It simplifies matters if he hands over the money because we can look the other way. If Mr. Smith knows what's good for him, he'll reimburse Mr. Stewart and leave Skagway forever."

Major Strong spoke next. "I want everyone to understand I'm calling a meeting of the full Committee of One Hundred and One at six o'clock to decide what to do. We'll meet here."

As we headed for the door, Roger grabbed me by the arm. "Tell me, Jesse, what you've got in mind for me tonight."

"Your greatest performance ever," I replied, "but it'll have to wait."

From the Union Church, Sehlbrede, Tanner, Reid and I marched to the Occidental Hotel and up the stairs to the deputy's office and lodging. I remembered the last time I'd climbed the staircase escorting Mattie Silks to her room. What she overheard that night and conveyed to me the next morning saved my life.

At the door, Sehlbrede rapped on the facing, shaking his head at the sign identifying the room as the lawman's office.

"What is it?" Taylor called.

"It's United States Commissioner Charles Sehlbrede on official government business."

Taylor opened the door and the moment he saw Tanner, Reid and me with the commissioner, the grin on his face collapsed.

"Hand over your badge, deputy," Sehlbrede said. "You're being relieved of your duties and placed under house arrest."

Taylor lifted his hand to his chest and unpinned the badge from his shirt. "You can't believe what these fellows said about me," he said, handing the insignia to the commissioner.

Sehlbrede took the badge. "Did a John Stewart complain to you about being robbed?"

The former lawman nodded. "I didn't believe him."

"And you never investigated the robbery, did you?"

"I've been busy with other work," he hesitated, "trying to find the murderer of a mulatto whore."

Angered by his reference to Ella Wilson, I pointed at his nose. "That's a lie. You haven't lifted a finger to arrest her murderer. You know who killed and robbed her because you shared in the loot. It was Soapy."

"You've got plenty to answer for, deputy," Sehlbrede said, giving the badge to Tanner. He gestured at the sign tacked on the door. "Remove this so no one thinks you have anything more to do with the law in Alaska. Stay in your room until we come back. If you leave here, you'll be treated as a jail escapee and shot on sight."

Taylor paled and bit his lower lip.

Sehlbrede turned to Tanner. "Let's go, deputies, and pay a visit to Mr. Smith."

Reid winked my way, as surprised as me we were being addressed as lawmen.

"Should we be sworn in?" Tanner asked.

The commissioner shrugged. "We'll decide on an oath later. Right now I want to get to Mr. Smith before he learns Taylor's been arrested."

We marched downstairs and out the Occidental, Tanner leading the way to Jeff Smith's Parlor as the commissioner fell in beside him, Reid and I trailing in their wake. We walked with such authority that people stopped and looked, several pointing to the badge on Tanner's chest as a sign that Skagway was changing for the better. Spectators even followed us to see the show.

At Soapy's saloon, Tanner marched inside, the rest of us following him in, me lifting my shotgun to convince Soapy and his cronies we meant business. Three men at the bar turned to face us and two at a table on the opposite wall looked up at us from their game of cards, none of them Soapy. Tanner pointed at the bartender. "Where's Soapy?"

"You mean Mr. Smith?" the barkeep responded.

I stepped beside the new deputy marshal and wagged the scattergun at his chest.

The counter man grimaced, answering meekly. "He's in the back room."

"Get Soapy out here," Tanner demanded.

"Jeff, you've got visitors up front," the barkeep called.

"Send them back," Soapy answered.

Tanner shook his head and motioned for the saloon keeper to get him.

"No, Jeff, you need to come up here."

Shortly, Jefferson Randolph Smith the Second came through the doorway, freezing in the doorframe when he saw his visitors. He studied us, shaking his head. "Get out of my place," he growled. "You're not welcome here now or ever."

I swiveled around, pointing my shotgun at Soapy's chest.

"Mr. Smith," said the commissioner as he stepped between me and Tanner, "my name is Charles Sehlbre-de, and I'm the new United States commissioner for the

Dyea District of Alaska, which includes Skagway. I'm following up on a robbery on these premises."

"I have no idea what you're talking about. Besides that, Marshal Taylor can investigate any accusations against me," Soapy replied, arrogance dripping from his words.

"No, he can't, Mr. Smith, as I have relieved him of his duties and arrested him until we look into his role in multiple Skagway crimes."

Soapy's smirk disappeared as if he had been slapped with two pounds of raw liver. He stepped behind the bar and grabbed a bottle. Uncorking it, he swallowed a healthy sip.

"A certain John Stewart, fresh from Dawson City, says he visited you and your men took him out back and stole his poke of gold with near three thousand dollars inside."

Slamming the bottle on the counter, Soapy waved his fist at the commissioner. "It's a damned lie. Stewart lost his gold in a game of chance."

"Return his money to me or Deputy Tanner, and we'll look the other way. If not, we'll settle this by the books, the law books."

"Go to hell," Smith responded, then suckled on the whiskey bottle again, downing the liquor in gulps. "I run this town."

"Not any longer," the commissioner answered.

"Get out," Soapy screamed, "or I start shooting."

"I'm unarmed," Reid offered

"You're fine, Frank," I said, tweaking my shotgun until the barrel pointed at Soapy's head. "If he pulls a gun, he'll have a headache for the rest of his short life."

"You've been warned, Mr. Smith," Sehlbrede said. "Return the gold or you'll suffer the full consequences of the law."

Soapy scoffed. "I can buy whatever law I need whenever I need it."

"Not anymore, Soapy," Tanner interjected. "Reimburse your victim by four o'clock or I'll arrest you." The new deputy turned to me. "Can I have him come to the Gold Dust to deliver the money?"

I nodded.

"You heard that, Jeff. Take the gold to the Gold Dust. Now, Jesse, you keep him covered until we get outside."

Tanner, Reid, and Sehlbrede exited.

Soapy scowled at me. "I should've killed you in Leadville, Lomax."

"I owe you for setting me up for a murder I didn't commit, Soapy, and for killing Ella Watson and my dog. I won't forget." I backed out of the saloon and turned down the street with the others. We went to the Gold Dust and waited past the four o'clock deadline. When Soapy failed to show, we stepped to an eatery for a meal, before heading to Union Church for the called meeting of the Committee of One Hundred and One.

When we turned toward the church, what we saw shocked us, a throng of men milling about the building and trying to get inside. The crowd represented more than the committee's members and included concerned citizens and, most likely, dozens of plants from Soapy's gang, each intent on determining our intentions and reporting back to Smith.

"Make way for the law," Tanner said, as he cleared a path through the crowd and led me, Reid and Sehlbrede to the front where Major Strong had saved us seats on the front row. As soon as we were seated, Strong called the meeting to order, saying due to the important matters before the committee, the session was open to every Skagway citizen.

Strong provided the background on the robbery and the implications such crimes had on Skagway's business and reputation. He asked Commissioner Sehlbrede to apprise folks of the situation. He drew cheers when he announced that Taylor had been removed as deputy, and that the law was indeed coming to Skagway and would remain as long as he was commissioner. At that point the conversation turned to combating Soapy. For two hours, the crowd argued over what course to take, most arguing against Soapy but a few taking up his side, including J. Allen Hornsby and William Saportas of the *Daily Alaskan* and Frank Clancy, who volunteered to go find Soapy and persuade him to return the money along with a promise not to swindle anyone else in Skagway. Though no one expressed enthusiasm for his offer, Clancy jumped up and raced out of the building, likely to inform Soapy that the mood had turned surly against him.

After two hours of fruitless debate, Strong announced that the committee had heard from the citizens and would meet privately that night to decide a course of action. He set the meeting for nine o'clock at the end of the Juneau Wharf to restrict access to members only and even then not all of them, like Frank Clancy, who had returned to the session after visiting with Soapy.

Clancy walked to the front and stared at Sehlbrede as he spoke, "Jeff's not returning the gold today, tomorrow or ever. He threatened to get even with anyone standing against him."

"It's true," cried a man I didn't recognize. "I saw him on the street carrying a Winchester in one hand and a whiskey bottle in the other. He was mumbling how a lot of people would die tonight, and he planned to kill them himself."

The crowd gasped, several merchants rising and striding to the door to return to their homes and the safety of their wives before Soapy took out his anger on them.

Strong adjourned the meeting and others scurried away. As the session broke up, I spotted Roger Meredith across the room and strode to him, pulling him to a corner and whispering what I wanted him to do so we could separate Soapy from his men.

Roger's face went white. "Do you want to get me killed?"

"I'm trying to save lives, including yours *and* mine."

As we marched to the Gold Dust, he kept shaking his head and repeating, "I don't know, Jesse, I just don't know."

Chapter Thirty

Reaching the saloon, I sent Roger backstage and informed the bartenders, the piano player, the working girls and our patrons we were closing for the night, explaining that Soapy Smith was on the warpath. As he had promised to kill me, I said I owed it to them to close the place so no one else would get hurt if he showed up. Everyone scurried away, and I locked the door behind them, then grabbed an open bottle of liquor from the bar and settled into a chair, awaiting Roger's return.

When he crossed the stage and descended the steps to meet me, I admired his costume from the black hat, wig and beard to the black suit and tie. I applauded. "You're the spitting image of Soapy. You'd fool his mother."

My partner shook his head. "I'm terrified, dressing like Soapy when feelings are running so high against him."

"We've got to separate him from the herd," I reminded him.

"It's my tail that's at stake." He crossed his arms. "I'm not doing it unless you go too."

I pushed my scattergun across the table. "Carry this, if it'll ease your fears."

"Accompany me, Jesse, or I'm not doing it," Roger said in a perfect imitation of Soapy's squeaky voice. "If you want to separate him from the herd, you've got to lend a hand."

"Why would I be walking with Soapy? It makes no sense."

"I'll tell them I captured you."

Cocking my head, I grinned. "And you plan to kill me.

That might work, Roger, it just might. Now you're thinking."

"I'm thinking how to survive, Jesse, but you'll never know if it works until you go along!"

"Okay, okay. Let me run upstairs and get a coat to hide my sidearm if I need it in a bind." I pointed to the whiskey bottle. "Swish whiskey around in your mouth and perfume your beard with it so you'll smell like you've been drinking."

As he picked up the shotgun, I bounded up the stairs, grabbing my coat and putting it on, then running back downstairs. As I approached Roger, I sniffed the air. "I can't smell liquor."

"I had to check the scattergun first. Didn't have time to do much with the bottle."

"You need more liquor." I grabbed the bottle, sloshing liquid on his clothes, then gave him the container. "Carry that in one hand and the scattergun in the other."

"What if we run into Soapy?"

"Shoot him and deal with the consequences later."

"What if he's got members of his gang with him?"

"We shoot as many as we can before we die like heroes."

"I'd rather be a bad actor than a dead hero. I've never been in a gunfight, Jesse."

"I doubt you'll be in one tonight, but this could be your greatest performance ever. You stay out of sight, Roger, and I'll watch from the window. Soapy's been wandering the streets and threatening folks. If I see him pass, we'll run the opposite way to his saloon and issue orders to his men. You know what to say?"

Roger nodded.

We waited forty-five minutes, then I saw Soapy weaving down Broadway, spewing threats and profanity. When he passed the Gold Dust, I unlocked the door, held it open long enough for Roger to jump out. Taking time just to shut the door but not to lock it, I scurried off with Roger. We doubled back on Soapy and headed for his Parlor, getting there breathless. As we collected our wind, Roger pulled his slouch hat low over his brow to disguise himself further in the dying light of day.

"Raise your hands," he whispered, poking me in the butt with the barrel of my shotgun.

I was three paces from the Jeff Smith's Parlor door when it opened and two of his men emerged, doing a double-take at seeing me with Soapy.

Roger spoke in his shrill impersonation of Soapy's voice. "Get back inside, boys, I've got something you and the others need to hear. Move it and get the others up front."

"Yes, boss," they said in unison, backing into the saloon.

Roger pushed me with the scattergun barrel toward the entrance. I stepped two paces inside and my captor stood in the doorway, waiting for men to crowd into the front room.

"Is that everyone?" he asked.

"Yeah, boss."

"Good," Roger replied in his squeaky impersonation. "I intend to settle scores tonight with Skagway, and I plan to do it myself, starting here with Jesse Murphy or whoever he is. I don't want any of you within fifty yards of me this evening because I want Skagway to know I'm the boss of this town."

"Any questions?"

"Yeah," said the bartender. "What happened to your Winchester?"

For a moment Roger hesitated, frightening me that he'd give away the game. "I clubbed Murphy here on the shoulder and broke the stock. I took his scattergun, and it'll work even better. Does everyone understand what I want?"

They nodded.

"Instruct all the boys what I said. If any of them come within fifty yards of me, I'll shoot them. I don't want to hurt any of you, so do what I say. When I'm done, Skagway will be open for us to pick clean."

The fellows cheered.

"That's what I like to hear, boys."

Roger lowered the scattergun and grabbed the collar of my coat, pulling me outside. I grabbed the doorknob as I backed out, closing the place behind me and turning on the walk as we retraced our path to Broadway. Fortunately, the streets were sparse with people, most having stayed inside to escape Soapy's wrath.

"Hell of a job, Roger," I said. "We should be home free."

I spoke too early. As we reached the corner, Professor John Bowers and George Wilder turned our way and met us. The professor stopped in wide-eyed disbelief.

"Get your hands up, Murphy," my partner ordered in Soapy's voice, and I lifted them.

Bowers looked at Roger, then down the street behind him. "I thought I saw you back there a moment ago, Jeff."

Glancing over my shoulder, I saw Roger lift the bottle and take a sip of liquor, stalling, then responding. "I've been with me the whole time," he said. "I tricked you like I did Murphy."

"You mean Lomax, don't you?" Bowers snarled.

"See, I tricked you again, professor."

Bowers and Wilder scratched their chins. Roger's voice was perfection and the twilight was helping disguise his true identity. "I'll tell you what I told the fellows back at the Parlor. Don't come within fifty yards of me tonight because I plan to settle scores, starting here with Lomax. I'll kill as many people as it takes so folks understand I run Skagway." He laughed. "Lomax here is first. You be sure and tell any of the other fellows you see to stay clear of me."

"You sure that's wise, Jeff?" Bowers asked.

"Hell, yes," Roger shouted back. "I just don't want to shoot one of you boys before I'm done. Stay wide of me and scat."

Bowers and Wilder nodded, spun about and raced down the plank walk toward the genuine Jeff Smith's Parlor.

Still chuckling over Roger's performance, we made the block, opened the unlocked door to our saloon and stepped into the Gold Dust. Our laughing stopped. There, standing in the middle of the otherwise empty room, was Jefferson Randolph Smith the Second in the flesh.

"I've been looking for you, Lomax," he screamed, then took a swig from his whiskey bottle. "I intend to shoot you like I should have in Leadville." He lifted his rifle, then froze as Roger stepped from behind me and pointed the scattergun at Smith's belly. Soapy shook his head like he was trying to clear the suds from his brain. He looked from Roger to his whiskey, then back to my partner again as he lowered his rifle.

Calmly, my partner said, "You're seeing double, Soapy. If you shoot me, you'll kill yourself because I'm you."

Soapy cocked his jaw and grimaced, then raised the whiskey bottle to his lips and took a healthy swig. "I want to shoot Lomax."

Roger shook his head. "I'll do it, so you'll kill him because I am you, and you are me, and we're one and the same."

Soapy looked as confused as a Democrat under oath. "Okay if that's what I said."

"That's what we said!" Roger answered.

Soapy lifted the liquor bottle, then hesitated and flung it across the room, the glass shattering against the bar. "I've been drinking too much."

"No," I interjected. "Have yourself another bottle, compliments of the Gold Dust." I marched behind our bar and retrieved our cheapest whiskey, yanked the cork free and carried the liquor to Soapy, who stood transfixed, blinking at the spitting image of himself. As I stopped at his side, I spat in the bottle, but the inebriated Soapy never noticed, so confused and fascinated was he with his mirror image. I lifted his hand and put the neck of the bottle in his palm, closing his fingers around the gift of elixir.

"Now," said Roger, "you need to go to Jeff Smith's Parlor—"

"That's me," he said.

Roger nodded. "Tell Professor Bowers, George Wilder, and the others to remember what you told them."

"Remember what I told them," he repeated three times.

"That's right," Roger replied. "Do that, and I'll shoot Murphy for you."

He stamped his foot. "No, shoot, Lomax. His name is Lomax."

"Not until you get moving and remind everyone to follow your last orders."

I eased behind Soapy and nudged him toward the door. He half-walked, half-staggered to the exit, walked outside and turned on Broadway to find his saloon. As soon as he reached the corner, I retreated inside and locked the door, then ran and slapped Roger on the back.

"Greatest theatrical performance I've ever seen."

My partner trembled. "I never was so scared in my life. My knees were shaking so."

"You weren't as frightened as he was confused."

"And drunk!"

"You should've shot him, then we could've said he killed himself, a case of suicide."

"I'm going to change my clothes before someone shoots me, but one question, Jesse. Who's this Lomax character?"

"Just a fellow I used to be," I replied, then looked out the window, judging by the twilight that it was a half hour until the called meeting of the Committee of One Hundred and One. "I best start for the Juneau Wharf and help Deputy Tanner with the security."

"You do that, Jesse or Lomax or whoever the hell you are."

"Let's keep it with Jesse so my past doesn't catch up with me again."

Roger nodded. "Lock the saloon when you leave. I'm skipping the meeting, figuring I've skated too close to death today to risk it again."

I removed my coat, tossing it on a table, and took my shotgun from Roger, thanking him for another exceptional performance and heading outside, locking the door behind me, then turning for Skagway Bay. The streets remained quiet, only a fraction of the normal traffic on this unusual night. I made it to the wharf in ten minutes and found Frank Reid and two men I didn't recognize guarding the foot of the pier.

"He's okay," Reid said to the other two. "It's Jesse Murphy from the Gold Dust. Tanner wants him and me farther along the wharf." He turned to me. "I feared Soapy had caught up with you since you were late showing up."

"He did," I answered, "but he was too drunk to do anything."

Reid informed me that Tanner wanted the two men posted at the steps to turn away anybody but committee members from passing that point, but not to force anyone to obey. "Tanner, you, and me will be stationed down the pier as the enforcers and the final safeguard against unwanted visitors that might spill our plans to Soapy."

"I expect Soapy will disrupt the meeting," I said.

"Tanner thinks so, too, and has told these boys to let him pass, if he does, and the three of us will handle him and any other troublemakers."

I turned to the other two guards. "Soapy's drunk and confused. Be careful if he shows."

They nodded to confirm they understood their instructions. Then Reid and I started to our posts, meeting Tanner a third of the way down the wharf.

"Jesse ran into Soapy," Reid informed the new deputy.

"He's slobbering drunk and unpredictable," I advised Si, "but Roger and I tricked enough of his men that Soapy'll probably be traveling alone tonight."

The new deputy marshal then explained that he wanted me and Reid to stay at this location and confirm every committee member that approached before letting each pass. "The only exception is Soapy. If he resists your instructions, let him by and I'll arrest him as deputy marshal. Are you both okay with that?"

I patted my shotgun. "I'm fine, and so's my scattergun."

"Me too," said Reid, patting his pocket. "My pistol's loaded and ready for anything."

"You'll recognize most committee members, but stop any unknowns from advancing."

"What about those aligned with Soapy?" Reid asked.

Tanner nodded. "I listed a dozen members to stop." He extracted a paper from his shirt pocket and handed it to me.

I unfolded the sheet and looked at the dozen names, including J. Allen Hornsby, William Saportas, and Frank Clancy. "Clancy'll throw a hissy fit when we halt him."

"If he doesn't turn back, I'll arrest him when he reaches me and chain him to the pier until we can get him to jail in Sitka." Tanner wished us luck and marched away to take up his position. In a few minutes, members of the committee began to arrive, Major Strong first, then a few others approached individually and in pairs.

Our initial challenge came with the *Daily Alaskan* men showed up, demanding to pass.

"Not tonight," I informed them. "Turn around and go home."

"It's an outrage," Hornsby protested. "I'm a bona fide committee member."

"And I'm a newspaper man," cried Saportas, "here to cover the committee's decisions for the public good."

"You've both been feeding information to Soapy," Reid said.

"That's a lie," the editor of the *Daily Alaskan* replied. "We've only been doing our duty on behalf of the fine citizens of Skagway."

"No," I replied, "you've been doing it *to* the town folks."

When my persuasiveness failed, I lifted my sawed-off shotgun and cocked both hammers. At that point, the two newspapermen saw the validity of my argument.

"You haven't heard the last of this," Hornsby shouted. "I will chronicle your treachery in tomorrow's issue of the *Daily Alaskan.*

"Perhaps," I replied, waving my shotgun at them, "but if you don't move along your obituaries will definitely be in the next edition."

Both men cursed, but turned around and retreated toward town.

When they marched out of range, I released the hammers on the scattergun.

"You think they'll tell Soapy?" Reid asked.

"Yes, if for no other reason than to let him know they've been shut out of the meeting and won't find out what the committee is planning."

"Do you suppose Soapy'll show?"

I nodded. "He will, though as drunk as he was I don't know if it will be by accident or by design."

We then stood silent guard, passing the legitimate members of the Committee of One Hundred and One, but rejecting two of Soapy's suspected spies. Though they protested, they acquiesced and stomped down the wharf.

Then Frank Clancy strode toward us, his eyes flaring with anger. Reid and I braced to face him, ready to prevent his advance.

"What's this I'm hearing about some committee members being turned away?" he shouted. "You don't have the right to do that."

"Stop, Frank," Reid commanded. "You're on the list, and you're not attending the meeting."

Clancy stopped opposite us, balled his fingers into fists and planted them on his hips, standing akimbo as he scowled. "I'm a charter member of the Committee of One Hundred and One with every right to attend and hear what's said."

"Not today, Clancy," I informed him.

"Let me talk to Major Strong and settle this," he insisted.

"It's no longer Strong's meeting," I advised him. "Deputy Marshal Tanner is in charge of things now, and he's prohibited you and a dozen or so others from attending."

"On what grounds, dammit?"

"Tanner says this is a legal matter. He's only inviting trustworthy members," Reid advised him.

"Trustworthy?" Clancy cried. "What do you mean?"

"He means men who can attend a meeting without reporting back to Soapy," I replied.

"This is an outrage," he said, stomping his boots on the wharf. "Let me pass."

"Can't do it, Clancy, unless you want to be arrested. The deputy is just up the pier and he'll arrested you and chain you to the pier. That's a poor place to be if firing breaks out because you can't dodge bullets or buckshot." I patted the barrel of my shotgun. "I could save you the worry and shoot you now."

Clancy retreated a step, acknowledging my eloquence, and my sawed-off shotgun! "I have nothing to do with Soapy."

"That's a lie," Reid replied. "You own the land and building that Soapy calls his Parlor. That's a fact. For all we know, you're his partner and taking a share of his thievery. You're certainly receiving rent from him."

"So what if I rent him property? That don't mean we're partners or I'm a crook." He pointed his middle finger at me. "Murphy sells liquor to customers. That don't mean he's their partner. It's commerce, strictly commerce."

Waving my shotgun at him, I offered a last suggestion as I cocked both hammers. "You'll boost commerce, Clancy, if I have to buy shotguns shells to replace the two that will send you to hell. You best leave." He hesitated until

I lifted the twin barrels of my weapon toward his nose.

He wagged his middle finger at me again. "You haven't heard the last of this, Murphy. You either, Reid."

"Maybe not," I replied, "but we've heard the last of you tonight or the final noise you'll hear is the sound of my scattergun blowing your brains away."

Clancy backed off cursing, then turned and jogged to the foot of the pier. I released the hammers on my shotgun. Shortly, several more legitimate members of the committee approached us, and we waved them on. We saw three more men climb the wharf steps, pause, then turn around and retreat. Moments later, we spotted why.

"Here he comes," Reid said, pointing toward town.

I watched Jefferson Randolph Smith the Second approaching like a demon from hell, sinister and unpredictable. A man consumed by anger, he cursed and stammered, slurring his words and threats. As he came toward us, he spun around and looked behind him, cursing the people in his wake. In the twilight, it was hard to tell if they were his men, other members of the committee or the curious wanting to see what awaited Soapy or us. The conman waved his gun at them and screamed. "Get back and leave me alone." The crowd hesitated. "Do it or I'll shoot." He pointed his Winchester toward them, only lowering it when the spectators vanished down the steps. Soapy resumed his march to us, cradling the barrel of the rifle in the crook of his left arm as he approached.

Reid and I took our stances to block his advance, angering him further when I spoke. "That's far enough, Soapy," I cried, re-cocking the hammers on my shotgun.

Smith cursed and blasphemed us and our mothers, then came to a halt within arm's reach of Reid. He turned to me. "I should've killed you years ago in Leadville," he snarled, then twisted to Reid.

"You're a bastard, too," he cried as he slid the rifle down his arm and toward Reid.

His eyes widening, Reid reached in his pocket and yanked out his revolver, instantly lifting it and pointing it at the conman.

"My god, don't shoot me," Soapy screamed as he lifted

the rifle barrel toward his foe.

Reid aimed his revolver at Soapy and squeezed the trigger.

CLICK! responded the pistol. The cartridge was faulty.

Soapy swung his rifle toward Reid, who grabbed the barrel with his left hand and shoved it away as he cocked his handgun for another shot.

I jumped to the side so I could fire my shotgun without hitting Reid. I pulled the first trigger, expecting the jolt of the discharge, but felt nothing and only heard another metallic CLICK. My first shell was defective as well. Soapy was the luckiest man I ever tried to kill.

Then Smith fired his Winchester just as Reid shot his pistol. The retorts came as one loud explosion, Reid doubling over as a bullet tore through his groin, and Soapy screaming as hot lead slashed his left arm.

As Reid fell to his knees, still firing at Soapy, I had a clear shot at the conman. I pulled the second trigger and heard the same empty metallic noise.

CLICK!

Dammit, I thought, Soapy would kill me as he swung the rifle toward my gut. I flung down my shotgun, lunged at him and grabbed the barrel, wrenching the weapon from his grip before he could squeeze the trigger. Grasping his bloodied left arm with his right hand, Soapy turned to escape.

I flipped his Winchester around, slid my index finger over the trigger, then my other fingers into the lever. I fired one, two, three shots, hitting him in the back, then the side. The scourge of Skagway fell on the walkway face down. I dropped the rifle at his side.

As the deputy marshal raced up, I retrieved my shotgun. Tanner fell to his knees beside Soapy and rolled him over. He grabbed the conman's beard and yanked his head up. When he released the whiskers, Soapy's head clunked against the wood. "He's dead," the deputy announced.

Between us we heard the groans of Reid, and from both ends of the wharf we caught the rumble of men dashing to see what happened. As he moved to Reid, Tanner looked up at me. "Don't say a thing, Murphy, to anybody about the shooting. I'll provide the details when the time is right."

Reid thrashed in agony on the walkway and screamed when Tanner ripped open his shirt and unbuttoned his trousers to inspect the wound. "Gut shot," he announced. As the curious rushed up and surrounded Soapy, Reid, Tanner and me, they shouted to everyone that Soapy Smith was dead.

"What happened?" demanded one spectator.

Tanner arose. "I'm investigating. No one is to say anything until I talk to every witness. Now someone find the doctor for Frank. All we know for certain is Jeff Smith is dead. And, I intend to arrest his cronies."

"There'll be hell to pay in Skagway," called a voice I didn't recognize. I turned and pushed my way through the crowd, wondering if Soapy's men would exact their revenge on me.

Chapter Thirty-one

Returning to the darkened Gold Dust, I let myself in and marched up the stairs to my room, passing Roger's where I could see lamplight seeping from under the door.

"Is that you, Jesse?" he called.

"Yep," I answered, entering to find my partner pointing a pistol at me.

Roger lowered the revolver when he confirmed it was me. "Can't be too careful with Soapy on the loose and drunk," he explained.

"He's not running around anymore," I said. "Soapy's dead."

Roger jumped up from his bed and ran over, grabbing my arms. "Did you shoot him?"

Breaking from his grip, I tossed the malfunctioning shotgun on his bed. "My scattergun misfired, both barrels, or I would've cut him in half." Following the deputy's orders, I didn't admit the detail that I had shot Soapy with his own rifle.

Roger grimaced, then cocked his head and bit his lip. "What's the matter?"

"I unloaded both barrels while you were upstairs grabbing your coat. I feared I might shoot you in the back by accident when I was impersonating Soapy, I was so scared."

"You should've told me."

"I was so shaken after encountering Soapy downstairs that I forgot."

"Soapy's dead, Frank Reid's gut shot, and I'm alive," I said. "So, it worked out well for me, at least, assuming I can survive when Soapy's gang comes after me."

Roger pointed to his bed. "Don't forget your scatter-gun." He reached in his pocket and pulled out the two shells he had removed earlier. "You may need these."

I took them, picked up the weapon, broke it apart, inserted the shells and snapped the breech shut. "Don't come knocking on my door tonight or in the morning, Roger, as I'm the one that'll be jumpy."

"I'm staying out of range," he said.

Nodding, I stepped out of his room, closed the door and retreated to mine. I yanked off my boots and removed my gun belt, hanging it over the bedpost so the holster was within reach. Then I placed the shotgun on my mattress, nearby if any intruders came for me. I slept restlessly, but stayed in bed until nine o'clock, then I got up, pulled on my boots, placed my gun belt around my waist and picked up my scattergun before heading downstairs, wondering who from Soapy's gang might try to kill on this new day. I hoped it was Professor Bowers or George Wilder since they had been involved in the Leadville killing and in Ella Wilson's death.

My worries, though, were unwarranted as gossip I overheard in the saloon from the morning crowd revealed that new Deputy Si Tanner and his posse of armed volunteers had scoured the town. Without Soapy around, his gang was as toothless as a newborn kitten. His confederates, terrified over his death, slipped quickly and quietly away, some heading into the forests and mountains, others trying to make it to Dyea and a few hiding in their dwellings. Crooked lawman Sylvester Taylor was cowering under his bed in his room when arrested, one of dozens that Tanner and his new deputies rounded up on criminal charges or advised to depart Alaska and never return. Even J. Allen Hornsby and William Saportas of the *Daily Alaskan* abandoned Skagway on the first steamship to Seattle. As for John Stewart's missing poke, which had started the cascade of events ending the conman's life, Tanner found it in a trunk in Soapy's room. Though the gold stash was short three hundred dollars, Stewart received a better return from his dealings with

Soapy's men than most before him.

The killing and its aftermath provided the grist for the gossip in the saloon. Our bartenders, piano player and several of the early arriving girls approached me, wanting details on my part in Soapy's death. Remembering Tanner's admonition not to disclose anything, I waved them away, telling them they should devote their thoughts to praying for Frank Reid's recovery.

Shortly after one o'clock, Tanner came in the saloon. The moment he entered, all the Gold Dust employees and patrons stood up and applauded the honest lawman. His face reddened in embarrassment, and he tipped his hat in gratitude as he made his way over to me. He shook my hand and extended an invitation, "Let's take a walk."

"Sure thing," I said, arising from my chair and grabbing my scattergun.

"In a day or two, you won't need your shotgun. Soapy's men are scurrying away like rats off a sinking ship." We stepped outside, though I was uncertain where we were heading, and turned down the street. "Let's visit about last night. As I saw what happened, I'm certain you shot Soapy, but that's not what I intend to tell the inquest. Frank Reid's gonna die from his wounds, though it may take a few days. I plan to announce that Reid killed Soapy so he will go to his grave believing he's the hero of Skagway. This way, you avoid credit or blame for the killing, however folks want to look at it."

As big a skunk as Soapy had been, I felt a tinge of disappointment in not receiving acclaim for his death. On the other hand, I was living under an alias instead of H.H. Lomax so my past wouldn't catch up with me. Too, there was the identically named Irishman Jesse Murphy, who'd probably get the credit anyway as time passed. Considering each disadvantage of claiming the kill, I decided Tanner's offer was sound. "I can live with that."

Tanner smiled. "Thank you, Jesse. It's the least we can do for Reid before he dies. Commissioner Sehlbrede is holding a preliminary inquest into Soapy's death at the undertaker's parlor. I want you to testify that you saw Reid shoot Soapy so we can make it official." Tanner escorted me to E.J. Peoples Undertaker's Parlor just down Broadway from the Gold Dust. Tanner rapped on the locked door. In a moment, the curtains parted slightly, then closed as the lock clicked. Tanner opened the door and motioned for me to step inside. Sehlbrede shut and secured the door the moment Tanner entered the darkened room. The commissioner led us into the back where Soapy was laid out on a table, a sheet covering him below the waist and the bullet wounds to the chest and arm readily visible. I studied the man I'd killed, knowing he deserved it for the anguish he had caused so many and for the twenty years of worry he had caused me after framing me in the death of a crooked lawyer. I snickered as I looked at him.

"What's so funny?" asked Tanner.

"It's the first time I remember seeing him without crumbs in his beard."

Tanner and Sehlbrede laughed. When I looked around the room, I saw three other men there, including the Reverend John A. Sinclair, who had performed Ella Wilson's somber funeral.

The commissioner turned to me. "In all seriousness, Mr. Murphy, I need you to tell me what happened last night on the Juneau Wharf."

"Yes, sir," I said, nodding at Tanner. "Frank Reid and I were screening men for the meeting on the wharf, when Soapy approached and demanded to pass. We told him no, and he lifted his rifle toward Reid, who drew his pistol, but it misfired. Reid fired a second time at the same moment Soapy shot him in the gut with his rifle. Staggered, Reid grabbed Soapy's rifle and yanked it from his hands, shooting at him a time or two more. It happened so fast that I couldn't count the shots fired, but both men collapsed on the pier, Soapy dead and Reid groaning."

Sehlbrede looked at me and pursed his lips. He nodded, then spoke. "Did you shoot at Soapy?"

"Yes, sir," I said, drawing a wild look from the deputy marshal. I held up my sawed-off shotgun. "I pulled both triggers on my scattergun, aiming at Soapy, but nothing happened. What I didn't know was my partner had unloaded it earlier. So it never fired."

Sehlbrede eyed me. "Another witness reported seeing you with the rifle."

"That's true, commissioner. Once Reid fell, I grabbed the rifle. Everything happened so fast, I was uncertain if Soapy was dead. I may have fired in the excitement, but I don't remember for sure."

The commissioner looked at Tanner. "That squares more or less what you said, deputy. Frank Reid fired the fatal shot that killed Jeff Smith, and that's what we'll report."

Tanner nodded. "What next?"

"We bury the bastard," Sehlbrede said.

"Where?" Tanner asked.

"The cemetery, I suppose," the commissioner replied.

"Hell no," I cried. "The saloon girl he killed is buried there. So is my dog that Soapy shot. I don't want their burials defiled by this rubbish being planted in the same cemetery."

Tanner, Sehlbrede and the Reverend Sinclair discussed my objection, but decided they had no place else to bury him. I suggested they take him out in the middle of the bay and weight him down with rocks for a watery grave.

"Every man deserves a decent burial," Sinclair said, "even an indecent man."

"Don't plant him in the cemetery," I replied. "He doesn't deserve to be in the same resting place as the fine people of this town or even my dog."

"That's all we need from you, Murphy," Sehlbrede said.

"If you're done with me, commissioner, I'll check on Frank Reid," Tanner said.

Sehlbrede nodded his approval, and the deputy marshal escorted me out of the undertaker's. I went with him to the hospital where Reid lay. We stepped softly into his room, and he looked up at us, his face pale and etched in pain. "Hi, fellas," he rasped.

"It was a brave thing you did, Frank," I told him, "killing Soapy Smith."

"The good citizens of Skagway thank you, Frank," Tanner said.

Reid grimaced. "If my pistol hadn't misfired, I might have got him without him getting me back."

"You did your best, Frank."

"Sorry I couldn't get a shot off sooner," I apologized.

"I'm not going to make it, am I, fellas? The doctor won't tell me, but it's true, and I'll be glad when death ends this pain."

"Skagway has no greater hero than you, Frank. You'll be remembered by the grateful citizens of this town. That's more than can be said of me and Murphy."

Reid smiled. "That means a lot to me, fellas." His face contorted and his body stiffened, then he cried out in agony, gasping for air with quick breaths before controlling the throbbing ache. "I'm sorry, but the pain in my gut burns like embers."

"We understand," I said, though we could never imagine the suffering he was enduring.

Tanner and I thanked him again for confronting Soapy and wished him well in his recovery, knowing his fate was sealed. Exiting the hospital, Tanner sighed. "I should've stayed with you both. Maybe I could've dropped Soapy before he shot Frank. That decision will stay with me for a long time."

"Don't let them bury Soapy in the cemetery with Ella and Buck and Frank when he dies," I replied. "They deserve a better neighbor."

"Not much I can do about that, Murphy. I'll have my hands full this week. There's already talk of lynching members of Soapy's gang, and I've got to stop that or the lawlessness we've tried to end will prevail. I'll designate you to handle the cemetery"

"I intend to," I said, then headed toward my saloon as Tanner went about his new responsibilities.

For two nights Tanner discouraged vigilantes from doing things they might regret and might get them arrested. While the noise of the civil tumult reached the Gold Dust, I stayed away, listening for details on Soapy's burial. Three days after the conman's death, I got word Reverend Sinclair planned to hold a brief funeral at the undertaker's parlor that morning. I grabbed my shotgun and headed up the street, pausing a moment to confirm the ceremony was underway. It was the least attended funeral service ever in Skagway, just Sinclair, the undertaker and a woman so shrouded in black that no one could identify her. Some gossiped she was a secret mistress, though I believed it was the ghost of Ella Wilson come back to inform Soapy that his new home would be much hotter than her spot in paradise. When I was certain that the ceremony was indeed for Soapy, I marched out to the graveyard and waited outside the fence for the freight wagon to arrive with the undertaker, two laborers, the reverend and Soapy's carcass.

I cradled my scattergun in the crook of my arm. As the wagon drew up beside the cemetery, I walked over and shook my head. "You're not burying him here," I informed them, patting my shotgun.

"We must bury him somewhere," Sinclair said. "Even a troubled man deserves a final resting place."

"What about outside the fence?" the undertaker asked.

"I'm fine with that as long as it's as far away from Ella and Buck as possible."

The undertaker pointed to a spot on the north side of the cemetery. "How about there?"

"As long as it's outside the fence. He'll not share this graveyard with Ella and Buck."

Sinclair nodded his approval as both he and the undertaker jumped from the wagon seat, and the two laborers climbed out the back. The two gravediggers placed their shovels atop the rough wooden casket, then slid it from the wagon where the undertaker and the preacher grabbed rope handles. The four men carried the box and Soapy around the perimeter of the cemetery to the designated spot. There the two laborers began their work, the going slow and difficult in the rocky soil. After two hours they had dug three feet before giving up. The quartet lowered the coffin into the ground. If the reverend said a prayer, he said it silently as the two gravediggers covered the grave and mounded dirt and rocks atop it. The undertaker pounded into the soil a wooden marker with his name, date of death and age painted in black. I would've thought he was older than the thirty-eight years listed for all the misery he had caused. Lingering by the grave and declining the offer to ride back to town, I waited until they departed so I could be the first to spit on his grave. Once the four pulled out of sight, I spat on Soapy's final resting place, then paid my respects to Ella and Buck. I walked back to Skagway.

Frank Reid lived for twelve agonizing days after the shooting. He drew the largest funeral in the history of Skagway, men and women forever grateful for him eliminating such a vicious scoundrel. His body lay in state in Union Church for three hours before his service began, giving time for the grateful citizens of Skagway to march by and offer their gratitude. The undertaker did an excellent job as Reid's placid face belied the excruciating pain he had endured before his death. As the man at his side when he was shot, I and other members of the Committee of One Hundred and One served as his pallbearers. The Episcopal minister Sy Wood headed the service as nobody wanted Reverend Sinclair because he had conducted Soapy's ceremony. The crowd was so big, though, that the church filled an hour before the service began and the overflow blocked the street outside, where Sinclair read a copy of Wood's remarks so those mourners felt a part of honoring Skagway's greatest martyr.

With the funeral's conclusion, I along with Tanner and the others carried Reid to the fancy black hearse with brass trim and polished glass. The conveyance was shipped in from Seattle in preparation for Reid's expected death so he would receive the honor his sacrifice deserved. After we closed the back, the undertaker climbed into the seat and began the drive to the cemetery. We pallbearers walked behind the hearse and the citizens of Skagway trailed us, their line stretching for a halfmile. When we reached the graveyard, we pallbearers carried the polished coffin from the hearse to the grave that had been dug the full six-feet deep, unlike Soapy's on the other side of the fence. It took twenty minutes for the entire crowd to reach the graveyard and encircle its latest resident. The minister said more fine words about Reid and the value of sacrifice, then offered a prayer and an amen that was echoed by hundreds of other voices. The undertaker instructed the pallbearers to lift the casket and lower with ropes the remains of Frank Reid into the Skagway earth as women cried and men stood with moist eyes. Then the same pair of gravediggers who had buried Soapy covered Reid's coffin. Several of us reminisced about Reid, Roger and I recalling how he helped us claim the property where we built the Gold Dust. My Irish twin brother Jesse Murphy spotted us and walked over to say he was enjoying his railroad work, though he still looked back fondly at conning Soapy's allies out of faro winnings. We wished him well and talked to other members of the Committee of One Hundred and One about Skagway's prospects in a new century just eighteen months away. After a half hour of visiting and consolation, the crowd drifted home. I saw several men and at least one woman walk by the fence where Soapy lay and spit on his grave for killing Frank Reid and staining Skagway with his corruption.

Reid's burial marked a spiritual resurrection for Skagway as people looked to a bright future without the dark clouds of Soapy and his thugs on the horizon. Men and women returning from Dawson City with their riches now passed through Skagway knowing that their gold and their lives were safe. Smiles decorated the faces of Skagway residents because most of those connected with Soapy had left, either voluntarily or not, or had been jailed to await trials for their crimes. A handful of men like Frank Clancy, who may have been Soapy's silent partners, tried to cover up any association with him and rebuild reputations as decent citizens.

In the days that followed Reid's funeral, I thought I had at last found a home where I could plant roots and succeed with a steady job in a semi-respectable occupation. As more women arrived in Skagway, I thought I might find a decent woman to marry, even at my age. Things were looking up for my future, and I might even retire as a respected member of a community, even if I was living under an alias. Business boomed at the Gold Dust that summer as more cheechackos arrived to make the trek to Dawson City and early stampeders returned from the Klondike with flush pockets or broken dreams. In fact, our profits grew, and I bought fancy clothes to reflect our growing wealth and marched around the saloon as if I owned it all, rather than just half. Roger kept drawing customers with his plays or dramatic readings. Things were going better than I could ever remember in my life, so much so that people wanted to meet me and shake the hand of the man that had accompanied Frank Reid when he killed the villain Soapy Smith. I enjoyed the reflected glory even though I knew it should all be mine, but at least I was alive while the man receiving the honors was buried in the cemetery.

Two weeks after Reid's funeral, I was enjoying my status as a saloon owner and near celebrity when a slender man with black, swept back hair approached me. I had noticed him eyeing me earlier and figured he was like the others, curious about my role in Soapy's demise, perhaps even a writer who might want to pen my biography or a dime novel. He came over and smiled, almost blinding me with a set of teeth so white and perfect that he must have stolen them from God.

As he approached, he extended his hand. "Might you be Jesse Murphy?"

"That's me," I announced, taking his hand and shaking it warmly, though his grip was stronger than mine. When he released my fingers, I grabbed the lapels of my coat and rocked back on my heels as if I owned the place or at least fifty percent of it.

"This is an honor," my new friend said, "I have been looking forward to meeting you for a long time."

I smiled, enjoying my spreading fame as I swayed on my feet.

"Might I ask you a question, Mr. Murphy, if you don't mind?"

"Why certainly," I responded, suspecting he was curious what I was thinking during the shootout on the Juneau Wharf.

"Well, Mr. Murphy," he began, "do you know where I might find H.H. Lomax?"

I stopped rocking so suddenly I almost fell over, my

grin melting like butter in a hot skillet. "H.H. Lomax?" I sputtered. "I can't say that I'm familiar with him."

My inquisitive acquaintance reached into his pocket and pulled out a calling card. "I've been looking for H.H. Lomax for a while, and I suspect you can help me find him." He placed the card between my fingers.

Taking a deep breath, I lifted it to my nose. The card read: DAYLE LYMOINE, SPECIAL INVESTIGATOR, WELLS FARGO & COMPANY.

Chapter Thirty-two

"Is there a place we could meet in private, Mr. Murphy?" The Wells Fargo man smiled as wide as a tomcat with his paw on a mouse's tail.

"What is this about, Mr. Lymoine?" I asked, offering his card back to him.

"Keep it," he said, "because we're going to get well acquainted, Mr. Murphy."

I sighed. "Why are you interest in H.H. Lomax?"

"A certain Wells Fargo strongbox at a California train depot," he replied, still smiling.

Nodding, I pointed to my office door at the end of the bar and started that way, Lymoine tailing me like he had done ever since San Francisco. Stepping into the room, I directed him to a seat across from mine behind the desk. Lymoine shut the door and settled into his chair.

"Your actual name, Mr. Murphy, is Henry Harrison Lomax, though you go by H.H. Lomax, to be sure. Am I correct?"

I nodded. "How'd you figure it out?"

"When the Wells Fargo money came up missing, I visited the hotels looking for anyone that checked in with an unlikely amount of cash for their position in life. I found your name on the register at the Palace and visited your room, finding instead Tom and Salome Lippy just returned from the Klondike. They confirmed your name and admitted they had swapped rooms with you to avoid the newspaper harassment. They told me you intended to head out to the Yukon and make your fortune, though you were grubstaked with Wells Fargo funds."

"I found the money."

He smiled. "In a Wells Fargo strongbox that had fallen off a baggage cart at the depot."

"That's true, though the padlock was never secured. It was easier than opening a Christmas gift. What would you've done had you come across that much money?"

"Returned it to its rightful owner, in this case Wells Fargo, my employer."

"Okay, so I made a mistake, but I'm not a thief or a badman."

"Well, Lomax, that's a matter of opinion. We dug around in your past, and what we found suggests you're no angel."

"Never claimed to be."

"Yeah, but what we turned up shows you rode with Jesse James for a spell, then with Billy the Kid before falling in with Doc Holliday and the Earps in Tombstone. You had a vendetta against Wild Bill Hickok that resulted in his death."

I shrugged. "I escaped them when I could, but some died, though not at my hand."

"Then there's Colorado."

Gulping, I wagged my head from side to side. "Don't remember being there." That was a lie, and Lymoine knew it, but my luck had just soured, especially if he arrested me for murdering Adam "Noose Neck" Scheisse because nobody would believe I was set up by Soapy.

"Our Colorado affiliates say you even went by the alias of Shotgun Jake Townsend and likely murdered an attorney in Leadville."

"Soapy Smith and his gang set me up in Leadville. They killed the lawyer."

Lymoine grinned. "I thought you just said you never visited Colorado."

"I guess I forgot. You got me."

"You know the most disturbing thing we uncovered in our investigation?"

"Do you intend to blame me for General Custer's misfortune at the Little Bighorn, too?"

Lymoine shook his head. "It's worse than that. Some reports say you courted Susan B. Anthony during her Colorado lecture tour, that you even asked her to marry you despite a thirty-year age difference."

"That's a lie," I answered. "I refused *her* marriage proposal." Knowing I could never change the facts since legends had a way of growing, I figured I just as well embellish the story.

"I don't see what she saw in you," he said, then paused, "or you in her."

"It was her *money,* but she wasn't as easy to get into as a Wells Fargo strongbox. What next, Mr. Lymoine? Prison?"

His smile never flinched. "That's up to you."

"How's that?"

"Wells Fargo's primary interest is in recovering the funds plus expenses for an investigation that's gone on for over a year."

"What does that amount to?"

"There's thirty-five hundred to start with, then costs that come to another two thousand dollars or more, including my pay, travel, meals and lodging plus fees for the investigators we hired to explore your past." Lymoine stood up from his chair and walked over to the door, opening it and looking out across a room full of patrons. "You seem to be prospering here, if you are indeed the owner of the Gold Dust Saloon and Opera House."

"I own half of it with my partner Roger Meredith. We split everything fifty-fifty."

Lymoine nodded and shut the door. "That squares with my investigation. You took thirty-five hundred dollars from Wells Fargo. You reimburse the company for that loss and for the expenses in recovering your theft, and we'll not file charges. A court case'll only increase our cost in resolving this matter, though we have lawyers that'd love to put you in prison, especially after they learn you back-shot one of their own in Leadville."

"Soapy Smith killed him."

Lymoine shrugged as he re-took his seat. "A Colorado jury will have to determine that, but only if Wells Fargo turns you over to state authorities. If you repay what you owe the company, what happened in Leadville is of no concern to us."

"So, I pay you the money and you clear my name, is that correct?"

"That's how it works with Wells Fargo, Lomax. Can't say about Colorado."

For a moment, I stroked my chin, taking the measure of Wells Fargo Special Investigator Dayle Lymoine. Could I trust him? "What guarantee do I have you won't run off with the money and never reimburse the company?"

"All you got is my word, Lomax, but I am a man of my word."

"I haven't always had good luck with lawmen," I answered. "For most of my time in Skagway, we've had to bribe a deputy marshal just to keep him from shuttering us."

"Not all lawmen have the integrity of a Wells Fargo investigator, I understand that. But your choices are limited. You can pay me and trust me to set your record straight with the company. You're welcome to accompany me to San Francisco and deal with the company lawyers, though they may not give you the same opportunity. Or, we can file charges and let the courts in California decide your fate before extraditing you to Colorado to stand trial for a murder you may or may not have committed twenty years ago."

I hesitated to give an answer, my mind a jumble of conflicting thoughts.

He arose. "I'll give you until noon tomorrow to think it over, Lomax, but don't leave Skagway. As you've learned, I'll find you wherever you go." He smiled with his perfect teeth. "Good day!"

I sat in the desk chair, stunned for a moment, uncertain what to do. So much of my past had caught up with me I couldn't sort out the details or decide my next step. There was no sense running. Since Lymoine had found me on sketchy information, he could track me down now. I remained in the office so long that my partner came in to check on me.

"Everything okay, Jesse?" he asked. "You look bewildered."

"My past caught up with me," I admitted.

He shrugged. "It catches up with most of us, even the dead."

"What are you talking about?"

"Word's going round that Frank Reid was a murderer back in the states. Don't know if there's truth to it, but that's the gossip."

"Probably Soapy's friends trying to dirty his memory."

"What's your problem? Does it have anything to do with the man leaving the office?"

"He was a special investigator with Wells Fargo."

My partner whistled. "Not good."

"You remember the money that grubstaked us when we first arrived?"

Roger nodded. "We wouldn't have been successful without it."

"It was Wells Fargo's."

Laughing, Roger shook his head. "I'd never taken you for a robber, Jesse."

"I didn't rob them of a thing. I just found an unlocked strongbox at a train depot outside San Francisco and helped myself to what was inside, thirty-five hundred dollars."

"And they want it back?"

"Yep, plus expenses, another two thousand or more. I don't have that kind of money."

"Of course you do, Jesse."

"How's that?"

"We've done well with the Gold Dust, Jesse. I could buy you out, cover your original investment plus profits. It might be enough to leave you some cash after you settle with Wells Fargo. I'd even hire you to stay on once you reimbursed Wells Fargo."

"It wouldn't be the same," I replied, "going from owner to hired hand. Too, if I pay Wells Fargo, I intend to ensure the agent doesn't pocket the money like Taylor always did."

"So you'd go back with him to San Francisco to settle up?"

I nodded. "It'd be nice to quit living under an alias and take up my old name."

"It's that Lomax fellow I've heard about from time to time."

"H.H. Lomax, Henry Harrison Lomax, if you must know."

"You'll always be Jesse Murphy to me, an honest man who did Skagway a great favor. I suspect you killed Soapy Smith and allowed Reid to get the credit. That was decent of you as he'll be remembered for a long time because of you."

"Thanks, Roger," I answered. "Tell me what you think you can pay for my share of the Gold Dust." I stood up and shook his hand.

"I'll give you a price first thing in the morning." He turned and exited the room, closing the door behind him.

I sat in my chair and leaned against the back wall, figuring in total I was lucky to be alive, but likely broke after this was sorted out. After a while, I decided to go for a walk. I grabbed my hat and left the office and saloon, walking along Broadway where White Pass & Yukon Railway crews were grading the center of the street for the railroad line. As I walked toward the wharves, I saw iron rails and bundles of railroad ties to be laid down Broadway. It seemed unbelievable that a year earlier I came to a town of tents, and now the place was thriving with structures and people who were poised for a grand future as long as the gold held out five hundred miles away. While Skagway had been mostly men when I arrived, it was easy to see the influence of women as several houses and a few stores had flower beds or hanging pots adorned with colorful plants.

At the four piers, I counted six steamships with two more in the harbor awaiting a berth. The ships daily unloaded supplies and dreamers who believed their fortunes were just over the horizon. Most, like me, would never realize their dreams, but at least I survived and would leave Skagway with money in my pocket, even if not for long. After spending a couple hours at the wharves, I started back toward the Gold Dust, making a loop through town and passing by Jeff Smith's Parlor, where the sign had been painted over and workers were reworking the building for a legitimate use. I ate supper at a restaurant, then returned to the Gold Dust and went to my room to pack two cases for the return to the states. I'd be leaving Skagway with a lot less gear than I had brought a year earlier.

The next morning after breakfast, I met with Roger who offered me sixty-two hundred dollars for my share of the saloon, saying he thought it was a fair price and would leave me a little money once I settled up with Wells Fargo. We shook hands on the offer, and Roger advised me he would arrange the sale. He asked if I wanted him to announce my departure and schedule a farewell with the other Gold Dust employees, but I declined, not caring to explain things. I asked him to delay announcing the purchase until after I had departed Skagway. He agreed and said he would bring papers for me to sign and my cash the following morning.

Dayle Lymoine came into the saloon at noon, just as he had promised, smiling as wide as ever. "Have you made up your mind, Lomax?"

I nodded and pointed him to the office. We walked inside and closed the door. "I'll pay the money," I said, "but I intend to return to San Francisco with you to confirm everything is clear between me and Wells Fargo. I don't want stories of this following me around."

"Like the tales of you and Susan B. Anthony."

"Yeah," I said, "malicious tales like that." I told him that Roger would have cash for me before noon the next day. While I agreed to give him the money, I expected a receipt and the right to accompany him to San Francisco to confirm that he indeed repaid my debt.

He nodded, and we shook hands on the deal. Lymoine informed me that a steamship was leaving for San Francisco at four o'clock the next afternoon, and he would pick me up at one to escort me and my money to the wharf. I asked him to make it at noon because I had a brief errand I wanted to run before I left town. Lymoine said he'd see me in twenty-four hours.

I spent the remainder of the day packing my belongings, including the sawed-off shotgun, in my two valises and slipped the bags one at a time down the stairs into the office and stacked them by my carbine in the corner. While I lingered in the room, someone rapped on the door. "Who is it?" I called, but the response sent shivers racing along my spine as I heard a squeaky voice from the grave.

"It's me, Soapy!"

I froze for a moment, as confused as a lawyer in church, then grinned. It was Roger doing his impersonation of the conman.

"Let me in," came the squeaky imitation again.

"The door's open, Roger."

He marched in, a big smile on his face. "Bet I had you for an instant."

I nodded. We sat down and talked about our partnership, the good times and the sad we had had running the Gold Dust. I thanked him for his solid and honest management that had separated our saloon from most of the others in Skagway over the last year. We visited until supper time, and then Roger bought my dinner at a restaurant down the street. After we returned, I went around the saloon speaking to the piano player, the bartenders and the girls, though not informing them I was leaving the next day.

After that, I retired for my last night in Skagway, awoke refreshed and met Roger in our office to sign the papers and receive the cash for my share of the Gold Dust. Then my partner and I killed time until noon when Lymoine knocked on the door. He came in, smiling as usual.

"Are you ready, Lomax?"

I nodded and stood up, introducing him to Roger Meredith, my former partner.

"Glad to meet you, Roger," he said, shaking Meredith's hand warmly. "I understand the two of you ran an honest place unlike many of your competitors."

"Where do you learn such things?" I asked.

"Wells Fargo has influence wherever it goes," he answered as he released Roger's grip. "You got the money, Lomax?"

I nodded. "I can pay you now or in San Francisco, as long as I get a receipt."

"Let's settle on the steamship," he said.

"I'm fine with that, but I need a couple favors first." I pointed to my two valises. "Would you carry those out for me so folks won't realize I'm leaving?"

"That I can do. What's your other favor?"

"Take me to the cemetery before we leave. That's why I wanted you here early."

Lymoine nodded. "Fair enough." He picked up the bags and headed out the door.

I shook Roger's hand a final time, then gave him a hug. "Best partner I ever had."

"You weren't so bad yourself, Murphy, or should I say Lomax."

Then I turned, grabbed my carbine and departed my former saloon.

"Don't get yourself shot in the back," Roger called after me in his high-pitched imitation of the late Jefferson Randolph Smith the Second.

Nobody paid attention to my departure, and I was relieved as I didn't care for any long goodbyes. Outside, I smiled that Lymoine had rented a buggy, a service that had not been available when I first arrived in Skagway. I put my carbine in the back between my two valises and climbed aboard. As soon as I did, the Wells Fargo agent shook the reins and started the horse moving along Broadway until he found a spot between the railway workmen and the traffic to turn around and head out of town to the cemetery. As we passed a house with a flower bed, I asked him to stop. When he did, I jumped down and knocked on the door, hoping to buy flowers from the owner. When no one answered, I reached in my pants and extracted a trio of silver dollars. I slid two under the unanswered door and stepped to the plot, taking out my pocketknife and cutting the stems of a half-dozen yellow flowers for a simple bouquet. Completing that, I climbed back in the buggy, and we continued to the graveyard. When we arrived at our destination, I asked Lymoine to wait for me as I attended personal matters.

Leaving him, I walked among the graves past Frank Reid's, whose plot was covered in dried flowers, to the far side of the cemetery where Ella Wilson lay. I removed my hat and spoke to her. "I'm sorry you never made it back to Louisiana, Miss Wilson. You deserved better. I brought you a few flowers." I squatted and laid them against the wooden cross that marked her grave. "Sleep well, Miss Wilson, sleep well." Sighing, I turned and moved to another grave, the smaller unmarked mound where I had left Buck. "Well, Buck," I said. "I'm leaving you behind. I saved you from starving or drowning on the mud flats in Dyea, and you saved me in the shootout with Soapy. Maybe we're even, but I still feel I owe you more." I dug into my pocket and pulled out my remaining silver dollar, which I placed atop his grave. "I left a dollar on your cage when I took you, and I'm leaving another dollar in honor of your name before we part ways. So long, Buck. You were the best dog I ever had!"

When I finished I plopped my hat back on my head and angled over to the opposite side of the cemetery to the fence that separated Soapy from the decent folks and dogs of Skagway. I spat over the barrier on his grave a final time, spun around and returned to the buggy.

"Who was she?" Lymoine inquired as I took my seat. "A woman that worked the saloon and my dog that saved me from an ambush by Soapy Smith."

He nodded. "She must've been a fine woman."

"She was a decent woman in an indecent profession," I answered, "but deserved better."

As we headed back to town, I asked Lymoine to drive along State Street instead of Broadway so I wouldn't pass the Gold Dust Saloon and Opera House again and think of what might have been.

At the wharf we unloaded and I stood over both of our belongings while Lymoine returned the buggy to the livery stable. We bought our tickets and boarded the steamer. Once I stepped up the gangplank and onto the deck, Jesse Murphy disappeared from my life and H.H. Lomax reappeared. It was good to be my old self again.

Over the next seven days on the way to San Francisco, I found Lymoine to be as straight and honest a man as I'd ever roomed or rode with. He didn't shade the edges like I had a tendency to do. That became apparent when we reached our destination late in the evening. He took me to a modest hotel, certainly not the Palace and advised me to clean up and put on a suit for the meeting with company attorneys. At nine o'clock the following day he took me to the Wells Fargo offices to confront the lawyers, four of them in a mahogany-paneled room with a matching table and leather-tufted chairs as comfortable as any I had sat in. The legal quartet took positions opposite mine and scowled at me across the wide table for having the audacity to take money from an unlocked strongbox that belonged to Wells Fargo.

As they settled into their seats, the lead steer of the bunch pointed his index finger at me and said, "I've got a question for you."

Shrugging, I replied, "I'm at your mercy, though it's been a while since the incident at the depot."

"Not that," he said, waving away my response. "Is it true you courted Susan B. Anthony?"

I looked at Lymoine.

"They've read the files."

Once something appeared in a Wells Fargo report, it didn't matter if it was factual or not. I had only known Miss Susan B. Anthony for a few hours at best, and now that acquaintance had come back to haunt me two decades later. "She was harder to get into than your strongbox."

My comment did not fall well on the ears of the lawyers, whose cheeks bloated and whose chests swelled. "We'll see about that," replied the head lawyer, "once we bring charges against you in court."

Lymoine interrupted. "Gentlemen, there will be no charges. Mr. Lomax has been cooperative all along and has already paid me and I have deposited in company accounts the thirty-five hundred dollars he took from the strongbox and an additional two thousand dollars for expenses. In exchange for that, I told him Wells Faro would not file criminal charges."

"You didn't have the authority to make an agreement," the lawyer harrumphed.

"And, you didn't have the skills to track Mr. Lomax over the last twelve months. I recovered the missing funds plus expenses as best I could estimate them. You weren't there to arrange a better deal on Wells Fargo's behalf, so either accept my terms or I'll return the money to Mr. Lomax and resign from Wells Fargo."

The four lawyers pushed themselves back from the table and rolled their chairs into a pow-wow, speaking in hushed tones, then chortling as they scooted back to the table.

"Mr. Lomax and Mr. Lymoine," the head lawyer said, "we've decided to accept your arrangement, once we get the accountants to confirm the actual expenses so we can collect anything else that is due on behalf of the company. As for pressing charges, we've decided courting Susan B. Anthony was punishment enough for any man's lifetime."

The lawyers laughed and slapped each other on the back as they stood up and turned for the exit.

"Wait here until our accountant can figure final expenses," said the lead lawyer over his shoulder as he left the room, then turned to his compatriots. "We'll have plenty to discuss over lunch."

Turning to Lymoine, I nodded. "Thanks."

"These lawyer types that sit in offices and have no idea what it's like in the real world. They discuss their legalities and have then have lunches at the Palace to show everyone how important they are."

We waited a half hour in the meeting room until a thin fellow wearing thick glasses came in and informed me I owed another hundred and thirty-seven dollars and eighteen cents. I counted out the money from my diminishing bank roll and gave it to the bookkeeper, who returned in ten minutes with my receipt showing my debt to Wells Fargo was paid in full.

When that was done, Lymoine escorted me outside and wished me the best, advising me to stay out of trouble and not to open any more Wells Fargo strongboxes. I promised him I would no longer shade the edges as we stepped out onto the street, though I remained uncertain what to do next. After thanking Lymoine for his honesty in settling my debt, I turned and walked away from the Wells Fargo investigator, calculating that I had a little less than four hundred dollars on me. Though it wasn't a fortune, it was more than I usually carried after a bout with trouble. I wandered the hilly streets not sure of my next step, but at least I wasn't going to prison. As darkness approached, I decided to spend the night at the Palace Hotel, treating myself to a final moment of luxury before moving on with my life.

I returned to the Palace still in awe of its luxury and waited at the desk for my turn to register for one of the more affordable rooms. When a clerk motioned me up to the desk, I told him I wanted a reasonable accommodation for the night, assuming one was available. Pointing to the register for me to sign in, he asked my name.

"H.H. Lomax," I responded as I reached for the pen

He glanced up, grinning. "There were some Wells Fargo lawyers in the restaurant today laughing about a thief named Lomax that had once courted Susan B. Anthony. Can you believe that a real man would squire that suffragist around? You wouldn't be that Lomax, would you?"

"Nope," I lied, fearful that rumor might follow me the rest of my life, a perpetual stain on my reputation. I dropped the pen, turned around and strode away from the desk.

"Say, fellow," the clerk called, "don't you want a room for the night?"

"No," I said, "I think I'd rather stay in a prison cell." I exited thinking a lot less of the Palace Hotel, though nothing could diminish my opinion of lawyers any lower than it already was.

A Look At: Preston Lewis
Western Collection, Volume 1

SPUR AWARD WINNING AUTHOR PRESTON LEWIS BRINGS YOU FIVE TIMELESS WESTERNS IN ONE!

Get swept away by five western heroes all on a bout of good versus evil. From fighting for freedom in the Texas Revolution to fighting the demons and secrets that have been holding one hero back, Lewis will have you captivated the whole time.

In Choctaw Trail, retired U.S. Marshal Doyle Hardy is called back into service to track down the culprit in a brutal double murder in Indian Territory. The no-nonsense lawman working out of Fort Smith, Arkansas, returns to the trail to track down the murderer, who he doesn't want to admit is his own son...Hardy must confront his own son and tough family truths that he had tried to avoid in all his years as a lawman.

The Preston Lewis Western Collection, Volume 1 includes: Blood of Texas, Lone Survivor, Choctaw Trail, Tarnished Badge and Sante Fe Run.

AVAILABLE NOW

About the Author

Growing up in West Texas and loving history, Spur Award-winning author Preston Lewis naturally gravitated to stories of the Old West and religiously read his father's copies of True West and Frontier Times. Today he is the author of more than 30 western, juvenile and historical novels as well as numerous articles, short stories and book reviews on the American frontier.

Preston Lewis is a past president of WWA and WTHA, which in 2016 named him a fellow. He has served on the boards of the Ranching Heritage Association and the Book Club of Texas. He and his wife Harriet live in San Angelo, Texas.

READ MORE ABOUT PRESTON LEWIS AT:
https://wolfpackpublishing.com/preston-lewis/

CPSIA information can be obtained
at www.ICGtesting.com
Printed in the USA
BVHW031834160820
586565BV00001B/162

9 781647 340513